HEX

ALLEN STEELE

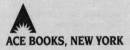

ACE BOOKS, NEW YORK

THE BERKLEY PUBLISHING GROUP
Published by the Penguin Group
Penguin Group (USA) Inc.
375 Hudson Street, New York, New York 10014, USA

Penguin Group (Canada), 90 Eglinton Avenue East, Suite 700, Toronto, Ontario M4P 2Y3, Canada
(a division of Pearson Penguin Canada Inc.) • Penguin Books Ltd., 80 Strand, London WC2R 0RL,
England • Penguin Group Ireland, 25 St. Stephen's Green, Dublin 2, Ireland (a division of Penguin
Books Ltd.) • Penguin Group (Australia), 250 Camberwell Road, Camberwell, Victoria 3124, Australia
(a division of Pearson Australia Group Pty. Ltd.) • Penguin Books India Pvt. Ltd., 11 Community
Centre, Panchsheel Park, New Delhi—110 017, India • Penguin Group (NZ), 67 Apollo Drive,
Rosedale, Auckland 0632, New Zealand (a division of Pearson New Zealand Ltd.) • Penguin Books
(South Africa) (Pty.) Ltd., 24 Sturdee Avenue, Rosebank, Johannesburg 2196, South Africa

Penguin Books Ltd., Registered Offices: 80 Strand, London WC2R 0RL, England

HEX

An Ace Book / published by arrangement with the author

PUBLISHING HISTORY
Ace hardcover edition / June 2011
Ace mass-market edition / May 2012

Copyright © 2011 by Allen M. Steele.
Alien glyphs by Allen M. Steele.
Hex graphics and diagram by Rob Caswell.
Cover art by Scott Grimando.
Cover design by Judith Lagerman.
Interior text design by Kristin del Rosario.

ISBN: 978-1-937007-51-5

ACE
Ace Books are published by The Berkley Publishing Group,
a division of Penguin Group (USA) Inc.,
375 Hudson Street, New York, New York 10014.
ACE and the "A" design are trademarks of Penguin Group (USA) Inc.

PRINTED IN THE UNITED STATES OF AMERICA

10 9 8 7 6 5 4 3 2 1

For mothers everywhere . . .
especially my own

It is easy to imagine a highly intelligent society with no particular interest in technology. It is easy to see around us examples of technology without intelligence. When we look into the universe for signs of artificial activities, it is technology and not intelligence that we must search for.

—FREEMAN DYSON, *DISTURBING THE UNIVERSE*

CONTENTS

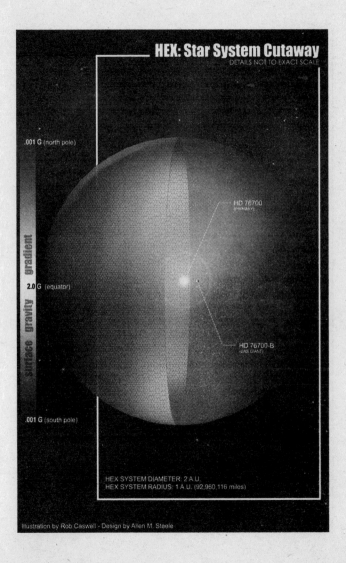

HEX: Star System Cutaway
DETAILS NOT TO EXACT SCALE

.001 G (north pole)

surface gravity gradient

2.0 G (equator)

.001 G (south pole)

HD 76700
(PRIMARY)

HD 76700-B
(GAS GIANT)

HEX SYSTEM DIAMETER: 2 A.U.
HEX SYSTEM RADIUS: 1 A.U. (92,960,116 miles)

Illustration by Rob Caswell · Design by Allen M. Steele

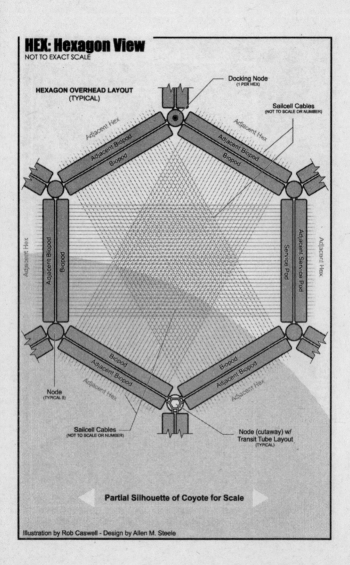

HEX: Hexagon View
NOT TO EXACT SCALE

HEXAGON OVERHEAD LAYOUT
(TYPICAL)

Docking Node
(1 PER HEX)

Adjacent Hex

Adjacent Biopod

Biopod

Sailcell Cables
(NOT TO SCALE OR NUMBER)

Adjacent Hex

Adjacent Biopod

Biopod

Adjacent Hex

Adjacent Biopod

Biopod

Service Pod

Adjacent Service Pod

Adjacent Hex

Node
(TYPICAL 5)

Biopod

Adjacent Biopod

Adjacent Hex

Biopod

Adjacent Biopod

Adjacent Hex

Sailcell Cables
(NOT TO SCALE OR NUMBER)

Node (cutaway) w/
Transit Tube Layout
(TYPICAL)

◄ **Partial Silhouette of Coyote for Scale** ►

Illustration by Rob Caswell - Design by Allen M. Steele

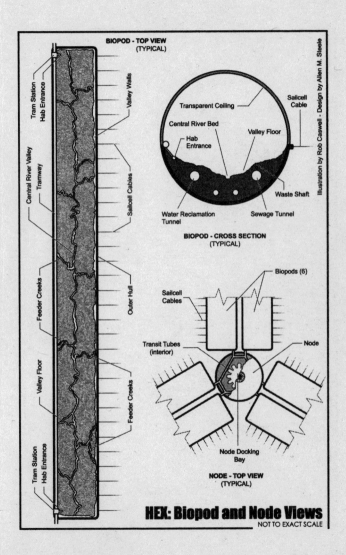

BIOPOD - TOP VIEW
(TYPICAL)

Tram Station
Hab Entrance
Valley Walls
Central River Valley
Tramway
Sailcell Cables
Feeder Creeks
Outer Hull
Valley Floor
Feeder Creeks
Tram Station
Hab Entrance

Illustration by Rob Caswell · Design by Allen M. Steele

Transparent Ceiling
Sailcell Cable
Central River Bed
Valley Floor
Hab Entrance
Waste Shaft
Water Reclamation Tunnel
Sewage Tunnel

BIOPOD - CROSS SECTION
(TYPICAL)

Biopods (6)
Sailcell Cables
Transit Tubes (interior)
Node
Node Docking Bay

NODE - TOP VIEW
(TYPICAL)

HEX: Biopod and Node Views
NOT TO EXACT SCALE

The following is an extract from a document submitted to the Talus High Council by Saromajah Saj Sa-Fhadda, *hjadd* Prime Emissary to the Coyote Federation. Translation by Dr. William Manofsky and Dr. Larry Manofsky of the School of Astroethnic Studies, University of New Florida. Due to differences in nomenclature and systems of measurement and chronological reckoning, certain names, dates, and distances have been substituted with Anglo approximations. Historical references are annotated by footnotes.

To the High Council of the Talus and His Holiness, the *chaaz'braan*: my most respectful greetings and salutations, with hopes that my humble words will be received with patience and understanding.

By now, I trust that the High Council has become acquainted with the race known as human, who have recently become members of the Talus. Although humankind developed starfaring technology in only the [last three centuries], with a large colony established in the [47 Ursae Majoris] system in the last [seventy years, Gregorian calendar], they have already come to be regarded as an ambitious and curious species, eager to make contact with other races and, whenever possible, establish trade or cultural relations. It is the yearning of this colony world—known in their dominant language as Coyote—to become a respected member of the galactic community that compels me to report on their current disposition.

In order to fully understand humans, a brief review of their recent history is necessary. Their homeworld, Earth, is located [forty-six light-years] from Coyote, or [54.4 light-years] from *Talus qua'spah*. Coyote was originally settled by political refugees from Earth, who stole their race's first starship, which had been built by an authoritarian local government.[1] Because this large but rather primitive vessel was powered by a ramjet-augmented nuclear-fusion engine, it was capable of traveling at only [20 percent] of light-speed. As a result, it took [270 years, Gregorian] for this ship to reach the [47 Ursae Majoris] system, where a habitable world, the fourth moon of a gas giant, had been detected by Earth-orbiting telescopes.

Despite the fact that they were confronted by an unfamiliar and often hostile environment, and possessed limited technologic resources, the settlers managed to successfully make a new home for themselves, their population suffering only relatively few fatalities during their [first year, LeMarean calendar] on Coyote. Yet the colony had barely become self-sustaining when it received an unwelcome surprise: the arrival of another starship from Earth, this one much larger and faster than the first. During the long period it took for the first ship to travel to Coyote, scientists and engineers on the human homeworld had managed to invent a warp drive that, while not capable of achieving light-speed, was none-

---

[1] The URSS *Alabama*, built by the United Republic of America in A.D. 2070

theless able to make the same journey in a fraction of the original time.

This second vessel was sent by a government that had succeeded the original one.[2] Unfortunately, this new government was just as authoritarian as its predecessor, and it soon became clear that it intended to take control of Coyote, by military force if necessary. Hopelessly outnumbered, and aware that more ships were on the way, the original colonists decided to flee into the unexplored regions of their new world. From their wilderness retreat, they waged a war of insurrection against the invaders. After a long and bloody conflict, they regained control of the original settlement, driving away their enemies while allowing newly arrived colonists to remain on Coyote.

At this same period, scientists and engineers of yet another government on Earth[3] managed to unlock the secret to hyperspace travel. As circumstances would have it, this occurred just when they also detected an object of unnatural origin passing close to the edge of their solar system. Using an experimental starbridge already placed in orbit around a minor planet in the outer system, a small starship[4] was dispatched to investigate this object, which the humans had named Spindrift.

Unknown to them, Spindrift was *Shaq-Taaraq*, a planetoid that had been transformed into an interstellar ark. It bore the sole remaining members of the *taaraq* race, whose homeworld in the [Lamba Aurigae] system had been destroyed by the rogue black hole colloquially known as the Annihilator. As the High Council may remember, when the *hjadd* discovered *Shaq-Taaraq* and found its passengers in long-term biostasis, my people placed a starbridge in orbit around the ark. This starbridge contained

---

[2] The WHSS *Seeking Glorious Destiny Among the Stars for the Greater Good of Social Collectivism*, built by Western Hemisphere Union in 2256
[3] The European Alliance
[4] The EASS *Galileo*, built by the European Space Agency in 2288

an automatic beacon programmed to transmit warnings to any vessels that approached *Shaq-Taaraq* without our permission and which would also alert us via hyperspace link if those warnings were ignored.

This is what occurred when the human starship approached *Shaq-Taaraq*. In hindsight, we now realize that we erred in assuming that any race that might find the ark would naturally belong to the Talus and thus would be able to translate our warnings. However, the humans erred as well in believing that any aliens they encountered would be hostile; their ship was armed with a nuclear weapon, which, although crude, nonetheless posed a significant threat to the ship my people dispatched to investigate the intrusion at *Shaq-Taaraq*. Our ship was forced to detonate the weapon launched at us, and the explosion destroyed the human vessel, with the loss of all aboard.

Before that happened, though, the humans had sent an exploration team to *Shaq-Taaraq*'s surface. One member of the team died while exploring its interior, and the other three were subsequently marooned when their mother ship was destroyed. Unable to return to Earth, they activated their landing craft's emergency beacon, then went into biostasis cells. Our vessel located their craft a short time later. We brought the survivors to *Talus qua'spah*, but did not revive them for [fifty-six years, Gregorian], during which time *hjadd* researchers sought to access their craft's computers and thereby translate their language.

Once this was accomplished, we were able to gain an understanding of who these strangers were and why they had come to *Shaq-Taaraq*. In this way, we also became aware of the possible existence of a colony in the [47 Ursae Majoris] system. However, it was not until we revived and questioned the survivors that we came to realize that their mission had not necessarily been hostile in intent, and that their weapon had been launched in haste by a panic-stricken commanding officer.

By then, the Earth government that dispatched the ship to *Shaq-Taaraq* had subsequently sent a similar vessel to

Coyote, where it had built the first starbridge linking the colony world to Earth. The colonists had only recently achieved political independence from their homeworld when the Talus allowed the survivors of the *Shaq-Taaraq* expedition to use the newly established starbridge to travel to Coyote. My predecessor, Mahamatasja Jas Sa-Fhadda, went with them. Heshe became the first Prime Emissary to Coyote, and it was through hisher efforts that diplomatic relations with humankind were established.

My people built an embassy on Coyote, yet we decided not to do the same on Earth. Although we were willing to make contact with humankind, we determined that their homeworld was dangerous. It had a long history of violence, its global environment was collapsing after centuries of neglect, and its political infrastructure was in chaos. So when we decided to let humans visit *Talus qua'spah* and meet the *chaaz'braan*, we were careful to make sure that they came from Coyote, not Earth.

Despite a cultural misunderstanding that arose during the initial trade negotiations[5], the disagreement was quickly resolved, and Coyote Federation was allowed to join the Talus. It was during this time that our first Cultural Ambassador, Jasahajahd Taf Sa-Fhadda, brought a *Sa'Tong-tas* to Coyote. In keeping with *Sa'Tong* tradition, heshe gave it to the first individual whom heshe determined to be receptive to its teachings. This person, a former criminal, embraced the wisdom of the *Sa'Tong* as expressed by His Holiness. He eventually became the *chaaz'maha* of humankind and began spreading the True Knowledge to his people.

Although many humans were receptive to *Sa'Tong*, some were not, with a few actively hostile. One of those who opposed *Sa'Tong* was a minister of a monotheistic religious sect that, until only recently, had denied even the

---

[5] The mission of the CFS *Pride of Cucamonga*, launched in c.y. 16 (A.D. 2249)

very existence of races other than humankind. When the
chaaz'maha announced his intent to visit Earth, this individual decided to stop him. He carried an explosive de-
vice aboard the ship scheduled to carry both him and the
chaaz'maha to Earth and detonated it just as the vessel was
about to enter hyperspace, destroying both the ship and the
starbridge.[6]

For the next [three years, LeMarean], Coyote was cut
off from both Earth and the Talus. However, the *hjadd*
embassy on Coyote possessed the technology necessary to
build another starbridge, and, therefore, my people were
eventually able to assist the humans in doing so. However,
we made a major stipulation: the new starbridge could only
be used as a means of travel to the Talus worlds. Once
again, Earth had proven itself to be dangerously immature
and needed to be left alone indefinitely.

Surprisingly, few humans objected to this isolation. By
then, Coyote's population was over a million, and in that
time a generation had grown up that had never seen the
world of their parents and grandparents (it should be noted
that humans generally participate in the raising of their
offspring). Even the older colonists had very little nostalgia for their homeworld, and most were happy that Earth
would no longer be able to cause problems for them.

As a result, over the course of the next [three years,
LeMarean], relations between the inhabitants of Coyote
and the races of the Talus have been both peaceful and
prosperous. Using ships brought to Coyote before the destruction of their first starbridge, they have successfully
established trade relations with several Talus races, most
notably my own people but also the *soranta*, the *kua'tah*,
and the *nord*. Humans have benefited from the introduc-
tion of advanced technologies, and despite the death of
their *chaaz'maha*, a significant number of them have em-

---

[6] The CFSS *Robert E. Lee*, destroyed c.y. 17 (A.D. 2252)

braced *Sa'Tong* as their spiritual philosophy. Although they are still the newest members of the galactic community, they are proving themselves to be worthy neighbors.

It has recently come to our attention, though, that a new development may soon occur. Through the *nord*, humans have recently made contact with the *danui*. However tentative this may be, it is possible that humankind may soon learn of the existence of *tanaash-haq*. This discovery may have major implications for their relations with not only their current allies and trade partners but also those races whom they have yet to encounter.

Therefore, it is my recommendation that we closely monitor the situation and perhaps coordinate our actions with the *danui*. If the humans prove themselves able to successfully cope with *tanaash-haq*, this will be a major boon to them. Yet the lessons of their initial encounter with the *hjadd* must not be forgotten.

They can be a wise and peaceful race, but we should never neglect the fact that they can also behave in rash and often foolish ways.

TWELVE
FROM COYOTE

CHAPTER ONE

"I'M BORED WITH MY JOB," SAID THE STARSHIP CAPTAIN.

Andromeda Carson took a sip of merlot as she waited for her comment to sink in. Theodore Harker raised an eyebrow, if only for a moment, and she was satisfied. Like Andromeda herself, Ted's normal expression was a poker face. People who commanded starships tended to be stoics; if she could get this much out of the Chief of Operations for the Coyote Federation Merchant Marine, it meant that he was listening.

"Well . . . that's not something I hear too often." Harker toyed with his drink, letting the dark red wine run around the inside of his glass. "I have a list of shipless captains who'd love to have your job. Want to see it? You might recognize a few names."

"I didn't say I'm ready to retire. I just said that I'm bored." Andromeda set her glass down on the blackwood deck beside her Adirondack chair and propped one sandaled foot on the low table in front of her. Beyond the deck railing, she could see sailboats on the Great Equatorial

River. It was late afternoon of a warm midsummer day, the sun dappling the blue waters of the New Brighton harbor. "Bored, bored, bored . . ." she added, singsonging the rest as if she were a schoolgirl.

"Really." There was little empathy in Ted's British-accented voice as he gave her a sour glance. "Perhaps you should count your blessings. You still have your own ship. The same one, in fact, that you used to get here . . ."

"Appropriately rechristened, of course."

Harker's gaze sharpened. "You have a problem with the *Carlos Montero*? Believe me, you would have never been allowed to keep your ship as *The Patriotism of Fidel Castro*."

"Not complaining at all." Too late, Andromeda realized that she'd said the wrong thing. Ever since his death seventeen Earth-years ago, Carlos Montero—original Coyote colonist, hero of the Revolution, former Federation president—had become something of a martyr, his name held in reverence particularly among those like Theodore Harker, who'd personally known him. It had just been Andromeda's misfortune that her ship, a Union Astronautica deep-space surveyor she'd brought to 47 Ursae Majoris following the collapse of the Western Hemisphere Union, had been the one picked to be rechristened in his honor. Andromeda may have fled the WHU and taken her ship and crew with her, but everyone in the merchant marine knew that she hadn't completely given up a long-held belief in social collectivism. Yet no one had asked for her opinion; one leader was to be immortalized, the other consigned to history's ashbin.

"Good." Another glance at her, more approving this time, then Harker went on. "You've got a good crew, a couple of whom have been with you from the beginning. And over the past few years, you've been to more places . . . a lot more . . . than you would've if you'd remained in the Union Astronautica."

Andromeda couldn't argue with any of that. Before she'd decided to take her ship through Starbridge Earth in the waning days of the Union, as so many other UA captains had done once it was apparent that the Union was doomed, the *Castro* had been used to survey the Jovian system, including the establishment and support of a small science station on Ganymede. So, yes, she and her original crew had seen the outer planets of their native solar system, and for a long time this had been the high point of her life.

All that paled, though, once the *Castro* was rechristened the *Montero* and refitted to serve as a merchantman. Since then, she'd seen worlds that made Jupiter and the Galilean satellites almost banal by comparison. The city-sized space colony of *Talus qua'spah*; the methane seas of Tau Boötis-C; the mountains of Sanja, in the HD 73256 system, which the native *soranta* had spent centuries carving into the likeness of a god.

"I realize that," she said. "And believe me, I'm grateful. You . . . the merchant marine, I mean . . . could have taken my ship, then mustered me and my people out and turned us into sidewalk beggars or something. Instead, you were good enough to let us keep . . ."

"No." Harker shook his head. "I appreciate your gratitude, Andi, but don't think for a second we did it out of the goodness of our hearts. Taking a ship while discarding its crew would've been a waste of resources."

"Nice to know," she murmured. *You're all heart,* she silently added.

"Think nothing of it," Harker said dryly. "Maybe that sounds cold, but speaking as one CO to another, the last thing I ever intend to do is ground a captain who isn't ready to stop flying . . . Unless you really are ready to retire, of course."

Andromeda was about to respond when, from the distance, her attention was drawn by an abrupt and distant roar. Turning about in her chair, she looked back to see, above the rooftop of her waterfront cottage, a slender finger of grey-white smoke rising into the deep blue sky, a tiny silver thimble at its tip. A spacecraft lifting off from the nearby New Brighton spaceport; judging from the character of the engine noise and the shape of the exhaust plume, she immediately knew that it was an Ares-class heavy lifter, probably belonging to one of the freighters parked in high orbit above Coyote. A few seconds later, the crackling roar of its engines reached them, causing a flock of sea-swoops to rise from the nearby river.

Some women do a double take when a handsome man walks by; Andromeda Carson looked at spaceships. She used to look at men, too, but that had stopped shortly after she'd left Dean. A psychiatrist of the old school might have said that there was some symbolic connection between her fascination with spacecraft and her lack of interest in men, but Andromeda knew that there was a simpler explanation: a broken heart, not for her husband, but rather for their son.

She watched the shuttle as it traced a long, hyperbolic curve that gradually faded from view, and once she'd heard its sonic boom, she turned back to her guest. "Sorry, Ted. You were saying something about retirement?"

If Harker noticed the ironic undercurrent of her question, he was careful not to let on. "Rumor around the spaceport pubs has it that you're thinking about getting out. Announcing your retirement, then sticking around only long enough to train your successor. That true?"

Andromeda hid her expression by picking up her glass again and taking another sip of wine. She tried to be lady-like about it, but she was tempted to chug the fine Midland merlot as if it were cheap ale. *Oh, hell,* she thought, *who talked?* Probably one of her crew; they were the only people with whom she confided anymore. Jason, her first officer, knew better than to reveal his captain's secrets, but someone else might have had their lips loosened by drink. Rolf, perhaps, or maybe Zeus . . .

"Only rumor," she replied. "Is that why you asked how I'm feeling these days?"

"Sort of." Harker bent forward as if to get some more wine, then seemed to think better of it and withdrew his hand, shaking his head when Andromeda silently pointed to the bottle. "Y'know, no one would blame you if you decided to cash in. You've been at this for . . . what, twenty-five years now?"

"Thirty-four, if you count the time I spent grounded after Black Anael." Andromeda knew he wouldn't. No one in the Federation Navy, its merchant marine, or Coyote's few private space companies included in their logbooks the nine Earth-years—three by local reckoning—that most of their spacecraft had been grounded following the destruction of Starbridge Coyote. The hyperspace bridge was eventually rebuilt with the assistance of the *hjadd*, but until then, only a few ships had lifted off from New Brighton, and then only to other places in the 47 Ursae Majoris system. "But no one counts nine years of gardening as flight time."

"But such a lovely garden." Harker glanced at the well-tended flower beds surrounding the deck. "I'm just surprised you've had time to look after it, considering how often you've been away . . ."

"I don't. My housekeeper takes care of it when I'm gone. My son, too, when he uses the house." *Which is the only time Sean visits anymore,* she thought, although that was something Harker didn't have to know.

"But you could be spending so much more time with it. Are you . . . ?"

"What are you trying to get at, Ted?" Andromeda put away the rest of her wine in a single gulp, then firmly planted the glass on the table. "You call to ask if you can drop by for a chat, and when you show up, you ask me how I'm feeling lately and whether I'm thinking about retirement. Yes, I feel fine. No, I'm not planning to retire anytime soon." The second was a lie, but she wasn't about to tell him the truth, at least not here and now. "Any other questions, or would you like to trade gardening tips instead?"

Theodore Harker didn't respond at once but instead merely regarded her with expressionless eyes. Andromeda regretted her flash of impatience; she should have stopped drinking when he did, but instead, she'd let the wine get the better of her. But she and Harker had known each other for years, and if not for the fifty-six years he'd spent in an emergency biostasis cell—a legend in itself, the part of the

Spindrift story that every spacer on Coyote knew by heart—they could have been approximately the same age. Not that anyone could easily tell, or at least not fairly recently. When Ted let his ponytailed hair go grey, Andromeda finally decided that she wasn't fooling anyone and had let the fake auburn coloring fade from her platinum locks. Oddly, the effect had been the opposite of what she'd expected; men started to look at her again, even a few Sean's age. But one person she'd never have to worry about making a pass at her was Ted. He was married to both a woman, Emily, and a ship, the *Pride of Cucamonga*, and whatever reasons he had for visiting, seduction wasn't one of them.

"You said you're bored with your job," Harker said. "You still haven't told me why."

Andromeda hesitated, then reached for the wine bottle. It was her house; she could get drunk if she wanted to. She'd just have to watch her mouth, that's all. "I'm a starship captain. Before that, I was in command of a long-range survey vessel. I'm trained for deep-space exploration, with all the risks that go with it. That's what I love, and if I've occasionally said something about retirement . . ."

"Which you haven't, as you say." There was a sly twinkle in Harker's eye.

"Let me finish." Andromeda poured the last of the bottle into her glass; fortunately, she had two more bottles of merlot in her liquor cabinet, so she shouldn't have to return to the neighborhood vintner before tomorrow. "What I'm trying to say is, my job is supposed to be about visiting new worlds, breaking new trails, and so on. But ever since I got my ship back and signed up with the merchant marine, I've been doing little more than hauling freight."

"I'd say it's more than that." Harker folded his hands together in his lap. "It's not like you were mapping the Jovian system for the first time . . . That was done long before you were born. The planets you've visited since then have been seen by very few people. And the races you've met . . . the *soranta*, the *kua'tah*, the *hjadd* . . ."

"Most of the time, I only see those planets from orbit.

And when my crew and I do get cleared to land, more often than not we're confined to quarters at their spaceports. As for the aliens themselves . . ." She shrugged. "They're less interested in who we are than in what we've got. As soon as we unload our cargo and take on whatever it is we're bringing back, they'd just as soon that we leave. The *hjadd* are the closest friends we have in the Talus, and I think that even they don't like us very much. You, of all people, should know that."

Of course he did. When he'd been an officer in the European Space Agency, Harker had been second-in-command of the ill-fated *Galileo* expedition that had made contact with the *hjadd*, the first intelligent extraterrestrial race encountered by humankind. A few years after he and the two other surviving members of the *Galileo*'s crew finally returned to human civilization, Harker had resigned from the ESA and was now the captain of the Janus Ltd. freighter that had made the Coyote Federation's first trade mission to the Talus, the so-called galactic club to which most of the known starfaring races of the galaxy belonged. That mission had met unexpected obstacles, but its eventual success meant that humankind was admitted into the Talus, albeit on a provisional basis.

The bombing of Starbridge Coyote by a religious fanatic had temporarily shut off Coyote from the rest of the galaxy, including Earth. While the starbridge was being rebuilt with the assistance of *hjadd* scientists marooned in the 47 Ursae Majoris system, the Federation Navy took the step of regulating its various competing private space companies by forming a merchant marine that would oversee all of them; it was hoped that, this way, disasters like Black Anael would be avoided. Not long afterward, Harker took on the job of the merchant marine's operations chief. He was still conning a ship, but only part-time; perhaps he was becoming tired of it as well. Chronologically speaking, he was more than one hundred Earth-years old; Andromeda figured that he'd probably had enough of wormhole-jumping and wanted the quiet life of raising his own garden.

"I don't think it's a matter of whether or not they like us," Harker replied. "It's their trust we're having a hard time winning. Considering that an Earth ship made an un-provoked attack on the first alien vessel it saw, or that one of our kind blew up our own starbridge because he thought God wanted him to . . ." He shrugged. "Anyway, you can't blame them for keeping us at arm's length. We're trouble."

"That's what I'm getting at." Andromeda picked up her glass, then stood up from her chair. The wine, along with the warmth of the afternoon, had made her a little light-headed; she leaned against the deck railing and gazed out at the river. "If I can't visit worlds because the natives don't trust me, then what good am I? I wasn't meant to be a truck driver. If that's all I've got to look forward to . . ."

"It isn't . . . and that's why I asked to come see you." Harker paused. "I've got a job for you and your crew. And, no, it doesn't involve hauling cargo. It's something else entirely."

Andromeda gave him a sharp look. "Exploration?" she asked.

He nodded. "Yes, it is."

"Hazardous?"

A shrug. "It could be, yes."

Andromeda smiled. "Tell me more."

TWO

HARKER HAD MORE ABOUT THE MISSION IN HIS DATAPAD, but the bright afternoon sun made its holo imager hard to use. Andromeda was tired of the deck, anyway, so she led Ted into the living room. After making sure he was comfortable, she excused herself to the kitchen to brew a pot of coffee, then made a side trip to the bathroom to find a sober-up patch. By the time she returned to the living room, her head was a little more clear, and she was ready to listen to his pitch.

Harker had linked his pad to the house comp. He accepted a mug of hot coffee from Andromeda, then settled into one of the bamboo swing-chairs suspended from the ceiling beams. "What do you know about the *danui*?" he asked, as Andromeda took a seat in an identical chair across the coffee table from him.

Andromeda thought it over a moment. "As much as anyone else, I suppose . . . not a lot."

"I thought so. Well, let's review what we do know." Harker raised his voice slightly. "Display *danui* emissary, please."

The holo projector in the ceiling responded by showing them a life-sized image of a *danui*. Andromeda had seen pictures of the aliens before, of course; nonetheless, she was glad that this was only a three-dimensional projection. If this one were actually in her house, she'd probably be reaching for the fléchette pistol she kept in a side-table drawer. A little more than seven feet tall, with a black, hairy body standing on six multijointed legs, two of which could also serve as hands, the *danui* would have borne a strong resemblance to a tarantula were it not for its elongated head, which had the mandibles and eyestalks of a lobster. Had it been naked, she might have mistaken it for some hideous animal, but the garments it wore—an outfit that looked like a cross between a vest and a six-legged pair of shorts, two bandolier-like belts with dozens of pockets, open-fingered gloves at the clawlike extremities of its limbs—clearly showed that it belonged to a sapient, tool-using race.

"This is the *danui* trade emissary to the Talus," Harker said. "Don't ask me to tell you its name . . . I've heard it once, and it's unpronounceable unless you can whistle and click your tongue at the same time. Even the word *danui* isn't their own . . . It's *hjadd*, meaning 'strange genius.' We can't speak their own name for themselves. The emissary knows we have problems with their language, though, so it chose a human name for our convenience. It calls itself George Jones."

"George Jones. Right."

"Yes, well . . ." Harker paused to take a sip of coffee. "You'll probably never meet him . . . it, I mean . . . anyway, so it hardly matters. What does matter is that our friend George has given us permission to make use of a piece of information that our people stumbled upon a short time ago."

"I take it you mean the merchant marine."

"Quite right . . . But we're getting ahead of ourselves. As you yourself said, there isn't much we know about the *danui*. They're one of the oldest member races of the Talus, but they're rather reclusive, seldom seen outside their home system. From what we've been told, they're renowned as superb engineers . . . the best in the known galaxy, if the *hjadd* are to be trusted . . . but aside from the occasional ship at *Talus qua'spah*, we've never seen any evidence of that."

Andromeda nodded. She'd once caught a glimpse of a *danui* vessel, while the *Montero* was making a port-of-call visit to the immense space colony in orbit above the *hjadd* homeworld that served as the central meeting place of the Talus. The ship looked like two spheres joined by a cylinder; one sphere was a fusion drive, the other was the crew module, and other than a few hatches and portholes, nothing else about it could be seen. The design was simple, efficient, and utterly enigmatic . . . just like the *danui* themselves.

"They trade with the other Talus races," Harker went on, "but only for raw materials. Apparently, they have no interest in the art and culture of other worlds . . . which, of course, is one of the reasons why we haven't had much contact with them since our culture constitutes most of the goods we offer. They have a minimal number of representatives on *Talus qua'spah* . . . four, maybe five or six; it's very hard to tell one from another . . . and no off-world colonies that we know of."

A last sip of coffee, then he put his mug on the table. "In short, they're mysterious and tend to keep to themselves. All the same, the other Talus members appear to respect them. In fact, our friends among the *hjadd* tell us that the *danui* are considered to be one of the most powerful races in the galaxy, one that no other race dares to even think about attacking."

"Not that anyone in the Talus is likely to start any wars," Andromeda said.

Long ago, the Talus had arrived at an elegant solution to the threat of interstellar war. Since the member races used starbridges to journey from star to star, with ring-shaped portals at both the embarkation and destination points creating the wormholes necessary for such jaunts, they agreed to equip those portals with keys. These small cards, which fit into a starship's navigation computer, contained frequencies for unique microwave codes that an outbound ship would transmit to the artificial intelligence controlling an embarkation starbridge. The AI would then relay the code via hyperlink channel to the destination starbridge, and if the AI at the other end recognized that code and authorized it, it would then allow a wormhole to be created and the incoming ship to pass through.

Thus, a vessel couldn't make the hyperspace jaunt unless it had an appropriate starbridge key for its destination, and the race who controlled the starbridge at that place could choose who received those keys and, therefore, who got to visit their worlds. Since the distances between inhabited systems were usually so great that it could take an invasion fleet, traveling at sublight velocity, a hundred years or more to reach its objective, this made surprise attacks all but impossible.

As a result, war was so difficult to wage that it simply wasn't worth the time or effort. Far easier to reach an accord with one's adversaries, or at least ignore them. So armed conflict between potential enemies was rare. Most races sincerely wanted to get along with one another, and even when first-contact situations occasionally went badly—such as when humans met *hjadd*—peace was nearly always seen as the first, and most preferred, option.

"True." Harker nodded, understanding what she meant. "Even so, there's something about the *danui* that none of the other races care to share with us, even though they all seem to know about it. Something or someplace that the *hjadd* call *tanaash-haq*, which astroethnicists at the university tell us translates as 'the living world.'"

"'The living world'?" Andromeda raised an eyebrow. "What the hell does that mean?"

Harker shrugged. "No idea . . . and the *hjadd* aren't telling us. Navy Intelligence has been trying to find out exactly what it is for quite some time, but only lately have they asked the merchant marine for help."

Andromeda nodded. There was a long-standing rivalry between the Navy and the merchant marine that went back to the time that private operators started competing with government ships for right-of-way through Starbridge Coyote. Ever since Coyote had begun trading with the Talus, the merchant marine had become the Federation's most-widely-traveled ships. Although the Navy handled most of the diplomatic travel between 47 Ursae Majoris and the rest of the galaxy, if there was any group likely to ferret out info about the *danui*, it would be a merchantman's captain and crew. "I'm surprised you haven't come to me before," she said.

"We would've, but you've been handling the *soranta* route the last couple of years. We figured that you probably wouldn't have learned anything more from them than we already have . . . which has been zero . . . so we didn't get in touch with you." Harker shrugged. "Nothing personal, Andi"—Andromeda winced; she hated that nickname—"but the intelligence boys have been trying to let as few people know about this as possible, and . . ."

"I didn't need to know. Right." Andromeda tried not to bristle, but this sounded like much the same sort of paranoia she'd had to put up with in the Union Astronautica. *So much for Coyote progressivism,* she thought sourly.

"Anyway, we put out the word that we wanted to open a dialogue with the *danui*, with the purpose of establishing trade relations with them, and eventually one of our other captains came through . . . Frank Lewin, of the *Bear's Choice*."

"I know Frank." Like most merchantmen captains, Frank also had a cottage in the Riverside neighborhood. They sometimes played cards together, along with other ship commanders or senior officers spending a little ground time between flights. "He usually alternates the Rho Coronae Borealis run with you, doesn't he?"

"Yes, he does." An ironic smile. "I might have learned this myself, except that Frank's ship gets out to *Talus qua'spah* more often than the *Pride* does these days, and that's exactly what happened." His smile faded. "But it wasn't from the *hjadd* or the *arsashi* or the *soranta* or any of the other usual suspects that we learned what we wanted to know, but from the race I would never have guessed . . . the *nord*."

"The *nord*?" Andromeda gave him a skeptical look. "I never would have guessed either. Are you sure?"

Of the many races humans had met since joining the Talus, the *nord* were easily the most obnoxious. Resembling—and sounding much like—wild turkeys who happened to be six feet tall and had arms and hands where wings should be, the *nord* had lost their homeworld several years ago, when the rogue black hole known as Kasimasta, or the Annihilator, passed through their solar system. They'd managed to evacuate most of their population before Nordash was destroyed, and since then, they'd become something of a gypsy race, their ships traveling from one system to another, taking advantage of other races' hospitality until they inevitably wore out their welcome through what seemed to be innate traits of arrogance and argumentativeness.

"We're sure . . . It was the *nord*, all right." Harker grinned. "They're a pain in the bum, but there's one thing you can say for them . . . They love our banjos."

"I've heard that. Our banjos sound a lot like some musical instrument of their own. Most of them were left behind, though, when they had to evacuate their world, and the trees from which they were fashioned were on Nordash. So they buy banjos from us as an acceptable substitute."

"That's right," Harker said. "Only don't ever ask a *nord* to play a banjo for you. Not unless you want a migraine that'll last all week." He became serious again. "Anyway, Frank traded them a container full of brand-new banjos, and during the exchange he learned something very interesting. The *nord* are no longer wanderers. The *danui* have recently given them permission to establish a colony on a world within their own system, and since then, the *nord* have been sending their people there."

"Well, that's generous, I suppose." Andromeda sipped her coffee. "But what does that have to do with us?"

"The *nord* captain told Frank that there may also . . .

very probably, in fact . . . be another world in the *danui* system that would be habitable by humans. And that if we approached the *danui* emissary and asked nicely, it might give us the hyperspace key for their starbridge."

For a few moments, Andromeda was speechless. Feeling the coffee mug about to slip from her hands, she leaned forward to carefully place it on the table. "You're joking," she said at last, then shook her head. "No, I'm sorry. I didn't mean it that way. What I meant to say was, *they're* joking, and *you* fell for it."

Harker neither smiled nor frowned. "No, I'm not kidding . . . and neither is Frank, or the *nord*, or even the *danui*. As soon as Frank let our people know what had been said to him, our Talus emissary went to see their Talus emissary, and the *danui* confirmed what the *nord* told Frank. Yes, there's a world in their home system that's human-habitable, and we're welcome to it."

Andromeda opened her mouth to respond, only to discover that she didn't know quite what to say. In the four hundred years that humankind had been exploring space, only one unoccupied world capable of supporting human life had been discovered, and that was Coyote. Every other planet humans had found or visited either required survival gear to cope with differences in atmosphere and temperature, or—as in the case of Sanja, the *soranta* homeworld—was already inhabited by oxygen-nitrogen breathers. Fortunately, Coyote's population was still small enough that no one expected to be bumping elbows with their neighbors anytime soon. All the same, though, the Navy had made the discovery of another world suitable for colonization a high priority.

"And that's it?" she asked. "The *danui* have a habitable planet in their home system, and they're willing to let us have it?" Harker nodded. "Just like that? No questions asked?"

"Only a couple of stipulations. We agree not to engage in hostile actions against them or any other races we may find there, and also that we accept their terms for future trade negotiations with them. But from what George Jones has told us, there's no one there whom we'd consider to be an enemy, and all they want from us is the same thing that they want from everyone else . . . raw materials like iron, copper, zinc, silicon, and so forth."

"I see." Andromeda slowly nodded. "And I take it that we've been given the planet's coordinates along with the starbridge key."

"The key, we have. George Jones said that the coordinates will be given to us once one of our ships makes the jump." Harker frowned slightly. "And that's something of a puzzle right there. Because, according to our data, there's not a lot in the *danui* home system, let alone planets habitable by us or anyone else."

He looked at his datapad again. "Display HD 76700 system diagram," he said loudly, and George Jones vanished, to be replaced by a three-dimensional schematic of a solar system. It was remarkably simple: a midsized star, with a single planet in a close yet highly elliptical orbit around it.

"HD 76700," Harker continued, reading from his pad's screen. "Type G6V star, same spectral class as 47 Uma but just a little larger, located 214.9 light-years from Coyote." He pointed to the sole planet circling the star. "In the early twenty-first century, optical inferometry found a small gas giant in close orbit around it. Since its semimajor axis is a little less than .05 AUs, that means HD 76700-B completes an orbit of its primary about once every four days."

Andromeda nodded. Hot Jupiters, while freakish, were not uncommon in the galaxy. They were usually gas giants that evolved in the outer reaches of a solar system, only to have their orbits gradually deteriorate over time. When that happened, the planets began long, slow falls toward their primaries, death spirals that took millennia to complete.

"Are you sure you've got the right system?" she asked. "I mean . . . look, I'm not an astronomer, but even I know that habitable worlds of any kind aren't usually found in the same system as a hot jupe. The whole system gets destabilized."

"Our people thought of that, too," Harker said, "but the

danui insist that this is their home system and that more than one habitable world exists there. But it's still strange as hell . . . Overlay HD 76700 remote image."

On top of the schematic diagram, a two-dimensional photographic image was transposed: the *danui* star, a small white blob brighter than the tiny dots of light in the background yet surrounded by a nimbus the color of verdigris on rusting copper pipes.

"That's what we see when we point a telescope at their system," Harker said. "We see their star, all right, and although HD 76700-B is too small to be seen directly, we know its there because of the gravitational effect it has on its primary. But if there's a planet located within a 1-AU radius, we can't make it out because of this thing"—he pointed to the nimbus—"which appears to be some sort of dust cloud or planetary nebula."

"A dust cloud?" Andromeda peered closely at the image. "Within 1 AU? Wouldn't that make any planets within the system . . . ?"

"Uninhabitable?" Harker finished. "Yes, at least that's what the science boys at the university told me when I checked with them." He paused. "But if there's no habitable planet anywhere in the system, why would the *danui* tell us otherwise? The *nord*, too, for that matter."

Andromeda absently tapped a forefinger against her lips. "I think I know where this is going," she said at last. "We've been given an awfully nice horse. Now someone needs to check its teeth, and that's why you've come to me."

"I was rather hoping that you'd say that." Harker smiled. "The Navy is reluctant to send a cruiser on a first-contact mission to a race as touchy as the *danui*. It might be seen as a hostile action, and they don't sound like a race we want to risk offending. On the other hand, you're a merchantman captain who also happens to have previous experience with survey missions. Your ship is designed for this kind of assignment, and you still have people in your crew who've done this sort of thing before."

"So have you, Ted."

"I'm too old for this sort of thing . . ."

Andromeda laughed out loud. "And I'm not?"

"A gentleman never inquires about a lady's age." Harker gave her a sly wink. "Besides, everyone knows you're barely eighteen."

"Is that in Earth or Coyote years?" She couldn't stand flattery, particularly when it came to her age. And since a year on Coyote was three times longer than one on Earth, the second guess was a lot closer to the mark than the first.

"Point taken." Harker shrugged. "Truth is, after the time I took a ship closer to Kasimasta than anyone thinking straight had a right to do and still live, I swore an oath to Emily that I'd never undertake a hazardous mission like that again. That's why I'm handling a milk run to Rho Coronae Borealis when I'm not flying a desk." A pause. "Besides, aren't you the one who just told me that she's bored?"

"I'm afraid I did." Andromeda slowly let out her breath. "All right, I'm in. When do you want me to leave?"

"Soon as you're ready, I suppose." Standing up from his chair, Harker leaned down to switch off his pad. "No need to rush. Take your time getting your crew together again. We're still putting together our own team."

"You're sending someone with us?"

"Of course . . . From the Corps of Exploration." As he slipped his datapad into his pocket, he seemed to notice the expression on her face. "Why, do you have a problem with that?"

"Oh, no," she lied. "None at all."

THREE

I T TOOK NEARLY NINE HOURS FOR THE CORPS OF EXPLORA-
tion gyro to travel from Hammerhead to Albion; the flight
included a brief refueling stop in Midland, the only time
the passengers had a chance to get out and stretch their legs.
Like the other four members of Special Survey Team
Three, Sean Carson spent most of the time either sleeping
or reading. A long mission was ahead of them, and no one
wanted to get on anyone else's nerves with unnecessary
chatter. Once the gyro was halfway across the Great Equatorial River, and the pilot announced that they would be
landing in twenty minutes, the others began to stir, looking
at one another as if it were the first time since they'd left
Fort Lopez that they'd become aware of the fact that they
were sharing an aircraft.

No. That wasn't entirely true. Sean was acutely conscious of the young woman seated beside him. The two of
them said little to each other, but there was a reason for
that; a few days earlier, he and Kyra had agreed that it was
probably best that they put their romance on hold until the

mission was over. It wouldn't be easy, particularly since they'd lately discovered that there was nothing they enjoyed more than each other's body. But the Corps frowned on sexual affairs among its members, and while most of their teammates politely looked the other way when Corporals Carson and Wright took off on their own, there was no sense in aggravating Lieutenant Cayce.

There was nothing wrong with talking, though, so as the gyro began to lose altitude, he felt Kyra's elbow nudge his own. "Colonial for your thoughts?" she murmured.

Sean looked away from the window beside his seat. "Nothing, really," he said quietly. "Just wondering how I'm going to handle my mother for the next few weeks."

Kyra glanced over her shoulder, making sure that neither Mark nor Sandy was paying attention to them. But Sergeant Dupree was studying his datapad while Corporal LaPointe gazed out the window on her side of the compartment, and if Lieutenant Cayce had overheard them from the gyro's front right seat, he gave no indication. "I wouldn't worry about it," she whispered. "She's probably just as nervous as you are." She caught the dubious expression on his face. "All right," she added, smiling slightly. "*Almost* as nervous."

Sean let out his breath. "You've never met my mother. She had her emotions surgically removed years ago."

Kyra raised an eyebrow. "You can't mean that."

"Just wait. You'll . . ."

"Something you'd like to share with the rest of us, Corporal?" From his seat in the cockpit, Cayce addressed him even though he continued to look straight ahead.

Sean felt his face grow warm, albeit more in anger than embarrassment. He could have sworn that the noise of the gyro's twin props would have drowned out their conversation, but apparently Amerigo Cayce had sharper ears than Sean thought. Either that or, more likely, he just didn't like having his people sharing secrets.

"Just talking about the assignment, sir," he replied, adopting an easygoing tone that he didn't feel. "Wondering why we're so lucky to get tapped for a first-contact job."

Lieutenant Cayce turned his head to look at him. "It's not a first-contact mission . . . or 'job,' if you want to call it that. Our people met the *danui* a long time ago. It's in the material you've been given if you haven't read it already."

There was a note of accusation in Cayce's voice, and it was impossible to miss the disdain in his eyes. Four days earlier, the survey team had been given intelligence reports pertaining to both the *nord* and the *danui*, with the expectation that the Corpsmen would study them thoroughly before the mission. Knowing Cayce, he'd probably read everything twice already, probably right after running twenty miles every morning at Fort Lopez.

"I've read it, sir," Sean said, meeting his gaze. "My mistake. This isn't the first time we've met the *danui* . . . only the first time we've been to their home system."

An abrupt cough from the seat behind him. From the corner of his eye, Sean caught Sandy covering her mouth with her hand. The cough was an attempt to keep from laughing out loud. Although Mark displayed no more emotion than he usually did, he was staring at his datapad screen just a little too fixedly, as if trying hard not to chuckle at Sean's subtle comeback. And while Kyra said nothing, Sean felt her slide her foot against his and, ever so gently, apply pressure against his toes.

Cayce didn't say anything. Then a smile slowly spread across his face. "That's all right, Sean," he said, assuming a cordiality neither of them had ever felt for the other. "I'm sure you have other things on your mind just now." A pause. "So . . . looking forward to seeing your mother again?"

Damn it, he had *been eavesdropping.* Either that, or he already knew that Sean's relations with his mother were not very warm. "I'm sure we'll be fine," he said, staring back at Cayce until the lieutenant looked away.

Behind him, he heard Mark and Sandy move restlessly. He half expected them to say something, but Mark's *Sa'Tong*ian beliefs prohibited him from any words or actions that might harm another, and, for once, Sandy refrained from the smart-ass remarks for which she was infamous. So they both remained quiet, and Kyra knew better than to ask him what she already knew: seeing his mother again was the last thing Sean wanted, let alone embarking on a mission with her.

But he hadn't been given a choice. Four days earlier, Sean and his teammates had just returned to Fort Lopez from a furlough, when they were summoned to a classified briefing for their next assignment: an expedition to a human-habitable planet located in HD 76700 system. Like the rest of the team, Sean was intrigued by the prospect of being the first people to visit a world that might possibly support a human colony; it was the sort of assignment for which he'd joined the Corps of Exploration. His enthusiasm waned, though, when they were informed that the ship that would transport them to the *danui* system was the *Carlos Montero*; he didn't need to be told who its commanding officer was even though it was a revelation to the others that Captain Andromeda Carson was Sean's mother. Sean had never told anyone in his team about his mother, and he was particularly reluctant to air the grievances between them.

A bump from the gyro's undercarriage caused Sean to return his gaze to the window. The coast of Albion was within sight, and the pilot had lowered the landing gear. A quick glimpse of the port city of New Brighton, then the aircraft made the left turn that would bring it toward the spaceport on its outskirts.

If I'm lucky, he thought, *I won't see much of her. And if I do, I'll just have to suck it up. But why the hell did it have to be her?*

The gyro swept over the spaceport, passing low above shuttles and freighters parked on its vast concrete expanse, until it came in for a touchdown near a row of hangars on the military side of the field. The pilot cut the engines, then reached up to yank the T-bar that unlocked the passenger hatch. "Here you go," he said. "Good luck."

"Thanks. Buy you a drink when we get back." Cayce unbuckled his seat belt and stood up. "All right, then," he said to the others. "Grab your gear and follow me."

Sean reached up to fetch his duffel bag from the rack above his seat, pulling down Kyra's bag as well. She was closer to the hatch than he was, so he waited while she followed the lieutenant from the aircraft. Once again, he found himself admiring her. Petite yet athletic, with olive skin and jet-black hair habitually tied back in a bun, she looked more like the university student she'd once been before enlisting in the Corps. Nonetheless, the Corps uniform suited her well; it was hard to ignore the way its blue unitard clung to her slim body. The contrast she made with Sandy—short and stocky, looking as if she wrestled creek cats for exercise— was striking; there weren't many women in the Corps as good-looking as the one with whom he'd shared a bed during their recent furlough. Unfortunately, that was another reason why he wasn't looking forward to the mission; once they were aboard the *Montero*, the two of them would have to refrain from their usual playtime. Sean didn't want to have to introduce his girlfriend to his mother.

The gyro had landed near two spacecraft. One was a Federation Navy shuttle, the recently built version of the type used to ferry passengers and freight to orbiting spacecraft; its side hatch was open, a ladder had been wheeled into place beneath it, and a small group stood below its port wing, apparently waiting for the Corps team. The other was a landing craft; a little larger than the shuttle and nearly thirty years old, with collapsible delta wings on either side of an indigenous-fuel nuclear engine, its midsection cargo hatch open to allow the ground crew to bring aboard the rest of the team's equipment.

"We'll be riding up with *Montero*'s crew," Cayce said, as they walked toward the shuttle. He had an annoying trait of explaining that which was already obvious. "Hand over your bags to the . . ."

"That won't be necessary." A woman stepped away from the group. "If those are your personal belongings, you'll want to keep them with you."

"Oh . . . all right, then." Cayce stopped in front of them, raised his right hand in a formal salute. "Lieutenant Amerigo

Cayce, commanding officer of Special Survey Team Three, Coyote Federation Corps of Exploration. You must be Captain Carson. Pleased to meet you, ma'am."

The woman smiled without returning the salute. Tall and slender, with dark hair twisted into a long braid that nearly reached her waist, she bore absolutely no resemblance to Sean. "Pleased to meet you, too, Lieutenant," she said, "but I'm not the skipper." A few chuckles from the people behind her, which she acknowledged with an amused wink before looking at Cayce again. "I'm Melpomene Fisk, the helmsman. Thanks for the salute, though."

"Oh." Cayce's face reddened as he dropped his hand. "I see. So who is . . . ?"

"I am." Another woman spoke up from the center of the group. "Don't bother with the salute. I'm not impressed."

How like her, Sean thought, as his mother stepped out from among her crew. *Let some poor schmuck make a fool out of himself just so her people can get a laugh at his expense.* He didn't realize it, but this was the first time he'd ever felt sympathy for Cayce.

"Captain Carson." Cayce did his best to recover from the gaffe although even his own team were hiding grins behind their hands. "Sorry, ma'am. I only assumed . . ."

"Yes, yes, I understand." A nonchalant flip of her hand brought an end to any unnecessary explanations. "I know this is when your people are supposed to be introduced to mine, but we're on a schedule here. The *Montero* has been given priority clearance through Starbridge Coyote, and before that we need to rendezvous with the gatehouse to pick up our last passenger."

"We have someone else coming along?" Cayce was puzzled. "I wasn't informed of that."

"Guess you haven't read the memo, then. A senior representative from Janus will be joining us. He'll have the hyperspace key to the *danui* system." Captain Carson was becoming impatient. "That means we need to get out of here soon, so if you'll get your people aboard . . ."

"Yes, ma'am." Pulling together what remained of his

dignity, Cayce turned to the others. "You heard the captain. Let's get moving."

"Yes, sir," Sandy muttered, barely able to suppress the sarcasm in her voice. The rest of the team hefted their bags and headed toward the shuttle. The five *Montero* crew members received a quiet nod from their commanding officer and fell in beside them; together, the two groups formed a line in front of the ladder leading to the shuttle's passenger hatch.

Sean avoided meeting his mother's gaze, and for a moment he thought he might be able to board the spacecraft without having to speak to her. She was having none of that, though. He was about to walk past her when he felt her hand on his arm.

"Sean?" she said quietly. "Aren't you going to say hello?"

Sighing inwardly, he paused to look at her. "Hello, Captain. Good to see you again."

As always, there was no expression on Andromeda Carson's face, yet the look in her eyes betrayed her surprise at the coldness of his tone. "Good to see you, too, Corporal," she replied. "I was surprised to learn that you're on this mission. I'm looking forward to . . ."

"Thank you, ma'am." Sean took a step forward, freeing himself from her grasp. "If you'll excuse me . . ."

"Corporal." From behind him, Mark Dupree spoke up. "Before we go, I think we ought to make sure our equipment has been properly stowed." Sean glanced at him, and Mark nodded toward the nearby lander. "The gyro, I mean."

Sean was about to tell Mark that he was sure the gyro was in fine shape when Cayce stopped at the foot of the ladder. "Good idea, Sergeant. Captain, with your permission . . . ?"

"I agree." Andromeda Carson nodded. "We have time for a quick inspection." She gestured to a large, red-bearded man wearing the insignia of a chief petty officer. "Zeus . . . please take their gear and put it beneath their seats."

Sean surrendered his bag to the crewman she'd called Zeus, as did Mark; then they turned to walk across the apron to the shuttle. Several ground crewmen were standing beneath the belly hatch; they waited while the two Corpsmen approached them. Mark glanced over his shoulder, then looked at Sean.

"So . . . want to tell me what's going on?" he whispered. "With your mother, I mean."

"Not really."

"C'mon, man. Don't make me give you an order." Mark was Sean's superior officer, but the two of them seldom observed the difference in status. They'd joined the Corps at the same time and gone through training together, with both qualifying for Special Survey, and it was only because Mark had scored a few points better on their final field test that he'd been made sergeant instead of Sean. They were friends first and foremost, though, and only rarely did Mark pull rank on his buddy. But this was one of those times. "Do you have a problem working with her that I should know about?"

Sean hesitated. "Look, it's not something I really like to talk about. Can I just say that we don't get along and leave it at that?"

By then, they'd reached the shuttle. Looking up at it, Sean read its name, stenciled across the port fuselage beneath the cockpit windows next to the Coyote Federation flag. Something else had once been there, and Sean vaguely recalled that it was the name of some Central American socialist or another. But that name, along with the Western Hemisphere Union flag, had long since been painted over, with a new one in its place: *Gilbert Reese*, after the United Republic of America colonel who'd been one of the original *Alabama* colonists, if Sean wasn't mistaken.

"You're going to be flying this thing, aren't you?" he asked, trying to change the subject.

A quick smile from Mark. "If I'm lucky and someone else doesn't beat me to it." He knelt to look at the tandem-mounted wheels of its forward landing gear, then stood up again. "I'm not trying to pry into your private life," he went on, speaking quietly. "I just need to know that if she gives you an order, you're going to follow it."

Ducking his head, Sean stepped beneath the lowered left-side door of the belly hatch and peered up into the cargo bay. Suspended from a trapeze within the bay was the expedition gyro; with an aft-mounted pusher-prop, winglike stabilizers, and a main prop whose four blades were neatly folded together above the narrow canopy of its cockpit, the small aircraft was just large enough to seat a pilot and four passengers. Even so, they'd practically be sitting in each other's lap.

"If she gives me an order, I'll follow it," Sean said, reaching high above his head to grab hold of the gyro's starboard skid. He shoved at it, and was satisfied to see that it barely moved; the trapeze would keep the gyro from banging around during launch and landing. "Just don't expect me to have tea with her." *Not that tea is what she usually drinks,* he silently added.

Sean and Mark took another minute to make sure the aluminum cases containing the rest of their gear had been loaded aboard the *Reese*, then they left the lander and trotted back to the shuttle. By then, everyone else had gone aboard, and the aft pods of the spacecraft's *hjadd*-made reactionless drive were already glowing. The ground crew held the ladder while Sean and Mark climbed aboard, then they wheeled it away, leaving it to Sean to close the hatch and dog it tight.

The rear compartment was cramped; the shuttle was meant only for ground-to-orbit sorties, with passenger comfort a lesser priority. Mark had already found a seat, so there was only one left; Sean was relieved to find that it wasn't next to his mother, who'd gone forward to join Melpomene in the cockpit. On the other hand, Zeus had decided to take the seat next to Kyra, which meant that Sean found himself having to sit with Cayce.

"Everything all right?" the lieutenant asked, as Sean pulled his harness straps around his shoulders and waist.

"Yes, sir." Sean clicked shut the six-point buckle and made sure the straps were tight. "Loaded and locked down."

Cayce nodded. There was a mild jar as a tractor attached itself to the shuttle's forward landing gear and began to tow the spacecraft out to the launchpad. Cayce gazed out the starboard window beside them, and for a few moments, Sean was able to hope that the team leader would leave him alone. But it was too much luck to count on because the tractor had just detached itself from the shuttle and moved away when Cayce turned to him again.

"That was a rather cold reception you gave your mother." His voice was none too quiet; on the other side of the aisle, two other *Montero* crewmen—the name patches on their jumpsuits read R. KURTZ and J. RESSLER—turned their heads slightly as if to listen in. "I hope this isn't going to be a problem."

"It won't be." Sean glared at Kurtz and Ressler until they looked away again, then he turned back to Cayce. "And forgive me for saying so," he murmured, "but how I get along with my mother is no one's business but mine . . . sir."

Cayce scowled at him, and for a couple of moments, Sean thought he was going to have a quarrel with his CO. Which was fine with him. He was willing to respect the lieutenant's position as team leader; despite his shortcomings, Sean also had found a few things to admire about Amerigo Cayce in the eight months they'd worked together. Yet there were times when Cayce could be overbearing; unlike Mark, he wasn't hesitant about pulling rank. There was nothing in Corps regulations that said Sean couldn't argue with a superior officer, though, and Cayce had already learned that Corporal Carson was willing to take him on.

"Very well, then." Cayce dropped his voice a little. "I'll let you two work it out on your own . . . so long as it doesn't get in the way of our mission."

Sean was about to reply when, as if on cue, his mother's voice came over the ceiling speaker: *"All hands, stand by . . . Launch in ten seconds."*

That ended the conversation, much to Sean's relief. Grasping the armrests with both hands, he lay back against the heavily padded seat, forcing himself to relax as much as possible. This wasn't the first time he'd been aboard a spacecraft; nonetheless, he still had to ignore the skeeters in his stomach whenever he went into orbit.

A low, hollow moan from the engines' pods rose gradually to a high-pitched whine, then there was a slight jar as the shuttle lifted off from the pad. There was no exhaust plume as it ascended to five hundred feet upon its negmass thrusters, then the nose tilted upward, and, with very little noise, the shuttle leapt toward the sky. Careful not to turn his head toward the window, lest the mounting g-force cause his neck to suffer whiplash, Sean watched from the corner of his eye as the sky gradually faded from blue to purple to jet-black. A green and brown horizon, gently curved and crisscrossed by the blue veins of rivers and channels, swept into view; moments later, the vast bulk of 47 Ursae Majoris-B appeared beyond Coyote, the silver sword of its ring plane lancing straight out into space.

They were on their way.

FOUR

TWO AND A HALF HOURS AFTER THE SHUTTLE LIFTED OFF from New Brighton, it rendezvoused with the *Montero*. From the copilot's seat, Andromeda Carson watched as Melpomene Fisk deftly manipulated the control yoke. Melpomene had been *Montero*'s helmsman ever since its original pilot retired and Andromeda was forced to recruit a replacement; Fisk had demonstrated her ability to fly anything that could leave the ground, including spacecraft retrofitted with reactionless drives. All the same, Andromeda quietly made sure that the shuttle was on course before allowing herself the luxury of gazing out the cockpit windows.

Even half-hidden within its orbital dry dock, the CFSS *Carlos Montero* was magnificent. Three hundred feet long, with a dry weight of nine thousand tons, it was a long, fat cylinder that gradually tapered at its midsection to a slighter smaller service module from which the nacelles of its four gas-core nuclear engines were mounted on outriggers. At the bow was the broad dish of its deflector array; just aft of the crew module were the maneuvering thrusters. Lights gleamed from portholes along the hull; as the shuttle came closer, Andromeda could see that the lander bay was already open in preparation for *Reese*'s arrival.

If any spacecraft could be called a tall ship, then the *Montero* met the definition for such an antiquated term. The ship was old, even obsolete by some measures; indeed, it was a starship in name only since it had been originally designed for travel within Earth's solar system and had made its first starbridge jump only after it had been refitted with a hyperspace-rated AI. Yet even after all these years, Andromeda hadn't become jaded to the sight of her vessel. It was one of the few pleasures she still derived from being a captain.

"Shuttle Romeo Navajo Six-Two to Dry Dock Alpha Six, requesting clearance for final approach and docking." Melpomene listened to her headset for a few moments. "Thank you, Alpha Six, we copy. Over." She glanced at Andromeda. "Port hatch, skipper? Or do you want me to use the bay?"

"Port hatch, please." Andromeda knew that the *Reese* was scheduled for launch a half hour after the shuttle's departure, and she didn't want the bay to still be occupied by the shuttle when the *Reese* arrived. Regulations mandated that a starship's landing craft should be flown to orbit by a harbor pilot; the rule was a nuisance, and she suspected that it had been put in effect mainly to provide employment for spacers who otherwise wouldn't have jobs. At least it meant that her crew would all board the ship at the same time; only two or three dockworkers were presently aboard the *Montero*, and they'd leave as soon as the captain and crew came aboard.

Andromeda stole a glance through the cockpit door. She'd hoped that her people would use the time to acquaint themselves with the Corps of Exploration team, but it appeared that only her chief petty officer, Zeus Brandt, had made the effort to do so, and probably because the Corpsman he'd chosen to sit next to was young, female, and good-looking; Andromeda hoped that Melpomene wouldn't notice her boyfriend's flirtation with another woman. Jason Ressler, her first officer, ignored the two Corpsmen sitting across the aisle from him. Rolf Kurtz, the chief engineer, and Anne Smith, the communications officer, were seated side by side, neither of them speaking to Lieutenant Cayce or Sean even though they were within arm's reach.

Andromeda looked away. On one hand, she couldn't blame her crew for being a little standoffish. They'd been on shore leave for the past six weeks, and most of them had spent the ground time with their families; Mel and Zeus were the only crewmen who didn't have spouses, and from what Andromeda had heard, Zeus made up for it with a long list of girlfriends, his relationship with Mel notwithstanding. The new mission had brought an abrupt end to their vacations; so as far as they were concerned, the Corps team was little more than a group of unwanted passengers.

Perhaps that would change once the ship was under way. It would take the *Montero* twelve hours to reach Starbridge Coyote and its gatehouse; in the meantime, she could call for a general meeting. No, even better . . . lunch in the wardroom. Much more informal. She'd made sure that the galley was stocked with a few gallons of wine; maybe that would be a good time to break out a bottle or two. Regulations prohibited the flight crew from drinking while on duty, but she was the captain, after all, and she could bend the rules a little if she . . .

Oh hell, woman, she thought, *admit it. You don't care about making friends with any of these people. You're just trying to find a way to talk to Sean, maybe make peace with him.* She winced. *Yeah, right. Fat chance . . .*

"Skipper?" Melpomene's voice interrupted her thoughts. "Coming in on final approach. Alpha Seven Control on Channel Two for you."

Andromeda snapped herself back to awareness. Through the windows, she could see that Melpomene had maneuvered the shuttle toward the dry dock's open forward end and was slowly guiding the small craft toward *Montero*'s port side. She tapped her headset mike. "*Montero* CO to

Alpha Seven Control. Request permission for rendezvous and docking."

"Roger that, Montero *CO."* The male voice on the other end of the comlink sounded bored. *"Welcome back. Dock crew standing by to hand over the ship."*

"We copy, Alpha Seven, thank you. *Montero* CO over." Andromeda muted her mike again. A needless formality, but it could be worse. When she'd been with the Union Astronautica, and her vessel was named after a long-dead Cuban president, she would've had to endure a final meeting with a Patriarch before being allowed to board her own ship. The traditions of Coyote's merchant marine were much less demanding.

Melpomene performed a 180-degree roll to align the shuttle's port hatch with *Montero*'s, then coaxed the craft the rest of the way in, carefully maneuvering past the dry dock's mooring cables. The hull gradually grew larger until there was a dull *clang* as the shuttle docking collar telescoped forward to mate with the *Montero*. Melpomene reached up to flip a couple of switches, and there was a soft hiss as the shuttle's internal atmosphere depressurized slightly. "Docking complete, Captain," she said.

"Thanks. Good job." Andromeda unfastened her harness and pushed herself out of her seat, reaching down to retrieve her duffel bag. The others were already pulling their own bags out from under their seats when she floated into the aft compartment. It was customary for the captain to be first to board her ship, so the crew and passengers waited for her to undog the hatch and pull it open.

On the other side of the gangway tunnel, *Montero*'s primary airlock was open, with three men already waiting for her in the narrow compartment. "Welcome aboard, Captain," said the harbor pilot as he handed her a datapad. "Ship's ready to launch. You're all set to go."

"Thank you." Andromeda slipped the pad into a thigh pocket; she'd read his report later. "See you when we get back." The pilot nodded, then he and the other two men pulled themselves aside and watched while *Montero*'s crew floated through the hatch, followed by the Corps team. Once everyone was aboard, the three men would board the shuttle and fly it to the dry dock's control module, where they would remain until the starship had successfully launched.

Just beyond the airlock was an access shaft leading forward. Barely touching the rungs of its ladder, Andromeda pushed herself forward to Deck Four, where the crew and passenger cabins were located. She opened another hatch, then entered a circular corridor that wound its way around the ship's interior; behind her, she heard the others coming up the shaft. The ceiling lights were already on, the passageway pleasantly warm. The dock crew had done a good job of bringing the *Montero* back to life; there was little to show that the ship had been cold and lifeless during the six weeks it had spent in parking orbit before being moved to the dry dock for preflight maintenance and refueling.

Grasping a ceiling rail, Andromeda pulled herself along the corridor until she reached her quarters. She slid open its pocket door and pushed herself inside. It wasn't much larger than any other cabin, which meant that it was about the size of her bathroom back home, but she'd done her best to make it comfortable: paper books secured to the shelf above her fold-down desk, a handmade quilt on the bunk, landscape watercolors by a favorite artist affixed to the bulkheads. There was an old picture of Sean on the bulkhead beside the porthole, taken on his tenth birthday; there had once been one of Dean, too, but she'd removed it long ago. It didn't do her any good to be reminded of her ex-husband.

Andromeda stayed only long enough to stow her bag and put on a pair of stickshoes before leaving again. As she pulled herself down the passageway, she saw her crew putting stuff away in their own cabins; Jason caught her eye, gave her a quick nod. "I'll be right up, skipper," he said in response to her unasked question.

"Very good," she replied, then moved on. In the next cabin, Mel was having a quiet conversation with Zeus. The helmsman and the chief petty officer fell silent as the captain went by. Andromeda ignored them, but once again she found herself wondering how much longer she could pretend not to know that the two of them were sleeping together during voyages. So long as it didn't affect their jobs, Andromeda was willing to look the other way; she didn't like it, but it wasn't any of her business.

Just before she reached the hatch leading to the main access shaft, Andromeda entered the part of Deck Three where the passenger cabins lay. Unlike her crew, the Corps team would have to share quarters. Even so, it looked as if Lieutenant Cayce had claimed one cabin for his own: another indication that his sense of leadership left much to be desired. But just as Andromeda was about to open the shaft hatch, Sean floated out of the next cabin. He caught sight of his mother, and for a moment the two of them silently regarded each other, as if waiting for the other person to say the first word.

Andromeda broke the silence. "Doing all right, Sean?"

"Fine, Captain." Again, his tone was stiffly formal. "No problems at all."

"Good. Glad to hear it." She paused, trying to find something else to say. "If you need anything, just . . ."

"Thank you," he replied, then he withdrew into his quarters. Andromeda had a quick glimpse of Sergeant Dupree, his cabinmate, then the door slid shut.

For a moment, Andromeda had an urge to pull herself over to Sean's cabin, knock on the door, ask Dupree to give them some privacy, then . . . well, what? Another fight with her son, with her crew and the Corps team as witnesses? Perhaps she could ask for forgiveness again, knowing well that it wasn't coming anytime soon. Or maybe she could just yank him out of there and haul him to the airlock while ordering Jason to call the shuttle back so that it could take home a troublesome passenger. After all, that was her prerogative; as captain, she could bounce someone from her ship without cause, and no one could do anything about it.

Or maybe none of the above. Which was the best option, really. *Leave it alone,* she told herself as she opened the hatch and pulled herself into the access shaft. *You don't have time for this. You're back on your ship, and you've got a mission ahead of you. So knock it off.*

Andromeda closed the hatch behind her, then glided up the shaft, passing the hatches for Decks Three and Two until she reached Deck One. The top hatch was closed; she pulled its lock-lever counterclockwise and shoved it open. The command center was empty, but the dock crew had switched on the consoles and screens before leaving, and the room was alive with light and sound.

Andromeda never got tired of that particular moment, when she had *Montero*'s bridge all to herself, if only for a few minutes. Inserting the toes of her shoes within a foot rail behind her wingback chair, she gazed around the bowl-shaped compartment. Surrounding her were the horseshoe-like carrels of the flight stations, with flatscreens arranged along the consoles below them. Within the shallow dome of the ceiling were portholes, and the forward bulkhead could become a massive wallscreen, showing whatever view she desired. Directly in front of her was the navigation table, a holotank within which *Montero*'s present position could be projected within a three-dimensional sphere.

This was her home, really; her place in New Brighton was only the house she stayed in when she wasn't on her ship. *It'll be a sad day when I leave this behind,* she thought, idly running her fingertips across the worn faux leather of her chair. *This may be the last time, though. I'm getting old, and I can't . . .*

Movement from the open floor hatch behind her; she looked around to see Jason coming up the manhole. "You're always the first one here, aren't you?" he asked, a smile upon his face.

"That's my job." A new thought occurred to her. "Did you tell Ted Harker that I was thinking about retirement?"

Jason raised an eyebrow. "No. Are you?"

Andromeda ignored the question. "Well, someone did . . . or at least someone told someone else, and word got back to him." She shook her head as she withdrew her toes from the foot rail; planting the soles of her shoes against the carpet, she carefully walked around to her seat. "Never mind. Doesn't matter. Let's get started."

Jason nodded, then pushed himself over to his chair, to the right of her own. Watching him, Andromeda felt a twinge of nostalgia. Jason Ressler had been her first officer for as long as she had been in command of the ship, back when both of them had been in the Union Astronautica. He was older now, too, his hair turning grey, and a small pot nestled in the place where a flat stomach had once been, but there was a time not so long ago, shortly after they'd taken the *Castro* through Starbridge Earth and announced their intent to defect to the Coyote Federation, when they'd had a furtive little affair of their own. It hadn't been good for either of them, though, more an act of desperation than anything else, and they'd amicably put an end to it. He'd married since then, to a woman he'd met in Liberty during the crew's involuntary sabbatical, and although he and Andromeda remained close friends, they seldom mentioned the brief period when they'd shared a bed. Indeed, that was the last time she'd had an affair with anyone; even when she'd been making love to Jason, she'd felt as if Dean were in the room.

Andromeda settled into her seat; fastening its waist strap, she then pulled the side-mounted console across her lap. In her thigh pocket was the datapad the harbor pilot had given her; she was still studying his report and comparing it to the data on her console when the rest of the flight crew showed up for work. One by one, they floated up the manhole and went to their respective stations: Melpomene at the helm to Andromeda's left; Rolf at the engineering console beside her; Anne at the communications station to the right of Jason; Zeus at the chief petty officer's carrel next to her. Two stations were vacant—remote survey and probe control—but it wouldn't be necessary to fill them until after the last passenger came aboard at the gatehouse and the ship had reached its destination. Once everyone was where they should be, idle chatter came to an end, and the serious work began; pulling on their headsets, the crew members murmured to one another as they started going through the prelaunch checklist.

It took nearly two hours, but at last Andromeda was satisfied that the *Montero* was ready to leave port. By then, the *Reese* had arrived, the dock crew securing it within the lander bay. The wallscreen displayed an aft view; the bay's double doors were shut, and the last couple of workers were moving away from the ship, the flash of their maneuvering units giving them the appearance of fireflies.

"Time to go," Andromeda murmured, and Jason nodded in agreement. Signaling Anne to open a channel, she prodded her mike. "Alpha Seven Control, this is *Montero* CO. All stations reporting green-for-go, requesting permission to initiate final launch sequence. Beginning five-minute countdown on your mark."

"We copy, Montero CO," the familiar voice replied. *"Initiate launch sequence . . . mark."*

Andromeda glanced over at Melpomene. The helmsman tapped codes into her keyboard, glanced at her screens, then nodded to Rolf. The chief engineer responded with a silent nod of his own, then entered the commands that would commence the main engines' primary ignition sequence. Across their consoles, lights went from orange to green; Andromeda glanced at her own lapboard, saw that there were no warning signals.

From here on, there was little for her to do except watch. It was up to her people to work in concert with *Montero*'s comps. She looked over at Zeus. "Inform the passengers that we're launching in five."

"Aye, skipper." The chief petty officer touched his mike and murmured something she couldn't hear, then touched a button on his console. Four bells rang through the ceiling speakers, announcing the five-minute warning. Down on Deck Four, the Corps team would be strapping themselves into their bunks. There would be little for them to see, though; their cabin flatscreens and the view through their bulkheads wouldn't show them very much. Sean was probably in his bunk, impatiently waiting for the ship to start moving. If only he could be on the bridge . . .

On impulse, she turned to Jason. "Call Sean," she said quietly, "and tell him to come up here."

The first officer blinked. This was an unusual order. "Any particular reason?"

"I'd like for him to be here, that's all." Andromeda paused. "Don't tell him it's my idea," she added. "Just say that his presence on the bridge is requested."

Jason said nothing for a moment. He was aware of the tense relationship Andromeda had with her son. Then he reluctantly nodded and prodded his mike.

The countdown had reached the two-minute mark when Sean appeared. He pushed himself through the manhole, stopped himself by grasping a bulkhead rung. "Something I can do for you, Captain?"

"Not at all." Andromeda looked over her shoulder at him. "Just thought you'd like to have a better view of the launch." She gestured to the vacant seat at the remote survey station, to her right next to Rolf. "Sit there."

Sean hesitated. "Thanks, but I'd prefer to be below."

"Too late now. Regs say everyone has to be strapped down. You can't get back to your cabin in time." Andromeda pointed to the empty chair. "Sit."

Sean scowled, and for an instant Andromeda thought he might disobey her and duck back down the shaft. He didn't argue, though, but instead pushed himself over to the unoccupied station. Andromeda waited until he'd fastened the lap strap. "See?" she said, offering him a smile. "Better than watching from your cabin, isn't it?"

Sean stared straight ahead. "Bigger screen," he muttered.

Butter wouldn't melt in your mouth, would it? Andromeda wisely kept her thoughts to herself as she turned to Jason. "Status?"

"T minus one minute, five seconds." There was a sympathetic look on the first officer's face; no one else in the command center appeared to have paid attention to what was going on, but Andromeda suspected that everyone had been quietly listening in.

"Detach mooring lines," she said. "Switch comps to full autopilot." Rolf and Melpomene moved to obey; on the forward screen, she saw the bow lines float away. She touched a stud on her console; above the nav table, a translucent blue sphere materialized, showing a tiny replica of the *Montero* hovering within its dry dock. "Anne . . ."

"Comlink open, ma'am," the communications officer said, anticipating Andromeda's next command.

"Thank you." Andromeda touched her mike again. "Alpha Seven Control, this is *Montero* CO. Launching in"—a quick glance at the chronometer on her console—"T minus twenty-nine seconds."

"We copy, Montero. *You're clear for departure. Good sailing. Alpha Seven over."*

"Thank you, Alpha Seven. See you soon. *Montero* CO over and out." Andromeda silenced the mike, slowly let out her breath. Yet another moment she relished: the ship leaving port, bound for the stars. Glancing around the bridge, she saw the same expectant expressions on the faces of her crew. No one who worked on a starship could be unmoved by that particular instant, no matter how many times they might have experienced it.

Sean remained stoical, though. His arms were folded across his chest as he continued to gaze at the screen. "Enjoying yourself?" Andromeda asked.

"Yes, ma'am," he replied.

Andromeda was still staring at him when the countdown reached zero, and *Montero*'s four engines fired. A dull rumble as the hull shuddered, then Andromeda felt a gentle but insistent hand push her against her seat. Looking away from Sean, she watched as the dry dock slowly moved away from the ship until there was nothing to be seen ahead except the broad blue-and-green curve of Coyote's horizon, shining bright against the pitch-black darkness.

For the next several minutes, the only words spoken in

the command deck were the occasional comments of the flight crew as the *Montero* eased itself out of high orbit and commenced the .05-g thrust that would take it to the starbridge. Coyote disappeared from sight, to be replaced by Bear, its rings no longer resembling a blade but instead becoming a silver ellipse around a blue-banded world. As the starship left Coyote behind, the stars began to come out, until space wasn't a black abyss anymore but instead a tapestry of distant suns.

Melpomene finally reported that the *Montero* had reached cruise velocity, and Andromeda ordered her to reduce thrust to one-quarter. Zeus rang two bells, signaling that general quarters was over. Andromeda unfastened her lap strap and rose from her seat; now that the ship was at low gravity, everyone would be able to stand and walk around, at least until the *Montero* reached the Lagrange point near Bear, where Starbridge Coyote was located.

Raising her arms above her head, the captain arched her back and stretched, then she turned toward the remote survey station. "I hope you . . ." she started to say, then stopped.

Sean was no longer there. The moment that two bells had sounded, he'd left his seat and exited the command center, without so much as a word to his mother.

"You're welcome," she whispered to the empty chair. "Come again anytime."

FIVE

THE LAST TIME SEAN CARSON HAD SEEN THE GATEHOUSE at Starbridge Coyote was when he was a small child aboard that very same ship, just after the *Castro* had made the hyperspace jump from Earth that would change his life. Although he'd been in space on several occasions since then, this was the first time in his adulthood that he'd visited the starport in trojan orbit near Bear.

Back then, the gatehouse had been little more than a spindle-shaped collection of modules that had once been the EASS *Columbus*, the first European starship to reach 47 Ursae Majoris. The original station was long gone, deorbited shortly after the second starbridge was built and sent spiraling into Bear's turbulent upper atmosphere. In its place was the new and much larger gatehouse: a ring of twelve cylindrical modules around a central docking hub, serving as both the starbridge's control station and also a port of call for the various alien vessels that came through hyperspace to humankind's sole colony world.

The gatehouse was primitive in comparison to *Talus*

qua'spah, the vast space colony in orbit above the *hjadd* homeworld; nonetheless, it was an impressive piece of engineering, particularly when one considered the fact that it had been built from scratch with materials extracted from Bear's other moons. From his cabin window, Sean saw another starship hovering on the station's opposite side. He recognized the seed-shaped form as being a *nord* merchant ship, its solar sails furled upon the spars projecting from its elegantly streamlined hull. Other than a couple of merchant marine freighters, it was the only vessel in sight.

Four bells rang, signaling the final burn of *Montero*'s maneuvering thrusters; the ship was about to enter parking orbit near the station. Adjusting his grip on the ceiling rail, Sean let his feet swing free as, a few seconds later, a vibration passed through the ship. The burn lasted less than a minute; when it was over, gone were the last vestiges of the low gravity he and the others had enjoyed during the long ride out from Coyote. Since the *Montero* didn't have diametric drive, it wasn't equipped with Millis-Clement field generators either. No more gravity until the ship was under way again.

Sean had just swung his legs down to plant his stickshoes against the carpeted floor when the cabin door slid open, and Mark Dupree floated in.

"You're right," Mark said, pushing himself to the other side of the narrow cabin the men shared. "You get a better view from the wardroom."

"Thought so." Sean looked back out the window. "I remembered the windows as being bigger on Deck Two."

"Well, you'll get another chance in fifteen minutes. We're meeting the Janus rep there as soon as he arrives. His skiff is already on the way over." Mark paused. "Cayce told me to tell you that you're expected to be there. No excuses this time."

Sean nodded. Lunch had been served in the wardroom a few hours earlier, but he'd skipped it. He'd claimed to be spacesick, but Kyra had smuggled him a sandwich anyway; she knew the real reason why he'd ducked the little get-together with *Montero*'s crew, as did Mark. His mother had tricked him into coming up to the bridge; he'd escaped as soon as it was safe enough for him to go back down the access shaft, but as much as he didn't want to give her another chance to corner him, he knew that another encounter was inevitable.

"Yeah, well . . . guess there's no getting around it." Sean zipped up his unitard, then unclipped his Corps waistcoat from a wall hook. "I could find a gun and shoot myself in the foot, but someone would just haul me to the autodoc."

"That someone would probably be me." A wry grin as Mark planted his own shoes against the floor. "And you don't want me to get pissed off at you."

"An empty threat, and you know it." Sean slipped on the vestlike waistcoat. "*Sa'Tong*ians are pacifists. You wouldn't do anything to me even if your own life was at stake."

"Wrong. I'm a pacifist only so long as my own life is concerned. But the Fourth Codicil gives me permission to kick your ass if it'll stop you from hurting yourself or others. And until you get over your problems with your mother . . ."

"Never mind." Sean sighed as he found his uniform beret in the waistcoat's side pocket. He thought about putting it on, then decided against it. Too formal. "Let's just drop it, okay? I'm sick of talking about it."

"Really? That's funny. As long as I've known you, you've never told me what this is all about." Mark folded his arms together. "What *do* you have against your mother, anyway?"

"It's a long story." Sean turned toward the door. "C'mon. Let's get upstairs before the lieutenant has a fit."

The wardroom didn't look like any other compartment on the *Montero*. Indeed, Sean reflected, it looked very little like the way he'd remembered it from when the *Montero* was called the *Castro*. Over the years, the crew had made it as homey as possible; the utilitarian furniture had been replaced with a long blackwood mess table and leather-backed chairs, and the floor was covered by a handmade carpet with an intricate Navajo design. The walls had faux-birch panels upon which artwork had been hung; there was a framed painting of the Gillis Range on Coyote, but also a crayon drawing of the ship that apparently had been done by the kindergarten-age child of one of the crew members. Someone had even tacked up a restaurant menu beside the galley serving window; it wasn't until Sean looked more closely that he realized it was a joke since everything on it was a gourmet version of the ship's standard fare: potage au chicken noodle, grilled ration bar, and so forth.

The chairs and table, of course, were useless until the *Montero* was under thrust; when he and Mark arrived, they found the rest of their team using hand and foot rails to keep themselves in place. Cayce glared at Sean as he came in. "I take it you're no longer feeling ill," he said, his tone suggesting that he suspected Sean's earlier excuse to be false.

"Not at all, Lieutenant. Thanks for asking." Using the wall rail, Sean pulled himself across the room until he reached Kyra's side. "Did I miss anything?"

"Only a chance to get acquainted with the crew." There was an amused glint in Cayce's eyes. "Of course, you probably know one or two of them already."

Ignoring the jab, Sean turned his head to gaze out the window, a broad oval that took up most of one wall; through it, he could see the gatehouse a little more clearly. As he watched, a skiff glided away from the *Montero*, heading toward the station. The small craft had apparently just dropped off the expedition's final member; he guessed that one of the crew was probably escorting the company rep to his quarters.

"So who is this guy, anyway?" Standing at the other side of the room, Sandy LaPointe gazed out the window past Sean and Kyra. "Not just a company suit, I hope."

"He's a senior vice president with Janus," Cayce said stiffly. "Which means that this better be the last time I hear you call him a suit, Corporal."

"Oh, okay . . . so he's a very important suit." Sandy winked at the others. "Glad to have that cleared up."

Sean and Mark chuckled, and Kyra bit her lower lip to keep from laughing out loud. Janus Ltd. was the Federation's largest private import company, and also the merchant marine's leading partner. Originally established on Earth, it had relocated to Coyote shortly after the new world's independence was recognized by the United Nations. After contact was made with the *hjadd*, Janus had become responsible for opening trade with both them and the other Talus races. As a result, the company continued to grow in prosperity and power even after the death of its founder, Morgan Goldstein.

Janus and the merchant marine—and by extension the Coyote government—had very close ties, and sometimes it was difficult to see where the dividing line lay. No wonder, then, that a senior VP would be accompanying the first expedition to the *danui* system. Sean just hoped that they weren't getting someone who'd try to micromanage the team as well.

So it came as a surprise that, when the wardroom door opened again, the person escorted in by Chief Petty Officer Brandt was a tall and rather thin gentleman in his middle years who looked more like a university professor than a business magnate. His close-cropped black hair thinned to a small bald spot at the crown of his head, and his gaunt face was framed by a pair of antique gold-wire spectacles; for some reason, he'd apparently decided not to undergo optical surgery. He wore a frock coat over a black turtleneck sweater and khaki trousers, and the quick, easygoing smile he gave everyone as he entered the room was relaxed and unpretentious.

Kyra uttered a small gasp. Glancing at her, Sean saw recognition in her eyes. "I know him," she whispered to him. "He's . . ."

"Shh!" Cayce gave her a stern look, and Kyra went silent again.

"Good afternoon, or whatever it is," the newcomer said, then glanced at the old-fashioned watch on his left wrist. "Whoops . . . By ship's time, it's already evening." A mildly embarrassed grin. "I must be off by a few hours. I could've sworn it was just after lunch."

"Doesn't matter," Mark said. "In space, it's always the middle of the night."

An old joke, but the exec laughed as if this were the first time he'd ever heard it. "So it is, so it is." He glanced at Zeus. "Thanks, Chief, I appreciate it. I think I can take over from here."

"Very good." Zeus started to back toward the door, then paused to raise a hand to his earpiece. He listened for a moment, murmured something Sean couldn't hear, and looked at the newcomer again. "Captain Carson sends her regards and says she'll be along shortly."

Sean suppressed a sigh. It couldn't be helped; this was his mother's ship, after all, and he couldn't avoid her indefinitely. Kyra briefly touched his hand and gave him a sympathetic look; everyone else pretended not to notice his discomfort. "Very good," the exec said, and once Zeus had shut the door behind him, he returned his attention to the Corps team. "Well, then . . . until the captain arrives, perhaps I should introduce myself. My name's Thomas D'Anguilo, and I'm the executive vice president of trade and development for Janus, Ltd."

"Suit," Sandy muttered. She feigned a cough into her fist to disguise the comment, but everyone in the room heard what she said, including D'Anguilo. He didn't look directly at her; nonetheless, he responded to her unkind remark.

"I'm sure some of you think I'm some kind of bureaucrat or corporate stooge," he said, his tone remaining mild and unflustered, "but don't let the job title fool you." With practiced ease, he planted his feet firmly against the carpet; Sean noted that his stickshoes, while apparently custom-made, were well-worn. "I prefer to think of myself as an astro-ethnicist, which is what I was doing at the University of New Florida before Janus hired me away."

A low chuckle from Kyra drew everyone's attention. "Sorry," she murmured, embarrassed by her own interruption. "It's just that . . . well, I thought I recognized you. I took one of your classes when I was at the university."

D'Anguilo peered at her, then he abruptly snapped his fingers. "Of course . . . Ms. Wright, isn't it?" She smiled and nodded, which he reciprocated in kind. "I remember you telling me once that you wanted to join the Corps after you graduated. Looks like you made it."

Kyra grinned, and it was Sandy's turn to look embarrassed; realizing that D'Anguilo wasn't just some corporate flack, she stared down at the floor. D'Anguilo paid her no mind as he returned his attention to the others. "Anyway, I'm here because I'm the company expert on the races we're dealing with . . . including the *danui*, or at least as much as we know about them."

"I take it, then, that you've met the *nord*," Mark said. D'Anguilo raised an inquisitive eyebrow, and the sergeant nodded. "We've already been briefed about this . . . I mean, that a merchant marine captain heard about the *danui* system from one of the *nord*, and . . ."

"I talked to the *nord*, yes. In fact, that's what I was doing here before you showed up." D'Anguilo gestured to the porthole. "You probably noticed their ship near the gatehouse. It brought one of their emissaries. I spoke with him just a few hours ago." He smiled. "Not that I had a chance to say much. You don't talk to the *nord*, really . . . You just listen, and hope that your translator can keep up with them."

"And the *danui*?" Kyra asked. "Have you met with them, too?"

D'Anguilo shook his head. "You can count the number of humans who've actually laid eyes on a *danui* on one hand and have some fingers left over, and I'm not one of them. For some reason, the *danui* preferred to let the *nord* act as their intermediaries. We've had no direct contact with them, and . . ."

The door behind him slid open. Sean's mother floated into the wardroom. "Dr. D'Anguilo?" she asked, and he nodded. "Andromeda Carson, captain of the *Montero*. Pleased to meet you."

"Likewise, Captain." He offered his hand, which she shook. "Happy to be aboard."

"Don't let me interrupt. Go on with what you were saying." Andromeda grasped a wall rail and pulled herself to one side of the room. Sean noticed that she seemed to be deliberately not looking his way. Which was fine with him.

"Thank you," D'Anguilo said. "As I was saying, we've had no direct contact with the *danui* . . . which is puzzling, to say the least. You'd think that, if they were interested in allowing humans to colonize a planet in their system, they'd want some say in the matter. But they seem to be rather indifferent about the whole thing."

"Not even trade negotiations?" Cayce asked.

"Oh, there has been some of that. We're not getting a planet for free." D'Anguilo shrugged. "But that's for later missions. For this particular expedition, all we've been asked to bring with us are transplantable specimens of native flora from Coyote . . . seeds, sprouts, young trees and shrubs, that sort of thing." He glanced at Andromeda. "The skiff that brought me here carried them as cargo. I assume they've been loaded aboard."

"Yes, they have," Andromeda replied. "But I'm just as confused about this as you are. Aren't the *danui* concerned that we may be introducing invasive species to one of their planets?"

"I asked the *nord* emissary about this, and . . ." D'Anguilo stopped, slowly let out his breath. "Have you ever heard a *nord* laugh? They don't do it very often. Maybe it's just as well, because it's pretty unpleasant, but . . . well, that's exactly what he did. Then he told me that it didn't matter. We could poison the place, he said, and the *danui* wouldn't care."

A low whistle from Mark, while Sean and Kyra traded an astonished glance. Cayce stared at the astroethnicist. "They don't care? What are they . . . ?"

"Lieutenant." Andromeda gave him a cold look, and Cayce shut up. She looked at D'Anguilo again. "So what else have the *nord* let us know? Surely they've supplied us with vital info. Mass, surface gravity, atmospheric composition . . ."

"No. Not even so much as a photo." D'Anguilo reached

into his coat pocket and pulled out a small black cartridge. "Just this starbridge key," he added, holding it out to the captain. "It's programmed to let us make the jump to HD 76700 . . . and, yes, before you ask, we've been promised that it'll work in reverse as well."

Andromeda took the key from D'Anguilo. "Will this put us out near the *danui* homeworld, or didn't the *nord* tell you that either?"

"The starbridge it opens is located one-half AU from our objective," D'Anguilo said, "or one and a half AUs from HD 76700." Andromeda opened her mouth, but he held up a hand before she could say anything. "I don't know if that means it's at a Lagrange point or in a trojan orbit or anything like that. All I've been told is that's where the *danui* starbridge is located, and that the world we're being allowed to colonize is within half an AU of that position." He hesitated. "I'm sorry, Captain Carson, but that's all the *nord* would let me know. They seem to take some amusement by keeping us ignorant."

"I don't like this." Sandy's voice was low; she'd folded her arms across her chest and was scowling at no one in particular. "There's no reason why we should trust them . . . and I don't know about you, but when someone tells me nothing about the place they want me to go, I get the feeling there's something there they're trying to hide."

Sean nodded, and to his surprise, D'Anguilo did as well. "I agree. I think the *nord* are hiding something, and so are the *danui*." A corner of his mouth ticked upward. "That's why I went through diplomatic channels and sent a private communiqué to the *hjadd* ambassador on Coyote, to ask himher what heshe knew about HD 76700."

"Well, that's resourceful," Andromeda said, and Sean reluctantly found himself agreeing with his mother. The *hjadd* were humankind's closest allies among the Talus races; if any of them were going to offer candid information, it would be them. "What did heshe say?"

"Nothing . . . or almost nothing." D'Anguilo turned to

look her straight in the eye. "Heshe wouldn't tell me what was there. Not in specific terms, at least. But what heshe did say was we'd find—and I quote—'the greatest wonder of the known galaxy, and we're honored to have the *danui* share it with us.'"

No one said anything for a moment until Sandy slowly let out her breath. "Yeah, that's a lot of help. And why should we believe anything the beakheads have to tell us?"

D'Anguilo glared at her. *Beakheads* was a racial epithet, usually directed at aliens in general and the *hjadd* in particular. Before he could retort, though, Mark cleared his throat. "Pardon me, but I know for a fact that the *hjadd* ambassador is a devout follower of *Sa'Tong*, just as I am. And the Third Codicil of the *Sa'Tong-tas* prohibits us from any actions—including telling lies—that would bring harm to ourselves or anyone else. So if the ambassador says we'll find the greatest wonder in the galaxy in the *danui* system, then believe me when I say that we can trust himher."

"I'm not entirely sure . . ." D'Anguilo began, then stopped. "That is, I have certain . . . um, suspicions . . . about what may be there. But I'd rather not share them until I know for certain."

"Fair enough." Andromeda looked at Mark. "So that's your job . . . to explore this new world and find out what's there. If it's what the ambassador says it is, then it's worth the risk."

"Yeah . . . or so we hope," Sandy murmured, and Cayce shot her an angry look.

Andromeda glanced at her watch. "All right, then . . . If there are no other questions, my crew and I have work to do. *Montero*'s scheduled departure is forty-five minutes from now, and we'll be making the jump at the top of the hour. You'll need to be in your cabins by the time we leave the station and safely strapped down before we go through the starbridge. Dr. D'Anguilo . . ."

"Tom," he said.

"Tom, I'd like to have you on the bridge when we make

the jump. Please report to Deck One in forty-five minutes. The rest of you are at liberty until then." Without another word, Andromeda turned to the door, slid it open, and pushed herself out into the corridor. Sean noticed that she barely glanced his way. It was as if he'd become just another passenger. Which was just as well with him.

"You heard the captain," Cayce said, sharply clapping his hands together to get their attention. "Everyone needs to be back in their cabins in forty-five minutes. Until then, do whatever you need to do, but do it soon. That's all. Dismissed."

He pushed himself toward the open door, with Mark and Sandy not far behind. Sean turned to Kyra as they started to leave. "So . . . you once had him as a teacher?"

"Uh-huh. Pretty good one, too. I learned a lot from his class." She hung back, giving the others a few more seconds to exit the wardroom, then took his hand. "I'm a little nervous about the jump," she murmured. "This is the first time I've ever done this."

"You don't have anything to worry about, really." Sean had been through hyperspace before, but he had to remember that it was Kyra's first time. Like the rest of their team, they had taken a rehearsal on the Corps simulator at Fort Lopez. It was only a facsimile of the real thing, though, and he couldn't blame her for being anxious.

"Yes, well . . . all the same, I'd rather not be alone." Kyra made sure no one else was listening, then moved closer to him. "I asked Sandy if she'd mind swapping cabins with Mark," she whispered. "She said she wouldn't. Do you think you can ask Mark . . . ?"

"I don't think he'll mind, either." Sean stared at her. "But I thought we'd agreed to stay away from each other until this was all over."

"I know, but . . ." Her expression was pensive as she bit her lower lip. "I'm getting the feeling this isn't going to be the usual survey mission. I mean, we don't know anything about where . . ."

"Don't worry. We'll be fine." Another glance at the door, then he gave her a kiss on the forehead. "Of course, if you're really serious about being comforted, we'll have to see if two people can fit in those bunks."

"Maybe." A fleeting smile that quickly disappeared. "I just hope you're right," she said, becoming solemn again. "I'm beginning to think we should have stayed in bed back home."

PART TWO

ANATOMY
OF AN
IMPOSSIBILITY

SIX

IN ALL THE MANY TIMES ANDROMEDA HAD GONE THROUGH
hyperspace, never once had she completely closed her
eyes. Oh, she'd blinked, all right, at the moment when a
starbridge's zero-point energy generators opened its torus
and a silent explosion of defocused light rushed through the
wormhole. That no one could look at without squinting. But
she always kept her eyes open during the fifteen seconds it
took her ship to make the jaunt from one star system to another. Although she told herself that, as captain, she needed
to be aware of what was happening, the truth of the matter
was that she was fascinated by the near-instantaneous tran-
sition from one place to another even though she'd experienced it dozens of times.

So the retinal afterimage of the spacetime kaleidoscope
hadn't yet faded when the *Montero* completed its plunge
through Starbridge Coyote. Peeling a sweaty hand from her
armrest, Andromeda pushed back her hair as she let out her
breath.

"Everyone okay?" she asked, speaking to no one in particular.

Around the command center, her crew groaned and muttered. Jason's face was pale, but at least he hadn't vomited; it had taken *Montero*'s first officer a long time to learn how not to get sick during jumps, and he still kept a plastic bag discreetly hidden beneath his seat. A weak smile and a shaky thumbs-up, then he prodded his mike wand and called below to check on the passengers. Only Zeus seemed unperturbed; perhaps it was only machismo, but the chief petty officer insisted that hyperspace didn't bother him. Andromeda had watched him in the past, though, and had quietly noted that he closed his eyes like everyone else. He just recovered more quickly than the others.

"Nice work, Captain." From behind her, Andromeda heard Thomas D'Anguilo's voice. "In fact, that was just about the smoothest jump I've ever had."

She half turned in her chair to look back at him. D'Anguilo was seated at the remote survey station, hands calmly resting at his sides. His complexion was normal; there wasn't so much as a drop of sweat on his face. She was impressed. Most passengers were upchucking by then, but D'Anguilo was as placid as if they'd only taken a gyro ride.

"Thank you," she said, then returned her attention to her crew. "Stations, report. Engineering?"

"All systems nominal, ma'am." Rolf didn't look away from his screens. "No structural damage. Main engines on standby, life support functional, ditto for all comps and primary AI."

"Very good. Mel?"

For a moment or two, Melpomene didn't respond. She was focused entirely upon her board, her hands moving across the console. "Melpomene?" Andromeda repeated. "Status, please."

"Aye, skipper." The helmsman finally heard her. "We're at our expected arrival point . . . HD 76700, 1.5 AUs from the primary. But . . ." Apparently puzzled by something on her screens, she hesitated. "Skipper, I don't get it. I'm not finding any planets."

"No planets?" Andromeda was confused. "Are you using the optical imaging system or the infrared rangefinder?"

"Both, but . . ." Melpomene pointed helplessly at her station's largest screen. "Well, see for yourself. No planets, only the starbridge in sight . . . but there's something else out there."

Andromeda didn't rise from her seat but instead tapped commands in her lapboard that linked the wallscreen to Melpomene's console. The forward bulkhead disappeared, replaced by a floor-to-ceiling starfield so realistic that it seemed as if a section of *Montero*'s outer hull had simply vanished. Distant stars against black space, all marked by translucent red numerals identifying them by their catalog numbers. None were unfamiliar, yet as Melpomene pointed out, neither were any of them planets.

Then the starfield slowly began to turn as the forward telescope twisted about, and something appeared that she'd seen before, but only as the grainy telescope photo that Ted Harker had shown her.

Directly in front of the ship, one and a half astronomical units away, lay HD 76700, a star just a little larger than 47 Uma. It wasn't clearly visible, though, for surrounding it was a translucent haze the color of old rust tinted with silver. It might have been a planetary nebula were it not for the fact that it was perfectly spherical. Indeed, the sphere was so immense that it almost completely filled the wallscreen.

Jason gasped in astonishment, and Zeus murmured something under his breath. "What the hell?" Andromeda stared at the object. "Mel, what's the scope's magnification?"

"Zero." Her voice was strangely hollow. "That's what we're seeing from our current position."

Andromeda wasn't in the habit of distrusting her crew. When Melpomene said this, though, she had to see for herself whether or not the pilot was mistaken. Unfastening her seat belt, she pushed herself out of her chair. The nearest porthole was directly above her; the ship's windows had automatically shuttered just before the *Montero* went through hyperspace, but she found the button that opened this one.

The shutter slid open and Andromeda peered outside. Her view was obscured slightly by the deflector array; nonetheless, it was the same she'd seen on the wallscreen. Whatever the object was, it was vast enough to completely surround the star at its center.

"Hell's bells," she whispered, "what *is* that thing?" Tearing her gaze away from the porthole, she looked down at D'Anguilo. "Are you getting any readings?"

The scientist was already bent over his console. "Whatever it is, I can tell you for sure that it's not a dust cloud. Mass spectrometer shows hydrogen, oxygen, nitrogen, carbon, iron, silicon . . . They're all there, along with carbon dioxide, argon, methane . . ." He looked up at her. "Everything you'd expect to find in the absorption lines of a planetary system, but the estimated mass is off the scale. That should be a planet, maybe even a superjovian, but . . ."

He suddenly stopped, his mouth falling open. "No," he murmured. "It can't be." Then he turned to Melpomene. "Give me a close-up!" he snapped, pointing toward the wallscreen. "Highest magnification you can!"

The helmsman gave Andromeda an uncertain glance. The captain nodded, and Melpomene turned to her console again. Still hovering near the ceiling, Andromeda twisted herself around until she was upside down; the wallscreen looked odd from that angle, but the display remained unchanged. For only another moment, though; then the optical system cast a new image upon the forward bulkhead, and she felt her heart skip a beat.

In the new image, HD 76700 had grown large enough that the polarizing filters automatically activated to prevent the bridge crew from being blinded. Even so, the alien sun was still obscured by whatever lay between it and the *Montero*. Yet the object no longer had a spherical shape. In close-up, what they saw was . . .

"That can't be right." Jason shook his head in disbelief. "That just can't . . . There must be something wrong with the scope."

A vast and seemingly endless network of hexagons, each having the same six-sided form, each identical to its six adjacent neighbors. The hexes weren't solid, though; they were open at their centers, with sunlight shining through. Linked together in perfect geometric pattern, at first glance they resembled a chicken-wire fence, much like that a farmer might put up around a roost to keep the hens from wandering away. But there were no chickens inside this immense pen, but a star instead.

"Apparent magnification is .01 AU from the outer perimeter." Melpomene's voice was hushed. "We're seeing it from approximately 930,000 miles."

The goddamn thing is made up entirely of hexagons, Andromeda thought. *There must be thousands, maybe millions of them. Hell, more than that . . .* billions, *even.* A cold chill went down her spine. *Whatever it is, it's not of natural origin. Someone actually* built *this . . .*

"I knew it!" D'Anguilo was no longer at his station; he had risen to his feet, his shoes barely anchored to the floor. "I *knew* it!" he yelled, laughing with almost adolescent delight. "Those crazy bastards, they actually did it!"

The flight crew stared at him. Until then, Tom D'Anguilo had been quiet and reserved, the very picture of a former university professor. Suddenly, it was as if an overexcited student had taken his place. Apparently forgetting where he was, he let the soles of his stickshoes leave the carpet; he began to float upward, not noticing or even caring.

Swearing under her breath, Andromeda pushed herself away from the ceiling. "Cut it out," she said, grabbing D'Anguilo by the shoulders. "You're on the bridge. You can't monkey around like that in . . ."

"Sorry. Didn't mean to get carried away." He shook his head as he calmed down a little. "It's just that . . . I mean, I suspected that the *danui* might have done something like this, but until now I couldn't believe that they . . ."

"Pardon me, Dr. D'Anguilo . . ." Jason pointedly cleared his throat. "If you already know that the *danui* are responsible for"—he motioned to the screen—"well, *that*, then why didn't you tell us?"

"I didn't really believe it was possible until . . ."

"Never mind that." Still holding on to D'Anguilo, Andromeda looked him straight in the eye. "What I want to know is . . ."

"A Dyson sphere."

"What?"

"It's a Dyson sphere. An artificial habitat, only with more room than hundreds, even thousands of planets." The astroethnicist glanced at Jason. "And, no, I didn't know for sure that the *danui* had built one. I suspected that they were engaged in some massive engineering project, but I couldn't be sure until we actually got here." His gaze traveled to the screen again. "I thought it might be a network of space colonies, like *Talus qua'spah*. Maybe even some sort of terraforming operation. But this . . ."

"Tell me later." Andromeda cut him off with a wave of her hand. "The *danui* invited us, so they're probably waiting for a message. I'm sure they must know we're here."

Letting go of D'Anguilo, she pushed herself toward the com station. "Anne, would you please transmit a text message? Standard Ku band. Umm . . . 'Coyote Federation starship *Carlos Montero* to *danui* homeworld. We have arrived in your system, request permission to land . . .' No, scratch that." She reconsidered her words, tried again. " 'Request permission to rendezvous at whatever coordinates you wish to give us. Captain Andromeda Carson, commanding officer.' " She looked at D'Anguilo. "Think that'll work?"

"It's as good as any, I suppose." Still hovering in midair, D'Anguilo continued to stare at the wallscreen. "They'll be able to translate it, of course. Whether they respond is another matter entirely."

"What do you mean?" The comps of starships of races belonging to the Talus were loaded with translation programs capable of deciphering the written languages of other member races. "If they receive a message in Anglo, they should . . ."

"They should, yes. The question is whether they *will*." D'Anguilo shrugged. "The *danui* have their own way of doing things . . . and it's often not what anyone else expects or even understands." He nodded toward the screen. "I think that should be obvious, don't you?"

Andromeda didn't reply. Anne's hands were resting on her keyboard, waiting for her captain to give her the final go-ahead. Andromeda gave her a silent nod, and the communications officer began to type the message. Planting her stickshoes on the deck, the captain carefully walked back to her seat. "Mel, set a course for . . . whatever that thing is. Set thrust at .05 g. That should give them enough time to respond while we figure out exactly where we're going."

"Yes, ma'am." Melpomene started to turn to her controls again, then she paused and looked over her shoulder at the captain. "Skipper? That's a rather large target. I know we haven't yet heard from the *danui*, but could you be a little more specific, please?"

"I'd say the equator," Jason said, before Andromeda could reply. "That way, we won't be very far off the mark, no matter where our hosts tell us to go . . . assuming, of course, they mean for us to somehow dock with the thing."

The first officer was making a guess, of course, but it was the best they had for the time being. "The equator sounds about right," Andromeda said. "Go ahead, Mel."

The helmsman nodded as she began entering coordinates into the nav system. Andromeda was about to take her seat again when she noticed that D'Anguilo was still floating above the holo table. Unable to reach either the ceiling or the floor, he flailed helplessly in midair. He might have been an experienced spacer, but this time his enthusiasm had gotten the better of him. Andromeda glanced over at Zeus and silently gestured in D'Anguilo's direction: *get him down from there.* The chief petty officer smirked as he unfastened his seat belt and pushed himself toward the hapless scientist.

Zeus had just hauled D'Anguilo back down to the deck when Andromeda heard someone coming through the hatch behind her. Looking around, she saw Lieutenant Cayce glide up the manhole from the access shaft. The team leader's eyes were wide, plainly astonished.

"Captain, where are we?" His gaze never left the wallscreen. Melpomene had returned the image to its previous magnification, so he was seeing the same thing he'd seen on his cabin comp screen or through a porthole, only much larger. "Are we in the right system? And what's that . . . ?"

"Lieutenant," she said, "in the future, if you want to visit the bridge, I'd appreciate it if you'd call ahead and request permission." He started to stammer an apology, but she went on. "To answer your questions . . . Yes, we are in the *danui* system, with the star positively identified as HD 76700. And no, we're not absolutely certain what that is, but Dr. D'Anguilo has tentatively identified it as something called a Dyson sphere."

"A what?" Cayce's expression was bewildered. Grabbing hold of a bulkhead rung, he turned toward the Janus exec, who'd just then resumed his seat at the remote survey station. "You mean you know what this is?

"Sort of." D'Anguilo grinned; he seemed to be happiest when he was explaining things to other people. "It's an old idea, really . . . and not really what a lot of people were expecting. Dyson spheres were thought to be solid structures, or at least by those who wrote about them."

Andromeda turned to look at him again. "And who would that be?"

"Science fiction writers, who else?" D'Anguilo chuckled at his own joke. "My late father was a literature professor who specialized in twentieth-century science fiction. I read a lot of the books in his collection." He pointed to the wallscreen. "But almost all those stories got the idea wrong. The physicist who came up with it in the first place—Freeman Dyson, one of the foremost visionaries of his time—never intended for such an object to be a solid sphere, but rather a series of individual habitats in orbit around a star."

He paused to study the screen. "But that doesn't quite appear to be what's happening here," he added, a little less confidently. "From the looks of things, this appears to be a linked network of hexes."

"Hexes?" Cayce shook his head, not quite understanding what he meant.

"Plural for hex." D'Anguilo reflected upon this for a moment, then looked at Andromeda again. "Come to think of it, that's not such a bad name . . . Hex."

"Whatever." At that particular moment, she was less interested in what they called the place than in what she and her people would do once they got there. "Mel, how long will it take for us to get there?"

"At our projected velocity"—the helmsman paused to enter numbers into her console and study the readout on one of her screens—"about seven days."

"Good. That gives us plenty of time to study . . . um, Hex . . . before we arrive. Maybe we can make sense out of the thing by then." She turned to Cayce. "In the meantime, I want your team to prepare for a reconnaissance mission. Before I commit my ship to anything, I'd like to make a flyby, to see what we're getting into, and maybe send down a survey team."

"Not a problem, Captain," Cayce said. "That's what we're here for."

D'Anguilo coughed into his fist. "Captain, with all due respect . . . I don't think the *danui* would've deliberately given us permission to visit their system if they thought the environment was hostile for us."

"I understand that." Andromeda gestured at the screen. "But I'm also keeping in mind the fact that the *danui* aren't exactly the most forthcoming race we've met. They didn't tell us that this wasn't a normal planet. There must be a reason for that, and until we know what it is, I'm not going to make any assumptions. So we're going to treat Hex as if it's potentially dangerous and study it before we jump into anything."

D'Anguilo looked as if he wanted to argue with her, but he wisely kept his mouth shut. Andromeda looked at Cayce again. "Do I remember correctly that one of your crew is a trained biologist?"

"Corporal Wright, ma'am." Cayce hesitated. "She's not actually a scientist. She just had scientific training before she joined the Corps. Her degree is in xenobiology, though, and she studied under Dr. D'Anguilo while she was at the university."

Kyra Wright. Andromeda wondered if she was the same young woman who'd been with Sean in the wardroom. Her maternal intuition told her that there was something between the two of them; at the very least, she certainly looked like Sean's type. "That's fine. We could use another hand up here once we get closer to that thing . . . That is, if it's all right with you, Tom."

D'Anguilo nodded. "Ms. Wright was one of my better students. I wouldn't mind having her help at all."

"I'll send her up here as soon as possible." Cayce started to turn toward the hatch again, then stopped. "Just one more thing, Captain. What do I tell my people?"

Andromeda blinked. "Come again?"

"They were expecting a planet, ma'am. Instead, we got . . . well, *that*." The lieutenant paused. "It's spooked a couple of them, to tell the truth."

Andromeda doubted that Sean could be made nervous by anything besides his own mother; she wondered if Cayce wasn't really speaking for himself. Yet she was aware of the uncomfortable silence that had fallen across the command center. Since they'd been together, *Montero*'s crew had visited nearly a half dozen alien worlds. Yet none were as strange as what lay before them. Hex was an appropriate name; it appeared to have spooked everyone.

"Tell them the truth," she said. "This isn't what we were expecting . . . and they'd do well to remember that as they get ready to go down there."

SEVEN

O VER THE COURSE OF THE NEXT SEVEN DAYS, THE
Montero made the journey to Hex. Andromeda would
later reflect that the least of her surprises was how
quickly her crew and passengers accepted the name that Tom
D'Anguilo had given this place. Hex, a human word, was
simple, easy to remember, and oddly appropriate. So when
she sent her first report to Coyote via hyperlink, that was the
name she used.

The response she received from the merchant marine
was terse:

COEX PRIORITY ONE 7/46/23 12:09:03 CMT
TO: Carson, A., Capt. (CO, *Montero*)
FM: Harker, T., Com. (MM)
GRADE: TS
RE: Hex

Intrigued by your discovery. Standing by for further
info. Please update when you learn more.

Ted

Reading this in the privacy of her cabin, Andromeda rolled her eyes. Intrigued, indeed; that had to be the understatement of all time. If Harker had been aboard the *Montero*, she would have loved to see the look on his face when the ship came through the *danui* starbridge.

Sure, Ted, I'll send you more info, she thought. *Soon as I figure out what the hell I'm dealing with.*

The closer the *Montero* came to Hex, the more mysterious the sphere appeared to be. Anne's original transmission went unanswered; nothing came through the com network even though she frequently retransmitted the text message on multiple wavelengths. With D'Anguilo's assistance, she rephrased the message in more diplomatic terms, using the translation program to reiterate it in the *hjadd*, *nord*, *kua'tah*, and *soranta* languages (the *danui* native tongue being still unknown). Still, there was no response. It was as if the *danui*—or, for that matter, anyone else who might be present—simply didn't want to speak with their newly arrived visitors.

And yet, near the end of the second day, the *Montero* discovered that they were far from alone in the *danui* system. Andromeda was having a late dinner in the wardroom when Jason's voice came through her earpiece, asking her to come to the command center. When the captain returned to the bridge, she found her first officer peering at the nav table.

Hex was so immense, it was impossible for the table's holographic imaging system to construct a model that wouldn't crowd out everything else, including *Montero*'s present position. In the end, a significantly downscaled version of the Dyson sphere had been projected instead. Ever since the *Montero* had fired its main engines to begin the long trip, the only images above the table had been Hex, the *danui* starbridge, and the tiny white dot of the *Montero* itself, with red and blue dotted lines showing the distance the ship had already traveled and the course it was projected to take.

But that had changed. About one-sixth of the way

around Hex, at a distance of 1.5 AUs, was a second ring, identical to the starbridge the *Montero* had come through. And next to it was another white dot, leaving behind a broken red trail of its own as it inched toward Hex.

"A second starbridge," Jason murmured, pointing to the new ring. "We didn't spot it before now because it wasn't active. It opened just a few minutes ago, when that ship came through."

Andromeda stared at the ring and the adjacent dot. "What kind of ship? Do we know?"

The first officer said nothing but instead glanced over his shoulder at Rolf Kurtz. In D'Anguilo's absence, the chief engineer had assumed his position at the remote survey station. "Still trying to get a visual fix, skipper," he replied, not looking up from his console. "Judging from its energy signature, though, I'd say it's using a negmass drive." He hesitated. "My guess is that it's *hjadd*."

Andromeda turned toward the com station, only to see that it was vacant as well. *Hell of a time for this to happen, with most of the bridge crew off duty and only a couple of officers standing watch.* Perhaps it was just as well that Anne was in her bunk; her failure to make contact with the *danui* had been giving her fits, and another unanswered communiqué would only vex her even more. Andromeda decided to let her sleep.

"Where's the second starbridge?" she asked.

"That, I can tell you." Jason typed a command into the nav-table keyboard. An instant later, numbers appeared beneath the new ring, with a green line appearing as a parabolic curve between it and the first starbridge. "How interesting," the first officer murmured, staring at the computations. "The two starbridges are in the same equatorial orbit, half an AU from Hex and exactly 14,602,140.88 miles apart." He hesitated, then pointed to an empty point in space one-third of the way around Hex. "I'll bet anyone here their dessert for the next week that there's another starbridge right there . . . same orbit, same distance."

"What makes you think that?" Rolf asked.

"With something this big, why settle for having only two starbridges to get here?" He shrugged. "Or even three, for that matter."

Neither Andromeda nor Rolf took him up on his wager, which was wise on their part. A day later, the existence of the third starbridge was confirmed when another starship—most likely *nord*, judging from its lightsails—came through it, and it wasn't long after that before they realized that the first officer was right. In all, six starbridges were in equatorial orbit around Hex, each one located at equal distances from its nearest neighbors.

It soon became apparent why the *danui* had chosen to build six different points of entry to their system.

By the fourth day, Hex completely filled the forward screen until nothing else could be seen. The sheer size of the thing was staggering: 93 million miles in radius, 186 million miles in diameter, with a circumference of 584,336,233.568 miles and an estimated volume of 1.086^{17} miles. As abstract as the figures were, they were the only way Andromeda could comprehend just how bloody *huge* the sphere was.

Except for the small gas giant in close orbit around HD 76700, the only other object in the *danui* system besides its sun was Hex. If Tom was right, and the sphere had been built more or less on the same principles originally postulated by Freeman Dyson, then any other planets that might have once existed here had long since been destroyed, their mass used for the sphere's construction. Indeed, the amount of matter and energy—not to mention time—required for such an effort was utterly mind-boggling. Andromeda knew that she would've deemed such a feat to be impossible had she not seen it with her own eyes.

Once the ship was within ten million miles of Hex, D'Anguilo was able to study its hexagons a little more closely through *Montero*'s optical telescope system. Their dimensions were identical; each of their six sides were one thousand miles long and one hundred miles in diameter, giving them a total perimeter of six thousand miles. By then, it was obvious that Hex revolved around HD 76700 at a rate that would produce an internal surface gravity of 2 g's for the hexagons at the equator and nearly none at all for those at its poles. It was difficult to tell exactly how many hexes made up the sphere, but D'Anguilo estimated that Hex was comprised of approximately six trillion hexes.

Even more astonishing, it appeared that the sides of a given hex were individual cylinders, joined together at their corners by spherical nodes, with the adjacent hexes linked to them by the same nodes. Examining them through the ship's telescopes, Kyra Wright arrived at the conclusion that these cylinders were hollow, and most likely were serving as habitats. She dubbed these objects *biopods*, since *biospheres* was not an accurate description of their shape. If D'Anguilo's estimates were correct, then Hex was made up of thirty-six trillion biopods . . . every one of them potentially habitable.

Now they knew why the *danui* had put six starbridges in orbit around Hex. The sphere was so large, multiple points of entry had to be provided in order to reduce the travel time to its far-flung habitats. And it was obvious that Hex was well visited; by the end of the sixth day, the bridge crew had counted nearly a dozen alien vessels coming and going through the starbridges they could see, and there was no telling how thick the traffic was on the other side of the sun.

And yet, the *danui* still hadn't made contact with them, nor had any other ship responded to Anne's attempts to communicate with them. It was as if the *Montero*, and the humans aboard, were being deliberately snubbed.

"I don't get it. I really don't understand." Absently gnawing at a thumbnail, Andromeda slumped in her seat as she scowled at the wallscreen. From a distance of less than eight million miles, Hex had all but completely lost its spherical shape; instead, it appeared to be a curved wall of hexagons that slowly moved from left to right, the sun behind them shining through like a distant spotlight. "If they wanted us to come here, then why give us the silent treatment?"

"The *danui* are naturally reclusive . . ." D'Anguilo began. He was standing at the remote survey station, Kyra seated beside him.

"I know. You've told me that over and over again." Andromeda glared at him from over her shoulder. "But this is downright rude. It's like . . ." She paused, searching for the right words. "Getting invited to a party, then being made to wait at the front door while all the other guests are let in."

"Not only that, but the other guests aren't saying anything to you either." From the helm station, Melpomene gave her captain a sympathetic nod; she didn't bother to hide her disgust. "I'm with you, skipper. This is really pissing me off."

Seated at the communications console, Anne quietly nodded in agreement. Andromeda was about to reply when Kyra shyly raised her hand. "Pardon me, Captain, but . . ."

She stopped, suddenly self-conscious. "Go ahead, Ms. Wright," Andromeda said, not unkindly. "You have something to say?"

"Well . . ." Kyra hesitated. "I think you're overlooking the obvious. The question isn't why the *danui* haven't communicated with us. It's why they built Hex in the first place."

That was one of the few times in the past six days that Kyra had spoken directly to her. Ever since she'd starting working with D'Anguilo in the command center, she'd been a quiet presence, sharing the console with the astroethnicist as the two of them studied Hex. But Andromeda had gradually become aware that, when she wasn't on the bridge, Kyra spent most of her free time with Sean. The captain had seen the two of them together in the wardroom, and on one occasion she'd spotted her emerging from Sean's cabin. It was probably just as well that Kyra hadn't seen her, or otherwise, D'Anguilo might have lost his assistant; Andromeda apparently intimidated her.

So Kyra was Sean's new girlfriend. On the one hand, Andromeda found herself liking her, albeit reluctantly. Before their relationship had gone sour, and Sean had moved out of the house, she'd met most of the girls Sean had hooked up with in the past, and the majority of them had had more beauty than brains. Kyra was good-looking *and* smart, and the fact that she had manners was a bonus. But Sean had probably told her all about his mother, and by then Kyra probably thought Andromeda flew a broomstick when she wasn't commanding a starship.

"The thought has occurred to me." Andromeda favored Kyra with an encouraging smile as she turned her chair toward her. "You have a theory, I take it?"

"Umm . . ." Kyra glanced at D'Anguilo. Her former teacher nodded, and she went on. "I've lately reread Dyson's original paper . . . the one he wrote back in the mid twentieth century, on searching for infrared sources in the galaxy as a way of detecting extraterrestrial civilizations. He said that an alien race might go to the effort of building something like this in order to solve two problems: overpopulation and diminishing energy resources. Such a habitat would not only meet all the population needs of the ones who built it, but they'd also be able to capture all the energy emitted from its sun." A rueful smile. "Dr. Dyson later insisted that he was only joking, and he was rather embarrassed that these things were eventually called Dyson spheres. I would love to see the look on his face if he could only see this."

D'Anguilo raised a finger, politely interrupting her. "Another scientist of the same period, Nikolai Kardashev, devised a classification system for advanced alien races. According to the Kardashev scale, the *danui* appear to be a Type II civilization . . . one capable of harnessing the entire energy output of its native star."

"Uh-huh." Kyra nodded in agreement. "By comparison, humankind rates as a Type I civilization . . . but just barely . . . because we've learned how to harness the entire energy resources of our own planet. And a Type III civilization would exploit the energy of an entire galaxy . . ."

"I understand." Andromeda tried not to sound impatient. "So what are you getting at?"

Another nervous glance at D'Anguilo, then Kyra rose from her seat and walked across the bridge until she stood in front of the wallscreen. "Let's assume Dyson was right," she continued, pointing to the image of Hex behind her, "and the *danui* built this place in order to deal with over-population and the subsequent rise in energy demands. If our estimates are correct, there are six trillion hexes here, with thirty-six trillion biopods among them, and each bio-pod is a thousand miles long." She shook her head. "Even if the *danui* bred like crazy, it's doubtful that they'd need all this space just for themselves."

"It's certainly scary to think that they would," Andromeda murmured, and both Melpomene and Anne chuckled at her dry comment. "I'm following you. Go on."

"So . . ." Kyra shrugged. "Why not call the neighbors and invite them over? Throw open the doors and let them in?" Again, she gestured toward Hex. "Like I said, there's more than enough room . . . and they'd have the entire energy output of a star, too."

Andromeda blinked, trying to absorb what Kyra had just said. It was utterly mind-blowing to think that a civilization would go to the effort of building something like Hex, only to practically give it away to any other race capable of getting there. It would be like humans placing an enormous sign above Coyote: INVADE US, PLEASE! As harebrained as Kyra's theory seemed, though, it appeared to fit what they'd already observed: six starbridges in orbit around the Dyson sphere, with alien vessels freely coming and going.

"I'll take your theory into consideration." Andromeda shifted uncomfortably in her seat, then stood up to stretch out a kink in her lower back. "In the meantime, we should get ready to make a flyby and send out the recon mission."

"Do you still think that's wise?" D'Anguilo asked. "With all due respect, Captain, if the *danui* haven't con-tacted us . . ."

"We didn't come all this way just to take pictures." Andromeda looked over at Melpomene. "Time to set course for final approach. I want to get in as close as we can to one of those hexes and look for a place where we can land, or dock, or whatever."

"Which one?" The helmsman cast an uncertain glance at the screen. "They all look the same."

"You can narrow down your choices a little." Although still reluctant, D'Anguilo was apparently resigned to the inevitable. He walked over to the nav table, where Hex's holo image continued to revolve on its axis. "If there's 2 g at the equator, I think it's safe to assume that we'll find 1 g at the hexes about halfway up the northern hemisphere and halfway down the southern hemisphere."

"Good call." Joining him at the table, Andromeda took a moment to study the projection. Hex didn't have an axial tilt, so they wouldn't have to worry about seasonal differences between the two hemispheres. "Let's try the northern hemisphere," she said at last, pointing to the holo. "About halfway to the north pole. Think you can do that?"

"Think you're being a little too picky, skipper?" Melpomene managed to keep a straight face, and Andromeda didn't know she was joking until she saw the amused glint in her eyes. The captain said nothing but simply stared at Mel until the helmsman cracked a smile. "Yes, ma'am . . . northern hemisphere it is."

Andromeda went over to the helm and watched over Melpomene's shoulder as the helmsman used the trackball to move a cursor across a comp-generated image of Hex. Careful to account for Hex's rotation, the pilot selected a series of hexes in the northern hemisphere that would move into range of the *Montero* once it closed in on the sphere. Behind her, she heard D'Anguilo and Kyra quietly murmuring to each other as they stood near the nav table. She couldn't make out what they were saying, but it didn't sound as if either of them was very happy with the captain's decision.

This is the way mutinies get started, she thought. Like everyone else in the Federation Navy and merchant marine,

Andromeda was familiar with the details of the Spindrift affair, and how a breakdown in the chain of command aboard the *Galileo* had had grave consequences when the ship made contact with the *hjadd*.

She couldn't risk letting that happen again. Leaving Mel to finish laying in the course correction, Andromeda walked over to the table. As she'd expected, D'Anguilo and Kyra went silent as she came near. "Do you have a problem you want to talk about?" Andromeda asked, fixing them with a frank and unwavering gaze.

Kyra's face became pale, and D'Anguilo shook his head and started to turn away, but Andromeda wasn't about to let them cop out like that. "No, really," she said. "If you have something to say, speak up. You're supposed to be the experts. I want to hear your opinions."

D'Anguilo slowly let out his breath. "Captain, I . . . we . . . have some misgivings about sending down a survey team without further communication with the *danui*. I realize that we've come a long way, but I'd rather go back home empty-handed than risk offending a civilization capable of"—he cocked a thumb at the wallscreen—"well, building *that*."

"I see." Andromeda nodded. "And you, Ms. Wright? What's your take on this?"

Kyra hesitated even longer than D'Anguilo. "I agree with Tom . . . Dr. D'Anguilo, I mean," she said at last. "There must be a reason for the *danui* to remain silent, and same for all the ships we've seen. Humans belong to the Talus. They know we're not hostile. And the *danui* invited us here. So there must be some custom or protocol that we've overlooked, and I'm afraid that if we take some action out of ignorance . . ."

"It could come back to bite us on the ass," Andromeda finished. D'Anguilo nodded gravely, and although Kyra's face colored, she managed a wan smile. The captain sighed as she turned to gaze at the screen. Again, she remembered the *Galileo* mission. The first contact between humans and *hjadd* had met with disaster because *Galileo*'s captain had made a rash and unwise decision. The last thing Andromeda wanted was to have history repeat itself.

"Y'know," she said after a moment, "you may have a point. So here's what I'm thinking. We'll continue our approach, and on the way we'll keep sending radio messages. When we're a little closer, we'll send out a recon sortie, just as we planned."

D'Anguilo started to say something, but Andromeda quickly held up a hand. "Let me finish. If we still haven't heard anything from the *danui* by the time we complete our flyby, I'll take it that the continued silence is their way of saying, 'Go away, don't bother us.' I'll recall the lander, tell Mel to turn us around and head for the nearest starbridge, and we'll go home."

"You'd do that?" D'Anguilo was obviously surprised.

Andromeda nodded. "I was told that this mission might be hazardous, but I'm not going to risk a major incident with an advanced race just because we can't talk to them. I'll report everything that happened, and let the diplomats hash it out with the *danui*." She paused. "Fair enough?"

"Yes, it is." D'Anguilo slowly nodded. "Thank you, Captain."

"You're welcome." Andromeda looked at Kyra. "Perhaps you'd better go below and let your team know what we're planning. If Lieutenant Cayce has any questions, tell him he can come up here and talk to me. Otherwise, I'll expect your people to be ready to go by"—she checked her watch—"1800 tomorrow."

Kyra nodded, then turned to leave. She'd almost reached the access shaft when Andromeda decided, on a spontaneous whim, not to let her off the hook so easily.

"Oh, and Ms. Wright?" she called out, and Kyra stopped to look back at her. "When you see Sean, give him my best, will you?"

Again, the corporal's face went pale. "Yes, ma'am," she murmured, then she fled down the manhole.

EIGHT

THREE BELLS RANG FROM THE AIRLOCK LOUDSPEAKER, and Sean reached up to grasp a ceiling handrail. The vibration of the ship's engines ceased a few seconds later, and he felt his feet leave the deck. The *Montero* had ended its braking maneuvers; once again, the vessel was in zero g.

Kyra jostled him from behind, nudging his life-support pack. "Sorry," she said, gently pushing herself away. "Wasn't ready for that."

With all five members of the Corps team crammed into the airlock, the narrow compartment was uncommonly crowded. Their cramped conditions weren't made any better by the Navy-issue skinsuits they were wearing. The outfits were lightweight and flexible, but their life-support packs and chest units made them cumbersome in tight quarters. Cayce and Mark were just in front of him, and Mark was so close that Sean could see the scuff marks on the back of his helmet.

"S'okay," Sean said. "Just relax and try to—"

A double beep in his headset, then First Officer Ressler's voice came over the comlink. *"All right, we're at zero thrust and preparing to commence rollover maneuver. You can board the* Reese *when you're ready."*

"Copy that." Cayce stared up at the ceiling as if he could actually see the bridge from three decks below. "Survey team proceeding to lander. Over." He then glanced back at the others. "All right, everyone . . . follow me."

Mark turned his head to look at Sean through his helmet's open faceplate, and the two of them simultaneously rolled their eyes; from behind Kyra, Sean heard Sandy quietly sigh. Lieutenant Amerigo Cayce, hero of the Corps of Exploration. For the past seven days, the rest of the team had been largely spared his presence; they'd been too busy making preparations for the mission to pay much attention to him. And Kyra had been in the command center most of the time, helping Tom D'Anguilo study Hex.

Sean hadn't seen very much of her, but at least he hadn't seen much of Cayce either. Now that the time had come for the team to start earning their pay, he'd decided to put on his lieutenant's bars again. Despite his curiosity about what lay down there, Sean found himself hoping that this would be a short trip. The less he had to deal with Cayce, the better.

Probably just as well, he thought. *He's nervous about this sortie, and he's compensating by making an ass of himself.*

Cayce bent forward to unseal the hatch to *Montero*'s hangar bay. A faint hiss, then it swung open, exposing the darkness that lay on the other side. As the team commander pushed himself through the hatch, sensors detected his presence; light panels flickered to life, revealing the spacecraft berthed within.

The CFS *Gilbert Reese* was nestled inside its launch cradle, its wings folded against the fuselage. Except for a couple of electrical umbilicals still attached to the hull, the lander was fueled and ready for launch. Sean and Mark had gone down there several times already to inspect the spacecraft and make sure that all the equipment packed aboard it was in good shape. The port hatch was already open, with a tether line stretched from the airlock to the lander. Pulling himself along hand over hand, Cayce led the way to the *Reese*; as team leader, he was the first to board the spacecraft, with Mark Dupree close behind.

Although not quite as cramped as the airlock, the lander's cabin was just large enough for five passengers and their equipment. Cayce and Mark sat up front in the cockpit, with Mark taking the left-hand pilot's seat; Sean settled in behind Cayce, while Kyra found her place behind Mark. That left Sandy in the rearmost seat, tucked in beside the equipment cases and backpacks strapped to the aft bulkhead. She'd groused about the seating arrangements earlier, but it was necessary for Kyra and Sean to sit close to the cockpit in order for them to assist Mark and Cayce.

Sean would be little more than a camera operator, but Kyra had an important role in the mission. She was the first to admit that, even after having studied Hex for the last several days, her knowledge of the place was only slightly less than zero. Nevertheless, over the last few days, she'd become the team's astrobiology expert. Sean suspected that she wanted him nearby as moral support.

As Sean pushed himself into the port-side seat, he found himself grateful that the padded couches were designed to accommodate life-support packs. This was only the second time he'd worn a skinsuit. A couple of days ago, he'd had an argument with Cayce, insisting that it was unlikely that they'd need EVA gear for what might well be little more than a quick flyby; the likelihood of actually landing on Hex was considered remote, considering the silent treatment the *danui* had given the *Montero* thus far. Yet the lieutenant was adamant; it was possible that they might attempt to land if they found a reason to do so. If that occurred, Navy regulations specifically stated that skinsuits were to be worn while entering an alien environment.

As always, Cayce was a stickler for following the book. Just one more thing that was irritating about him.

Sean had just finished buckling his harness when Sandy pulled the hatch shut. Mark was making his way down the rest of the prelaunch checklist. He reached to the panel between him and Cayce and snapped a couple of toggles. Green lights lit across the board, and from the lander's aft section came the dull *thrum* of the nuclear engine coming to life.

"Hatch sealed, main cabin pressurized," Mark said. "Internal power on, comps reset, primary ignition sequence initiated." He glanced at Cayce. "Ready when you are, Lieutenant."

Cayce reached up to the com panel above the cockpit's wraparound windows, pressed a button. "*Montero*, this is *Reese*. Pilot reports all systems are green, and we're ready for launch."

"*We copy, Reese.*" Again, Sean heard Ressler's voice through his headset. "*Bay depressurization sequence initiated. Main hatch open in ninety seconds.*"

"Roger that." Mark flipped two more toggles. "Umbilicals detached. Starting mission clock."

Kyra unzipped a thigh pocket of her skinsuit and removed a datapad. She used an adhesive patch to fasten it to the seatback in front of her, then ran a slender cable from the pad to a serial port on the side of her helmet. "Lieutenant, would you patch me into the comlink, please? I need to talk to Tom."

Cayce pushed a button on the com panel. "You're on."

"Thank you. *Montero*, this is *Reese* Survey One. Tom, are you there?"

"*Right here, Kyra.*" Sean heard D'Anguilo's voice through his headset; everyone in the lander was sharing the same com channel. "*Ready for download?*"

Kyra tapped a command into her pad. "Yes, I am. Go ahead." A moment passed, then data began to scroll down the pad, replaced a few seconds later by a menu screen. "Very good," Kyra said, studying the information. "Looks like it's all here."

"What's that?" Sean asked, peering over her shoulder at the pad.

"The data Tom and I collected the last few days." Kyra

ran her finger down the menu, and a window opened to display another set of figures. "This way, not only can I access everything we've already found out, but we can also send new info to each other as we go along."

As if in response, Anne Smith's voice came over the com. *"I'm linking Montero's telemetry to Tom's board. You'll get everything we're seeing from up here, too."*

"Thanks. That'll help." Satisfied, Kyra touched the pad again, and the display returned to the menu default. She looked at Sean. "Don't expect much conversation from me once we get started. I'm going to be pretty busy."

D'Anguilo laughed. *"I certainly hope so. If we find nothing but a big ball of chicken wire, I'm going to be very disappointed."*

Sean said nothing but instead turned his gaze toward the oval porthole beside him. The lander bay had apparently just become depressurized, because he looked outside just in time to see the hangar doors start to open. As the massive doors parted at the center and rose upward, raw sunlight flooded the bay. Now that the braking and turnaround maneuvers were completed, the *Montero* was oriented bow first, with its hangar facing Hex. From where he was sitting, though, Sean still couldn't see their destination, only the bay's inside walls.

"Bay doors open, Reese," Ressler said. *"Ready to elevate cradle on your command."*

"We copy, *Montero*." Cayce gave Mark a quick look, and the pilot nodded. "Elevate cradle, please."

A faint shudder, then Sean felt the lander start to rise. Through his porthole, he could see the hangar walls slowly fall away. There was a loud, sudden snap against the hull, and he looked through Kyra's porthole in time to see a familiar nylon line float away.

"Aw, damn!" Sandy hissed. "I think I forgot something."

"Corporal!" Cayce turned his head to glare at her. She didn't say anything, but when Sean glanced over his shoulder at her, he saw that her face was red with embarrassment.

"You didn't detach the tether before you shut the hatch,

did you?" Mark was more forgiving than the lieutenant. "Don't worry about it. No harm done."

The cradle continued to rise until it elevated the lander to a position where it was level with the open hangar doors. When it came to a halt, Mark flexed his hands within his gloves, then grasped the control yoke. "All systems go, *Montero*. Ready for separation. Open cradle, please."

An abrupt *thump* from outside the lander, then a sensation of floating free. Mark gently pulled back on the yoke, and the lander's reaction-control thrusters silently fired, pushing the *Reese* away from the *Montero*.

"Separation complete." He reached up and flipped a pair of switches. A faint whirring sound, and Sean glanced out his window to see the port wing lowering into position.

"We copy, Reese." This time, Sean heard his mother's voice over the comlink. *"You're go for launch."*

"Roger that." Mark moved the yoke to the right, and the *Reese* made a 180-degree starboard roll. Through his porthole, Sean watched as the *Montero* swung into view, its hangar bay yawning open below them. With his right hand, Mark grasped the throttle bar on the center console. "Firing main engine on three . . . two . . . one . . ."

A faint rumble, then the *Montero* suddenly disappeared. *"Reese* away," Mark said.

"Affirmative," Andromeda said. *"We've got you on our scope. Good luck to you all."*

From the corner of his eye, Sean noticed Kyra giving him a sidelong look. Although his mother hadn't specifically mentioned him by name, she'd doubtless meant her son to be included in her well-wishes. Sean said nothing, and after a moment, Kyra returned her attention to her pad.

Mark let the deorbit burn continue for fifteen seconds, then pulled back on the throttle and pushed the stick forward. As the lander began to descend in a wide parabolic arc, Hex came into view. Earlier in the day, the *Montero* had assumed a low orbit eight hundred miles above the sphere's outer surface. From that altitude, Hex no longer resembled a sphere but instead appeared to be a vast and seemingly endless expanse of hexagons, stretching so far that its horizon was little more than a thin and distant line.

No one aboard said anything, save for a low and awe-struck whistle from Sandy. The view stunned everyone into silence. None of them had ever seen anything as magnificent as Hex, or as chilling. After a few seconds, Cayce found his voice.

"All right, people," he said, his tone uncharacteristically hushed, "we've got a job to do. Stop gawking and get to work." He looked back at Sean. "Corporal?"

"I'm on it, sir." Loosening his shoulder harness, Sean reached beneath his seat to retrieve the camera he'd stashed there earlier. Although the *Reese* was equipped with wing cameras, mounted on the leading edge of its port and star-board canards, they weren't designed to pick up anything except what was straight ahead. So it was Sean's task to take close-up shots of Hex as the lander made its flyby, with the images to be transmitted in real time to the *Montero*.

Unspooling a cable from the camera to his helmet, he mounted the unit on his right shoulder and pointed its lens toward the porthole beside him. He swiveled the viewfinder so its eyepiece fit through his helmet's open faceplate, then peered through it. The image he saw was an indistinct blur. "Getting some glare from the glass," he murmured. "Can we turn off the inside lights, please?"

Mark reached up to the overhead console, and a moment later the cabin fluorescents went dark. There was hardly any loss in illumination, since the sun was shining brightly through the windows, but the glare immediately vanished. "Thank you," Sean said. "Ready to patch in, Lieutenant."

"Very well." Cayce pushed another button on the com panel, and Sean's video output was added to *Reese*'s telemetry. "You're on."

Sean pointed the camera out his window again, this time tilting it downward so that he could record what was be-neath the lander. He had to refrain from gasping out loud. One of the hexagons lay directly below, and what had once been tiny was now immense. The biopods were enormous cylinders, each a thousand miles long and a hundred miles in diameter, joined together by spherical nodes fifty miles in diameter. Dull grey, they were featureless save for a row of black panels running along their dorsal midsections.

From the lander's present altitude, Sean couldn't see the far side of that particular hex; the cavity at its center was big enough to encompass even Coyote's largest continent. But the fact that he could make out two biopods of the nearest adjacent hexagon was enough to remind him that there were trillions of them, each one the same size.

He apparently wasn't the only person to be amazed. Through his headset, he heard an unintelligible yet nonetheless astonished babble of voices. Then his mother's voice came online: *"Sean, is that you operating the camera?"*

He hesitated. "Yes, it is."

A pause. *"Nice work. We're impressed."*

"Thank you, Captain," he said, his tone deliberately cool.

"No, really . . . This is utterly breathtaking." A dry chuckle. *"And that's just what we're seeing on the bridge screen. I can only imagine what it's like for you."*

Despite himself, a smile stole across Sean's face. "It is awesome, all right. I—"

"Sean? Corporal Carson, I mean." The new voice was Tom D'Anguilo's. *"Don't mean to interrupt, but there's something down there I'd like to see a little more closely. Can you zoom in toward the center of the hex you're heading toward?"*

"Wilco." Pointing the camera toward the open middle of the hexagon, he touched the magnification stud. As the viewfinder image grew larger, he saw what had drawn D'Anguilo's attention. The hexagon's center wasn't as empty as it seemed; instead, it appeared to be crisscrossed by cables or wires. From the lander's altitude, they were so narrow that they became visible only when sunlight touched them from a certain angle. Resembling the strings of a tennis racket, they were tightly strung from one side of the hexagon to the other, making up a dense net where they intercepted one another.

"Structural cables?" Sean peered at them through the eyepiece. "That's what they look like to me."

"Could be," D'Anguilo said, *"but . . . Whoa! Did you see that!"*

A shimmering, translucent blue wave had just raced across the cables. Resembling St. Elmo's fire, it was gone in half a second. It repeated itself a few moments later, but in a different part of the hexagon's inner perimeter.

"Am I imagining things," Kyra said, "or did I just see an aurora?"

"Could be," D'Anguilo said. *"I'm picking up faint electric discharge from them. I think they have another purpose besides structural support. Perhaps they're radiators . . ."*

"I don't think so." Kyra pointed to a false-color image of one of the biopods on her screen. "I'm picking up infrared emissions from those panels on the backs of the pods. If the pods have radiators to shed excess heat, you'd think that's where they'd be located."

"She's right." It was Rolf Kurtz's turn to chime in. *"The panels are probably radiators. If that's so, then the cables must have some other function."*

"Maybe they're magnetically charged," D'Anguilo said. *"The biopods may not have magnetic fields to ward off cosmic radiation the way planets usually do, so the cables perform that function."* He paused. *"That's just a guess, of course."*

"It's a good one," Rolf said. *"You may be right. But we're not going to know for sure unless we get a lot closer."*

"I agree." Cayce hadn't spoken much until then; apparently he'd just remembered that he was in command of the sortie. "Captain Carson, I'd like to fly through this hexagon and see what's on the other side. With your permission, of course."

Andromeda didn't respond at once. Sean pictured his mother sitting in her chair on the bridge, weighing all the options. *"What do you think, Sergeant Dupree?"* she asked at last. *"Do you think you can make it through without endangering your craft?"*

Mark studied the small screen on his center console where the image from Sean's camera was displayed. "I believe so," he said after a moment. "The cables appear to be spaced pretty far apart. It'll be a little tricky, but so long as I match course so that we have the same lateral movement, I should be able to pass between them. I'll have to get the timing just right, though, and . . ."

"Yes or no," Cayce said impatiently. "Can you do it or can't you?"

"Sure." Mark was barely able to hide his annoyance. "Piece of cake."

Sean pursed his lips together. Cayce had bullied Mark into giving an immediate answer. If he knew his friend, though, Mark would have preferred to spend a few more minutes studying the problem before committing himself. But it wasn't Sean's place to object, so all he could do was accept the situation and hope for the best.

"Very well, then," Andromeda said. *"But take it easy, and abort at once if you don't think you can make it."* Another pause, then she added, *"I don't think that I should have to remind you that rescue is going to be very difficult if you run into any problems."*

Sean knew what she meant, and that she'd intended her words more for Cayce than anyone else. Although the *Montero* was equipped with an EVA pod, the tiny one-man craft was only meant for repair work, not search-and-rescue operations. And since the *Montero* itself was hard to maneuver in tight situations, any attempt to steer it through that cable-net would be treacherous at best.

"We copy, *Montero*." Mark took a deep breath, slowly let it out. "Okay, folks, hold on to your butts. I'm going to take us in."

One hand on the throttle bar, he carefully inched the yoke forward. Through the cockpit windows, Sean watched as the hexagon hove into view. "I'll try going through near one of the pods," Mark said. "The cables don't seem to be as closely strung together at the edges as they are at the center."

No one objected. They trusted the pilot to know what he was doing. All the same, Sean couldn't help but notice that Mark's lips silently moved as he recited a *Sa'Tong*ian prayer to himself.

The lander was closing in on the cables when they heard from D'Anguilo again. *"Can you switch on your wing cams, please? I'd like to get another look at them before you go through."*

Sean knew what he meant. From his seat on the cabin's starboard side, he wouldn't be able to supply D'Anguilo with a clear view of the cables until the *Reese* was actually among them. Mark nodded to Cayce, and the lieutenant reached up to the overhead consoles and pushed a couple of buttons. "Sixty-five miles and approaching," the pilot said. "We should be going through in another minute or so."

"Thank you, Sergeant." D'Anguilo sounded satisfied. Another few moments went by, then he spoke again. *"Kyra, I'm picking up something strange. Looks like there are some objects attached to those cables. Can you . . . ?"*

A sudden rush of static blurred his voice, making the rest unintelligible. "Damn," Cayce muttered as he reached up to the com panel. *"Montero*, this is *Reese*, do you copy? We're getting interference here. Please respond if you . . ."

Almost as if a switch had been thrown, the static abruptly ceased. But when the comlink became active again, the next voice they heard wasn't human, but a high-pitched string of clicks and squeals.

"What the hell?" Almost as if stung, Cayce quickly pulled his hand away from the panel. "I don't . . ."

"Oh, my God!" Kyra exclaimed. Sean looked at her, saw that her eyes were wide. "I don't know what they're saying, but . . . that's *danui*!"

NINE

THE STUNNED SILENCE IN *MONTERO*'S COMMAND CENTER lasted only a couple of moments. Then Jason spoke up. "I don't know what they're saying," the first officer said, "but it sounds like they're pissed off."

Andromeda glanced over her shoulder at Tom D'Anguilo. He shook his head; no, he didn't understand the *danui* transmission either. She turned to Anne and gestured for her to patch her into the comlink. Anne tapped a couple of commands into her touch screen, then gave her captain a quick thumbs-up. Andromeda prodded her headset mike.

"This is Captain Andromeda Carson of the Coyote Federation merchant vessel *Carlos Montero*," she said. "We've received your message, but we do not understand what you're saying. Please repeat in our own language or that of another Talus race. Over."

There was no immediate response. The wallscreen displayed three overlapping images. The largest was the view of Hex as seen from *Montero*'s bow cameras, a vast plain of hexagons stretching as far as the eye could see. At the top right side of the screen was a straight-ahead view of the hexagon that the *Reese* was approaching as seen through the lander's wing cameras; on the top left side was Sean's close-up view of the cables stretched across its center. The last jiggled constantly—her son was having trouble holding the camera—nonetheless, it was the most detailed of the three images.

"Montero, *this is* Reese." Cayce's voice came through her earpiece. *"We just received a signal from . . ."*

"I know. We got the same thing." Andromeda looked at Anne again; the com officer met her gaze, shook her head. "We've asked them to repeat what they said in Anglo, but haven't heard anything yet."

"Roger." A pause. *"I'd like to continue our approach unless specifically told otherwise."*

"I'm not sure I'd recommend that, Captain." D'Anguilo turned around in his seat. "Mr. Ressler is right. We may not know what the *danui* was saying, but the tone suggests that it may be a warning . . ."

"Do you know what an angry *danui* sounds like?" Andromeda muted her mike as she looked at D'Anguilo again. He didn't reply, and she went on. "Neither do I. For all we know, it could have been a welcome, or landing instructions, or anything at all. If they want us to stay away, though, they've had plenty of chances to tell us before now. And I'm tired of waiting for them to make up their minds."

D'Anguilo's expression suggested that he didn't agree with her, but when Andromeda gave him a chance to make his case, he chose to remain quiet. *Some expert you're turning out to be,* she thought as she activated her mike again. "Affirmative, *Reese.* Continue your present course. Over."

Crossing her legs, Andromeda returned her attention to the wallscreen. By then, the lander was only a couple of miles from the hexagon, and it was clear that the cables of its inner perimeter were as thick as those of a suspension bridge. Although they reflected the distant sun, the objects attached to them seemed to absorb the light.

"What are those things?" she asked aloud.

Arranged in rows on either side of each cable were large black rectangles, their major axes running parallel to the cables themselves and their ends nearly touching one another. Several hundred feet long, the rectangles were thin, flat surfaces that appeared to be rigged to the cables by slender wires. Although they were slanted inward, no two had exactly the same angle; instead, they seemed to be oriented toward the sun in an almost random order.

"Radiators?" Jason asked. Sitting quietly beside Andromeda, the first officer absently rubbed his lower lip between thumb and forefinger.

"I don't think so," Rolf replied. "We spotted radiators already, on the outer surface of the biopods. No point in being redundant for no reason. Those look kinda like . . ." He suddenly snapped his fingers. "Solar collectors!"

"Yeah, that might make sense, but . . ." Jason pointed at the upper-left screen. "Look at the way they've been rigged. They're not all facing directly toward the sun. Most are, but some aren't. And it looks like they're mounted on gimbals. If those are solar-cell arrays, that's a pretty haphazard way of placing them, don't you think?"

Rolf scowled at Jason, as if to ask *Since when did you become an engineer?* From the other side of the compartment, Zeus Brandt chuckled softly. "Now, boys . . ."

Andromeda tapped her mike again. "Sean, can you point your camera straight at one of those big black things and zoom in, please? We're trying to figure out what they are."

"Yes, ma'am," he said, and again Andromeda bristled at the not-well-disguised sarcasm in her son's voice.

"We'll be making a close pass in just a few seconds," Mark Dupree said. *"I think we should be able to give you a good shot then. But"*—a moment of hesitation—*"judging from what I'm seeing here, I think I've got an idea what they are."*

"Love to hear it, Sergeant." Andromeda smiled. "Someone here thinks they're photovoltaic arrays, but the jury's still out."

"Yes, well . . . they may be that, too. But judging from their shape and size, and the weird way they're attached to the cables, my first guess is that they're solar sails."

Rolf and Jason traded looks; apparently that thought hadn't occurred to them. "It would make sense," Rolf said grudgingly. "You'd need some sort of attitude-control system to keep Hex in proper alignment as it rotates. You could mount engines all over the thing, but that would use a lot of energy. If you had a passive system . . ."

"You could use the solar wind instead." Andromeda nodded. "The magnetic charge attracts it to the cables, then the sails harness it. You'd need a lot of 'em, of course, but I suppose it's plausible."

The lander was beginning to make its passage through the hexagon's center. Andromeda used her fingertips to manipulate a trackball on her lapboard; the image on the upper-left side of the wallscreen expanded, displaying Sean's close-up view of the nearest cable. The black panels did indeed look very much like the thin polymer of solar sails, but she noticed that they also had the hexagonal patterns of photovoltaic arrays. Perhaps Dupree's theory was correct; the panels might serve two functions at once. If so, then it was further proof of *danui* ingenuity . . . as if any more proof were needed.

"Don't get too close to those panels," D'Anguilo said, apparently addressing the lander pilot. "You don't know how . . ."

"I'm getting another transmission!" Anne snapped. "A text message this time . . . in *hjadd*!"

"Send it over to Tom," Andromeda said, "and put it up on the screen. Tom, can you translate, please? I want Anne to concentrate on maintaining contact with the lander."

"I'm on it." D'Anguilo quickly turned back to his console, where the new message was already appearing on one of his comp screens. A second later, a window appeared at the bottom of the wallscreen, and the message unscrolled in vertical bars upon it:

Andromeda had seen *hjadd* script before. As always, she considered it to be strangely beautiful, more a work of art than an alien language. She had no idea what it meant, though, but she barely had time to wonder why the *danui* had sent something in *hjadd* before D'Anguilo used the translation program to divine its meaning.

"I've got an approximate translation," he said, his voice low, "but you're not going to like it."

"Let's see it," Andromeda said, and a second later several lines of Anglo text appeared beneath the *hjadd* script:

> To human starship: please immediately withdraw your craft from the [center of the hexagon]. It is trespassing upon arsashi territory and poses a hazard to [vital components]. Arsashi inhabitants have noticed its presence and are threatening to [retaliate?/respond with force?]. Please withdraw immediately and await further instructions.

"Oh, hell," Jason murmured. "This is not good."

"Tell me about it," Andromeda said. But the warning seemed to confirm Kyra's theory that the *danui* were allowing different races to occupy various hexagons. *So this is what they meant when they told us that there was a habit-*

able world in their system, she thought. *We assumed that they meant a planet . . . not this!*

No time to consider that now. She started to prod her mike before she remembered that the comlink was still active. "*Reese*, this is *Montero*. We've just translated that message from the *danui* . . . at least we think it's the *danui* . . . and they're ordering us to withdraw the lander at once. Do you copy?" Not waiting for a reply, she looked at Anne. "Replay that on the same frequency you received the warning. I want the *danui* to hear it."

"Already done," Anne said.

Cayce's voice came over the comlink. "*Montero, this is* Reese. *We copy, but couldn't you have told us this fifteen minutes ago? We're already . . .*"

"I know where you are, Lieutenant." As she spoke, Andromeda intently watched the multiple images on the wallscreen. In the midst of a thicket of cables, the lander was more than halfway through the hexagon's inner perimeter; it was as if the *Reese* were a fly finessing its way through a spiderweb. "According to . . . ah, whoever sent that message . . . you're violating some sort of territorial agreement. You need to . . ."

"Another transmission, Captain!" Anne yelled. "Audio, this time . . . and it's not *danui*!"

"Patch it through the whole comlink," Andromeda said. "Tom, get ready to translate."

A second later, she heard a growling, guttural voice, its tongue laden with vowels; it was somewhat like how she imagined a large dog would sound like if it tried to speak Latin. "That's *arsashi*, all right," D'Anguilo said. "I'll try to get us a translation, but I bet I know what they're saying."

"So do I," Andromeda said. "Lieutenant, you heard it, too. There's an *arsashi* down there who's righteously pissed off. Get out of there *now*."

Dupree came on the line again. "*Easier said than done, Captain. If I attempt to turn around now, I'll probably run into one of the cables. Even if I do a retroburn and back out, there's a strong chance of collision. The best way to make a safe return is to continue going the way we are now, then turn around once we're clear of the cables and go back the way we came."*

"He's right, skipper." Melpomene had been quiet until then, but apparently she felt compelled to speak up for a fellow pilot. "If I were in his place, that's what I'd do."

Andromeda glanced at Jason. The first officer's face had gone pale. Tight-lipped and tense, he slowly nodded. She darted a look at D'Anguilo. "You got that translation yet?" she demanded.

"Still working on it." D'Anguilo didn't look up from his console. "Their language has about twenty or thirty different dialects, though, and . . ."

"Keep on it," she said. "*Reese*, continue on course, but turn around as soon as you're in the clear and get back here ASAP. Anne, send a message . . . in Anglo, I guess." Tom was too busy to translate it into *hjadd* or *arsashi*, and she trusted his language skills more than Anne's, albeit reluctantly. "In any case, tell whoever it is down there that we're withdrawing our lander, but we need to make sure that it'll be able to safely return."

"Roger that, Montero," Mark said. *"We'll return as soon as we're out of the woods."*

The pilot sounded distracted. On the upper-left side of the wallscreen, Andromeda noticed that Sean had turned his camera away from the porthole and was now aiming it between the seats. Mark had both hands on the yoke, and his gaze was fixed on the lidar display just below the middle cockpit window. Apparently Sean had decided that what was happening inside the lander was more interesting than what was going on outside. The camera turned for a second toward Kyra, sitting quietly behind Mark as she stared out the window beside her, before it was directed at the pilot again.

"Sean, point the camera out your window again," she said.

He didn't reply, but the view shifted back to the porthole, and once more she saw what was on *Reese*'s starboard side.

The lander was almost clear of the cables; beyond them, she could make out the far side of the hexagon, where three of the biopods came together at their respective nodes to form what looked like little more than a distant line. Aurorae occasionally raced across the cables like miniature blue lightning storms. But it appeared that only the outer half of the hexagon was opaque; the side facing the sun seemed to be translucent, like it was . . .

A startled gasp from Kyra: *"Sean, look over here!"*

An instant later, Sean himself: *"Wow! That's . . . Wow!"*

"What are you . . . ?" This from Sandy LaPointe in the lander's rearmost seat. *"Let me . . . Oh, my freakin' God . . . !"*

"What's going on?" Andromeda demanded. Although Sean had turned his camera toward the port-side porthole, Kyra blocked the view; very little could be seen through the small window save for a vague silver hump. "Sean, give Kyra the camera so we can . . ."

"Hold on a moment, Montero," Mark said. *"Soon as I turn us around, you'll be able to see what we're look-ing at."*

A couple of seconds went by, then *Reese*'s bow-angle view shifted to the right as the lander turned to starboard, and Andromeda caught her first glimpse of the image captured by the wing cameras. Her fingers fumbled at her lapboard until they found the controls to expand the image so that it filled the wallscreen. When that happened, everyone on *Montero*'s bridge cried out in astonishment.

Just past the edge of the cable web, only about twenty or thirty miles away, was the nearest biopod. From the lander's vantage point, the cylinder was tremendous, so long that its endcaps were lost to sight. But the near side of the biopod wasn't the featureless grey hulk that they'd seen from orbit; instead, it appeared to be open to space, with only a semicircular curve of reflected sunlight revealing the transparent roof that formed a ceiling above the cylinder's vast interior.

Beneath that ceiling was another world.

From an altitude of about fifty miles, they looked down
upon a winter landscape. Snow-covered plains lay on either
side of an icy river that flowed down the middle of the cylinder, fed by narrow estuaries that wound their way through
low hills. On both sides of the river, the terrain gradually
rose in elevation until it formed the walls of an immense
valley a hundred miles wide, which in turn were bordered
by the window edges.

The roof was so high above the valley floor that they
could see filmy cirrus clouds in the sky above the valley;
within the shadows cast by one of those clouds, tiny lights
glimmered. A settlement, most likely. Indeed, other signs of
habitation could be seen: threadlike roads, tiny motes here
and there upon the river that might be boats, a large central
dome that didn't appear to be natural in origin.

An entire habitat, far bigger than anything even re-
motely like it that humans had ever built. The great crater
cities of the Moon would easily fit inside the thing, with
plenty of room to spare. *And this is just one,* Andromeda
thought. *How many did Tom estimate are here? Over a
trillion?* She swallowed hard, feeling her heart beat against
her chest. *This is impossible. How could anyone build anything this big?*

A low, awestruck whistle from Rolf. "That's it," he muttered. "I give up. I'm retiring. I have no business calling
myself an engineer. They . . ."

"Captain, I have the translation." Along with Rolf's
comment, D'Anguilo's voice broke the silence of the command deck. "The *arsashi* say that, if we violate their air-
space . . . I guess that means the area above their biopod, if
this belongs to them . . . then they are within their rights
to . . ." A momentary pause. "I'm not sure of the last word,"
he finished, "but I think it means *retaliate.*"

A chill swept down Andromeda's back. "*Reese*, did you
get that?"

"*Loud and clear,* Montero," Mark said. "*I'm . . .*"

Suddenly, the images on the wallscreen jiggled violently

as if something had struck the lander. *"What the hell?"* Cayce snapped. *"Where did that . . . ?"*

"Reese, what's happening?" Andromeda hunched forward in her seat. "Do you copy?"

A crackling rush of static. On the screen, the images from the lander cameras froze for an instant, then disintegrated into random pixels. When Cayce's voice returned, it was broken and distorted.

"Mayday, May . . . caught in force . . . or beam of some . . . control compromised, pilot . . ."

"Boosting gain, Captain," Anne said, "but I'm getting some wicked interference."

"Try harder. Switch to another band if you have to." Andromeda glanced over at D'Anguilo. "Send a message . . . any language, just so you make it fast . . . and tell them we're not hostile and . . ."

"You think I haven't thought of that?" For the first time, D'Anguilo lost patience with her. "I've already tried! Everything I send just gets bounced back . . . !"

". . . is Reese, *do you copy?"* Dupree's voice again. *"We've been caught by a force beam of . . ."*

More static, followed by an uncharacteristic curse from Anne as she struggled to regain contact with the lander. *"Reese*, this is *Montero*, do you copy? You're breaking up. Please repeat. Over."

Instead of the pilot's voice, the next thing she heard was a harsh electronic squeal, so loud that it caused Andromeda to swear and jerk away her headset. Anne cried out in pain; she stared at her console, then glanced over her shoulder at the captain. "Receiving some kind of transmission," she said, "but damned if I know what it is. It's not . . ."

"Never mind that," Andromeda snapped. The video feed from the *Reese* was gone; the only thing on the wallscreen was the image from *Montero*'s own bow cameras. "Can you reach the lander?"

The com officer frantically worked her console. "Negative. Loss of signal from the *Reese*."

Andromeda clutched her armrests. For a moment, she found herself on the verge of panic, not understanding what was going on and unable to decide what action to take. Then cold pragmatism snapped her mind back into focus. The survey team was in trouble; it was her responsibility to save them.

"Mel, take us down," she said.

Melpomene turned to her. "Captain? Excuse me . . . ?"

"You heard me." Andromeda didn't look back at the helmsman but instead stared straight ahead at the screen. "Break orbit and follow the lander. Use their last available coordinates to plot a trajectory for rendezvous and retrieval."

"But . . ."

"Don't argue. Just do it." Andromeda knew exactly what she was telling Mel to do: fly the *Montero* through the web of cables that the smaller ship had barely been able to penetrate. Regardless of the risk of collision, though, or the fact that the *arsashi* had reacted to the *Reese* coming too close to a hexagon that they apparently claimed as their own, Andromeda knew that she had little choice.

I can't abandon Sean, she thought. *He'll never forgive me if I let this happen again . . .*

She noticed that her headset was dead. Pulling it back over her head, she listened to the earpiece. The static was gone. She thought for a moment that Anne had managed to squelch it, but then the com officer turned to her again.

"Another text transmission, skipper. In Anglo. It says . . ."

"Damn it!" Melpomene yelled. "My board's frozen!"

"What?" Ignoring Anne for the moment, Andromeda looked at Mel. "What do you mean, it's . . . ?"

"I'm getting no helm response." In frustration, Melpomene stabbed at the touch screens of her navigation console, then reached up to try the same thing with the toggles and buttons of the overhead control panels. "I'm completely locked out, skipper. It's like someone just pulled the plug or . . ."

"That's what I'm trying to tell you, Captain." Anne

waved a hand at her own console. "We just received a clear-text signal from Hex."

Before Andromeda had a chance tell her to do so, Anne put the transmission up on the main screen:

> To human starship: navigation of your vessel has been assumed by local traffic control network. Your ship will be automatically maneuvered to the harbor node of a nearby habitat. Please refrain from making any attempt to resume control of your vessel or catastrophic damage may result. Your crew will be allowed to disembark once your ship has reached its destination. Further contact will be made with you at some future time.

A moment later, there was a sudden rumble from *Montero*'s aft section, and she felt a familiar vibration pass through the soles of her shoes.

"Main engines firing," Rolf said, gazing at his console. "One-sixth maximum thrust . . . just enough to budge us from our present orbit."

"Can you . . . ?"

"Scram the reactors?" The chief engineer flipped back the candy-striped cover of the main engines' emergency shutdown control, flipped the four toggle switches beneath it. "Negative. Same as with the helm, skipper . . . we have no control."

"Bastards probably sent us a Trojan horse," Zeus murmured. The chief petty officer's arms were folded across his chest, his eyes cold as he glared at Hex. "Piggybacked on that last transmission, fed new commands into the comps and AI, then locked us out."

Andromeda and Anne glanced at each other, and the com officer shrugged and quietly nodded. Zeus's theory was probably as good an explanation as any.

Andromeda read the message once more. She was tempted to ask where it came from, but the answer was obvious. It was just as pointless to ask why it had taken the *danui* so long to send a transmission in her own language. The aliens clearly had their own agenda, and the desires of their human visitors were moot at best.

The *Montero* was being hijacked, and she had no idea what had happened to the *Reese*. And there wasn't a damn thing she could do about any of it.

TEN

THE FORCE THAT ATTACKED THE *REESE* WAS INVISIBLE, undetectable, and without apparent source. Nevertheless, it seized the lander like a ghostly hand, pulling the small craft away from its intended course with an intransigent power that defied resistance.

Cayce wasn't about to surrender without a fight. "Full thrust!" he yelled at Mark. "Give it all you've got!" Then he stabbed at the com panel again. "Mayday, mayday! *Reese* to *Montero*, do you copy? Please respond, over!"

From his seat behind Cayce, Sean watched as Mark pushed the throttle bar forward. Despite Cayce's insistence, the pilot wasn't pushing the main engine to its limits . . . or at least not yet. Perhaps he was deliberately holding back to keep something in reserve. Yet the lander trembled, creaking and shaking as if it were caught in an unseen windstorm.

"Mayday, mayday . . . !"

"Forget it, sir. You're not getting through." Unlike Cayce, Mark remained calm. Panic wouldn't get them anywhere, and shouting only made things worse. "If you want to help, then keep an eye on the engine temperature. I don't want it to start overheating . . ."

A sudden lurch, and Kyra yelped as her datapad was suddenly wrenched from her hands. Sandy cursed as it sailed past her head, and Sean heard the pad smack against the aft bulkhead. His camera began to slide from his grip, and as he clutched it tight to keep from losing it, he felt his helmet tug at his skinsuit collar.

"What the hell?" He held the sides of his helmet with both hands. "What's . . ."

"Must be some sort of magnetic beam." Kyra glanced back to where her pad had crashed into the bulkhead. "Sorry about that, Sandy. Are you okay?"

"Yeah, sure." Sandy's face was ashen. "Can we go home now?"

"Working on it." Left hand gripping the yoke, Mark gently inched the throttle forward a notch. Another lurch, then the lander suddenly rolled over. "Damn. It's dragging us."

Dragging? Hugging the camera against his chest, Sean looked out the porthole beside him. The lander was no longer above the biopod's sunward side; instead, he saw that they were being pulled toward the spherical node at its end. A cable was only a hundred or so yards away, so close that he could see *Reese*'s exhaust plume reflected in the glossy black panel of its solar wing . . . and the luminescent white smear was not going forward but backward.

Mark was right. The beam was hauling them away from the biopod. "I think they want to bring us into that node," he said. "That might be where . . ."

"I don't care what you think!" Cayce couldn't turn his head around enough for Sean to see his face, but he could hear impatience in the lieutenant's voice . . . and panic. "I just want to get the hell out of here!" He looked at Mark again. "Did you hear what I said? *Full power!*"

And then, before the pilot could react, the team leader reached forward, grabbed the throttle bar with his left hand, and shoved it all the way forward.

An abrupt surge threw Sean against his seat. The back of his skull connected with the inside of his helmet; despite the padding, he felt a jolt of pain, and fireflies swarmed before his eyes. The blow must have stunned him for a moment, because when the tiny sparks of light finally vanished, he became aware that Kyra was grasping his hand and asking if he was okay. Somehow, he'd lost his camera; it was no longer in his hands.

"You *idiot!*" From a distance, he heard Mark's voice; it sounded as if he'd finally lost his cool. "Do you know what you're . . . Oh, *shit*, hang on!"

Sean barely had a second to brace his hands against the back of Cayce's seat before something slammed against the lander's starboard side. Another painful jolt told him that he'd sprained his left wrist, but at least he'd prevented a second blow to the head. But when he felt a rush of air against his face, and the decompression alarm began to shriek, he knew that minor injuries were the least of his worries.

"*Blow-out!*" Mark yelled. "Everyone, close your helmets! Now!"

Sean reached for his helmet faceplate. The moment that it snapped shut, the suit automatically activated its internal air system. Cayce might have been a fool, but at least he'd done one smart thing by ordering his team to wear skinsuits during this sortie.

Sean glanced out the porthole again. It was whiskered by dozens of hairline fractures, but Sean caught a glimpse of the cable that the *Reese* had just hit. Its nearest black panel was ripped lengthwise, and it appeared to be barely hanging on by its rigging. Then the cable disappeared, and the biopod's sunward side came back into view.

"What . . . ? How . . . ?" Cayce stammered. "Did we hit something?" He apparently had little idea what was going on.

"A cable. We sideswiped it." Mark hauled at the yoke, struggling to regain control of his craft. "We broke out of that beam, but I think . . ." His voice trailed off as he reached up to hastily snap toggles on the overhead console.

"Uh-oh . . . I'm getting nothing from the starboard RCRs."
He glanced back at Sean. "Can you look out there, tell me
what you see?"

Sean peered out the window again, craning his neck to
see the lander's aft starboard side. Remarkably, most of the
wing was still intact, but its canard had been sheared away,
and the outboard spoiler appeared to be warped. He reported the damage to Mark, and the pilot tested the flaps.

"No good," he muttered. "I've got no control over that
wing. Landing is going to be tricky."

"Landing?" Cayce stared at him. "We're not landing anywhere. We're returning to the ship. That's an order."

Sandy brayed laughter.

"With all due respect, sir, I think not." Mark nodded
toward the cockpit windows. He'd managed to stop the
lander's spin, and the biopod had reappeared through the
forward portholes. Its transparent roof was upside down,
but closer than it had been before. Much closer. "That stunt
you pulled has yanked us out of the beam, all right . . . but
the damage we've sustained gives me only partial control.
With the starboard RCRs out of commission, there's no
way I can turn us around, let alone maneuver through the
cables again. Not safely, at least."

"Then . . . then we sit tight. Wait for the *Montero* to
rescue us."

"We've lost most of our cabin pressure." Mark nodded
toward the cabin environment readout; Sean couldn't see it
clearly, but its top bar was flashing red. "The suits won't
keep us alive and breathing longer than six hours. That, and
the fact that we've lost contact with the ship, makes rescue
unlikely."

"You don't know that!"

"Listen to me, Lieutenant." Mark squeezed the left handle of his yoke; the port RCRs silently fired, and the lander
slowly rolled over until the biopod was right side up again.
"That's about as much lateral control as I still have. If I
try to get us back to the *Montero*, we're screwed, and if

we try to wait for rescue, we're screwed, too. Like I said, we're out of options. We're going down, whether we like it or not."

"But . . ." Cayce began, then stopped himself. Sean caught a glimpse of his face, reflected in the glass of the cockpit windows. Although his expression was distorted by his helmet faceplate, the lieutenant was obviously frightened by the prospect of a crash landing. "How do you think you're going to make it through the roof?"

"He's got a point, Mark," Sean said. "You don't know how thick it is, or even what it's made of. For all we know, it might be some kind of transparent metal."

"I know that." Again, Mark let out his breath. "All we can do is hope for the best."

Sean traded a look with Kyra, then the two of them cinched their seat harnesses as tight as they could. Behind them, Sandy had become uncommonly quiet, but when Sean glanced back at her, he saw her lips silently moving behind her helmet faceplate; she'd wisely muted her com-link before giving voice to the thoughts in her mind, and Sean had little doubt that they included nothing nice about Lt. Amerigo Cayce.

For the next fifteen minutes, the *Reese* descended upon the biopod in a steep, perpendicular dive. As the massive cylinder grew ever larger beyond the cockpit windows, the snow-covered landscape beneath its roof gradually gained detail. Sean began to make out what appeared to be forests surrounding what were either meadows or, more likely, frozen lakes. At least there was plenty of uninhabited area for Mark to land . . . if he could get them through the roof in one piece.

The pilot kept an eye on his instruments all the way down, even as he fought to keep the lander on a smooth and consistent approach pattern. The biopod roof had become a vast, concave expanse only a few miles away when he spoke again. "Good news. According to the lidar, the ceiling is just a few inches thick, and the spectrometer's not showing any metallic traces. Looks like it's some sort of polymer . . . not glass, but not quite plastic either."

"So what?" Cayce's voice was hollow. He hadn't said anything since losing his argument with the pilot but had only stared straight ahead with blank, hopeless eyes.

"It means I might be able to punch through that thing if I give it enough juice." Mark hesitated, then he glanced back at Sean. "What do you say? Roll the dice?"

"Roll 'em." Sean shrugged. What else did they have to lose?

"All right, then." The pilot nodded, then he reached for the thrust bar. "Hold on tight. We're going in."

He pushed the bar all the way forward, and the lander trembled as they were all pushed back in their seats again. As Sean gripped his armrests, he was startled to find Kyra's hand upon his own. One look at her expression through her helmet faceplate, and he knew that she was scared out of her wits. Wishing he could do more for her, he took her hand within his and prayed that it wouldn't be the last human contact he ever made.

He wasn't alone. As the lander hurtled toward the biopod, he heard Mark murmuring something just under his breath. Sean couldn't hear what he was saying, but nonetheless he knew what it was: a prayer-poem from the *Sa'Tong-tas*. Sean had never thought very much of *Sa'Tong*, but for the first time he found himself envying his friend for his beliefs, if only because they seemed to help keep him calm.

If we get out of this alive, Sean thought, *I'm going to ask him to lend me his copy. It can't be that—*

And then the *Reese* hit the biopod roof.

The impact wasn't what he'd expected. Not a crash, but instead a loud and violent *riiiiiip*, as if the lander was tearing through some fibrous membrane. A moment of resistance, then the small craft went through . . . only to have some giant foot kick the lander in the side.

"Hang on!" Mark yelled. "We're . . . !"

Another sudden jolt, then the lander went into a flat spin.

Screaming, Kyra clutched Sean's hand so hard that his knuckles hurt. Through the cockpit windows, he could see the ground spiraling toward them as if the lander were caught in a kaleidoscope. Fighting an urge to vomit, he clenched his teeth as he shut his eyes. That only made the vertigo worse; he opened them again, to see Mark fighting the controls.

"C'mon, you bitch!" he snarled. "Straighten out . . . straighten out . . ."

A muffled shriek of wind on the other side of the fuselage, then it slowly diminished as the lander's wings grabbed at the atmosphere. Another abrupt slam, a little less violent that time, then the spinning ceased.

"We're out of it!" Cayce shouted.

"Not yet." Mark didn't relax. As if to confirm what he'd said, the lander quivered as it encountered more turbulence. "I can try to glide in, but with the starboard flaps out of commission, I'm not going to have much say over where we're going to land. Or how fast."

Sean glanced through his porthole. The ruined glass made it difficult for him to see the ground clearly, but the white landscape was closer than he liked. "How far up are we . . . ?"

"Can't tell you. Forward array got knocked out when we went through." Mark reached for the middle console and snapped a row of toggles. Below their feet, there was the thud of the landing gear coming down. "That'll slow us down a little," the pilot added. "As soon as we're close enough, I'll kick in the . . . Ah, damn."

"What's going on?" Cayce demanded.

"I was afraid of this. The starboard VTOL is shot, too." Another shudder, and Mark returned both hands to the yoke. "Sorry, folks, but we're in for a rough landing."

"Just keeps getting worse and worse." Sandy sighed. "Man, I knew I shoulda gone to med school."

Kyra laughed out loud, but there were tears spotting the inside of her faceplate, and Sean heard an edge of hysteria in her voice. The lander was through the clouds, and the ground was getting closer by the second. Their descent had become more horizontal than vertical, but there was no comfort in the sight of snow-covered terrain rushing toward them. Forests, hills, frozen ponds, the central river . . .

"There. That open area straight ahead." Cayce pointed to the left through the middle cockpit window. "Think you can make it?"

Mark didn't reply, but instead twisted the yoke to port. The lander veered slightly to the left. "I might," he said at last, "but we're still going to come down hard." He raised his voice to be heard over the roar of the wind. "Sean, Kyra, Sandy . . . bend over, put your heads between your knees and hands over your heads."

"And kiss your—" Sandy began.

"Shut up!" Sean snarled. Kyra was frightened enough as it was, and Sandy's fatalism was only making it worse. He reached across the aisle to push Kyra's head down, then he did the same himself. The harness dug into his chest and stomach, and he suddenly became conscious of the pull of gravity. Just then, gravity was something of which he could use a little less . . .

Long, long minutes went by during which he couldn't see anything except the toes of his boots and heard nothing but the rush of the wind and an occasional mechanical noise. Sean was almost ready to think that it might be a smooth and uneventful landing when Mark suddenly shouted, "Brace yourselves!" And then . . .

The harsh and ugly screech of the landing gear coming into contact with snow and ice. The craft shook violently, tossing him back and forth within his seat. He was just beginning to hope that the *Reese* might simply drag itself to a stop when there was the loud snap of the port-side landing strut breaking free.

When the lander fell over on its left side, the port wing was the only thing that prevented the craft from going completely upside down and crushing the cabin. But although the wing remained connected to the fuselage, its leading edge dug deep into the ground, causing the aft end to fish-tail around. The bow caught the worst of it; Sean heard glass shatter, then something that sounded like hail rained down upon his shoulders and the top of his helmet.

Kyra and Sandy screamed. He did, too, although later he couldn't remember having done so.

The lander spun across the ground, its broken landing gear and wing dragging through snow, mud, and rock until it gradually came to a halt. For several long seconds, Sean heard only the slow, awkward tick of relaxing metal, the tinkle of a loosened piece of glass falling from its frame.

Then silence.

Sean let out his breath, took another one. He was alive . . . and, at least so far as he could tell, unharmed. Carefully sitting up, he looked over at Kyra. She'd been thrown back in her seat, and for a moment he thought she wasn't moving. But then her helmet turned toward him, and he could see her eyes through the faceplate, wide and terrified.

"You okay?" he asked, and she slowly nodded. The lander was listing to its port side. With the deck slanted toward the left, it would be difficult for her to move from her seat.

First things first. The lander's prow appeared to be half-buried in the snow; the cockpit windows were shattered, and pieces of ice and rock were scattered across the consoles. Mark lay back in his seat, hands in his lap, head cocked to one side. It looked as if he were resting from his exertions.

Sean thought Cayce had been knocked out, but then the team leader stirred in his seat. "Everyone all right?" the lieutenant asked, his voice weak and dazed. "Sound off."

"I'm good," Sandy muttered. "Nice landing, Mark. I mean it."

"Yeah . . . good job, man," Sean said.

No response. Sean hastily released himself from his harness, then leaned forward between the front seats. "Hey, Mark," he said, prodding his friend's shoulder. "Are you . . . ?"

No, he wasn't. At Sean's touch, Mark Dupree's head swung toward him upon a broken neck. Through his helmet faceplate, his eyes gazed sightlessly at the world to which he'd given his life to bring his friends.

THE TESSELLATED SKY

ELEVEN

WHEN ANDROMEDA CARSON WAS A CADET AT THE *Academia del Espacio* of the Union Astronautica, she'd learned to fly in the academy's flight simulator, an exact replica of a spacecraft cockpit. With an instructor sitting beside her and the voices of the control room piped in through her headset, Ensign Carson flew missions ranging from simple launch-and-landing exercises to more complex orbital sorties.

At first, the simulator was a lot of fun, at least for a girl from New Mexico who aspired to command her own deep-space vessel. But her instructor and the controllers were aware of her ambitions, and after it became apparent that Andromeda was a quick study, they stopped taking it easy and began throwing in-flight emergencies at her: main-engine failures, cabin decompressions, computer glitches, docking aborts, power brownouts, telemetry blackouts, on-board fires, space-junk collisions, even bizarre scenarios like alien attacks or crew mutinies. Sometimes the controllers would come up with two or three things at once while her instructor sat calmly in the copilot's seat, eating a sandwich as he quietly watched Andromeda cope with looming catastrophe.

Andromeda did the best she could. Not only was she at the top of her class, but it was obvious from the beginning that she had an instinctive talent for flying, displaying reflexes and intuition beyond the minimum requirements for flight certification. Yet the simulator staff seemed to take an almost sadistic pleasure in making life tough for her, and since they held all the cards, it was only inevitable that, every so often, they'd deal her a lousy hand. And when she found herself in a situation she simply couldn't handle, they would punish her in a singularly cruel manner: they would shut down her controls and put the simulator on full autopilot. So Andromeda would have to sit in her seat, quietly fuming as she watched the simulator solve her problems for her in the wink of an eye before completing the mission without her input. But while her instructor was aware that she was humiliated, he didn't know that what she hated even more was the sense of helplessness that went with the loss of control.

Simply put, Ensign Carson always wanted to be able to choose her own destiny. Which was why, many years later, Captain Carson tortured the armrests of her chair as the *Montero* was guided by forces unknown to a destination uncertain.

No one in the command center was happy about what was happening. Melpomene Fisk fidgeted at the helm, unable to do anything that mattered, while Rolf Kurtz appeared to be grinding his teeth as he scowled at the wallscreen. Anne Smith continued trying to regain contact with the *Reese* even though the hexagon where the lander had gone down was a long way behind them. Thomas D'Anguilo closely monitored the remote survey console, searching for any clues as to where the ship was going or why it was being taken there. On captain's orders, Zeus Brandt had gone below to the small-arms locker on Deck Two, where he opened the cache of fléchette pistols just in case . . . well, just in case.

Yet Andromeda was more tense than anyone else aboard, and only Jason Ressler knew why. From his seat beside her, *Montero*'s first officer quietly observed his captain from the corner of his eye. He was particularly intrigued by her fingers; they alternately dug and drummed at the armrests, occasionally curling into fists white-knuckled with suppressed anger.

Catching Jason watching her, Andromeda glared at him. "What?" she demanded.

"Nothing." He forced a smile. "Except we're going to need to reupholster your chair if you keep up like that."

"Take it out of my salary," she muttered, then returned her attention to the wallscreen. Without telemetry from the lander, the only image it displayed was Hex's outer surface, a seemingly endless plain of hexagons slowly rolling beneath them. Melpomene had put their flight track up on the nav table. It appeared as a tiny red line running across the holographic sphere; although it was only a couple of inches long, Andromeda was aware that the line represented the forty thousand miles the *Montero* had traveled since its guidance system had been taken over by the *danui* . . .

With every passing mile taking her farther away from Sean.

"I'll make a note of it in my log." Jason paused, then added, "I've got some friends at the shipyard back home. Maybe I can get them to cut us a discount."

"Knock it off," Andromeda growled.

"Sure. You first." Jason sighed. "Look, there's nothing you can do, so you might as well take a break." He cocked a thumb toward the hatch. "Go below. Grab some lunch, or take a nap. Something other than sit there and fret."

An angry retort hovered on Andromeda's lip; she restrained the urge to say it out loud. Jason meant well, but there was no way she could leave the bridge. Not until she knew where they were going, or what had happened to her son and his team. Until then, lunch and a nap were out of the question.

Instead, she pushed aside her lapboard and unfastened

her seat belt. Planting her stickshoes against the floor, she stood up and walked over to D'Anguilo's station. She was about to ask—again—whether he'd learned anything new when she felt the deck make a small yet noticeable movement, a motion that she recognized at once.

"Forward thrusters firing, skipper." Melpomene stared at the comp screens of her console, hands on either side of the frozen controls. "We're braking, and"—another motion, this time in a lateral direction—"turning about, ninety degrees to port."

Forgetting what she was about to ask D'Anguilo, Andromeda turned toward the wallscreen. Hex no longer appeared to be a flat plain but instead a wall of hexagons slowly moving by. As she watched, the wall seemed to grow larger.

"Are we heading toward it?" she asked.

"Appears so, ma'am." Melpomene didn't look at her. "Lateral velocity decreasing, forward velocity increasing."

"It's drawing us in," Jason said quietly.

Andromeda glanced at Anne. "Anything new?" she asked. The com officer silently shook her head, and the captain turned to Rolf. "What about those engines or RCRs? Can you . . . ?" Rolf shook his head as well, and Andromeda took a deep breath. "Damn. Damn, damn . . ."

"Captain?" Jason was still seated in his chair, calmly gazing at the wallscreen. "There's nothing we can do about it. Might as well wait and see what happens next."

"I have to agree," D'Anguilo said. "Whatever the *danui* have in store for us, I don't think it's necessarily hostile."

"And what leads you to that conclusion?" Andromeda asked. "Your fine grasp of alien psychology?"

D'Anguilo let the sarcasm pass. "If they meant us harm, don't you think they would have acted by now?" He nodded at the screen. "The *danui* could destroy us in seconds . . . Of that, I have little doubt. Yet their actions so far have been nonviolent, if rather mysterious. In any case, we're entirely in their hands."

"Or claws." There was a wry smile on Jason's face. "He's right, skipper. It's entirely up to them, so we might as well relax and wait."

Wait, yes . . . but Andromeda was damned if she was going to be passive about it. She tapped a finger against her headset wand. "Zeus, are you there?"

"Right here, skipper." The chief petty officer didn't need to tell her where he was. *"I've got the weapons out. Want me to bring them upstairs?"*

"Negative. I'll have Jason come down to fetch them." Her first officer started to say something, but Andromeda silenced him with a raised forefinger before he could speak. "You know what's happening, don't you?"

"Yes, ma'am." Zeus's tone became menacing. *"They're not taking us without a fight."*

D'Anguilo blanched, and Andromeda suppressed a smile. At least she wasn't alone; someone else was suspicious of the *danui*. "I'm not looking for a fight," she replied, giving D'Anguilo a sidelong glance. "At least not for the time being. Right now, I want you to prepare for docking. Suit up and board the pod."

"Yes, ma'am." There was newfound enthusiasm in Zeus's voice; apparently he, too, was tired of doing nothing. *"I'm heading below."*

"Good man." The lander's bay doors had been left open after the *Reese* had departed, so Zeus should have no problem taking out the pod. She muted the mike, then turned to Jason again. "Go collect the fléchette pistols from Zeus and bring them up here, along with holsters. I want everyone to have one before we . . ."

"Captain, I object!" D'Anguilo stood up from his seat and took a step toward her. "This endangers the very purpose of this mission! The *danui* have no history of hostility. They . . ."

"Dr. D'Anguilo, your opinion has been noted." Andromeda stared him straight in the eye. "As commanding officer, it's my duty to take whatever measures I deem necessary to protect my vessel and crew. You say the *danui* haven't acted in a hostile fashion. I disagree. They've refused to respond to nearly all our messages, allowed another race to act against our survey team, then captured this ship and brought it to an unknown location. And now they're preparing to do something else . . . dock the ship, and possibly even board us . . . against our will. As far as I'm concerned, those are hostile actions, and I'm taking the minimum precautions."

"Captain . . ."

"Sit down and shut up . . . or I'll have Mr. Ressler confine you to quarters."

Jason was already on his feet. He stood beside D'Anguilo, waiting for Andromeda to give him the word. Everyone else in the command center stared at them; no one dared to speak. The astroethnicist regarded Andromeda for another moment, then he looked away and sat down again without saying another word.

Jason headed for the access hatch, but not before he paused beside Andromeda. "I hope you know what you're doing," he whispered.

Andromeda quietly nodded. Jason left the bridge, opening the hatch to glide headfirst down the access shaft. She let out her breath, then returned to her seat and sat down again. She could feel D'Anguilo's eyes upon her back, but she refused to look at him.

Hex grew larger, no longer resembling a wall but instead a latticework of six-sided spaces with HD 76700 gleaming as a captive star within its center. The *Montero* came closer, thrusters firing periodically to correct its approach vector, and it soon became clear that the vessel was being guided toward a hexagon about halfway up Hex's northern hemisphere. If D'Anguilo's estimates were correct, that was the zone where the biopod gravity would be approximately 1 g. Whoever had reprogrammed *Montero*'s comps were apparently aware of human environmental tolerances.

The *Montero* was less than fifty miles from the hexagon when a small red spot of light appeared upon the outer surface of the node at its upper-left corner. As the light grew larger and brighter, the thrusters fired again, maneuvering the ship toward it. The lidar was still active, and Melpomene reported that the light was coming from within a circular hatch that had just opened. Apparently, that was the place where the *Montero* would be docked.

Jason returned to the bridge, bearing an armload of fléchette pistols. He passed them out among the crew. Andromeda checked to make sure her weapon was fully loaded with its arrowhead-like slivers, then clipped its holster to her belt. D'Anguilo made a sour face when Jason gave him a gun; he shoved the holster into his chair's cupholder and stared back at Andromeda when he caught her watching him. She decided not to make an issue of it. Perhaps it was just as well; if the *danui* were as peaceful as he insisted, then it might be a bad idea if their chief negotiator approached them with a weapon on his hip.

As the *Montero* made its final approach to Hex, the spherical node filled the wallscreen. Realizing that the bow cameras might not reveal everything she wanted to see, Andromeda left her seat again, pushing herself up to the ceiling portholes so that she could get a better view. The ship slowly passed through the outer hatch, and she caught a glimpse of the recessed flanges of its sphincterlike doors; the hatch was big enough to admit a vessel ten times the size of her own. Scarlet light gleamed from the other end of a broad, circular tunnel; in the sullen green glow of *Montero*'s port formation lights, she saw that its walls were grey and seamless, and appeared to be composed of some stony material.

"What the hell is this place made of?" she asked aloud, speaking to no one in particular. "Whatever it is, it's not metal."

"Restructured matter," D'Anguilo said, and Andromeda looked around to see that he'd joined her at the windows. "Possibly carbon nanotubes, but even if that's so, it probably started as something else."

Nice to know that D'Anguilo didn't bear grudges. Either that, or his sense of wonder outweighed any desire to indulge in a feud. "What do you mean by that?" she asked.

He shrugged, still staring out the window. "If the *danui* built this place the way I think they did, then what we're looking at is native material from their homeworld . . . or what used to be their homeworld, that is. After they tore their planet apart . . . along with just about every other planet and asteroid in this system . . . they broke its matter down to the most basic elements and compounds and used it as raw material." He paused. "Don't ask me how they did it. They just did."

Andromeda felt something stick in her throat. "You make it sound easy."

"Didn't mean to." A wry grin. "I'm sure it can't have been as . . ."

He stopped, his mouth falling open in amazement, and when Andromeda followed his gaze through the windows she saw why. The *Montero* had reached the end of the tunnel; before them lay a vast spherical chamber, tinted red from glowing red threads upon its walls and lined with deep, broad indentations that appeared to be docking bays. Apparently a harbor of some sort, yet so large that it could have held the Coyote Federation's entire merchant fleet. Within it, the *Montero* was little more than a toy.

She barely had time to comprehend the size of the place when she felt the RCRs fire again, that time to brake the ship. A sudden jolt from the starboard side, followed an instant later by another one from the port side, and the *Montero* began slowly gliding into the nearest bay.

"What in . . . ?" she began, then Rolf looked up at her.

"Skipper, you gotta see this!" he snapped.

He pointed to the wallscreen, and Andromeda pushed herself away from the ceiling to see what he was looking at. As the *Montero* coasted to a halt, thick cables uncoiled from recesses within the bay walls. Serpentine and swift, they lashed out toward the ship, wrapping themselves around the hull like the tentacles of some unseen kraken.

Andromeda couldn't believe what she was seeing. Within seconds, the cables formed a snare in which the ship was suspended. Her headset had become dislodged during her fall; pulling it up from around her neck, she jabbed at the wand. "Zeus, are you seeing this?"

"Aye, Captain." There was an irate undertone to his voice. *"I'm watching from the pod. They've got us trapped, but good."*

"I don't like this," Melpomene muttered. "Not one bit."

Andromeda nodded. She didn't like it, either; it felt too much like being imprisoned. But there was no point in asking Mel if she could fire thrusters and dislodge the ship. Perhaps there was another way . . .

"Zeus," she said, "go out and see if there's any way you can detach those lines."

"Captain . . ." D'Anguilo began.

She shot him an angry look. "Don't start with me again."

"I'm not trying to." D'Anguilo raised his hands in surrender. "Just let me point out that this might be normal docking procedure. It might seem like we've been captured, but . . . well, you don't know for sure."

"You've got a point," Andromeda said. "But since we don't know for sure, I'd like to see if we can escape, just in case your pals aren't as harmless as you say they are."

D'Anguilo's gaze traveled meaningfully to her holstered pistol. "Why are you assuming that everything they've done constitutes enemy action?"

Andromeda was tired of arguing with him. Turning away from D'Anguilo, she walked over to Rolf's station. One of his screens displayed the hangar bay's interior; the chief engineer had activated the pod's hull camera.

"Pod ready to undock," Rolf said quietly. Andromeda nodded, and Rolf murmured something into his mike. The screen changed, showing the hangar walls as they silently fell away beneath the service pod.

"Captain?" Anne said. "Receiving another text message. It's in Anglo."

"Put it up on the wall," Andromeda said. Anne's hands darted across her keyboard, and a moment later the message appeared on the wallscreen, superimposed over the forward view of the node harbor:

> Your vessel has been secured. An enclosed walkway will soon be extended for your convenience. Please do not interfere with docking operations.

"Captain, I recommend that you order your man back inside," D'Anguilo said. "I don't think they want us sneaking around outside our ship."

"No one's sneaking around. We're just making sure that we can leave when we want to." Andromeda continued to watch the smaller screen. The service pod had left *Montero*'s lander bay. As it turned toward the bow, she could see the tentacle-like cables wrapped around the command module's cylindrical hull. "Zeus, can you get close to one of those things? I'd like to get a good look at it."

"Wilco, Captain." A moment passed, then the screen showed the hull coming closer, with one of the cables in the hatched crosshairs of the camera's focal point. The cable didn't have any visible seams; although it had a metallic sheen that dully reflected the pod's floodlights, there was something about it that was disturbingly organic.

Apparently, Zeus was curious about the tentacle as well, because when he'd brought the pod close enough, Andromeda saw one of the remote manipulators move into view. Its claw opened, then it gently touched the side of the cable.

"Feels like rubber," Zeus said, and Andromeda noticed that the cable's surface dented ever so slightly where the manipulator claw touched it. *"Going to try to get hold of it, see if I can . . ."*

Suddenly, almost too fast for the eye to catch, the cable whipped free of the claw's grasp. *"Hey, what the hell?"* Zeus exclaimed as it disappeared from view. *"It just . . ."*

Then the screen view shuddered, as if something was violently shaking the pod. "What's going on?" Rolf snapped. "Are you . . . ?"

"Goddammit, it just grabbed me! I . . ."

"Get out of there!" Andromeda bent low over the console. "Zeus, fire your thrusters and . . . !"

"Captain, I . . . !"

"Zeus!" Melpomene screamed. "Get out of . . . !"

And then the screen went dark, and they heard nothing further from the pod.

TWELVE

ARK DUPREE'S LAST ACT HAD BEEN TO BRING THE *Reese* down in a long, flat plain not far from the bio-pod's central river. His flying skills probably saved the lives of everyone else aboard. Sean reflected upon this as he and Cayce pulled the pilot's body from the wreckage and laid it on the snow-covered ground.

"Thanks, buddy," he said quietly as he covered his friend with the emergency blanket he'd found among the lander's survival equipment. "I owe you one." Then he turned to look around.

Were it not for the ammonia-rich atmosphere and the weird trees that looked rather like immense broccoli, he could have sworn that he was on Coyote's north polar tun-dra. But only for a moment. To the west—the only way he could tell the direction was by checking the digital compass of his helmet's heads-up display—the landscape seemingly stretched away to infinity, with no apparent horizon. To the east, beyond the long furrow left by the *Reese*, the terrain ended in what appeared to be a hemispherical wall, so high that its upper reaches were hidden behind the cirrus clouds; it looked as if they'd come down closer to one end of the biopod than the other. To the north and south, the land gradually sloped upward until it reached mountainous ridgelines that seemed to run the entire length of both sides of the biopod.

In effect, he and the others were in a giant valley a thousand miles long and a hundred miles wide. The landscape wasn't the most disturbing thing about the place, though, but rather the sky.

It was easy to detect the point where the lander had penetrated the biopod ceiling. Many miles above them was what appeared to be an upside-down tornado: a small yet distinct funnel cloud, off-white and rotating clockwise, its mouth open to the ground and its spout tapering upward. The storm was too far above them for it to cause anything more than a steady breeze where they stood, yet as Sean watched the phenomenon, he knew that a much more dire situation was developing.

The biopod was leaking its atmosphere into space . . . and their crash landing was the reason why.

Sandy's right, he thought. *We should have stayed aboard the ship.*

"Sean?" Kyra said, and he lowered his eyes and turned to find her standing behind him. "Here. Got something for you."

A parka, a pair of insulated trousers, knee boots, gloves, and an airpack. While he and Cayce were removing Mark's body from the cockpit, she and Sandy had managed to pry open the cargo hold and locate the expedition gear. Kyra had already discarded her skinsuit and helmet; she was wearing cold-weather gear over her Corps unitard, its hood pulled up over her head, and the lower part of her face, from her eyes down to her chin, was concealed by the airpack's goggles and respirator, its hoses leading over her shoulders to the pack itself.

Sean gaped at her, surprised by her abrupt change of appearance. "How did you . . . ?"

"Sandy helped me." He couldn't see her mouth, but the

crinkling of the corners of her eyes behind the goggles told him that she was smiling. "C'mon . . . no time to be modest. You'll be a lot more comfortable in this."

He rather doubted that. The skinsuit had its own built-in heating system. But while the airmask might be cumbersome, even goggles would beat looking at the world through a helmet faceplate. Besides, he didn't have much of a choice. In a few hours, the skinsuit's oxygen supply would be gone, while the airpack could distill breathable oxygen and nitrogen from the atmosphere almost indefinitely.

Sandy had changed out of her skinsuit as well, and she was continuing to rummage through the equipment cases. But when Sean glanced over at Cayce, he saw that the team leader was making no effort to put on winter gear. Instead, he'd walked a few yards away from the wrecked spacecraft and was looking west, as if searching the horizonless distance for something.

Fine. Sean could have cared less what he was doing. In fact, if Lt. Amerigo Cayce wanted to continue wearing his skinsuit until he asphyxiated, that was okay with Sean. *Dumb bastard is the reason why we're in this mess in the first place . . .*

He and Kyra walked around behind the lander, where she and Sandy had already spread another silver-coated blanket across the snow. Then, while she held his airpack and mask at the ready, he took a deep breath and removed his helmet. The atmospheric ammonia stung his eyes; he squinted through the tears until he managed to get the goggles and respirator over his face. That done, the rest was simple. His bare skin was goose-pimpled in the few seconds that he was nearly naked, but once he pulled on the unitard, trousers, boots, gloves, and parka, life seemed to be a bit easier.

If only that were true. As he pulled up the parka hood, Sean studied the lander. The spacecraft had come to rest at an awkward angle, with its intact starboard landing gear tilting it to one side. Although Kyra and Sandy had been able to open the cargo hatch far enough to remove the equipment cases, it remained partially blocked. They wouldn't be able to get to the expedition gyro; if they had to walk far in order to leave the biopod, that would complicate matters greatly.

First things first. "I guess I'm going to have to help the lieutenant now," Sean said aloud. His voice was muffled slightly by the airmask, and he remembered to switch on its amplifier.

"Only if you want to." Kyra's voice dropped a little. "Actually, I think Sandy wants to do that. She wants to make him change clothes in front of a girl . . . and I don't think she's going to help him very much."

Sean smiled, but only for a moment. They were in a jam, no question about it. Marooned in a strange place, with one person dead and their craft totaled. That, and the fact that they were facing an environmental catastrophe, put their odds of survival against them. If he could only get in touch with the *Montero* . . .

"Have you found the wireless?" he asked.

"Not yet, but I'm sure it's in there somewhere." Kyra looked over to the other side of the lander. Sandy had opened another case and was rummaging through it. "Do you think it's going to work? I mean, the ship is on the other side of Hex. The outside, I mean."

"It might work." *It'd better,* he silently added. No doubt the lander's com system was down for the count, so the portable long-range radio that was part of the expedition equipment was their only hope of getting a message to the *Montero.* "Soon as Sandy finds it, I'll set it up and try to . . ."

Suddenly, they heard a muffled shout. Sean looked around, saw Cayce urgently waving to them. The lieutenant looked absurd in his skinsuit and helmet, but Sean bit his lip against the remark he was tempted to make.

"Lieutenant?" he asked, once he, Kyra, and Sandy hurried over to him. "What did you . . . ?"

"Something's coming." Cayce pointed to the west. "Look."

At first, Sean couldn't see what the team leader was talking about. Then he made out a small plume of icy fog moving toward them at ground level, a small black dot at its base. A vehicle of some sort, he guessed. The lack of a perceptible horizon hindered his estimation of how far it was from them; it could have been a mile away, or five, or even ten.

Regardless of the distance, though, he knew that Cayce was right. Someone had seen their craft come down, and *arsashi* were on the way to investigate.

"Anyone know *arsashi*?" he asked, even though he already knew the answer.

"This isn't funny, Corporal." Cayce glared at him from behind his helmet faceplate. "We're trespassers . . . and they're going to blame us for what's happened to the pod's ceiling."

Sean had to admit that Cayce had a point, but before he could say so, Sandy spoke up first. "Funny you should mention that . . ."

He looked around to see her staring up at the sky. Sean followed her gaze, and was immediately bewildered by what he saw. The upside-down funnel cloud caused by the escaping atmosphere was still there, yet in only the last few minutes it had diminished to a fraction of its former size. Even as he watched, its mouth was closing, the longer finger of its spout collapsing in upon itself. As if . . .

"I'll be damned," he murmured. "I think the hole is disappearing." He looked down at Cayce. "You were watching when we hit. You tell me . . . how big a hole did the lander make when we went through?"

Cayce paid no attention to either him or the dying tornado. "We may need to defend ourselves. Corporal LaPointe, have you found our weapons yet?" Sandy didn't say anything but only pointed to one of the open equipment boxes. "Good. Everyone, take out a fléchette pistol and load it. I want the *arsashi* to know we're prepared to defend ourselves."

Not waiting for a response, he jogged over to the box. No one followed him. "Lieutenant," Kyra asked, "do you think it's a good idea to be arming ourselves? As you said, we're the trespassers here, not . . ."

"Shut up and grab a gun. That's an order." Kneeling beside the box, Cayce reached in and pulled out a fléchette pistol. As he slapped a clip into its grip, he seemed to take notice of himself. "Carson! Don't just stand there . . . Find another winter outfit and help me get out of this skinsuit!"

"Oh, allow me, sir," Sandy said. "I've already put one aside for you."

Sean looked back at the distant plume. It didn't seem to have grown much larger in the last minute or so; he figured that it was probably several miles away. "She'll help you, sir. I'm going to see if I can find the wireless."

"Yes. I mean, no . . . That is, I . . ." Quickly rising to his feet, Cayce teetered back and forth, as if uncertain what to do next. "All right," he said at last, still flustered. "Do it. But make sure you're armed." He paused. "Those are *arsashi*. They're reputed to be warriors."

He turned to follow Sandy to the other side of the lander. Sean and Kyra looked at each other, and Kyra shook her head. "Don't listen to him," she said softly. "The *arsashi* have a violent history, but their wars were only among their own kind, and that stopped when they adopted *Sa'Tong*. There's never been an instance of their attacking another race."

Sean hoped she was right. But when he glanced again at the approaching vehicle, he couldn't help but notice that it was approaching very quickly.

The fléchette pistols were in the same box as the portable wireless. The transceiver was a small case with a shoulder strap, a miniature dish antenna folded against its side. Pulling it out of the box and placing it on the ground, he pushed the power button. A red light came on, showing that its battery was fully charged.

"I'm going to try reaching the *Montero*," he said. "If we're lucky, maybe we'll be able to get in touch with them before the *arsashi* get here." He paused. "Not sure how much good that'll do, but . . ."

"Try it anyway." Kyra was watching the alien vehicle. "If we can get through to them, they might be able to relay a message to the inhabitants, let them know that we're not hostile." She glanced down at the pistols still in the box. "I'd rather do that than greet them with a loaded gun."

Sean nodded as he raised the antenna. He had no idea which way to point it, so he oriented it upward and to the east, the direction from which they'd come. He switched the frequency-finder to the VHF channel reserved for emergency transmissions, then unclipped the mike and held it to his airmask mouthpiece. "CFS *Reese* to CFSS *Montero*. Repeat, this is CFS *Reese* to CFSS *Montero*. Do you copy? Please respond. Over."

Only static from the speaker. He reiterated the message two more times, then switched to the Ku band used for ground-to-space transmissions and tried again. Again, no response.

"They're getting closer," Kyra murmured. "I don't think . . ."

"What the hell are you doing?"

Sean looked up from the transceiver to see Cayce emerge from behind the lander. He was wearing winter gear, the parka hood pulled up over his head. The lieutenant's expression was hidden by his mask and goggles, but his voice betrayed irritation as he stalked toward them.

"We found the wireless," Kyra said. "Sean's trying to raise the *Montero*, see if they can . . ."

"Oh, for God's sake!" Before Sean could object, Cayce snatched the mike from his hands. "You're wasting time! The *arsashi* will be here any second now, and we've got to be ready for them!" Dropping the mike, he bent down to the box and pulled out two holstered pistols. "Here . . . take these and put 'em on! Make sure your parka doesn't cover them!"

Sean noticed then that Cayce's own parka wasn't zipped shut but was open to reveal the gun holster clipped to his trouser belt. The team leader insistently shoved another gun at him, a silent demand that he take it without question.

A sidelong glance at Kyra, then Sean shook his head, refusing to take the fléchette pistol. "Sir, that may be a bad idea. There's no reason to believe that the *arsashi* mean us any harm. If we act as if we're . . ."

"I didn't ask what you think! I gave you an order!" Cayce looked at Kyra. "You too. Take the gun and . . ."

"No, sir, I won't." Kyra's voice remained calm even as she stared at him in defiance. "Sean's right. If this is their territory, then we're visitors. It won't do us any good to be looking for trouble."

Behind his goggles, Cayce's eyes widened in anger. "If you don't . . ."

He fell silent as a mechanical growl reached their ears. By then, Sandy had walked up from behind him. "Hate to interrupt, folks," she said, "but we're about to have company."

She pointed behind Sean, and he turned to see that she was right. All but unnoticed during the argument, the *arsashi* vehicle had covered the remaining distance to the crash site. Twelve feet tall and nearly twenty feet in length, at first glance it appeared to be a boat mounted atop a broad caterpillar tread, until Sean realized that the V-shaped blade at its front was a plowhead. White vapor rose from a stack behind its forward cabin, and he guessed that the vehicle had a steam engine. Indeed, in many ways it resembled one of the sledges used in Coyote's mountain regions during wintertime.

"Steady, people," Cayce said quietly as the sledge rumbled to a halt, forgetting the quarrel he'd just been having with his teammates. "Don't be afraid."

"We're not afraid," Sandy murmured. "You are."

Yet Sean had to admit to himself that he was more than a little nervous. And when the sledge's cabin doors opened, and its passengers climbed out, he wondered if it might not have been such a bad idea to arm themselves.

It was one thing to see a 3-D image of an *arsashi* and be reminded of imaginary depictions of the legendary Tibetan yeti; it was quite another to see one of the creatures striding toward him. Bipedal and almost eight feet tall, with thick brown fur covering heavily muscled bodies, their eyes intense yellow orbs with rectangular pupils that looked very much like those of a goat. The *arsashi* wore knee-length kilts, short-sleeve tunics, and ankle boots made of some leathery material, and the manelike fur of their heads was braided with multicolored beads. It was hard to ignore the sharp fangs protruding from the corners of their lipless mouths.

There were three of them, and as they came closer, Sean noticed that the largest of the trio had four large breasts bulging beneath its . . . or rather, her . . . tunic. The two males took up positions on either side of her, as if to offer protection. Remembering something he'd once read about the *arsashi*, he turned to Kyra. "Maybe you should do the talking," he whispered. "Woman to woman, so to speak."

She nodded and started to walk forward, but Cayce raised a hand for her to stop. "That's my job. I'm in charge, remember?"

Kyra sighed, not bothering to hide her annoyance. "It would be better if Sandy and I did this. The *arsashi* are a female-dominant race, and they expect women to be the leaders in all things." She paused, then coldly added, "Sir."

Cayce hesitated, then reluctantly stepped aside. Kyra motioned for Sandy to join her. "Just do as I do," she whispered, as they slowly approached the three *arsashi*, who appeared to be patiently waiting for them. The two women stopped a few feet away; Kyra bowed, and Sandy did the same a moment later, but neither of them spoke before the *arsashi* female did.

The first thing she said came as a surprise to Sean. Raising her left hand, she spread her palm outward. *"Sa'Tong gro,"* she growled.

Despite the mispronunciation, Sean recognized what she'd said: *Sa'Tong qo*, a *hjadd* expression favored by *Sa'Tong* followers as a form of greeting. Kyra wasn't a *Sa'Tong*ian, but she imitated the gesture. *"Sa'Tong qo,"* she said.

The *arsashi* leader's yellow eyes slowly blinked, then her

mouth opened and an obscenely long tongue lolled out from between sharp teeth. The guttural *hyuck-hyuck-hyuck* that followed couldn't have been anything but a laugh, then she looked at the male to her right and, pointing at Kyra, said something in their own language. Sean couldn't understand what she said, of course, save for one word she repeated twice: *human*, which she pronounced as *who-mahn*.

"So far, so good," he muttered to no one in particular.

"Shh!" Kyra gave him an admonishing glance, then looked at the *arsashi* leader again. "Humans," she said, gravely nodding as she swept her hand to encompass Sandy and the men behind her. Then she pointed to the crashed lander. "Coyote," she added. "Humans from Coyote."

The *arsashi* leader had opened her mouth as if to say something when the male to her right spoke up. Raising a hand to point to the sky above, he said something that, judging as best as Sean could from his tone, sounded angry.

"I was afraid of this," Cayce said quietly, ignoring Kyra's earlier warning. "They're upset about the damage we've caused." He paused, then looked at Sean. "Be ready, Corporal. This might get ugly."

Sean started to nod in agreement, but then he happened to glance up at the sky. To his surprise, the tornado had vanished. Only a small swirl of filmy white clouds remained where the breach in the biopod ceiling had once been.

"I don't think so, Lieutenant," he said quietly. "Something . . ."

"Will you two please shut up?" Kyra's eyes blazed as she glanced over her shoulder at them. "I'm trying to work things out, and you're not making it easy." She stared at Sean and Cayce for another moment, then returned her attention to the *arsashi*.

While that was going on, though, the leader had unbuttoned a pouch on the right side of her belt. Pulling out a disk-shaped pendant, she hung it by a slender thong around her neck; a small headset came next, with a mike wand that looped in front of her mouth and an earpiece for her right

ear. When she spoke again, another voice came almost simultaneously from a small grille in the pendant's center.

"Heh-yo?" she said. "Can woo hear me?"

"Hot damn!" Sandy exclaimed. "She's got a translator!"
Delighted, she started to clap her hands.

Kyra cried out in horror. "Sandy, *no* . . . !"

Too late. Seeing this, the two male *arsashi* immediately
darted forward.

"Down!" Cayce yelled, then he knocked Kyra aside. But
he'd barely laid a hand on his fléchette pistol before both
warriors reacted.

Quicker than the eye could follow, each of them flung
his right arm forward in a rapid motion that resembled a
baseball pitcher throwing a fastball. One after another,
Sean thought he heard thin, reedy sounds—*phutt! phutt!*—
then Cayce suddenly staggered back, hands clutching at his
right eye and neck. A quiet, agonized gasp as blood spurted
from between his fingers, then his legs gave way beneath
him, and he collapsed upon the snowy ground.

Sean rushed to his side, but there was nothing he could
do for him. The quills had gone in deep, one piercing the
goggles to penetrate his brain, the other burying itself in his
neck.

Within seconds, Lieutenant Amerigo Cayce was dead.

THIRTEEN

M ELPOMENE WAS STILL SHOUTING ZEUS'S NAME WHEN
Anne reported another text message. It appeared on
the wallscreen a few seconds later:

Be prepared for restoration of gravity.

It wasn't until then that it occurred to Andromeda that
the node contained some sort of gravity-nullification field.
It made sense; otherwise, ships like the *Montero* would be
unable to dock safely. She barely had time to return to her
seat before weight returned to her. The ship groaned as
its sixty thousand tons settled into the tentacle-like mooring lines wrapped around its hull, but the cables held the
Montero as if it were in a cat's cradle, and a few moments
later, everything was quiet and still.

Andromeda let out her breath, then pulled up the lapboard and reactivated the exterior cameras. Once again, the
wallscreen revealed the node's vast interior. No sign of the

service pod, but sometime in the last minute or so, a tubular walkway had been extended from the docking bay to the ship's starboard side, where it had attached itself to the Deck Four airlock.

"They're nothing if not efficient," Jason said quietly.

Andromeda was too worried about Zeus to be impressed. "Anne, ask them where . . ."

"I already have, Captain." The com officer shook her head. "No response, except that warning about gravity."

"And that's truly amazing." There was admiration in Rolf's voice; catching the look on Andromeda's face, he shook his head. "Sorry, skipper, but . . . look, it's one thing to have a field generator to give a ship artificial gravity, but another entirely to be able to nullify centrifugal force at will. The *danui* really have some very advanced technology . . ."

"Right now, I don't care. I just want to find out what they've done with my man." Shoving aside the lapboard, Andromeda stood up from her chair. "Jason, you've got the conn. Anne, I want you here with him. Everyone else, you're with me . . . We're suiting up and going out to find Zeus. Bring your sidearms."

Melpomene and Rolf nodded and rose from their stations without comment. D'Anguilo was more reluctant. "Captain, this is a delicate situation," he said, remaining seated. "It's not going to do any good to charge in there with guns blazing. There must be an explanation for all this . . ."

"I agree. And you're going to help me find it." Andromeda glared at the Janus executive. "This isn't a request. This is an order. On your feet and down the ladder . . . now."

For a moment or two, they stared at each other. D'Anguilo was the first to look away. A frustrated sigh, then he stood up and followed Andromeda to the access shaft.

The starboard docking port had skinsuits in its readyroom lockers, but Andromeda decided that they would take too long to put on and were probably unnecessary anyway.

When Rolf entered the airlock and checked the atmosphere gauge, he confirmed that the gangway had been pressurized with an oxygen-nitrogen atmosphere and that the bio-sensors picked up no obvious contaminants. But merchant marine regulations specifically stated that EVA gear was to be worn whenever a landing party entered an alien environment for the first time, so the captain had everyone don pressure suits instead. The bulky garments were more cumbersome than skinsuits, but they could be worn over their clothes, and their life-support packs could supply them with purified air for six hours. Enough time to find out where they were and what had happened to Zeus, or so Andromeda hoped.

Once everyone was suited up, Andromeda took a minute to make sure that their com systems were linked to the *Montero* and that Jason and Anne were in the loop. She wasn't so successful when she checked to see that everyone was armed. Melpomene and Rolf had brought their fléchette pistols; like Andromeda, they had clipped the holsters to their utility belts. D'Anguilo had left his gun in the command center. Andromeda had accepted his argument that if he was going to negotiate with the *danui*, it would be best if he did so without a pistol at his side, but she was still reluctant about it. Zeus's disappearance had done little to ease her misgivings.

"If we get in trouble out there," she said, "don't count on us to defend you."

"Very well." He calmly regarded her from behind his helmet faceplate. "And if you get in trouble because you decided to carry weapons, don't say I didn't warn you."

Rolf snorted, and Melpomene peered at him. "What makes you so certain we're not in danger?" she asked. "Have you been asleep the last few hours?"

D'Anguilo's face turned red, and Andromeda had to bite her lip. Melpomene wasn't the sort of person to scold someone, but her tongue could be sharp when she wanted it to be. She was probably more worried about Zeus than anyone else; Andromeda mused that she'd naturally be concerned about her lover's fate.

"I just think it's a mistake to assume hostile intentions," D'Anguilo replied. "As I said, there's probably a reasonable explanation for all this."

"Very well. Let's see if you're right." Andromeda motioned to the open airlock. "You first."

D'Anguilo hesitated. "Captain's privilege," he said quietly, then stepped aside to let her be the first one to leave the ship.

The gangway was a tube with opaque grey walls that appeared to be made of some sort of plastic. Its floor had a certain spongy texture that gave slightly beneath the soles of their boots, and dim light came from concentric rings spaced at regular intervals between its ribs. The gangway led straight away from the ship for about a hundred yards and came to an end at a circular door that opened like a sphincter at their approach.

Walking through it, they found themselves in a bare room whose walls, ceiling, and floor appeared to be made of the same stony material as the rest of the node. Another sphincter door was on the other side of the room; a large screen was set in one wall, and near the entrance door was a large window through which they could see the *Montero*.

The entrance swirled shut as soon as they were inside. An instant later, a narrow ring lit up upon the walls near the ceiling. The ring slowly traveled down the walls, its beam touching the four people gathered in the room, until it reached the floor, then it moved back up to the ceiling before disappearing.

"I think we've just been scanned," Rolf murmured.

Andromeda nodded, but before she could say anything, the screen on the nearby wall lit up, and a human face appeared on it. Obviously a comp-generated image, the face could have belonged to either an effeminate male or a masculine female, and the voice that accompanied it was just as androgynous.

"Welcome to tanaash-haq,*"* the image said, smiling as it spoke perfect Anglo. *"Scans indicate that three people in your group are carrying weapons. Inhabitants are not permitted to bring in weapons of any sort. Please surrender them immediately, or you will not be allowed to enter."*

A panel opened within the wall beside the screen, exposing what appeared to be a disposal chute. Andromeda glanced at D'Anguilo; the astroethnicist didn't say a word, but there was no mistaking the smug grin on his face. She grimaced, then nodded to Rolf and Mel before unclipping the holster from her belt. They did the same, and the three fléchette pistols went down the chute.

"Thank you," the image said, its expression annoyingly beatific. *"Scans also indicate that all persons in your group are wearing pressure suits. They are permitted, but you should be aware that they are not necessary within the habitat you are about to enter. You may remove them and leave them here. They will be returned to you later, along with your weapons."*

Andromeda's heads-up display showed that, like the walkway, the room contained an oxygen-nitrogen atmosphere, its pressure just above one thousand millibars. She opened her helmet faceplate, took a deep breath. The air tasted fine.

"Thank you," she said, "but I have a few questions of my own." The image said nothing as it continued to smile at her. "While our ship was docking, one of my crewmen disappeared after he left our ship to investigate. What happened to him?" The image remained silent. Andromeda waited for an answer, then went on. "My ship's controls were overridden by some sort of remote system, and we were brought here against our will. Why did you do that?" Again, no response except for the same maddening smile. "You called this place *tanaash-haq*, and said that it's a habitat. What did you mean by . . . ?" And then the screen went blank.

"Talkative, isn't he?" Rolf said.

Andromeda slowly let out her breath. She was stymied, and the time had come to stop being stubborn and ask for help. She turned to D'Anguilo. "All right, I'll admit it . . . We should have listened to you about the guns, and also about not letting Zeus take the pod outside. My apologies. Now . . . do you have any other insights you'd like to share?"

"Believe me, Captain, I'm not keeping score. And as far as insights go . . ." D'Anguilo shrugged. "We've already offended them once by carrying weapons. I think we'd only offend them again if we continued wearing these suits. If we remove them, it may go a long way toward establishing some sort of mutual trust."

"Trust?" Melpomene stared at him. "Do you seriously think we should . . . ?"

"Ms. Fisk . . . Melpomene . . . I realize that you're frustrated, and that you feel like I'm asking a lot of you. But you have to remember that we're not dealing with other humans, but *danui*. They're reclusive, suspicious, argumentative, and obviously powerful enough to do whatever they damned well please. We're going to have to demonstrate that we're trustworthy if we expect to get any sort of cooperation from them . . . and that begins here and now."

Melpomene continued to glare at him. Andromeda stepped between her and D'Anguilo. "Mel, I want to find out what happened to Zeus, too . . . and my son. But he's right. This is their game, and we've got to play it their way. So let's get rid of these suits, and . . . well, see what happens next."

The helmsman reluctantly nodded, then reached up to unlatch her helmet from its collar ring. Andromeda turned to gaze out the window. *"Montero*, do you copy?"

"Loud and clear," Jason replied.

"Good." Andromeda gave him a quick rundown of everything that had happened, tactfully leaving out the part about the latest disagreement with D'Anguilo. "We've got a transceiver, so we won't be out of touch for long. Sit tight. Understood?"

"Roger that, Captain." Jason's voice was tense. *"Be careful. Montero over."*

"Thanks. Over and out." Andromeda switched off the comlink, then went about removing her pressure suit. Once everyone was back in shirtsleeves, they proceeded to the inner door.

It opened without a problem, and they found themselves on a platform within what appeared to be a long, narrow tunnel. A cylindrical craft was parked in front of the platform. With a blunt nose, rectangular windows, and a single hatch at its front, it bore an uncanny resemblance to a subway car.

The hatch bisected in the middle, allowing them to enter. Andromeda hesitated. "A tram?" she asked, speaking to no one in particular. "Is that what this is?"

"Looks like it." Rolf shrugged. "Makes sense. Hex is a pretty big place, after all. You'd need some form of rapid transportation to get around." He got down on his hands and knees to examine the bottom of the car. "Can't tell for sure," he said, straightening up again, "but I bet there's a maglev rail down there."

There didn't appear to be any choice but to step aboard. Once inside, they found little resemblance to a human-built tram. Instead of seats, there were benches on both sides of the interior; they appeared to have a thin layer of padding upon them but otherwise were bare. Another exit hatch was located on the opposite side of the tram, with a small door in the wall beside it. Next to each of the doors were large vacant areas with recessed rungs in the floor; Rolf guessed that those spaces were reserved for cargo.

There didn't appear to be a control cab, but on the wall beside the entrance door was a backlit panel. Upon it was displayed what appeared to be a diagram of a hexagon:

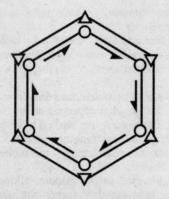

Andromeda noted that the node at the top left corner was glowing red. It wasn't hard to guess that the hexagon represented the one they were in and that the illuminated node was the harbor where the *Montero* was docked. But she could only guess what was meant by the rest: the geometric forms along the sides of the hexagon, the clockwise arrows within its inner perimeter, the short arrows pointing away from the other nodes, or the long arrows pointing away from the upper-left and lower-right corners.

"A map?" she asked aloud.

"Could be." Rolf shrugged. "Makes sense. Maybe the arrows show possible directions we can take. But I have no idea what this means." He pointed to two rows of figures at the bottom of the panel:

"I think I do." Standing behind them, D'Anguilo smiled knowingly. "Those might be *danui* numbers." Reaching forward, he pointed to the figure at the right end of the bottom that looked like a crosshatched diamond. "See? Four sides, with vertical and horizontal lines in the middle. Six sides, with no shapes more complex than that, except for a square every now and then."

"So?" Melpomene asked.

"Ever looked closely at a picture of a *danui*? Their two forward legs . . . the ones they use most frequently as manipulators . . . have three fingers each. That would indicate that they've developed a base-six numerical system, just as we have a base-ten system because of the number of fingers on our hands. The square must be zero."

Remembering the holo of the *danui* that Ted Harker had shown her, Andromeda had to admit that D'Anguilo might be onto something. "Okay, I'll buy that. But that still doesn't tell us what . . ."

"Wait a minute. I think I got it." Rolf moved a little closer to the panel. "If this is a map, then the numbers around the edge might tell us which pod is which. And if that's the case"—he pointed to the two rows of numbers—"this might be some sort of navigation system."

D'Anguilo slowly nodded. "Yes . . . yes, I believe you may be right." He studied the panel for another couple of moments, absently tapping a finger against his lips. "Which would mean that the top row, since it's longer, represents our present coordinates, and the bottom row is our means of entering new coordinates. So the map itself may be our way of getting around within this particular hexagon."

"Might be," Andromeda murmured. "Of course, there's only one way to find out." Raising her hand to the panel, she poised a finger above the top left surface of the hexagon, the one nearest to the red-lighted node. "Brace yourselves. Here goes nothing."

She pushed the hexagon.

The tram doors slid shut with barely a whisper, and a second later the vehicle began to move. At first, its motion was so slow that they barely noticed, but then it quickly accelerated. Yet the movement was eerily smooth; no bumps or jars, just an effortless plunge down the tunnel, whose rocklike walls raced by the windows so fast that they soon became nothing more than a grey blur. There was only the slightest hum; otherwise, the vehicle was nearly silent.

"Just as I thought," Rolf said. "Magnetic levitation."

"Yes," said D'Anguilo, sitting down on the nearest bench, "but I wonder why they couldn't have put in a pneumatic system instead. They . . . *Hey!* What the hell . . . ?"

The moment he sat down, the bench's padding started moving beneath him. As if it had a mind of its own, the material reshaped itself to conform to his buttocks. As Andromeda watched, a slender hump rose behind D'Anguilo, becoming a chairback for him to rest against.

"Some sort of smart material," Rolf said, bending down to examine the bench. "It figures out what's comfortable for you and reshapes itself for your needs."

"Makes sense." Andromeda pressed the bench next to the control panel with her fingertips. "Probably designed to accommodate different body forms."

Rolf nodded as he carefully sat down across from D'Anguilo; he grinned as his seat adapted itself to him. "Efficient . . . just like using maglev rails instead of pneumatic tubes. If these tunnels run through all of Hex, you'd have to maintain high air pressure for billions of tunnels."

"Sounds plausible." Andromeda carefully took a seat on the bench, with Melpomene sitting down beside her. Its transformation was unnerving at first, but in a few seconds she was as comfortable as if she were sitting in her seat in *Montero*'s command center. "But you've still got to wonder . . . How old is this place, anyway? For something this big and complex, it must have taken thousands of years to build."

"Uh-huh. At least a couple of thousand years . . . maybe more." D'Anguilo was quiet for a moment, then he went on. "Y'know, I've been thinking about that, and I wonder if it has anything to do with—"

He was interrupted by the tram's abruptly moving to the left. Through the windows on the right side of the car, the tunnel walls disappeared for a split second. They caught a brief glimpse of another tunnel, branching away from the one they were in and receding into the distance. Then it vanished as the rock walls closed around them again.

"Must be another line," Melpomene said. "Maybe leading to another hexagon."

"Habitat, you mean." D'Anguilo smiled. "Don't mean to split hairs, but that's what our hosts call them." He paused, then looked at Andromeda. "Come to think of it . . . Remember what the screen avatar called this place? *Tanaash-haq?*"

"Maybe that's the *danui* word for it," Andromeda said, although it sounded more like *hjadd* than anything else. "I think I like Hex better. Anyway, what were you about to say?"

"Well, it seems to me that . . ."

Suddenly, the tram began to slow down. Forgetting the discussion, Andromeda gazed through the windows. She couldn't see anything except the tunnel walls, but they appeared to be moving past the tram a little more slowly.

"Looks like we're about to stop." She carefully rose from the bench, wishing that the *danui* had supplied poles or ceiling straps for riders to hold on to. "Maybe we'll get some answers."

Before anyone could reply, light abruptly streamed in through the right-hand windows. The walls had vanished again, and it appeared that the tram had left the tunnel. The vehicle slowly coasted to a halt; a second later, the doors at the front end of the tram slid open. Andromeda looked at the others, then turned to walk forward. Melpomene, Rolf, and D'Anguilo got up from their seats and followed her toward the open doors.

They emerged on a broad platform that was open on three sides, with tiled floors and a high ceiling with luminescent panels. Just past it was an open veranda; a long railing ran along its edge. Andromeda was about to walk over to it when she noticed another control panel, identical to the one aboard the tram, recessed into the platform wall near the tunnel entrance. Pausing to examine it, she noted that the *danui* numbers on its top row had changed slightly. If D'Anguilo was right, and these were coordinates of some sort, it would be wise to copy them for later reference. She was about to pull her datapad from her thigh pocket when Rolf whistled out loud, followed by a startled cry from Melpomene.

"Oh, my God . . . Skipper, look at this!"

She was standing at the railing, Rolf and D'Anguilo beside her; all three were staring at something below them. Leaving the datapad in her pocket, Andromeda hurried over to join them . . . and felt her heart skip a beat.

Beyond the railing lay a vast valley, larger than any she'd ever seen. With a long range of low mountains sloping down into it from each side, it stretched away without any visible horizon until its farthest end disappeared in atmospheric haze.

The mountainsides and the valley floor were verdant with forests and open plains; grass and trees grew alongside creeks that flowed downhill toward a river that ran straight down the middle of the valley. The air was warm and unbelievably fresh, faintly scented with chlorophyll and wild spices.

Andromeda realized that they were overlooking a biopod from the vantage point of a tram platform. To their right, close to where they were standing, was a mammoth wall; apparently comprised of the same stony material as Hex's outer surfaces, it towered into a blue sky. There appeared to be circular vents evenly spaced within the wall, each large enough to drive the tram through. Air ducts, perhaps?

Before she could study them further, D'Anguilo tapped the back of her hand. "Captain . . . look at the sky."

It was blue and cloudless, with a bright sun at its zenith, but like none Andromeda had ever seen before in all the worlds she'd visited. Surrounding the sun on all sides were countless hexagons—very large near the mountain ridges, incrementally becoming smaller the higher they went—that formed a tessellated pattern across the heavens. Gazing upward, Andromeda realized that she was seeing Hex from its inner surface: a vast collection of hexagons, each the same as the one in which she was standing, that stretched to the far side of its captive sun, almost 186 million miles away.

Feeling the light-headed dizziness of vertigo, Andromeda grasped the railing and took slow, deep breaths. Until then, she'd been able to assimilate everything she'd seen since the moment the *Montero* had entered the *danui* system. But this was too much. She suddenly felt very, very small, like an ant standing at the lip of a chasm. Stunned by what she was seeing, she almost missed the insistent electronic chirp coming from her breast pocket.

"Skipper?" Melpomene murmured. "The radio . . ."

"Right." Wrenching her gaze from the weird sky, Andromeda fumbled at the pocket flap until she was able to pull out the small transceiver. She raised its aerial and spoke into its mouth. "Carson here."

"Montero, Captain." Anne's voice was surprisingly clear. Despite the distance between them and the docking node, the ship's VHF signal apparently had no trouble getting through the rock walls. *"Are you okay?"*

"Fine . . . we're fine." Andromeda took another deep breath, trying to clear her head. "You and Jason aren't going to believe this place. It's completely . . . I mean . . ."

"Captain . . ." Anne's voice was hurried, almost impatient. *"I've just heard from Sean. He's alive, but his team is in trouble."*

FOURTEEN

THE SIGNAL SEAN RECEIVED FROM THE *MONTERO* WAS weak, but strong enough that he was able to hear his mother's voice. *"Glad to hear that you're still . . ."* she began, then stopped herself.

Alive, he thought. *She was about to say, "Glad to hear that you're still alive."*

"Jason tells me that you've crashed," she said instead. *"Where are you, do you know?"*

"Somewhere on Hex," Sean replied, as if this explained everything. *Or maybe I should say "in Hex." Whatever.* "We came in through the roof of the biopod we were investigating and landed in a field not far from its eastern end. I told your first officer the rest . . . He's probably filled you in already. Anyway, we lost our pilot when we crashed, and shortly after that our team leader was killed."

"By an inhabitant, yes." Andromeda's voice was scratchy, and Sean adjusted the gain on the transceiver slung beneath his arm. *"Are you in any immediate danger? From them, I mean."*

Sean looked around. The *arsashi* stood nearby, with one of the males silently watching the female leader as she conversed with Kyra. He didn't like the way they towered above her, but they didn't appear to be hostile. The other male had returned to their sledge; the sunlight was reflecting off the cab windows, so Sean couldn't tell what he was doing.

"I don't think so," Sean said. "It was a . . . a misunderstanding. I think they know that now. Kyra didn't have a chance to tell Sandy that it's unwise to clap your hands around *arsashi*, because in their culture it's a signal to attack. And since Cayce had his hand on his gun . . . well, one thing led to another."

"I understand."

Yeah, I bet you do. "Your first officer told me you're docked in a hex some distance from here . . . where we are, I mean. Any chance you can pick us up?"

"Sean, I'm just like you. I haven't a clue where we are." A short pause. *"No, that's not quite true. There appears to be some sort of maglev system that runs from one hexagon to another. I'm standing on the tram platform of the hexagon . . . or habitat, as the* danui *call it . . . where we've docked, and it appears to be marked by a set of coordinates. They look like geometric shapes . . . dots, squares, triangles, diamonds, and so on . . . but Tom D'Anguilo thinks they're* danui *numbers. If you can reach the tram system in your habitat, and figure out how to plug in these coordinates, maybe you can get here."*

"Maybe." Sean's fist tightened around his hand mike. "So I take it the answer's no."

This time, his mother's response was not immediate. Sean looked over his shoulder. Mark and Cayce lay upon the snow-covered ground, and Sandy stood above them, staring at their covered bodies. He couldn't see her expression through her airmask, but Sean had no doubt that she was still blaming herself for Cayce's death even though both he and Kyra had taken pains to assure her that it had been only an accident.

When his mother spoke again, her tone was noticeably harder than it had been just moments before. *"Sean, you're on your own. I don't like it any more than you do, but you can't count on our coming to your rescue . . ."*

"What a surprise," he said dryly.

He knew that she must have known what he meant by that, but she let it pass. *"So I'm putting you in charge of your team,"* she went on. *"Your job is to get them out of there and lead them to where the* Montero *is docked. That's your first and only priority. Do you copy?"*

Sean stared at the handset as if his mother were about to jump out of it. It never ceased to amaze him just how callous she could be. Pragmatism was one thing, but . . . "Affirmative, Captain," he said, regretting that she wasn't there in person so that he could give her a sardonic salute. "Is there anything else?"

"Yes. I want you to keep in touch at all times . . . particularly if you run into any more situations like the one you're in. I know you've got Kyra there to help, but D'Anguilo knows even more than she does. Between the two of them, they should be able to figure out what's going on."

Sean knew that she was right. Their predicament would be even worse, if that were possible, if Kyra weren't with him and Sandy, or if Tom D'Anguilo wasn't with his mother and her people. "Affirmative. You said something about some coordinates?"

"Yes. Report back as soon as you reach a tram station, so I can describe what I've found. It may be the key to understanding how the trams work. And Sean . . . ?" Her tone softened a bit. *"Take care of yourself. I want you back, safe and sound."*

Tell that to my father. "Affirmative, Captain," he replied, deliberately cool in his response. "Survey team over and out."

He shut off the transceiver and folded the antenna, then walked over to Sandy. She was still staring at the bodies and didn't notice him until he put a hand on her arm. "It's all right," he said quietly. "You didn't . . ."

"I know. 'It's not your fault' . . . Everyone's said that already. Including them." She glanced at the *arsashi*, then raised a hand to her head as if to wipe tears from her eyes. Her fingertips bounced off the goggles, and she mumbled, "Damn, can't I do anything right?"

"Take it easy." It wasn't doing Sandy any good to be there, so Sean led her away from the bodies, over to where Kyra was talking to the two *arsashi*. Sandy was reluctant to approach them, but she'd have to get over that. The biopod belonged to its inhabitants, and Sean knew that he'd need their help if he and his team were ever going to get out of there.

Kyra turned to him and Sandy as they came closer. "Did you talk to your mother?" she asked.

"Uh-huh. I'll fill you in later." Sean cocked his head toward the *arsashi*, hoping that this wasn't another common human gesture they'd misinterpret. "Have you learned anything?"

"Quite a bit, actually." Kyra pointed to the female. "Allow me to introduce you to Lusah Sahsan . . . all one name, incidentally, so don't use just one or the other. She's the matriarch of one of the major tribes living here. Their tribes are more like extended families than political groups, so that makes her an important . . . um, woman."

Lusah Sahsan stared at Sean with unblinking yellow eyes and favored him with a nod that was surprisingly humanlike. "The males are two of her husbands," Kyra continued. "She hasn't bothered to tell me their names, but that's normal." She dropped her voice a little. "Men are chattels in their society and are regarded as being good for breeding, fighting, and lifting heavy objects, and not much more. Or at least that's what I was told at the university."

"Sweet." A new thought occurred to him. "So when Sandy clapped her hands . . . ?"

"They recognized her as being a female, yes, and assumed that she was in charge. And since the lieutenant was a male and also armed . . ." She hesitated, glancing again at the *arsashi*. "They reacted the way they normally would," she finished, reluctant to say anything that might offend Lusah Sahsan.

Apparently the tribal leader understood what Kyra said, because she spoke to her husband in her own language. He raised his right arm, and once again Sean saw the row of slender six-inch quills nestled within the fur between his elbow and his wrist. Evolution had provided *arsashi* males with a natural weapon; they could hurl these needlelike quills from their bodies with a single flex of their forearms, and since *arsashi* menfolk practice from childhood, the best of them could hit the smallest of targets at a distance of fifteen paces or more. Killing Amerigo Cayce had been no challenge at all . . .

"She says she's . . ." Kyra began.

"Aye yam sorree," Lusah Sahsan said. As before, the low growl of her voice was translated by the *hjadd*-made disk around her neck into a heavily inflected form of Anglo that Sean could barely understand. "Aye dint meen ta keel yer leeder. Et wuzza meesunnerstanning, an eye howp yew wall forgeev yus."

"She said . . ."

"I got it, thanks." Nevertheless, Sean was glad that Kyra had carried on most of the conversation and not he. He looked straight at Lusah Sahsan. "We apologize as well," he said, speaking slowly and hoping that the translator worked better for her than it did for them. It was *hjadd* technology, so it probably would. "It was not our intent to trespass on your territory, or to cause any damage to your . . . uh, habitat."

He figured that Kyra had probably said this already, but it couldn't hurt for him to reiterate the apology. Particularly not if Lusah Sahsan was now aware that human males weren't drones and could even occasionally be tribal leaders themselves. The *arsashi* female slowly blinked, then her long tongue spilled out of her mouth again and she gave the same gulping *hyuk-hyuk-hyuk* laugh they'd heard when she and her husbands had first emerged from their sledge.

"Et es nawt ah prowblem," she replied, apparently amused

by something Sean had just said. "Yew arr straynjurs hare, an yew havnut larned yer way bout or tha roolz ov tha wold." She paused, then pointed to the sky. "Ass yew see, *tanaash-haq* heels etselve, ass et always duz."

Tanaash-haq . . . *that must be their name for Hex,* Sean thought. *But what does she mean by learning the rules, or the bit about this place healing itself?*

Again, he looked up at the sky. The upside-down tornado caused by the *Reese* had disappeared, and even the clouds that had been formed by it had faded away. Only a deep blue expanse remained; beyond the immense ceiling, the hexagons of countless other habitats formed a vast pattern across the sky. He wished he'd had a chance to find a pair of binoculars and have a closer look at what had happened up there; he suspected that something had instantly reacted to repair the gap in the ceiling before too much of its atmosphere could escape.

"Tanaash-haq *heals itself, as it always does.*" *That's what she said . . . but what did she mean?*

"I've also spoken with her about finding a way out of here," Kyra said, "and she's willing to help us." A quick smile, then she dropped her voice to a near whisper. "Frankly, I think she'd be only too happy to see us go."

"I'm sure she would be," Sean murmured. "We're probably nothing but trouble."

"Uh-huh. Anyway, her husband . . . her other husband, I mean . . . has returned to their sledge to call for assistance. She told him to request a vehicle that can lift the lander high enough for us to open the cargo hatch and unload the gyro."

"That would be great." Sean breathed a sigh of relief. If they could retrieve the gyro, and it wasn't too damaged to fly, it would save them a long hike to the tram station his mother had instructed him to find. "Thank you," he said to Lusah Sahsan. "We would appreciate that."

The tribal leader nodded, then turned to point to the southwest. "Ta leeve hare, yew need ta gow datway, t'ward tha cornah ufda habbydat. Ah twam es dere, atta toppa da ramp."

"The tram station is located at the top of a ramp?" Sean repeated, making sure that he correctly understood her. Lusah Sahsan nodded again. "How far?"

The *arsashi* growled something that the translator was apparently unable to interpret; all that came from its grille was a disjointed string of consonants. Apparently it wasn't programmed to interpret *arsashi* units of distance as miles. "Um . . . yes, I see," Sean said, trying to be polite. He looked over at Sandy. "Better start packing up," he said, pointing to the boxes and the equipment they'd already pulled out. "We're going to need to put everything aboard the gyro as soon as . . ."

Another growl from Lusah Sahsan. "Noh weponz. Yew may noht tayk yer gunz. Dey muhs bey leff hare."

"She said . . ." Kyra began.

"I know what she said." Sean shook his head as he looked at Lusah Sahsan again. "I'm sorry, but I don't understand. Why don't you want us to take our weapons?"

She stared at him with the square pupils of her yellow eyes. "Noh weponz ar'lowd in *tanaash-haq*," she said, her scowl becoming even more menacing when she showed him the fangs at the corners of her large mouth. "Dis issa rule dat cahnot bey browken."

"Whose rule?" Kyra asked. "Yours?"

Lusah Sahsan shook her hairy head. "Noh. *Danyew'ee.* Noh rayce hare may hahv weponz." She pointed to the open case in which the fléchette pistols were plainly visible. "Leev dem. Wew'll depohz ov dem foh yew."

Sean understood what she meant, but nonetheless he was puzzled. "The *danui* say that no weapons are allowed here?" he asked. "Why?"

Lusah Sahsan didn't respond but instead looked away from them and toward the nearby forest, as if seeking answers from the strange, ice-covered trees that grew along the banks of the frozen river. "Yew muhst noht hahv spohken ta *danyew'ee*," she said at last, more a statement than a question. "Yew wuhd noh dis ef yew deyud."

"No," Kyra admitted, "we haven't spoken to the *danui* . . . not directly, at least. The person on our ship who has isn't with us, and he doesn't know much more than we do."

The *arsashi* leader gave her a sharp look. "Deyud da *danyew'ee* envaht yew hare?"

"Yes, they did."

"Buht dey tol yew nuthen bowt *tanaash-haq*?" Her eyes slowly blinked, as if disbelieving what she'd just heard.

"No, they didn't," Sean said. "We were only told that there was a habitable world in this solar system, and that we were free to colonize it."

For the first time during the conversation, Lusah Sahsan turned to look at her husband. The nameless *arsashi* male stared back at her as if in amazement. Then they laughed again, their long tongues curling upward from their mouths in undisguised hilarity.

"Glad to see that we're so amusing," Sandy muttered. "Maybe we can show them a few card tricks next."

Kyra shushed her, but Sean was becoming annoyed. The *arsashi* were beginning to remind him of hillbillies who'd come across city dwellers lost in their neck of the woods: hospitable to a certain point, but also willing to enjoy a laugh at their expense. "Sorry," he said, unable to keep the edge from his voice, "but it looks like this is their idea of a practical joke, and we've fallen for it."

Although her husband continued to laugh, Lusah Sahsan calmed down. "No jowk," she said. "Wee laff 'cuz *danyew'ee* deyud da sayhm ding ta'uz, mannee"—another jumble of consonants—"ago. Et es thar wahy."

"Did what to you?" Kyra peered at her. "I don't understand."

"Yew well . . . en ty'yum." She raised both her hands, palms spread open and outward. "Sayah noh moh. Yew muhst fohnd truff foh yohsehylves."

Sean and Kyra glanced at each other. For whatever reason, Lusah Sahsan wasn't willing to explain everything she knew. But it also appeared as if the *arsashi* hadn't been told everything about Hex—or *tanaash-haq*, as they called it—when they'd come here for the first time. Sean wondered how long ago that had been; again, the translator was unable to interpret the *arsashi* measurement of time into human terms.

"All right, then," he said. "I guess we'll just have to . . ."

"What about Mark and the lieutenant?" Sandy asked. "We need to do something about them."

Sean nodded. Like it or not, they wouldn't be able to take the bodies with them. The gyro had limited cargo space, and as much as he hated himself for thinking this, he wasn't keen on the idea of sharing its tiny cabin with two corpses. He turned to Lusah Sahsan again. "Before we leave, we'd like to bury or cremate our dead." He hesitated, then added, "This is what we do in our culture. You may have another way of . . ."

"Don't say that," Kyra murmured, urgently shaking her head. "The *arsashi* don't like to talk about their practices, but we believe that they ritualistically eat their dead."

Sean felt something cold slither down his back, and Sandy scowled in disgust. But Lusah Sahsan merely regarded him with what seemed to be sympathy. "Wee haf ouh custums, buh we donoh spec yew ta fallah dem." Her hand swept toward the covered bodies in an almost dismissive gesture. "Et duzzent mattah. Leev dem dere. *Tanaash-haq* well claym dem ass ets owhn."

Sean blinked, not quite understanding what the tribal leader had just said. "Just . . . leave them here? Just as they are?"

Lusah Sahsan slowly nodded. "Yesh. Ass dey ah. *Tanaash-haq* well tayk dem." She pointed to the bodies. "Luk . . . see foh yoh-selvz."

Sean suddenly found himself hesitant to look beneath the silver emergency blankets. Something that Lusah Sahsan had just said gave him the creeps. But Sandy didn't share the same reluctance. She walked back to where the bodies lay and bent down to pull back the blanket from Mark's body . . . and screamed out loud, dropping the blanket as she recoiled in horror.

Sean dashed to her side. Sandy was trembling, and from behind her airmask he heard nauseated gasps. "Easy, easy," he said, grasping her by the shoulders and turning her away from the uncovered body. "Whatever you do, don't throw up. You'll clog up your mask and suffocate."

Sandy nodded and let Sean hold her in his arms; she was shaking, her eyes tightly shut behind her goggles. Hearing another startled cry, he looked around to see Kyra staring down at Mark.

"Sean, come over here." Her voice was unsteady. "You need to see this."

Sean took another moment to make sure that Sandy was all right—she wasn't, but at least she was no longer on the verge of vomiting—then he left her and walked over to where Kyra stood. He didn't want to see what the two women had found, but he knew that he had to. When he did, though, he was sorry that he'd made that choice.

When he and Cayce had pulled Mark's body from the lander, one of the first things they'd done was to remove his skinsuit helmet to make sure that his neck was broken and that he really was dead. They hadn't put it back on again, but had simply closed his eyes and stretched him upon the ground, placing his hands at his sides and leaving the rest of his skinsuit on. Sean figured that, once they had a chance, he'd find a place to bury his friend and perhaps say a few words over his grave.

Obviously, that wasn't to be.

Above the skinsuit's neck ring, Mark's flesh had taken the appearance and texture of cottage cheese. His hair was almost completely gone, his eyes had shriveled deep within their sockets, and the outline of the rest of his skull was visible beneath skin that had become as white and mottled as the snow upon which it lay.

Sean was glad that he couldn't smell anything through the mask; otherwise, he had little doubt that the odor of mortification would have overwhelmed him. But when he forced himself to bend down to look closer, he saw that what was going on was more than just decay, as accelerated as it might be.

Beneath the back of Mark's neck and head, tiny crystalline formations, vaguely resembling coral yet a ghastly shade of pink, had grown up from the ground, rising from beneath the snow to touch, embrace, and pierce the flesh of the dead man.

Sean pulled the blanket away a little farther. The same formations hadn't yet grown up around the skinsuit, which indicated to him that they weren't fond of inorganic matter. But the delicate crystals had crept into the bottom of the helmet ring, and he had no doubt that, were he to unzip Mark's suit and open it, he'd find the same process taking place across the rest of his body.

"My God," Kyra said quietly. "He's dissolving."

"Heh ef bing tahken ba *tanaash-haq*." Accompanied by her silent husband, Lusah Sahsan had walked over to join them. "Dis es da way daded ah claymed hare. Wen der bohdees ah fownd, dey . . ."

"Disintegrate." Sean swallowed a mouthful of bile, then made himself walk over to Cayce's body and pull back its blanket as well. The lieutenant hadn't been dead as long as Mark, so he was still reasonably intact. Nevertheless, it was apparent that the same process had already begun; coral-like formations were touching the back of his head and neck, along with his bare hands, and his skin looked like it had developed a postmortem case of acne.

"Yesh," the *arsashi* leader said, and when Sean looked up at her, he saw that her mouth had stretched back in a broad grimace that looked frightening until he realized that it was a smile. "Do noh greev. Et es ah fon def. Dey ah becohmin won widda wold."

They are becoming one with the world. Again, Sean wondered what Lusah Sahsan meant, until he realized that his own culture had an expression that was a close parallel to what the *arsashi* had said. Something that he probably would have said over Mark's grave had he been given a chance to do so.

"Ashes to ashes, dust to dust," he whispered.

FIFTEEN

ANDROMEDA EXAMINED THE APPLE IN HER HAND.
It was small and, while not perfectly round, fit comfortably into her palm. Tinged with autumnal streaks of dark red and pale gold, it resembled an Empire or a Cortland, the kind of apples she'd grown up eating, but in fact was a Midland Tart, a hybrid of a couple of different Earth varieties that had been created by botanists to produce a fruit that could survive Coyote's cool climate.

She'd pulled the apple from a lower branch of one of the trees she'd found upon stepping off the escalator that had carried her and the others down from the tram station. Of all the things she'd seen since the *Montero* had docked with Hex, this small and rather mundane item had surprised her the most. Not because of what it was but simply because it was there.

"This is impossible," she said softly. Then she bit into the apple; for an impossibility, it certainly tasted sweet.

"Yes, it is." Tom D'Anguilo studied another apple that

he'd picked up from the ground beneath the tree. It appeared to have recently fallen; most of the other apples on the ground were in various stages of decomposition. He turned it around in his hand to show her the small wound in its skin. "And I bet, if you cut into this, you'd find a little brown impossible worm deep inside."

Andromeda grimaced. "Thanks for ruining my appetite," she muttered, and was about to toss her apple away before reconsidering. After a week of processed ship's rations, a fresh apple was an unexpected treat. "This shouldn't be here," she added. "Same for the worm."

D'Anguilo dropped his apple on the ground, gazed up at the tree from which it came. It was about twenty-five feet tall, the same height as the others around it. They belonged to a small grove at the base of the biopod's southern range, with a few younger ones growing from the mountainside's lower slopes. A nearby creek meandered downhill, quietly gurgling as it passed through the grove and into the broad, grassy plains on the valley floor, eventually flowing into the biopod's central river. Rolf had already surmised that the creek, along with others like it, captured condensation trickling down the ceiling window and fed it into the river.

"If you think this place was created yesterday . . . yeah, I agree," he said. "But apple trees take years to grow to maturity, and it looks like this one has been here awhile. So unless *danui* bioengineering methods are as advanced as their construction techniques . . . not that I'd put it past them . . . someone seeded this place long before they knew we'd arrive."

Andromeda didn't reply. Munching on the apple, she sauntered out from beneath the tree to look up at the escalator ramp. A long monorail made of the same stony material as the biopod's outer walls, the ramp led straight up the mountainside to the tram station. A flatbed lift, open except for a safety rail around its edge, was slowly moving up the escalator; it was large enough to carry twenty or more passengers at a time, or a few people and a lot of cargo. There was a footpath, too, running parallel to the ramp, but it would probably take someone an hour or more to hike all the way to the top; the escalator was an obvious necessity.

The lift was about halfway up the mountainside; she couldn't see Melpomene or Rolf, who were on their way back to the node. Since the *Montero* sometimes traveled to worlds whose inhabitants had made little or no provisions for human guests, the ship carried equipment they'd need in order to set up camp on an alien planet: pressurized dome tents, sleeping bags, a portable stove, lamps, collapsible chairs and tables, even a chemical toilet. No sense in remaining on the ship if they didn't need to; Andromeda asked Melpomene and Rolf to return to the *Montero* and fetch the supplies. She'd told Jason that he was welcome to join them if he wanted to do so; however, Anne would have to stay behind in order to watch the ship and maintain the communications relay with Sean's team.

Which left Andromeda alone in the biopod with D'Anguilo, or at least for the time being. Although the astroethnicist was sometimes an annoying presence, Andromeda could put up with him for a while if it meant that she might get some answers to a few puzzling questions. Like why they were finding apple trees in a place where no human had ever gone before.

"So what do you think?" she asked, turning away from the escalator. "The *danui* knew we were coming, so they created a bipod suitable for us?"

"Isn't that obvious?" D'Anguilo left the tree to wander over to the creek. Squatting on his heels, he reached down to pull up a handful of the tall grass growing on its banks. "Just as I thought," he said, a smile upon his face as he examined their roots. "Sourgrass . . . same subspecies as the stuff in Midland's mountain valleys." He looked around himself. "If we were to conduct a natural census, my guess is that we'd find that almost every plant and animal here comes from the same part of Coyote . . . because that's where the original specimens were collected."

"The *danui* have never been to Coyote."

"No, but the *hjadd* have. Although they've usually kept to themselves in their embassy on New Florida, when I was at the university, I read reports that they'd occasionally sent some of their people to places like Midland and Great Dakota." He shrugged. "So it wouldn't have been much trouble for them to gather living specimens, then send them to the *danui* for this very purpose."

"I hope that didn't include boids." The flightless predatory avians that inhabited the lowlands of Coyote equatorial regions had been the nemesis of early settlers; the thought of finding them in Hex made her nervous.

"I hope not either." D'Anguilo brushed bits of grass from his hands as he stood up. "But if the purpose of all this is to provide us with a safe and comfortable place, it doesn't make sense to stock it with man-eaters. Especially when we've also been deprived of the means to defend ourselves."

"You think that's why they built Hex? To give us . . . I don't know, a home away from home?" Andromeda was skeptical. "Seems like they went to a lot of trouble for something as simple as that."

D'Anguilo didn't immediately respond. Instead, he strolled over to the escalator ramp and sat down on the low parapet surrounding its base. "I don't know," he said at last. "It's a mystery to me, too . . . why we weren't told exactly what was here, why no one contacted us until we'd sent out the survey team, why we haven't heard from the *danui* themselves. It's like we've been handed pieces of a puzzle, and we're expected to put them together ourselves."

"I thought you said you had a theory."

"I do, but I'd rather see more before I tell you what I think." He raised a hand before she could object. "Look . . . first and foremost, I'm a scientist. That means it's my responsibility to make observations and gather evidence before forming a hypothesis, not vice versa. It's like when I first saw the pictures of this system. I thought it might be possible that there was a Dyson sphere here . . ."

"But you didn't say so until we actually arrived."

"Right. When I saw for myself that I'd made the right

guess, I said so." He smiled. "You're going to have to be patient with me, Captain. Sorry, but that way I don't have to apologize for making a wrong guess."

"I suppose you're right." Andromeda finished her apple. For lack of anything else to do with the core, she tossed it beneath the tree. "I guess we can only hope that Sean learns more . . . if he gets here safely, that is."

D'Anguilo slowly nodded. He regarded her with a pensive gaze that she found discomfiting. "You're worried about him, aren't you?"

"He's my son. Shouldn't I be?"

"Of course. It's just that"—he hesitated—"if I didn't know better, I wouldn't know the two of you were even related." Feeling her face grow warm, Andromeda cast him an angry look. "Sorry," he quickly added. "I'm not trying to pick a fight here. But it's pretty obvious that the two of you don't get along. I mean, you can barely stand to be in the same room . . ."

"Not because I haven't tried," she shot back. "If you're half as observant as you claim to be, you'd notice that Sean's been the one who's been hostile."

"Yes, I suppose you're right, now that you mention it." He was quiet for a few moments before he spoke again. "So . . . what's going on between you two? If you don't mind my asking, that is."

"I do mind." Even as she said this, though, Andromeda had a compulsion to answer his question. It had been a long time since she'd talked about Sean with anyone except Jason and Melpomene. One was a former lover, and the other was the closest she had to a best friend, but both were members of her crew and thus couldn't be expected to be impartial to their captain's feelings. Although D'Anguilo sometimes irritated her, Andromeda realized that it wasn't entirely his fault. He meant well; he simply had a tendency to put curiosity before common sense.

She looked up the ramp. The lift had almost reached the top. It would be a while before Melpomene and Rolf returned from the ship; meanwhile, she and D'Anguilo had time to kill. They could either talk about apples and aliens, or . . .

"If I tell you," she asked, "can you keep your mouth shut? This is personal, and I don't want this getting back to your company or . . ."

"I promise. It's just between you and me."

"All right, then." Andromeda let out her breath, then walked over to the ramp base and sat down beside him. "It goes back to when I was in the Union Astronautica, and Sean and I were living in New Havana with Dean, his father . . ."

"Your husband?"

"We were married, yes . . . or at least we'd been, once upon a time." She shrugged. "But it didn't work out, so a couple of years after we had Sean, he and I decided to call it quits."

"Sorry to hear that."

"Don't be. Other than the fact that he helped give me a son, marrying him was the biggest mistake I ever made." *Almost the biggest,* she silently added. "Fact of the matter is that I got hitched to him more as a career move than anything else. Dean was the son of a Patriarch, which meant that his old man was in a government position where he could help me get what I wanted . . . namely, my own ship."

"That's how you became the *Montero*'s captain?" D'Anguilo stared at her in disbelief.

"It was called *The Patriotism of Fidel Castro* back then, and no, it wasn't entirely a matter of patronage. I'd already earned my commission and was certified for command rank. But there was a long list of other people who also wanted their own ships, so Dean's father pulled some strings to have me bumped to the front of the line." A grim smile. "All I had to do was marry his son."

D'Anguilo had a guarded look in his eyes. "That sounds rather . . . opportunistic."

"Don't get me wrong," Andromeda said, a little more hastily than she meant to. "I liked Dean . . . I just didn't love him. Or at least not enough to want to remain married to him. And I think he felt the same way about me, too, because he didn't fight the divorce." She paused. "Only one problem . . . he wanted Sean, and I wasn't about to give him up."

"You had custody?"

"I did, but it was only temporary. After the divorce was finalized, I moved to Copernicus Centre on the Moon, and took Sean with me. Dean didn't like that, so he decided to fight it in court. Since he had his father on his side, I pretty much knew Grandpa would use his clout to make sure that the magistrate would reverse the earlier decision and give Sean to Dean."

"Uh-huh." D'Anguilo nodded. "And how did Sean feel about that?"

"He was too young to really understand what was going on, except that Dad was no longer with us and Mom didn't like to talk about him. But he loved Dean, and Dean loved him, and . . . well, I wasn't sure he wouldn't go with his father if given a chance to choose for himself."

Andromeda slowly let out her breath. "Anyway . . . the lawyers were still duking it out when the WHU collapsed. When the government fell, it took both the Union Astronautica and the legal system with it." She looked at him askance. "I'm sure you remember what that was like."

"Not really . . . or at least not the way you do. I'm a second-generation colonist . . . My folks came to Coyote aboard the *New Horizons*, the second Union ship to reach 47 Uma." A shrug and a smile. "I knew what was going on, of course, but I've never been to Earth."

"Yes, well . . . believe me, you haven't missed anything. The global environment had gone to hell by then, and all the old governments and coalitions were breaking down. Anyone with any sense was getting out of there if they could. And I had a ship . . ."

"So you escaped."

"Uh-huh. I took the matter to my crew, and after they voted unanimously to defect to Coyote, I approached the

Federation consulate on Highgate about having a hyper-space key installed in the nav system. They were only too happy to oblige—they were eager to acquire ships since Coyote wasn't able to build any of their own—and so we took the *Castro* before the Union Astronautica knew what was going on." She shrugged. "It wasn't hard, really. By then, a revolution had broken out in New Havana, and the social-collectivists were being overthrown. So the government had a lot worse things to worry about than someone's hijacking a ship."

"And, of course, you took Sean with you."

"Damn right I did." She looked him square in the eye. "When the *Castro* was ready to leave, I went back to our apartment on the Moon, grabbed him and a few belongings, and caught the next shuttle to Highgate. Sean didn't know what was going on until we were actually aboard ship and about to launch."

"What did you tell him?"

"That we were going far, far away, but it was going to be to a happy place, where he could run and play and . . ." Andromeda sighed. "Well, you can probably imagine the rest. The sort of thing you'd tell a little boy when you're yanking him away from everything he's known and taking him to another world."

"And what about his father?"

Andromeda hesitated. This was the part of the story she didn't like to talk about, and she found herself wondering why she was telling it to a relative stranger. But it was too late to stop, so she went on.

"I told Sean that his father would be joining us later. That he had a few things he still had to do on Earth, but once he settled his business, he'd be taking another ship to Coyote." She shrugged. "And, of course, Sean believed me. Why shouldn't he? I was his mother, and I'd never lied to him before."

She shook her head. "Funny thing is, I kinda believed it myself. I figured that Dean would eventually find out where we'd gone and that he'd pull strings to get aboard the next

Union Astronautica ship to Coyote. But since I'd already requested political amnesty from the Federation, and the Union didn't have any extradition treaties with them, he'd have a tough time taking Sean away from me. Unless he wanted to defect to Coyote himself, of course."

"And did he?"

"No." Andromeda let out her breath. "When New Havana went up in flames, I lost contact with him. The *Castro* . . . the *Montero*, I mean . . . was one of the last ships to leave Earth before Starbridge Coyote was destroyed. So I never heard from Dean again." A wry smile. "Weird thing is . . . once he was gone, I realized that I missed him. If he hadn't tried to take Sean away from me, we might have even gotten back together again. But . . ."

"But that didn't happen."

"No." Her smile faded. "Anyway, I thought my problems were over. And they were . . . but only for a while."

D'Anguilo said nothing, but only waited for her to go on. Feeling restless, Andromeda stood up. "I bought a place in New Brighton, and Sean and I settled in, and I got to watch him grow up while I waited for the starbridge to be rebuilt. He had only one parent, but he didn't seem to mind so long as he was able to continue believing what I'd told him . . . that his father was supposed to be joining us but had been left behind when the starbridge was destroyed. He never knew that Dean and I had broken up or that I'd abducted him, and I didn't intend to tell him. And he might have gone on believing just that if he hadn't found my old logbook."

"You'd written about it in your log?" D'Anguilo asked.

She nodded, not looking at him but instead gazing up the mountainside. "It was all there, in my personal log from the *Castro*. By then, the starbridge had been rebuilt, and I was back in the captain's chair. Sean had grown up, but he was still living at home while he finished school. I was on a mission for the merchant marine when he accessed my old logs through our home comp. Just curious, really, to read what his mother had been doing way back when. And that was when . . . well, that's when he found out that I'd been lying to him."

Tucking her hands in her jumpsuit pockets, Andromeda stared at the ground. "I'd forgotten how much he'd loved Dean. I'd tried as hard as I could to be a good mother, but the kid had grown up without a father, and he'd done so thinking that it was only an accident that Dean had been left behind. So when he found out that I'd deliberately taken him away and never really had any intention of letting his father see him again . . ."

"He was upset."

Andromeda gave him an annoyed glance. "Now there's an understatement. He felt . . ." She stopped, searching for the right words.

"Betrayed?" D'Anguilo said tentatively.

"That's one way to describe it. *Infuriated* is another. We had it out as soon as I returned home, and some things were said that probably shouldn't have been, and . . ." Andromeda looked away again. "He moved out. He got a place of his own in New Brighton and stayed there until he finished school, and the next day he enlisted in the Corps of Exploration. He's got a key to the house, of course, and sometimes he drops by, but only when he knows I'm not going to be there. I've sent him letters, but he's never answered them, and when I've tried to apologize, he doesn't listen."

"I see." D'Anguilo was quiet for a moment. "And now the two of you are on this mission together."

"Not my choice, believe me. But when Ted Harker told me that I'd be escorting a Corps of Exploration survey team, I knew that he'd be aboard, and that there was nothing I could do about it."

"But if he . . ."

D'Anguilo suddenly stopped. Because she wasn't looking at him, Andromeda didn't realize that he was staring past her. "It's tough for both of us, yeah," she said, still gazing at the ground. "And now that he's gone, I'm afraid that I'll never see him again, or tell him . . ."

"Tell me what?" a voice behind her said.

Her eyes widened, and for a moment Andromeda thought it was Sean who had spoken. But when she turned around to look, she saw that it wasn't her son who was walking toward them from the nearby grove but Zeus Brandt.

For several heartbeats, Andromeda was unable to breathe, let alone speak. His EVA suit was gone, and he wore only his jumpsuit, but *Montero*'s chief petty officer appeared to be unhurt. Indeed, there was a wide smile across his face as he strolled out from under the apple trees.

"Hi, skipper," he said. "Did you really think you'd never see me again?"

Behind her, D'Anguilo brayed laughter, but Andromeda was too astonished to mind. "I . . . I . . ." she began, then swallowed hard as she tried to collect herself. "I wasn't talking about you, but . . . yes, as a matter of fact, I did. Where the hell have you been?"

"It's a long story." A grin and a casual shrug, then Zeus held up a hand before she could go on. "I'll tell you everything, but first, there's a message I've got to give you."

For the first time, Andromeda noticed that he had a small paper scroll in his other hand. "What's that?" she asked as he held it out for her.

"Like I said, it's a message. The *danui* told me to deliver it to you . . ."

"The *danui*?" The captain's mouth fell open. "You've met them?"

"Yeah . . . well, sort of." Zeus held the scroll out to her. "Anyway, here it is."

There were a dozen things she wanted to know, but Zeus seemed insistent that she first take the scroll. It appeared to be made of some brittle parchment, like old hemp paper, and it was tied together by a slender blue ribbon.

She untied the ribbon and unrolled the scroll, and for a moment she thought this was all a joke; the paper was blank. Then, as she watched, words materialized upon the scroll:

To Captain Andromeda Carson of the CFSS *Montero*—

When you are ready to have your questions answered, please board the transportation network and enter the following habitat identification:

❘△·◇◇❘⊕□·❘△·◇❘⊕·❘□△

Prepare for a long journey.

We are waiting for you.

FOUR

BIG
SMART
OBJECT

SIXTEEN

NIGHT CAME AS A SLOW DIMMING OF THE SUN. HD 76700 didn't move from its position in the sky; instead, the biopod's transparent ceiling gradually polarized over the course of a few hours until it was completely opaque, leaving the cylindrical world in darkness. No stars, no moon: only a jet-black expanse.

By then, the *Montero*'s crew had set up camp near the bottom of the escalator, the lamps they'd brought from the ship casting a luminescent circle around the tents. Standing just outside the tent ring, Andromeda realized that the campsite was the only source of light in the valley. But while the biopod was dark, it was anything but silent: the chirp of grasshoarders in the underbrush, the harsh cries of swoops, even the distant growl of a creek cat. When Rolf had come back from digging a latrine pit, he'd reported having seen a pair of glidemunks playing in the upper branches of a judas tree not far from the creek.

Apparently the *danui* hadn't only imported some of Coyote's flora and fauna but had also gone so far as to make sure that the habitat had an identical twenty-seven-hour day-night cycle. Which made sense; the natural patterns of its creatures and plants would be severely upset if they lacked a nighttime, particularly the nocturnal species. But Andromeda still hadn't heard any boids, which lent credence to D'Anguilo's theory that the *danui* wouldn't have brought any animals against which an unarmed human would have been defenseless.

Andromeda glanced at her watch—3:39 P.M., the middle of the afternoon . . . but that was according to the ship's chronometer, which was set to the hour at Coyote's meridian. She'd have to reset her watch so that it accurately reflected local time. For the moment, more important matters demanded her attention.

Melpomene had set up the portable stove in the center of the campsite. She sat before it on a folding stool, stirring the pot of lamb stew she'd prepared with water Zeus had fetched from the creek. The chief petty officer himself was eagerly waiting for the evening meal; bowl and spoon in hand, he impatiently watched as the helmsman moved the soup ladle around the steaming pot. Apparently his disappearance had done nothing to abate his appetite.

Mel looked up as Andromeda reentered the camp. "Dinner's about ready, skipper. Grab your eatin' irons and come get some chow."

"Be delighted to . . . Thanks." Bowls, utensils, and cups were stacked atop one of the supply boxes. Andromeda picked up a bowl and a spoon but decided to pass on the coffee even though a fresh-brewed pot stood upon a nearby hot plate; it would only keep her awake longer than she wanted. She found herself wishing she'd asked Jason to fetch her liquor flask from her quarters. Probably just as well; it wouldn't do her crew any good for them to see their captain having a snort at a time when they were still unsure about where they were or what lay before them.

Sitting cross-legged between Jason and Rolf, Andromeda handed her bowl to Melpomene, who gave it back filled with stew. For something that had been freeze-dried who-knew how long ago, it wasn't bad; Rolf had used a test kit to check the creek water before he allowed Mel to cook with it, and he'd proclaimed it to be as pure and fresh as if from a mountain spring. Andromeda let everyone eat in peace; they made small talk—like the odd way night fell there or how the glidemunks Rolf had seen behaved just like the ones back home. When they were done, she placed her bowl on the ground beside her and cleared her throat.

"All right, now that we've had a bite to eat, let's get back to business." Andromeda looked over at Zeus. "You've already told Tom and me how you got here, but I don't think the others have heard it yet . . . or at least not the whole story. So you might want to take it from the beginning."

"Sure, skipper." Zeus wiped his bearded mouth with the back of his sleeve and grinned at Melpomene. "Thanks, sweetheart. That hit the spot." Mel smiled and nodded, and Zeus looked at Andromeda again. "Not much to tell, really, but . . ."

"Indulge us." Jason peered at him. "Start at the place where we thought you were dead."

"You mean when the cables grabbed my pod and hauled it into a hole in the wall?" Zeus gazed back at the first officer. "Believe me, I thought I was dead, too . . . or soon would be. And I don't know what happened to the comlink except that they did a fine job of jamming my signal."

He absently scratched at his beard. "Anyway, I was pulled through a hatch into a . . . I guess it was an airlock, because as soon as the hatch sealed, the gravity field kicked in, and the room began to pressurize. The cables released the pod and retracted into the walls, and I was left alone. After a couple of minutes, I decided to take a chance and get out of the pod."

"That *was* taking a chance," Andromeda said. "If I'd been you, I would've stayed put and tried to contact the ship."

"That was my first thought, too. But I was getting nothing over the com except static, so . . ." Zeus shrugged. "Except for a wallscreen and a door, the place was empty. The pod sensors told me that it had an oxygen-nitrogen atmosphere, so there wasn't much point in staying buttoned up. So I climbed out, took off my helmet, and waited to see what happened next."

He put his bowl down and stretched his legs. "The screen lit and some guy . . . a human, I mean, although I think he was really a sim . . . told me that it was okay to get out of my suit. I went along with that, and as soon as I did, a beam came from the walls and ran down my body. I figured it was some sort of scanner . . ."

"It was," Rolf said. "Same thing happened to us when we came in."

"Right. So I stayed still and let them check me out. When it was over, a panel opened in the wall next to the screen. I looked in and found the rolled-up paper I gave the captain."

Andromeda had left the scroll in her tent. The others had seen it already, along with the cryptic message that had appeared on it. "And you were told to bring it to me?"

"Yeah . . . but not by the guy on the screen. It was blank when I unrolled it, but then words appeared on it . . . 'Give this to Captain Andromeda Carson when you find her.' "

Andromeda's eyes widened. "You mean it changed messages?"

"Uh-huh. Skipper, I was as surprised as you were when you opened it and found something different. I don't know how it did that, but . . ."

"Electrophoretic print," Rolf said. "Looks like normal paper, but it's actually a comp that changes display on command." An uninterested shrug. "Nothing new there."

"Maybe not," Andromeda said, "but how did they know it was time to deliver a message meant for me?"

"Perhaps it's linked to a communication network," Rolf said.

Andromeda looked at him sharply. "You mean to say that it heard me?"

The chief engineer slowly nodded. "Either that, or it was triggered by your touch. Your fingerprints . . . maybe even your DNA. They wouldn't have been any harder to acquire than anything else here." Seeing the look on her face, his mouth tightened. "Anyway, you might want to be careful what you say when you handle it. Someone may be listening."

The thought that something in her possession might be capable of eavesdropping on them was chilling. For all they knew, they might be under constant surveillance. "I'll keep that in mind," Andromeda said, suddenly glad that the scroll was somewhere else just then.

"Yeah, well . . . whatever it is, I was meant to take it with me," Zeus said. "That much was obvious. Then the door opened, and I went down a tunnel to where I found something that looked like a subway . . ."

"Probably the same tram station we found," Melpomene said.

"Maybe." Andromeda brushed aside her comment with a wave of her hand. "Go on, Zeus. What then?"

"Not much, really. I got on the tram, and it carried me here."

"You didn't touch the control panel?"

"No. It brought me here on its own. I got off at the next station, found the escalator, and took it down here. I didn't have anything else to do, so I decided to walk around a bit and check out the place." A smile and a shrug. "I wasn't too concerned. Kinda figured it wouldn't be long before someone else showed up, and I was right. You know the rest."

Andromeda didn't respond, yet she carefully studied her chief petty officer. Zeus had always been unflappable, but he was taking his ordeal a little more calmly than she would have expected. Not for the first time, she wished that merchant marine vessels carried their own physicians as part of their crews instead of relying on autodocs and the first-aid training of its officers; she would've liked to have Zeus examined by someone with psychiatric training, if only to make sure that he wasn't suffering from some sort of poststress trauma.

On the other hand, though, perhaps she should simply

accept his story at face value. His service pod had been carried into the node, where he'd been scanned, given a message to bring to her, then transported to the biopod and released. Simple as that. And Zeus was no coward; the situation in which he'd found himself was frightening at first, but once he'd realized that he wasn't going to be harmed, he'd accepted it and did the best he could.

"Thank you," she said at last. "I'm glad to see that you weren't harmed and that you're back with us safe and sound." The others murmured much the same thing, and Melpomene smiled as she reached over to briefly grasp Zeus's hand. "So let's talk about where we stand. We've found this place, whatever it's called . . ."

"Nueva Italia," D'Anguilo said quietly.

"Pardon me?"

"Just a suggestion." For once, the astroethnicist seemed to be embarrassed by his tendency to interrupt others. When he found Andromeda waiting for him to go on, he continued. "We're going to have to call this place something, right? To me, at least, it looks sort of like pictures I've seen of northern Italy, where my family is originally from. So I've been thinking of it as Nueva Italia . . . 'New Italy.' "

"I like 'New Coyote' better," Rolf muttered.

"No, no," Andromeda said. "I don't want it to get mixed up with Coyote. Nueva Italia it is . . . and let's move on. We've set up base camp, and it doesn't look like there's anything here that might threaten us, but we've still got two important issues before us." She raised one finger, then another. "The first is getting back our survey team. The second is finding out what's going on with the *danui*."

"Skipper?" Melpomene raised a hand, and Andromeda acknowledged her with a nod. "I totally agree with you about the first, but the second . . . I don't know. Maybe we should keep the *danui* at arm's length. Every time we mess with them, something bad happens."

"She may be right." Jason nodded toward the helmsman. "Whenever we've done something they don't want us to do, we've ended up paying for it. Perhaps we should learn our lesson and just . . . I dunno. Stay away."

"As much as I'm inclined to agree," Andromeda said, "I'm afraid that's not an option. Our mission is to survey this world and find out whether it's suitable for colonization. So far, all we know for sure is that it's not what we thought it would be. The only way we can learn the rest is by making contact with the *danui* . . . and they've clearly invited us to do just that."

D'Anguilo nodded even though the others appeared reluctant. Andromeda went on. "There's also the matter of our missing team. We haven't heard from Sean again lately, but he told me that he'd try to get the *arsashi* to help him find his way here. I told him that he's on his own, and he accepts that, but all the same, he may need us. So that's another problem."

She let out her breath. "So I'm thinking that we should split up. I'll go . . . well, wherever it is the *danui* want me to go . . . and find out whatever it is they want to tell me." She looked over at D'Anguilo. "Tom, I want you with me. You know more about them than anyone else, so . . ."

"Of course, Captain." He smiled. "It'll be my pleasure."

"Glad to hear it." Andromeda turned to Zeus. "I'd like you along, too. You've made contact with them, if not directly, and judging from what you've told us, they seemed to accept you. So they might react well to a familiar face."

Melpomene frowned, obviously reluctant to give up Zeus again, but the chief petty officer nodded. "Ready when you are, skipper."

"What about the rest of us, Captain?" Jason asked. "You want us to mind the fort?"

"Pretty much, yes." Andromeda noticed his sour expression. "I know that sounds boring," she added, "but someone needs to stay behind. Sean may call again, so you'll need to be ready to assist him . . . and if Tom, Zeus, and I get in trouble, you may have to come to our rescue. Anne will stay on the ship to facilitate communications among the three groups."

"She's not going to like that," Melpomene said. "She's itching to see this place."

"There'll be plenty of time for sightseeing later. She's the com chief, and right now, I need her at her post."

"How do you know you'll even be able to reach us?" Jason asked. "That message told you to prepare for a long journey. In case you've forgotten, Hex is a helluva big place."

"And in case *you've* forgotten," Rolf said, "we're standing on the inside of a sphere, not the outside. No visible horizon means longer line of sight, and that means increased range for VHF transmissions."

"He's right," Melpomene said. "The survey team went down at least forty thousand miles from here, and Sean was still able to use his transceiver to reach the ship." She looked at Andromeda. "They're designed for ground-to-space transmissions. So long as the antenna is pointed in our general direction, you should be able to keep in touch with the ship, and Anne can relay signals from the camp or Sean's team."

"I'm still not . . ." Jason began.

A soft chirp from the radio hooked to Andromeda's belt. "Speak of the devil," she said, then lifted a finger for silence while she pulled the headset up from around her neck and nestled it against her ear and chin. "Base camp here," she said, then smiled. "New call sign," she added. "Nueva Italia."

D'Anguilo preened as Rolf rolled his eyes. A moment's pause, then Andromeda heard Anne's voice. *"Acknowledged, Nueva Italia. Skipper, I've just received a hyperlink transmission from Coyote. Captain Harker is on the line. Would you like for me to put him through?"*

Andromeda hissed beneath her breath. It had been more than twenty-seven hours since the last time she had reported in; no doubt Ted Harker would be irate with her. "Affirmative," she said, then looked at the others. "It's Harker. I better take this in private."

The others nodded as she stood up and walked away. A few seconds later, Harker's voice came through the headset. *"Andromeda, where the hell have you been?"*

"Sorry, Ted. Things have been busy here." Andromeda gave him a brief rundown of all that had happened since the *Montero* entered orbit around Hex, concluding with the establishment of the base camp at Nueva Italia and the message she'd received from the *danui*. Harker listened without interrupting her; when she was done, Andromeda heard his voice again through her earpiece.

"This doesn't sound good. The Corps team has lost two people, and the rest have gone missing, and the danui *have captured your vessel and transported it to another location."* A pause. *"I'm tempted to call this mission a failure and order you to return, if only for your own safety."*

"You're not serious, are you?" Andromeda stared into the darkness. "I've got three people out there." *One of whom is my son,* she was tempted to add, but decided not to; Harker knew that already, and she didn't want him to think that she was letting personal motives cloud her judgment. "I can't just leave them behind because I'm worried about my ship."

"Captain, the safety of your vessel and its crew are your top priority," Harker replied, and Andromeda couldn't help but notice that he'd taken to addressing her by her rank. *"If necessary, you must be willing to get them out of harm's way."*

"Captain, my crew is not in danger. Chief Petty Officer Brandt was returned unharmed, and the message he relayed to me from the *danui* indicates that they're interested in speaking to us. When you called, I was making plans for Tom, Zeus, and me to go to the coordinates we'd been given."

"What about the survey team? What's their present condition?"

Andromeda hesitated. "I haven't heard from them in several hours," she admitted, "but my son is now in charge of the team. He told me that they've reached an accord with the *arsashi*, and they're willing to help him reach our location." She paused. "I'm not going to abandon him, Ted. Don't ask me to do so."

A few more seconds passed, longer than could be accounted for by the time lag of hyperlink transmissions. *"I'm not going to,"* Ted said at last, *"but neither am I willing to let the* danui, *or any other race, hold them hostage."*

You poor fool, Andromeda thought. *You really have no idea how powerful they are, do you?* Yet the implications of what he'd said puzzled her. The Federation Navy could dispatch another vessel to Hex, this time as a rescue mission. So long as Sean had an active transceiver, another Corps team—or even a squad of Federation Militia—could zero in on his signal. But how would they get here in the first place? So far as she knew, the *Montero* had the only starbridge key that would allow a starship to make the jump from 47 Ursae Majoris to HD 76700 . . .

Unless there's another key that we haven't been told about, she thought.

"I understand," she replied, choosing her words carefully. "But I think it would be wise to exhaust our alternatives before we . . . ah, exercise that option. If only for the sake of diplomacy."

Another pause. *"I agree. I'm willing to give you more time to work things out for yourself, Captain, but I expect regular reports from now on. If there are any more delays or unfortunate incidents, you may expect an order to withdraw at once. Do you copy?"*

"Affirmative. I'll report back sometime tomorrow and let you know how things stand."

"Very well. I'll be waiting to hear from you. Harker over and out."

Andromeda sighed as she pulled out the earpiece and switched off the transceiver. On top of her other problems, she'd just been handed a ticking stopwatch. All of a sudden, she had a feeling that this wasn't going to end well . . .

"Trouble, Captain?"

Startled, she turned around to find D'Anguilo standing behind her. She didn't know how long he'd been there, but it was a good bet that he'd been listening in.

"No," she said, deciding that a lie was all he deserved

for eavesdropping on her. "Just a little disagreement with my boss." She started to walk past him, then a new thought occurred to her, and she stopped. "By the way, Tom . . . when the *danui* gave you that starbridge key, was it the only copy?"

"So far as I know. But if you're asking whether our people could have used it to make others . . ." D'Anguilo hesitated. "I suppose it's possible that an effort may have been made to reverse engineer it," he went on, his reticence plain in the guarded way he spoke. "It wasn't in my possession the entire time I was at Starbridge Coyote. It's conceivable that someone may have sought to crack its code and duplicate it." He hastily shook his head. "I can't be sure, of course."

Andromeda nodded. Yes, he could, even if he wasn't about to confess everything he knew. Between the time that the *danui* emissary had given D'Anguilo the starbridge key and the time he'd boarded the *Montero*, someone from the Federation Navy had closely examined the key, perhaps even hooking it up to an AI that replicated a starship's hyperspace system. In that way, they might have been able to crack the code for the hyperspace coordinates and thus fashion a second key that would enable another human ship to make the jump to HD 76700. Just in case the *Montero* ran into trouble.

"Well . . . if someone did, then I hope they're careful in how they use it." Andromeda continued toward the circle of light cast by the lamps. "We've made enough mistakes already. I don't think we can afford another one." She glanced back at D'Anguilo. "And Mel's right. Messing with the *danui* may be a bad idea."

SEVENTEEN

THE LIGHT WAS BEGINNING TO DIM AS SEAN BROUGHT the gyro in for a landing. Lusah Sahsan had warned him that this might happen; the *arsashi* homeworld had a day of only twenty-three hours, and their Hex habitat imitated its sunrises and sunsets. So Sean wasn't surprised when night began closing in; hoping to reach the eastern end of the biopod before it became too dark to see, he'd wasted no time leaving the place where the *Reese* had come down.

He clutched the stick tight within his right hand, feeling every shudder and jounce the gyro made. So far, the survey team had been lucky. The second *arsashi* vehicle to arrive at the crash site was equipped with a crane, and it had managed to raise the lander high enough for Sean, Sandy, and Lusah Sahsan's two husbands to pry open the cargo hatch and lower the gyro from its trapeze. Although the aircraft was still flightworthy, nonetheless it had sustained some damage. The aft pusher-prop's blades were out of alignment, but he and Sandy were able to fix that;

however, they couldn't do anything about the cracked reserve hydrogen fuel cell or the hairline fracture in the canopy.

So the gyro was good for one short-range flight, and its cabin couldn't be pressurized. Sean knew that they would have to abandon it once they reached their destination. So long as it held together long enough for his team to reach the nearest tram station, though, that was fine by him. He didn't admit it to Kyra and Sandy, but the truth of the matter was that he barely knew how to fly the damn thing.

Once the team thanked Lusah Sahsan and her tribesmen for their help, they climbed into the gyro's narrow cockpit, where they squeezed themselves into its small, tandem-mounted seats. The miniature aircraft wasn't built for comfort, but Sean expected their trip to take only two or three hours. In any case, he was relieved that he was able to start the engine. The aft prop made a noisy clatter as it wound up to speed, but at least it worked, and as soon as the main prop was an invisible blur above their heads, he pulled back on the stick, and the gyro made its clumsy ascent.

Sean had received only minimal flight training from the Corps, and thus had only logged fifteen hours in gyros. Minimal experience as a pilot hadn't been an issue when he was picked for the expedition because Mark Dupree was supposed to fly the gyro, but it mattered now. So Sean didn't spend much time admiring the landscape; his attention was entirely focused upon his instruments, and within his airmask, he chewed his lower lip. The few times he allowed himself to gaze out the canopy, though, he was impressed by what he saw. Like a planet in a bottle, the wintry terrain spread out below them was a microcosm of the *arsashi* homeworld. Despite his strong desire to get the hell out of there, he found himself wishing that he could remain longer, if only to explore.

Sure . . . and he'd be like a kid in a candy store who wanted only licorice jelly beans and nothing else. If Tom D'Anguilo was right, Hex contained hundreds of billions of miniature worlds—perhaps even trillions. The possibilities were staggering. *We could spend generations exploring this place,* he thought, *and never see them all.* And then the gyro lurched again, and he returned his mind to the instruments.

So, nearly three hours after leaving the crash site, they'd reached their goal. Through the canopy, Sean spotted what appeared to be a narrow, tan strip leading straight up the steep side of the southern mountain range. Lusah Sahsan had told him to look out for something like that; it would be the escalator that would carry his team to the tram station.

"Wow . . . Now that's weird." Sandy's voice, coming from two seats behind him, was muffled slightly by the prop noise.

"The escalator?" Sean gently pushed the stick forward as he pulled back on the throttle. The pusher-prop growled like an angry dog as the gyro began to descend. "I suppose, but they'd have to get down here somehow, wouldn't . . . ?"

"No, that's not what I'm talking about," Sandy said. "I've just spotted the source of the river, and it looks like it's coming from a hole in the wall."

"You're right." Kyra was sitting directly behind Sean, so he could hear her more clearly. "I see it, too . . . There's a hole in the wall, and that's where the water is coming from."

Sean didn't dare look at what the two women had seen, but from the corner of his eye he could make out the titanic concave wall that marked the biopod's endcap. It had loomed before them for the past three hours, steadily growing larger with every passing mile, but he hadn't been able to make out any significant details other than some large round holes evenly arranged in a circle near its edge. He and Kyra had thought that they might be ventilators—after all, the atmosphere had to come from somewhere—but it appeared that Sandy might have found another explanation.

However interesting her discovery might be, studying it was the furthest thing from his mind. "I can't look at it just now," he said, a little more peevishly than he intended. "Get some pictures. I'm busy."

"Okay . . . sure," Kyra said quietly, as if chastised. "Didn't mean to bother you."

Great, Sean thought. *Keep it up, and you'll turn into Cayce.* "Sorry," he added. "It's just that I'd like to get us on the ground in one piece, that's all."

He'd been careful to keep the gyro at an altitude of no more than eight hundred feet; if the aft prop failed, he could turn off the engine, switch the main prop to unpowered autodescent mode, and make an emergency touchdown. Sean glanced at the altimeter; they were at 450 feet. The aft prop sounded as if tin cans were tied to its blades, though, and he carefully throttled it back a little more. *Please don't go out on me now,* he thought, gritting his teeth as he gripped the stick with both hands. *I don't need two crashes in one day . . .*

But he didn't need to worry. The gyro held together, for the seven minutes it remained airborne, and settled upon its wheels as though it were a feather drifting to the ground. The pusher-prop rattled loudly as it spun to a halt, then it was still.

Sean sighed and closed his eyes in relief as he let his head sink back against the seat. His pulse hammered in his temples, and he felt Kyra's hand reach forward to give him a reassuring pat. "Good work," she said. "I knew you could do it."

"Thanks. I appreciate it." He gave her hand a brief squeeze, then he switched off the rest of the gyro's systems. Behind him, Kyra and Sandy were already turning the canopy latches. He waited until the main prop stopped turning, then said, "Okay, we can get out now."

He'd brought the gyro down on a flat place not far from the escalator. Lusah Sahsan had told him that she would try to have members of another family there to meet them when they arrived, but apparently she'd failed to do so because there were no *arsashi* in sight. Which was probably just as well; even with translator disks, the way they spoke made his ears hurt, and he didn't want to risk any more innocent mistakes of the kind that had cost Amerigo Cayce his life.

In any case, the *arsashi* would be given the gift of one slightly used gyro. The flat bed of the escalator's lift looked as if it was just big enough to take the aircraft, but Sean didn't want or need it anymore. If everything worked out right, their next stop would be the biopod where the *Montero* had docked.

Before they left the crash site, Sean, Kyra, and Sandy had sorted through their equipment, collecting everything they'd need to take with them—sleeping bags, rations, water bottles, lanterns and flashlights, datapads, a dome tent, various hand tools—and either stuffed it into the backpacks or strapped it to their frames. The rest was given to the *arsashi*. The fléchette pistols posed a small problem; Lusah Sahsan insisted that they were contraband, and when one of her husbands volunteered to dispose of the weapons, Sean had no recourse but to surrender them. Perhaps guns were forbidden on Hex; nevertheless, he felt defenseless without them.

Lifting his pack from the back of the gyro, Sean slipped his left arm through one of its straps and let it dangle awkwardly from his shoulder. His airpack prevented him from carrying it on his back; Kyra started to put on her backpack, but Sandy shook her head.

"We're not climbing that mountain, y'know," she said, nodding toward the nearby slope. "The lift will carry us up. And I bet a hundred colonials that, when we reach that tram, it'll be pressurized oxygen-nitrogen, and we can take off these stupid masks."

Kyra thought about it a moment. "You're right," she said. "Screw it." She unbuckled the pack's belt and shrugged out of the straps, then slung it under one arm as Sean had.

A greenish grey twilight was settling upon the mountains as they carried their packs to the escalator and dropped them on the lift. A safety rail surrounded the lift, waist height for an *arsashi* but shoulder height for a human; Sean nearly had to stand on tiptoes to see the control panel attached to the rear rail. Fortunately, it was simple enough for any race to understand: three buttons in a vertical column, one with a triangle that pointed up, another with an inverted triangle that pointed down, and between them a button with a horizontal line. Sean reached up to push the top button, and with the mildest of jolts, the lift began to move.

The ascent took nearly forty-five minutes, long enough for the remaining light to fade from the biopod. Sean was startled by the starless black of the sky above the ceiling; if not for the glimmer of lights from *arsashi* settlements spread out below, the habitat would have been plunged into total darkness. Kyra opened her pack and pulled out a lantern; once she switched it on, Sean and Sandy were able to retrieve lanterns from their own packs. The combined luminescence helped a little, but there was still a spooky sense of traveling through an abyss.

"I hope you're right about the trams being pressurized," Kyra said. "I'm starving."

Sean nodded. Although his airmask was fitted with a small valve at the mouth that could be opened to admit a water bottle's nipple, eating was impossible without removing the mask entirely. It was frustrating to have a rumbling stomach but be unable to do anything about it even though there were enough food bars in his pack to feed him for three days.

"That'll be the first thing we do once we get there," he promised her.

"No, it won't." Sandy shook her head. "The first thing will be to see if we can get out of here at all." She paused. "Sorry, but I'm not at all confident that the tram stops here."

As it turned out, she was right. When the lift reached the top of the escalator, they saw from the light of their lanterns that the station was vacant, with a dark, empty tunnel where they'd expected a vehicle to be parked.

"I suppose we'll have to call for it," Kyra said. "Question is, how?"

Dropping his pack on the veranda, Sean searched with his lantern until he found what appeared to be a control panel set within an enclosed wall near the platform. It had two screens, both glowing with a soft luminescence. The one on top displayed a hexagon whose inner and outer edges were ringed by half arrows pointing in various directions; he figured that it was a map of the *arsashi* habitat. On the lower screen were two rows of geometric shapes. His mother had said something about the tram using a coordinate system of *danui* numerals; Sean wondered if this was it.

"Give me the transceiver," he said to Kyra. "I'll call the ship and see if they can patch me through to my mother."

Kyra opened her pack, removed the transceiver, and brought it over to him. Slinging it over his right shoulder, Sean switched it on, then unfolded its antenna and pointed it toward the sky. "Survey team to *Montero*," he said into its hand mike. "Survey team to *Montero*, do you copy? Please respond."

He had to repeat himself a few times before Anne Smith's voice came through the transceiver's speaker. *"We copy, survey team."* She interrupted herself with a yawn. *"Sorry for the delay. I was catching a few winks."*

It seemed like days since the last time Sean had slept; he was envious of the communications officer for having that luxury. "Would you please patch me through to Captain Carson?"

Another yawn. *"Sure . . . Hold on."*

A long delay, as much as a minute or more, during which he heard nothing but static. Then a brief crackle, followed by his mother's voice. *"Sean, is that you?"*

Who else would it be? he almost asked, until he realized how tired she sounded. "I'm here," he said instead. "Sounds like you're asleep."

"I was. It's night here. We've set up camp in the biopod . . . we're calling it Nueva Italia, by the way . . . and just about everyone is sacked out. Where are you now?"

"It's night here, too . . . or at least what passes for night. We've made it to the tram station. I flew the gyro, but had to abandon it at the bottom of the escalator. No room for it on the lift, and it's pretty much a loss anyway." He paused, then added, "There's no tram here. Just an empty tunnel."

"Don't worry about the gyro," Andromeda said. *"You won't need it if you can get a tram to come to you, and we think we've figured out how to do that."* A short pause—it seemed as if she'd muted her headset to speak with someone else—then her voice returned. *"Tom D'Anguilo is on watch. He wants to know if you've taken any pictures or gathered any specimens."*

Sean nearly laughed out loud. "Tell him that I'm sorry, but I've had other things on my mind."

A dry chuckle. *"That's what I thought. All right, have you found the control panel? There should be one there."*

"I'm looking at it now."

"Good. Okay, there should be two rows of figures . . . dots, squares, triangles, diamonds, and so forth . . . on it. Do you see that?"

"I see it."

"Good. Tom thinks the bottom row are danui *numbers, zero through six, and the top row are the coordinates for the biopod you're in. So if you want to reach another biopod, you have to use that bottom row to plug in the numbers for the top row. Understand?"*

"Uh-huh. How do I do that?"

Another pause, then D'Anguilo's voice came over the comlink. *"Sean, we've never done this before, but I think that if you push the digits on the bottom row, it'll change the coordinates on the top row. Your mother . . . Captain Carson, I mean . . . copied down our coordinates, so she's ready to repeat them to you whenever you're ready."*

"Hang on a sec." Sean clumsily shifted the transceiver's carry-strap from his right shoulder to his left. Once its mike was in his left hand, he was able to use his right to operate the control panel. "All right, I'm ready."

"Okay, here goes," Andromeda said. *"Two dots joined by a vertical line . . . That's two."*

Sean found a figure on the bottom row that matched this description. He carefully pressed it with his forefinger. Nothing happened; the digit didn't give way beneath his fingertip, and the top row remained the same.

"Nope," he said. "No change. Are you sure you . . . ?"

"Wait a minute." Sandy was standing behind him; like Kyra, she was watching over Sean's shoulder. "If the bottom row is a keypad that's sensitive to body heat instead of pressure, wouldn't it make sense to take off your gloves first?"

Sean muttered an obscenity under his breath. He hadn't thought of that. Handing the mike to Sandy for a moment, he peeled off his gloves, then took the mike back from her and tried again. This time it worked; the top row vanished, then the *danui* numeral appeared on the screen.

"That did it," he said. "All right, go on."

An audible sigh of relief, then his mother continued. *"Next is an open diamond. That's four . . ."*

It took a while for Sean to enter all nineteen digits into the keypad. His mother had to describe them to him, and there were great similarities between the diamond-shaped figures that corresponded with four, five, and six. One by one, the *danui* numerals gradually appeared, and when the sequence was complete, he was rewarded by seeing them flash twice before disappearing, to be replaced an instant later by the original sequence.

Sean let out his breath. "I guess that means . . ."

Just then, a brilliant shaft of light came down from the ceiling above him and the two women, capturing them within its radiance. Startled, Sean nearly jumped an inch. "What the . . . ?"

"Did a light come on above you?" Tom asked. *"If it did, just hold still. That's a scanner checking you out."*

"Same thing happened to Mel and Jason when they used the tram to return to the ship," his mother added. *"It*

identifies which race you belong to, so it'll know what sort of environment your tram will need. Or at least that's what we think it does."

A glowing circular band moved down the sides of the shaft until it reached the floor, then it rose to the ceiling again, whereupon the light vanished. Sean blinked against the retinal afterimage left upon his eyes. "Now what?"

"Now you wait. The tram should arrive any minute."

Sean peered down the tunnel. He didn't see anything coming. "How long do you think it'll take for us to get there?"

"I don't know. Probably a while. Mel thinks you're a long way from here. Perhaps as much as forty thousand miles."

Sean glanced at Kyra and Sandy. Their expressions were stunned; until then, none of them had had any idea they were so distant from the *Montero*. On the other hand, forty thousand miles—if that figure was correct—was barely an inch compared to Hex's total circumference. "Practically in the neighborhood," he said. "Want me to fetch some ice cream on the way home?"

His mother laughed. *"Thanks, but I may not be around when you arrive. Long story, but I'm going to be doing some exploring of my own. But there will be someone here to meet you, and Anne will continue to relay any transmissions we send to each other."*

"Good excuse," Sean muttered.

"What?"

"Never mind."

As Andromeda predicted, before long a cylindrical vehicle appeared from the tunnel. With little more than a whisper, it glided to a halt in front of the platform. Windows revealed a lighted interior, and Sean saw that the tram was vacant.

"It's here," he said into the mike. "Signing off now."

"Good luck," his mother said. *"Over and out."*

Sean switched off the transceiver, then bent down to pick up his pack. Kyra and Sandy did the same, but as they approached the tram, they noticed that its door remained shut. He was wondering why when he heard a sound behind him, and turned to see a transparent barrier slide down from the ceiling, sealing off the platform from the rest of the station.

"What's going on?" Kyra's eyes widened in alarm. "Why . . . ?"

A moment later, there was the sound of rushing air as vents opened within the ceiling. Sean suddenly understood; the tram didn't have its own airlock, so this part of the station had become one; the vents were flooding the platform with an oxygen-nitrogen mix while removing the ammonia-rich atmosphere of the *arsashi* habitat. As if to confirm this, he felt his ears pop as the pressure decreased slightly.

"Nice arrangement," he said. "They think of everything, don't they?"

Kyra nodded but didn't speak. She seemed apprehensive about boarding the tram. Stepping closer to her, Sean took her hand, gave it a reassuring squeeze. As before, he couldn't see her expression through her airmask, but she gripped his fingers tightly within her own.

The rush of air slowly faded, then the tram's doors slid open. They carried their packs inside, dropped them in a vacant area in front of the doors. The benches looked rather uncomfortable, but at least they were padded.

"Whoa. What is this?" Sandy jumped up from the bench she had just attempted to sit upon. "This thing just grabbed me!"

Kyra was a little more brave. She tentatively rested her rump upon another bench, and watched with interest as it re-formed itself around her body, gradually transforming itself into a comfortable chair complete with a backrest. "Not bad," she said to Sandy. "Try it."

"Like hell . . . !"

"Do it." Sean nodded toward the doors; they remained open, and the tram was still at the platform. "I don't think

this thing is going anywhere until we're seated." Sandy
scowled, then tentatively sat down beside Kyra, making a
face when the bench flowed up around her.

They'd barely taken their seats when the doors shut, and
the tram started moving. It didn't reenter the tunnel, though,
but instead continued on its way through the biopod.
Through the windows on the right side of the car, Sean saw
the dark landscape they had just crossed. Clusters of light
glimmered here and there upon the terrain; judging from
their distance, it appeared that the monorail led across the
top of the biopod's southern mountain range, just below the
lower edge of the ceiling.

"Can we take these off now?" Sandy asked.

Sean didn't reply, but instead carefully pulled down his
mask. He hesitated, then took a shallow breath. He didn't
start choking; the air was cool and breathable. He grinned
and nodded, and the two women gratefully removed their
own masks.

"Thank God." Kyra pushed back her parka hood and
pulled off her goggles. "I was getting really tired of that."

"You and me both." Sandy unzipped the front of her
parka and shrugged out of it. "It's warm in here, too." She
chuckled. "All we need is a hot shower and a cold brew, and
we're set."

Sean had been wearing his goggles for so long that they
were stuck to his face; he winced as he peeled them off.
Standing up to remove his parka, he noticed for the first
time another control panel, this one on the tram wall opposite the door they'd come through. It was identical to one
they'd found on the station platform, only this time a tiny
yellow light slowly traveled across the upper-left edge of
the hexagon.

It was impossible to tell how fast the tram was going.
With the windows showing little but the darkness outside,
he couldn't even guess at their rate of speed. But if the
biopod was a thousand miles long, and if the tram was traveling at—say, three hundred miles per hour, the average

rate of a maglev train—it would take a little more than three hours for them to reach the other end of just this one biopod. No telling how long it would take for them to get to Nueva Italia.

"I wouldn't count on getting a shower anytime soon." Reaching for his pack, he unstrapped his sleeping bag and dropped it on the floor. "Might as well make ourselves comfortable. I think we're in for a long ride."

EIGHTEEN

BY THE TIME ANDROMEDA, D'ANGUILO, AND ZEUS
reached the tram station, morning—or at least something that resembled morning—had dawned within
Nueva Italia.

"I don't think I'm ever going to get used to this." Andromeda gazed down upon the biopod as the lift approached the top of the escalator. As the artificial sky
gradually depolarized, sunlight filtered in through the ceiling, erasing the darkness that had lain across the rolling
terrain. "I like it when the sun actually comes up, not . . .
well, this."

D'Anguilo gave a wry smile but said nothing. He was
bent over his backpack, nervously checking it again—as
he'd already done twice already—to make sure that he
hadn't left anything behind. By contrast, Zeus was stifling
a yawn; he hadn't removed his pack since they'd boarded
the lift, and it looked as if he was ready for a hike.

"I'm sure you're not the only one, skipper," the chief

petty officer said. "Isn't it the *soranta* who have some elaborate religious ceremony every morning?"

"That was before they adopted *Sa'Tong*." D'Anguilo zipped shut a side pocket of his backpack, then opened another to peek inside. "Most of them ceased their sun rituals a long time ago." He glanced up at the ceiling, beyond which countless other hexagons were beginning to make their appearance. "That's assuming, of course, that they have their own habitat."

Andromeda followed his gaze. Again, she was reminded of the fact that humans were far from alone on Hex. Elsewhere in the vast Dyson sphere were other races: not just *danui* and *arsashi*, but also *hjadd*, *kua'tah*, *nord*, and no telling how many more. So far, humankind had met only a handful of other Talus races; there were dozens more yet to be encountered. Was it possible that they were all there? Only the *danui* knew . . . and they weren't telling.

"I'm sure we'll soon find out," she murmured. "If all goes well, I mean."

D'Anguilo straightened up from his pack. "I wouldn't worry, Captain. The *danui* asked you to come meet them. It wouldn't make sense for them to extend an invitation if they didn't—"

He was interrupted by a soft chime from the control panel, signaling that the lift had reached the top of the escalator. It slipped into a broad slot within the station veranda and came to a halt. Andromeda reached down to pick up her pack; without a word, she hefted it over her shoulder, then led the others off the lift and across the veranda to the platform.

As expected, the tunnel was empty. "Guess they want us to enter those coordinates before they send a tram," Andromeda said. Putting down her pack, she reached into a side pocket for the scroll that Zeus had brought her, then walked over to the station control panel. The same message that she'd read yesterday was still there when she unrolled the scroll, its long string of *danui* numbers unchanged.

She was about to enter the first digit into the panel's top

row when D'Anguilo reached forward to stop her. "Wait a minute," he said, blocking her hand with his own. "You're getting it wrong."

Andromeda frowned at him. "What do you mean?"

"Look at the bottom row." He pointed to the seven digits at the bottom of the screen. "If we're right, and that square is their version of a zero and the crosshatched diamond is their six, then they read from right to left, not left to right." He moved his finger to the scroll. "You were about to start with the figure on the far left, when you should start with the one on the far right."

"That makes sense, yeah." Zeus was peering over their shoulders. "If the bottom row is their way of showing us their numerical system, the top row would be entered the same way."

Andromeda nodded. Once again, she found herself being forced to admit that, however irritating Tom D'Anguilo might occasionally be, the expedition couldn't have gotten as far as it had without his intuition. Yet as she started over again, carefully entering the coordinates the way he'd indicated, she couldn't help but feel that something was wrong. She couldn't put her finger on it, but . . .

Never mind. She forced herself to concentrate on entering the nineteen-digit string in proper sequence. *Whatever it is, it can't be important.*

Andromeda entered the final digit, and the top row flashed in acknowledgment as, once again, a circular panel in the platform ceiling lit to capture the three of them in a shaft of light. They stood patiently while the station scanned them. A couple of minutes went by, then there was a rush of air from the tunnel as a tram appeared. It coasted to a stop at the platform, and its forward door cycled open, a silent invitation to board the vehicle.

Zeus started to step forward, but Andromeda raised a hand to stop him. "Just a sec," she said, then she touched the headset of the long-range transceiver slung beneath her left arm. "Team Two to Nueva Italia. Com check. Do you copy?"

"We copy, Team Two. Over." Jason Ressler's voice was clear in her earpiece; if she'd wanted to, Andromeda could have walked to the veranda railing and waved to her first officer in the base camp far below.

"Affirmative, Nueva Italia. Over." Andromeda switched to a different channel. "Survey Two to *Montero*. Com check. Do you copy? Over."

A few seconds passed, then she heard Anne's voice, a little less clear than Jason's. *"Montero to Survey Two. Roger that. Good luck, Captain. Over."*

"Thank you, *Montero*. Over and out." Satisfied that their radio lifeline was operational—at least for the time being—Andromeda switched off the transceiver, then bent over to pick up her backpack. "All right, then . . . let's go."

The tram was identical to the ones that *Montero's* crew had ridden before; Andromeda suspected that it might even be the same vehicle. As soon as she stepped aboard, though, she realized that it was different. Her nose caught the faint aroma of ocean surf; the windows had water on them, and the benches were slightly moist. It appeared that the interior been soaked recently and hadn't completely dried.

"What gives?" Zeus asked. "Did they hose down this thing before they sent it to us?"

D'Anguilo noticed a small puddle on the floor. He knelt beside it and, before Andromeda could stop him, dipped a fingertip into the puddle and laid it on the tip of his tongue.

"Salt water," he said. "What do you want to bet that the last habitat this thing visited has an aquatic environment?"

"Your guess is as good as mine." Andromeda set down her pack. The doors shut behind them, but the tram didn't move. Perhaps it was waiting until they were all safely seated. She picked a bench near the windows that looked a little drier than the others; as before, the memory-material of its pad began conforming to her body as soon as she sat down. D'Anguilo and Zeus dropped their packs in the cargo space and took seats beside her, and without any further the delay, the tram started forward.

This time, though, it didn't reenter the node from which it had emerged but instead shot down the track until it entered a transparent tube running across the top of Nueva Italia's southern mountain range. Through the windows, they could see the valley spread out below them. Clouds had begun to form below the ceiling, casting shadows across grassy plains and wooded hills. No sign of habitation; the base camp was already lost to sight. Andromeda wondered if this was what Coyote had looked like to the crew of the URSS *Alabama* when they'd set foot on the new world for the first time.

"Funny," Zeus said. "You'd think that, if we're being taken to meet the *danui*, they'd pick a more direct route."

Andromeda nodded. The biopod was a thousand miles long; it would take hours to cross it. No wonder she'd been told to expect a long journey. "Maybe they want us to look over the real estate." She turned to D'Anguilo. "What do you think? Is the rest of the hexagon going to look like this part of it?"

"Maybe . . . but I sort of doubt it." He folded his arms across his chest, assuming a professorial posture. "If what I suspect is true, and the *danui* adopted geospheric design principles in building Hex, then we'll probably have a number of different environments. Desert, arctic tundra, maybe even miniature seas . . ."

"Okay, stop right there." Andromeda held up a hand. "Tell me what you think is going on here."

"I'm not ready to . . ."

"Oh no, you don't." She shook her head. "This is at least the second or third time you've said that you suspect something about this place, but when I've asked you what you meant, you've backed off. Quit stalling."

D'Anguilo gave her a sidelong glance; he appeared to realize that she was serious because he shrugged as though resigning himself to the inevitable. "Very well, then, but understand that this is all still tentative. Until we meet the *danui*, I'm not sure how much any of this is true."

"Understood."

"Okay . . . we know this is a Dyson sphere, and that it's comprised of billions of habitats, with each one probably unique to the race that inhabits it. Something of this scale and complexity not only suggests extraordinary engineering skills . . . It also suggests environmental control to a degree that we can barely imagine. If the *danui* hadn't accomplished that, then there's no way that Hex could function. It would become uninhabitable, no matter how well it was built."

"All right, I follow you. Go on."

"Good. Now, think about what we've seen so far. The solar sails and magnetic cables, and how they work together to keep Hex in proper rotation while supplying energy and shielding the biopods from cosmic radiation. The way the *Montero* was automatically . . . or, rather, autonomously . . . guided to this habitat, and the way that it was docked in the node. How the ceiling darkens by itself to furnish night and lightens again to provide daylight. How the tram stations operate . . . scanning us before we climb aboard, then sending a tram that has our own atmosphere, even though the race that used it last might have gills instead of lungs. Even these seats"—he patted the bench they shared, which had risen to provide a cushion for their backs—"change according to our needs. What does all that tell you?"

"That they've got one hell of an AI running this place," Zeus said.

"Maybe, but think about that, too. Hex is . . . how big? One hundred eighty-six million miles in diameter? The biggest and best AI we've ever built would be able to control only this one habitat, and it would be a strain to do so. The *danui* are well ahead of us, technologically speaking, but I haven't heard of their being capable of building AIs of such magnitude. Sorry, but I have a hard time believing in *deus ex machina*."

"What?"

"Literally, the god from the machine . . . and I don't believe that gods can be built." D'Anguilo shook his head and went on. "No, I think they've developed something less . . . well, mechanistic . . . than a mere AI." He paused. "I think Hex may be a geophysiological superintelligence."

Andromeda blinked. "Come again?"

"A living world." He took a deep breath. "I think Hex is alive."

She said nothing for a moment but instead stared out the windows at the scenery rushing by. No one spoke until Zeus coughed in his fist.

"You gotta be kidding," he muttered.

"I know it's hard to swallow. Believe me, the first time I heard about this sort of thing, I didn't believe it either. But the Gaia hypothesis . . . which is what this is all about . . . has been around since the late twentieth century, when it was first put forth by James Lovelock and Lynn Margulis. No one was able to prove or disprove it at the time because the only available test subject was Earth, and so there was no real means of comparison within its own solar system." He shrugged. "It didn't help that it was embraced by mystics and pseudoscientists who carried on about Goddess Earth and so forth while completely misunderstanding what Lovelock and Margulis were saying . . . that Earth itself is a living organism, capable of regulating its own environment." A brief smile. "Besides, remember what the *hjadd* call this place. *Tanaash-haq* . . . 'the living world.' "

"And you think that's what Hex is? A living world?" Andromeda was having trouble hiding her skepticism.

Zeus gazed up at the tram's ceiling. "Hello, Hex? Thanks for the hospitality, but we'd like to go home now . . ."

"That's not what I mean." D'Anguilo glared at him before turning to Andromeda again. "Hex isn't sentient, or at least not in the way we normally define conscious self-awareness. But we've already seen that it's capable of regulating its own environment . . . or environments, as the case may be . . . and the more I see of this place, the more I believe that the *danui* adopted something akin to biospheric principles when they designed it."

Andromeda thought about it for a moment. "So let me get this straight. Hex is a living . . . um, organism . . . but not one that we can communicate with . . ."

"Not in the way we usually communicate, no." D'Anguilo looked at Zeus. "You can talk to this tram all you want, but it's not going to answer you. But it will recognize that you're human and adjust itself to accommodate your needs."

Zeus frowned. "Any decent comp could do that."

"True . . . but for how many trams, all working at once? And not just trams, but also for everything else that goes into maintaining billions of habitats." D'Anguilo nodded toward the landscape whipping past the windows. "As I said, this is beyond the capability of any AI, no matter how powerful it might be. Something more organic, more adaptive is required for that."

Andromeda stood up. "I'm going to have to think about this. I'm not saying that you're wrong, Tom. I'm just not sure that you're right, either." She walked back to where they'd left their packs. "In the meantime, we might as well settle in. I have a hunch we've got a long ride ahead of us."

As it turned out, she was correct. They soon became bored with gazing out the windows, and although the benches were reasonably comfortable, they found that they needed to unroll their sleeping bags and lay them out across the floor in order to take a nap. They'd brought food with them—compressed rations, along with some apples they'd taken from the orchard near the base camp—and around midday, Zeus made lunch for them. They made small talk while they ate, wondering how much farther the tram would travel before it reached its destination.

Not long afterward, Andromeda felt the call of nature. Figuring that she'd have to find a bench to squat behind—messy and with very little privacy, but it couldn't be helped—she ventured to the other end of the tram. She was about to kneel behind the rearmost bench when she noticed the door behind the tram's aft cargo area.

She'd seen this door before, the first time she'd ridden the tram, but hadn't taken the moment to see where it led. Curious, she walked toward it. The door slid open, revealing a small compartment the size of a public toilet. Inside was a padded bench, with what appeared to be a round hatch in its center.

"No," she whispered. "It can't be that easy."

But it was. When Andromeda entered the compartment, the door quietly shut behind her. And when she tentatively laid a hand upon the bench hatch, it opened like a sphincter, exposing a funnel leading into darkness. A rank odor wafted up from the hole; she hesitated before carefully sitting down on top of it, and the bench re-formed itself to match the contours of her body.

The purpose of the compartment was obvious. And as odd as it might seem, that was when she realized that D'Anguilo might be right.

It took a little more than three hours for the tram to travel the length of Nueva Italia. She had just woken up from a nap to see the vehicle rush past what appeared to be another tram station, this one positioned at the eastern end of the biopod. The tram didn't stop, though, but hurtled through the station and entered the tunnel leading into the adjacent node. A second later, the tram made a left turn; through the windows on either side, she saw tracks appear to both the left and right of the one they were on.

She was about to say something to Zeus and D'Anguilo when, all of a sudden, another tram swept past to the left. It was headed in the opposite direction, so she barely had time to see it. Through its windows, she had the briefest glimpse of figures, bipedal yet four-armed, peering back at her. Then the other tram was gone, as quickly as it had appeared.

"Did you see that?" she asked no one in particular.

"Uh-huh." Zeus's voice was little more than a whisper.

"I'm just surprised that we haven't seen this before."
D'Anguilo was trying to affect a matter-of-fact tone, but
Andromeda could tell that he was just as startled as they
were. "It would make sense that there would be other
trams."

Another tunnel branched off to the right, but their tram
wasn't taking it. Instead, it continued to follow the middle
track; it appeared that it was making its way around the circumference of the node that it had just entered. Something
about the direction it was taking seemed familiar to Andromeda; remembering what it was, she grinned.

"I think we're on an express line," she said. "Sort of like
subways on Earth. You've got two local lines . . . one track
going one way, another going the other . . . Between them
is an express line that cuts past all the stations until the
train reaches its destination, when it switches back to the
local lines."

D'Anguilo nodded. "That makes sense. I guess we had
to go all the way across Nueva Italia until we were switched
to the express line in this node."

Andromeda thought about it a moment. "If that's correct, then we should be leaving the node and entering another habitat."

"But we haven't left the node," Zeus said. "Look . . .
we're still in a tunnel."

He was right. The tram had just made another turn, this
time to the right. Instead of emerging into another biopod,
though, it continued to hurtle down a tunnel, with opaque
walls on both sides of the track.

"Maybe you can't see the biopods from the express
line," Andromeda said. "We're in another habitat, but we
have no way of telling which one."

"I suppose that would make sense if you want to maintain privacy between adjacent habitats," D'Anguilo said.
"You know what they say . . . Good fences make good
neighbors. And you don't necessarily want to see what's
going on in your neighbor's backyard."

Andromeda settled back on her sleeping bag. "In any

case, I think we're probably going to be riding this thing for a while longer." She crooked her elbow across her eyes. "Wake me up when we get there."

Yet when she woke up again, several hours later, the tram was still in motion. D'Anguilo was asleep by then, but Zeus was awake. He told her that the tram had crossed another node and entered yet another tunnel. They were still on the express line, but he couldn't tell whether the tram was still in the same habitat or if it had entered another. And the control panel was of little use to them; the map displayed only the local lines on the hexagon through which the tram was traveling, with the top row of *danui* digits their sole means of identifying which one it was.

That was the way things went for the next ten hours. Andromeda, D'Anguilo, and Zeus slept in shifts; when they were awake, they shared meals together, although Andromeda was careful to make sure that they preserved their food and water for as long as possible. D'Anguilo had a chess program loaded into his datapad; they took turns at playing games on its holo screen, and that was the only thing that kept them from going crazy with boredom.

Andromeda tried to contact the *Montero*, but received only static; apparently radio waves were unable to penetrate the tunnel walls of the express line. Staring out the windows at the darkened tunnel, she found herself wondering whether Sean and his party had yet managed to make it to Nueva Italia and what she'd say to him once they saw each other again.

She was thinking about that very thing when the tram entered another node. Another tram rushed by in the opposite direction; judging from the quick glance she had of its windows, she had the impression that it was empty. Then their tram swerved to the right, and she realized that it was beginning to decelerate.

Zeus had been asleep on the floor. He must have felt the change in velocity because his eyes opened. "Are we stopping?" he asked.

"I think so." D'Anguilo was peering out the windows. "We're on a local line again."

Standing up from the bench where she'd been sitting, Andromeda hurried over to where she'd left her gear. "Get your things. I think we're getting off here."

The three of them barely had time to stuff their belongings back in their packs before the tram slowed down as if to enter a station. As it glided to a halt, Andromeda gazed through the windows on the tram's right side. Although she could see the illumination of a station control panel, there was only darkness beyond. Indeed, it didn't appear as if they'd entered a biopod; the station looked more like the one inside the node where the *Montero* was docked.

Andromeda quickly walked over to the control panel and examined its map. She was right; a node in the top left corner was illuminated. So they weren't in a biopod. Yet the coordinates appeared to match the ones she'd been given. She was beginning to wonder why the tram was stopping there when the doors opened.

"We're here." Picking up his pack, D'Anguilo stepped through the open door. "Let's go see . . ." His voice trailed off as he stopped outside the tram, apparently astonished by something he'd just seen.

"What are you looking at?" Hoisting her pack across her left shoulder, Andromeda hurried to follow him, with Zeus close behind. "Is this . . . ?"

Then she found herself unable to speak as well, leaving it to Zeus to say what she and D'Anguilo felt.

"Oh, my God," he whispered.

At the edge of the platform was a transparent barrier. Beyond that, though, was . . . nothing.

No veranda. No station. No biopod. Not even a hexagon.

There was simply a vast, empty space, thousands of miles in diameter and bordered on all sides by the biopods and nodes of adjacent habitats. Beyond that distant horizon lay the tessellated sky of Hex: countless hexagons curving upward and outward, gradually diminishing in size before the farthermost disappeared within the glare of HD 76700.

If there had ever been a hexagon there, it had long since vanished.

"What the hell happened here?" Andromeda murmured.

"For some, it was the end of the world," a voice behind her replied.

NINETEEN

EVEN BEFORE THE TRAM REACHED ITS DESTINATION, Sean realized that something was wrong.

The journey took a little more than twenty hours. Although it didn't take long to figure out that the tram was on an express line that went through hexagons without stopping, he soon lost count of how many nodes it had passed through and had no idea how many miles they had traveled. They could see little through the windows except tunnel walls, and the occasional tram that sped past in the opposite direction.

Sean took turns with Kyra and Sandy standing watch while the others slept. Although the benches changed shape to accommodate the human form, he found it hard to get comfortable on them. He and Kyra spread their sleeping bags out across the floor and zipped them together, which enabled them to sleep in each other's arms while Sandy politely sat at the other end of the vehicle. They ate as little as possible, conserving their rations in case the trip took longer than expected; keeping their Corps survival training in mind, they only sipped at their water bottles.

They should have been getting closer to the hexagon where the *Montero* was docked, but after twelve hours it dawned on Sean that this wasn't happening. At first, he thought it was only some sort of illusion that he was beginning to feel lighter, but when Sandy happened to mention the same thing and Kyra chimed in to say that she didn't feel as if she weighed as much as she normally did, Sean tried an experiment. Pulling a survival knife from his pack, he held it at shoulder height, then let it drop from his fingers. It was hard to tell for certain, but it seemed as if the knife took a half second longer than normal to hit the floor. Three hours later, though, when they repeated the experiment again, they were sure: the knife was taking longer to fall.

That could mean only one thing: the tram wasn't heading toward Nueva Italia, where the surface gravity was 1 g, but farther away from Hex's equator, where the gravity would become incrementally less. But as to exactly where they were going, they had no clue.

There was no way to contact the *Montero*; apparently the express line's tunnel walls blocked radio transmissions. Nor was there any way for them to change the tram's direction; even if they'd known the correct coordinates for Nueva Italia, Sandy discovered that any attempts to enter new *danui* numbers into the control panel were futile. Once the tram was on its way, apparently it didn't stop for anything. They had little choice but to wait for it to arrive at the destination for which it had been programmed and hope that they weren't in trouble once they got there.

One thing was clear, though. Somehow or other, Sean's mother had given him the wrong coordinates.

He had just finished using the lavatory in the rear of the tram—he'd never get used to it, as ordinary as it seemed—when he felt the vehicle begin to slow. Hastily zipping shut his fly, he opened the door and trotted back up front.

"Are we stopping?" he asked.

"Looks like it." Kyra was peering out the windows on the tram's right side. "We entered another node about a minute ago and switched tracks right after that."

Sandy was already kneeling to roll up her sleeping bag. "'Bout time. I don't care where we are, just as long as we get off this damn . . ."

"I want to get off, too, but it doesn't change the fact that we're lost." Sean hated to put it as bluntly as that—one look at Kyra told him that she was as frightened as she'd been when they'd crash-landed in the *arsashi* biopod—but there was no point in sugarcoating the situation. "If we do, it's going to be just long enough for us to . . ."

"Attention, please . . ."

The new voice startled Sean so much that he almost fell over a bench as he swung around to see where it came from. It spoke Anglo, without any trace of accent or even gender, and appeared to be coming from the control panel.

"Attention, please." The map on the upper half of the panel had vanished, to be replaced by an androgynous human face. *"You are entering a habitat with an atmospheric composition different from your own . . ."*

"Where?" Sean rushed to the screen. "Where the hell are we?"

The face ignored him. *"It is strongly recommended that you don breathing apparatus before leaving the transportation system,"* it continued, smiling as calmly as if it were delivering a weather forecast. *"If you do not have proper equipment, please remain in vehicle."*

"What if we don't . . . ?"

The face disappeared as if Sean had never spoken. Apparently it was an automatic recording, not designed to interact with passengers. The map reappeared; Sean noticed that the node in its lower center was lighted, with an arrow pointing to the biopod to the lower right. That was where the tram was headed, whether he liked it or not.

"Airpacks," he said. "Get 'em on, fast."

Kyra and Sandy scrambled for their backpacks. Along

with their winter gear, they'd put away their airpacks shortly after leaving the *arsashi* habitat, figuring that they wouldn't need them again. The tram was still decelerating as Sean retrieved his breathing gear and goggles. Like the women, he wore only his Corps unitard, waistcoat, and boots; he adjusted the airmask's regulator and tested its flow, and muttered a curse against the fact that he'd have to breathe through a mask again.

The tram left the node and came to a stop at a platform. Through the windows, Sean saw a station that superficially resembled the one in the *arsashi* biopod except that it appeared that another transparent barrier was in place between the platform and the veranda. The doors opened, and he and Kyra started to pick up their backpacks, but Sandy hesitated.

"What if we don't get out?" she asked. "I mean . . . if this isn't where we're supposed to be, why don't we just stay on the tram and wait until it takes us where we want to go?"

"And how do we find out where *that* is?" Sean shook his head. "We've got to get in touch with the ship and have someone relay the transmission to my mother." He paused. "She gave us the wrong coordinates . . . That much is obvious. But we won't know what the right ones are unless we talk to her . . ."

"And we can't do that unless we leave the tram because the transceiver doesn't work here." Kyra nodded, understanding what he meant. "He's right. It's the only way."

Sandy let out her breath. Sean couldn't see her expression through her mask, but he had little doubt that she was scowling. "Yeah . . . okay," she muttered, reluctantly bending down to retrieve her pack from the floor. "Let's do it and get out of here."

The tram doors closed behind them. A few seconds later, it moved away, disappearing down the tunnel. As it did, the ceiling scanner came on again. Its beam swept across them; when it was done, the transparent barrier moved upward, allowing the biopod's atmosphere to enter the platform.

Heat, uncomfortably humid and cloying, hit them like a wave. Putting down his pack, Sean removed his waistcoat and rolled up his unitard sleeves; Kyra and Sandy did the same. He touched a stud on the side of his mask; the red type of the heads-up display appeared within his goggles, showing the atmospheric composition. Mainly oxygen, but with larger than normal amounts of nitrogen; the pressure was only 235.6 millibars, thin by Coyote standards. They'd be able to breathe the stuff, but only for a short time; without airpacks, they'd soon succumb to decompression sickness.

They wouldn't need their goggles, at least. He pulled them off and hung them from a belt loop. Then, curious as to where they'd landed, he walked out onto the veranda, with Kyra and Sandy close behind.

Beyond the railing lay what appeared to be jungle, but unlike any he'd visited in Coyote's more remote equatorial regions. The slope leading down from the tram station was dense with foliage: enormous ferns, bushes with serrated, sharp-looking leaves, trees that resembled oversized weeds. The humid air was alive with the cries, chirps, and grunts of birds, insects, and animals invisible yet nonetheless present. The light was dim and had a greenish tint; a thick, wet mist prevented them from seeing anything clearly beyond a few dozen yards, and even the biopod ceiling was cloaked by a solid wall of clouds.

"Oh, man," Sandy murmured, "this place looks nasty."

"I think it's beautiful," Kyra said.

"You would." Sandy glared at her, then turned to Sean. "Hurry up with the radio. I don't want to hang around."

Sean pulled the transceiver from under his shoulder and propped it up on the railing. Unlike Sandy, he was intrigued by the place, almost reluctant to leave. It had a certain primeval majesty, and compared to the cold terrain of the *arsashi* biopod, its warmth was something of a relief. Indeed, this was close to how he'd originally imagined the habitable world of the *danui* system to be before the expedition had discovered otherwise.

Sandy was right, though. The fact remained that they

were lost; the sooner they found a way out of there, the better. He turned on the transceiver and pointed its antenna toward the ceiling, guessing at the direction in which it should be oriented, then switched to the VHF band and unhooked the hand mike.

"Survey team to *Montero*," he said, "please come in. Repeat, survey team to *Montero*, Carson speaking. Do you copy? Over."

He had to reiterate the hail three times before Anne Smith's voice came through the static. She sounded more tinny than before, and Sean guessed that he was probably at the edge of the reception range. *"Montero to Survey One, we copy. Corporal Carson, where are you?"*

Sean couldn't help himself; he laughed out loud. "Damned if I know. We followed the coordinates my mother . . . the captain, I mean . . . gave me, and wound up someplace other than where we ought to be."

"You're not at Nueva Italia?"

"No. We're most definitely not." His lip curled. "I just wanted to thank her for the directions. They were really useful."

"Sean . . ." Kyra began.

A long pause, then *Montero*'s com officer returned. *"I'm sorry, Corporal, but I can't reach the captain. She boarded a tram yesterday morning, and we haven't heard from her since. It appears that something is interfering with her signal."*

Sean closed his eyes. It was the same problem he'd had earlier; the transceivers didn't work in the tram system. From the corner of his eye, he saw Kyra and Sandy watching him. "Well . . . all right, then," he said at last. "When you hear from her again, let her know what the problem is, and that she screwed up somehow. Until then"—he glanced at the others—"I guess we'll try to figure out things from our end. Maybe see if we can find someone who can help us."

"Wilco. Good luck."

"Thanks, *Montero*. Survey team, over and out."

Sandy grabbed his arm as he folded the antenna and put away the mike. "What do you mean, see if we can find someone? You don't mean . . . ?" Her voice trailed off as her gaze turned toward the green chaos beyond the veranda.

"I don't see why not." Sean was careful to leave the transceiver switched on as he slung it beneath his arm again. Just in case his mother should call; he was looking forward to having words with her. "Odds are, this place is inhabited."

"That's probably a good bet," Kyra said. "Look . . ."

She pointed to the edge of the veranda. Just as in the *arsashi* biopod, an escalator led down the mountainside from the tram station, its lift conveniently parked at the top. Beside it was what appeared to be a footpath.

"There. You see?" Sean cocked a thumb at the escalator. "With any luck, we'll find someone down there who'll help us out. Just like the *arsashi*."

"You're counting on a lot, aren't you?" Sandy stared at the escalator. "Sean, I've followed your lead until now, but . . . man, this place gives me the creeps. I think we ought to wait here until your mother gets back to us and . . ."

"And does what? Give us some more bogus coordinates?" Sean turned away from the railing. "Sorry, but I'm not counting on her again." He grinned. "Besides, we're explorers, aren't we? So let's explore."

Figuring that they wouldn't be there long, they decided to leave their packs at the station. But when they stepped aboard the lift, Sean noticed that its control panel showed signs of not having been used in a while; its surface was spotted with rust and mold, and the descent button stuck a bit when he pressed it. The escalator was still functional, though, and the lift slowly began making its way down the incline, shuddering every now and then.

As it descended, Sean examined the path running alongside the escalator. It was paved with stepping-stones that appeared to be almost randomly placed, overlapping one another in a crazy-quilt pattern, with no two exactly alike.

If they were stairs, then it didn't seem as though they had been made for bipedal feet. Wondering who—or what— lived there, he found himself suddenly nervous about meeting the residents of this particular habitat.

The foliage became more dense the farther down they went, and when the lift finally reached the bottom, they found that the escalator ended at the edge of a vast swamp. Murky brown water lapped against an overgrown shoreline; a river curled away from the escalator base, leading into mist-covered wetlands. A large red bird, ostrich-necked and with broad serrated wings, took off from its hiding place behind one of the oversized ferns and flapped away, screeching in alarm.

There didn't appear to be any paths leading through the brush; when Sean stepped off the escalator, he noticed that the ground trembled and sagged beneath his boots and realized that he was walking on a thick bed of floating moss. If there was any dry land in that biopod, there probably wasn't much of it. But just as he was beginning to wonder whether they should turn around and go back to the tram station, Kyra pointed to something floating in the water on the other side of the escalator.

"Does that look like a boat to you?" she asked.

They carefully picked their way across the floating moss to the object, which was tied up to a small, twisted tree. Yes, it was a boat, no doubt about it; about twelve feet long, shallow-hulled and flat-bottomed, it was fashioned from reeds that had been tightly woven together. It seemed like a frail thing, but when Sean tentatively climbed aboard, he discovered that it was watertight. Two double-bladed paddles lay athwart its bow and stern; they resembled those of a kayak, except longer and with two deep grooves on either side of their centers.

"I think it can carry all of us," Sean said. Although there were no seats, the boat was obviously meant to be used by two individuals, sitting fore and aft, with enough room in the middle for a passenger.

"I don't know about this." Again, Sandy was hesitant. "Maybe we should just leave it alone. It probably belongs to someone else . . ."

"Of course it belongs to someone else." Carefully sitting cross-legged in the stern, Sean picked up one of the paddles. It was lighter than it appeared, but he couldn't fit his hands into the grooves; whoever used it had a smaller grasp than a human. "If we find them, we'll apologize for borrowing it for a little while."

"Assuming we're able to talk to them."

"Only one way to find out." Sean nodded toward the front of the boat. "C'mon, get in. We'll go just a little way and turn back if we don't find anyone."

Despite her reluctance, Sandy climbed into the bow; she was stronger than Kyra, and they'd need her muscles for the other paddle. Kyra took the middle position; although the gunnels were only a couple of inches above the water, the boat didn't sink under their combined weight. It took Sean a couple of minutes to untie the mooring line—its clumsy knot could only be described as a double granny—but once the boat was floating free, he used his paddle to push away from the tree.

The river was more narrow than the one they'd seen in the *arsashi* habitat. It branched off in all directions, with tributaries sometimes rejoining the main channel after flowing around small floating islands but more often disappearing entirely from sight. The landscape was a labyrinthine swamp, potentially confusing to anyone but its inhabitants. As they followed the channel, Sean carefully memorized landmarks—a particularly tall fern here, a strange-looking weed-tree there—to prevent getting lost on the way back.

The current was with them, though, and it wasn't long before the escalator disappeared from sight. By then, they had company. What appeared to be clumps of floating wood drifted away from the shoreline and slowly converged on the boat until they moved alongside it on both sides. Kyra had allowed one hand to dip into the river, idly letting her fingertips skim across the top of the brown water. The nearest of the clumps suddenly darted forward, and Sean barely had time to shout a warning when a blunt head emerged from the driftwood and sharp-toothed jaws snapped at Kyra's fingers. She squeaked in alarm and jerked her hand away before the creature could take off a finger or two. She kept her hands out of the water after that, but the creatures continued to follow the boat all the same; Sean realized that they burrowed into fallen pieces of wood and used them to hide themselves from their intended prey.

Tall, strange-looking trees grew at the riverbank: gnarled, slender roots rose from the water to support a thick trunk from which oval fronds hung almost all the way to the river. Nearly sixty feet tall, the trees loomed above the waterway like sentinels. What appeared to be eggs floated in clusters near their bottoms; Sean was about to suggest that they paddle closer to examine them when he saw one of the driftwood-disguised predators approach a tree. As before, it swam slowly, as if mimicking river debris, but it was only a couple of feet from the eggs when the tree abruptly moved forward on its roots, and its middle frond stabbed down into the water. A violent splash, a harsh cry, then the frond—which Sean now saw to be an immense beak—rose from the water, the creature impaled on its tip. The walking tree tossed the smaller predator up in the air; its beak opened wide, revealing a leathery-looking maw, then caught the creature on its way down and swallowed it whole, wooden shell and all.

"A mimic," Kyra said quietly. "An animal evolved to resemble a plant." She pointed to the egg cluster. "Those are probably its eggs. It protects them and uses them as lures at the same time."

"I don't care." Sandy's voice shook as she glanced back at her and Sean. "Let's get out of here. I'm serious."

Sean ignored her. Something else had caught his eye. Not far ahead, he saw something on the left side of the river: two large, cone-shaped mounds, resembling immense anthills, that rose above the ferns and weed-trees along the river-bank. The longer he studied them, the less natural in origin they appeared to be.

"I want to check those out," he said, pointing to the mounds. "If there's nothing there, we'll turn back. But I've got a feeling . . ."

"They're dwellings?" Kyra gazed at them. "You may be right. Let's go see."

"Let's not," Sandy grumbled, but she thrust her paddle into the water. "Oh, hell. No one listens to me anyway."

Careful to avoid the walking trees, they paddled farther downstream. As they came closer to shore, they could see the mounds more clearly, and it soon became obvious that Sean was correct. Narrow, ramplike terraces wound their way up their sloping walls, and holes that could have been either windows or doors were spaced irregularly along the ramps.

There was no movement from the dwellings, though, even when Sean and Sandy maneuvered the boat close enough that it could have been easily spotted by the occupants. Along the riverbank, foliage had been cleared away to make room for a wharf. Boats much like the one they were using were tied up at a floating dock, and woven baskets on the beach were further evidence of habitation.

"Maybe it's deserted," Sandy said quietly.

"Or maybe it's not, but whoever lives here doesn't want to meet us." Kyra's voice was almost a whisper. "I don't like this."

The silence of the place made Sean uneasy. They hadn't traveled very far from the escalator, perhaps no more than a mile or two; it wasn't too late for them to turn around. "Maybe you're right," he murmured. "Perhaps we should . . ."

A quiet splash from the right, followed by a muffled creak. Looking over his shoulder, he saw that they were no longer alone.

So quietly that Sean hadn't heard them, three more boats had emerged from behind the ferns growing along the op-posite shore. Within each boat sat three creatures that resembled giant insects: elongated heads with four bulbous compound eyes, two on either side of narrow snouts; chitin exoskeletons covering angular bodies that looked much like those of grasshoppers or mantises; four multijointed arms, which grasped boat paddles within pincherlike claws. Their long antennae constantly twitched as they rowed toward the human intruders; as they came closer, Sean could hear the rapid clicking of their mandibles.

Kyra and Sandy saw them almost the same moment Sean did, and Sandy yelped in alarm before Sean was able to stop her. "Quiet!" he snapped, raising a hand to shush her. "Just be calm. They may not mean us any harm." But it was hard to miss the fact that the creatures riding in the middle of each boat held javelin-like weapons, or that it looked as if they were ready to hurl them at the slightest provocation.

Another sound brought his attention back to the village. Other creatures were coming out of the mounds. Dozens, perhaps hundreds, swarmed from the holes along the ramps, moving quickly upon four legs; the purpose of the strange steps he'd noticed earlier was now apparent. Many of them carried the same weapons as those on the boats, and as they rushed toward the wharf, the staccato clicking of their jaws filled the humid air.

"This is impossible." Kyra's voice was low, and her eyes were wide, but she didn't seem to be afraid as much as fascinated.

Sean glanced at her. "Why? Because this place is inhabited?"

"No." Staring at the creatures, she shook her head. "I recognize these things . . . and they're supposed to be extinct."

TWENTY

ANDROMEDA TURNED TO SEE A *HJADD* STANDING BE-hind her.

Resembling a shell-less tortoise standing upright on its hind legs, heshe wore a togalike outfit embroidered with intricate designs and a translator disk suspended by a slender chain from around hisher long neck. The *hjadd* wasn't wearing any breathing apparatus, though, and it wasn't until Andromeda caught her faint reflection from a transparent pane between them that she realized heshe was standing inside an enclosed booth.

"Greetings, Captain Carson." The *hjadd* raised hisher left hand, six webbed fingers spread apart. As heshe spoke, the croaks, grunts, and whistles of hisher natural voice emerged from the translator as a gender-neutral, Anglo-speaking human voice. "Many apologies if I have startled you. It was not my intent to do so."

The hell it wasn't, Andromeda thought. The *hjadd* had a tendency to sneak up on people unannounced. But she forced a smile as she raised her own left hand. "Not a bit . . . just a little surprised, that's all."

A long, stuttering hiss from the lipless beak that Andromeda recognized as the *hjadd* equivalent of laughter. "Then you will forgive me for making an unexpected appearance," heshe said. "I arrived just a little while before you did." The *hjadd* gestured to the transparent barrier between them. "It gave our hosts time to provide this enclosure so that I would not have to wear an environment suit as my people do when visiting your world. The *danui* are inscrutable, but they are also capable of common courtesy."

"If you say so." Andromeda dropped her pack to the platform floor, then stepped a little closer to the booth. "I was under the impression that we were going to be meeting one of them. Instead . . ."

"Instead, you found me." One of hisher heavy-lidded eyes winked at her. "Allow me to introduce myself. I am Sashatasma Jahd Sa-Fhadda, and I am my people's Prime Emissary to *tanaash-haq*. You may call me Jahd."

Andromeda started to nod; remembering that the gesture had an opposite meaning for the *hjadd*, she stopped herself. "Obviously, you already know who I am," she said, and Jahd's head swung back and forth upon hisher neck. She turned to D'Anguilo and Zeus. "Then let me introduce my companions. This is . . ."

"Dr. Thomas D'Anguilo, formerly of the University of New Florida and currently an executive vice president of Janus, and Zeus Brandt, your chief petty officer." Again, the sibilant hiss. "There is little we do not know about your ship or its crew and passengers, Captain. In fact, we have been closely monitoring your mission ever since you entered this system." Independent of each other, Jhad's eyes swung toward D'Anguilo and Zeus. "Nevertheless, it is a pleasure to meet you both."

"Likewise," Zeus said quietly, his tone distrustful.

D'Anguilo tactfully cleared his throat. "The message

sent to us . . . Captain Carson, I mean . . . led us to believe that we would be meeting with the *danui*. Why are you here? Are the *danui* coming, too?"

The serrated fin on the back of Jahd's head lifted slightly; a sign of agitation, if Andromeda's knowledge of *hjadd* emotional responses was correct. "The *danui* will not be attending. They have asked my people to act as intermediaries between your race and them, at least for the time being. Whether or not they will allow you to meet with one of their representatives will depend on the outcome of this meeting."

"Of course. I understand." D'Anguilo shared a glance with Andromeda. "The *danui* do have a certain reputation for shyness."

Andromeda wasn't satisfied. "When my ship entered this system and approached Hex . . . *tanaash-haq*, that is . . ."

"*Tanaash-haq* is what we call this world, just as Hex is what you have come to call it." Again, Jahd's head went back and forth. "Every race here has its own name for this place."

"Whatever you say." Andromeda impatiently shook her head, not caring how the Prime Emissary interpreted the gesture. "Our first attempts to make contact were ignored, and subsequent attempts were met with text messages in your language. Are you saying that you've been . . . ah, intermediaries . . . all along?"

"The *danui* asked us to speak with you because our race has the longest history of communication with your own." Jahd's head rose a little higher upon hisher neck. "You probably would not have learned about this place for quite some time had it not been for the *nord*. They told your people about *tanaash-haq* before the *danui* were ready to reveal it themselves. That is unfortunate, but when the *danui* found out that it had happened, their emissary to the Talus requested that we act as . . . 'go-betweens,' as I understand your term for our role."

"So why all the mystery?" Andromeda asked. "Why not simply tell us what we'd find when we got here and what we should expect?"

"The *danui* have their reasons," Jahd said. "You'll learn them soon enough . . . if they want you to do so."

"But why . . . ?"

Another hiss. "So many questions, Captain . . . and yet you fail to ask the most obvious one." Jahd raised hisher left hand again, this time to beckon toward the broad window at the edge of the platform. "What is this place, and why were you directed to come here? I would think you would want to know that."

"I'm sure you're going to tell us," Zeus said dryly.

The fin rose again. "So I shall," Jahd replied, hisher left eye flickering toward him, "but you first must learn the history of *tanaash-haq.*"

Heshe turned toward the window. "Hex is very old," heshe continued. "By your reckoning, the *danui* started building it nearly five thousand years ago, after a natural calamity occurred within their solar system. The orbit of its outermost planet became unstable because of the close passage of a transient body . . . a rogue planet that briefly entered the system from interstellar space . . . and began to spiral inward toward its sun. The transient is long gone, but the destabilized planet is still here."

"The gas giant in close orbit around the sun," D'Anguilo said.

Jahd's head made a sideways movement. "That is correct. Its inward migration began tens of thousands of years ago and was detected early by ancient *danui* astronomers. The *danui* are an old and wise race . . . one of the oldest and wisest in the galaxy . . . and they quickly realized that, as this outer planet began to move through the system, it would perturb the orbits of the inner planets, including their own. In time, massive climate changes would render their world uninhabitable, and their race would perish."

"So why didn't they just move?" Andromeda asked. "Or

maybe they didn't know how to build starships," she added, trying to answer her own question.

"When the crisis began, the *danui* had not yet achieved the technology for interstellar travel. Even if they had, it would not have made any difference. The nearest system with a planet habitable by their species is almost a hundred light-years away . . . and theirs was a large race even then, with a population of over seven billion. They could not relocate, and so they were forced to seek another solution."

Jahd raised his hand toward the vast array of hexagons visible through the window. "This is it . . . *tanaash-haq*, an effort to which the entire *danui* race committed itself. For more than five thousand years, they have been creating a new world from the remains of their old one and its neighbors."

"The entire race?" Andromeda stared at the emissary. "They all worked on this?"

"They have a reputation as engineers . . ." D'Anguilo began.

"They are superlative engineers, yes," Jahd said. "Yet they also have an interesting cultural trait. Although they are reclusive and frequently uncommunicative, they are also capable of focusing their attention completely upon one particular problem, working on it obsessively until they achieve a solution."

"We have something like that in our own race," D'Anguilo said. "We call it Asperger's syndrome. Among our kind, it's usually considered an affliction."

Once again, the stuttering hiss of *hjadd* laughter. "For the *danui*, this same trait was important to their survival. No one knows exactly how they achieved this, for the *danui* have kept their technological secrets to themselves; but the fact remains that their entire race worked in concert for millennia to construct a world that could survive the destabilization of their solar system. Indeed, their efforts continue to this day."

"Hex isn't finished yet?" Zeus asked.

Jahd didn't look at him, but instead continued to gaze

through the window. "Nothing as vast as this could ever be finished. Many of the hexagons are mere shells, built for the sole purpose of maintaining structural integrity. Others are complete habitats, but as yet unoccupied. Like your own habitat, they await the arrival of races who do not yet know about this world."

"We've been wondering about that," Andromeda said. "Our habitat looks very much like Coyote. It has many of the same plants and animals. Did you . . . the *hjadd*, I mean . . . have a hand in this?"

"We did, yes." Jahd turned away from the window. "Shortly after your race made contact with my own, the *danui* asked us whether we thought humankind might be suitable candidates for a colony here. By then, we had begun trading with your race and discovered that your people have a certain promise. We told the *danui* that your kind were potential colonists, and so they asked us to quietly collect specimens of your plant and animal life so that a habitat could be prepared for your eventual arrival." One of hisher eyes twitched toward her. "The *nord* let you know about *tanaash-haq* before we or the *danui* had a chance to do so, but that is of little consequence. Your habitat was finished by then."

"I see." Andromeda thought about it for a moment. "So the things we were asked to bring with us? Crops, seeds . . . ?"

"Not for their consumption, but for your own," Jahd said. "There are six modules in your habitat—you call them *biopods*—five of which are habitable. Only the one you have visited so far is complete. The others have yet to be thoroughly planted. Those you will need to finish yourselves."

"What about the sixth?"

"A biogenesis module, meant for creation and reclamation of natural resources . . . atmosphere, water, soil, and so forth. As in all of the habitats, nothing is allowed to go to waste. Microassemblers in the soil constantly break down dead organic matter and other waste material and transfer it via underground arteries to the biogenesis module, where it is restructured as usable material."

"I'd love to see that," D'Anguilo said.

"Unfortunately, you may not. One of the conditions that the *danui* impose upon their guests is that we refrain from trying to enter or explore those modules. Like their engineering secrets, they do not wish to share their knowledge of ecopoiesis."

"Eco . . . what?" Zeus asked.

"Ecopoiesis." D'Anguilo glanced over his shoulder at him. "The transformation of dead worlds into living ones. Terraforming, in other words." He looked at Andromeda. "I was right. Hex is a geophysical superintelligence . . . a big smart object, to use an old term."

"I'm sure you're dying to tell us what you mean by that," Andromeda said.

Zeus snorted behind his hand, and even Jahd responded by raising hisher fin, but D'Anguilo seemed oblivious to her sarcasm. "It comes from twentieth-century science fiction. 'Big dumb objects' . . . alien structures found in space that don't seem to have any immediate use or purpose." He nodded toward the window. "Hex is sort of like that, only it's not dumb. There's an intelligence behind it, and a purpose."

"You are correct, Dr. D'Anguilo." Jahd's head moved back and forth in an affirmative. "In many ways, *tanaash-haq* is as much a living organism as you or me. Its habitats could be considered to be akin to individual cells, functional on their own yet necessarily supported by those around them. Just as our bodily functions . . . respiration, circulation, and so forth . . . are not the result of conscious, deliberate actions, so Hex maintains itself."

"And its purpose?" Andromeda asked. "I understand that the *danui* built this place to preserve their own race. But why are all the others races here, too?"

Another hiss. "The *danui* will have to explain that to you themselves, once you are allowed to meet them."

"So I take it that they're going to let us do that?"

"They will . . . but first, they wanted me to show you this

place." Jahd's eyes swiveled toward the window. "As an object lesson, so to speak."

Heshe pointed toward the empty space beyond the window. "This was once occupied by the *morath* habitat. Like yourselves, the *morath* were invited to establish a colony on *tanaash-haq*, under the terms imposed by the *danui*. One of those stipulations is that the races here must respect the right of others to live in peace, without fear of hostile actions from their neighbors. That is one of the reasons why no weapons may be brought to *tanaash-haq*, although some races are allowed to fashion their own for the purpose of hunting native animals within their own habitats."

"That must have been difficult for the *morath*," D'Anguilo said. "They're not known to be a pleasant people."

Andromeda nodded. She had never been to the *morath* homeworld, located in the HD130322 system, but a fellow merchant marine captain who had traveled there had once told her that the natives were suspicious of outsiders, even those with whom they regularly traded. They were one of the few races in the Talus that had not embraced *Sa'Tong*, and it showed in their behavior.

Jahd's fin lifted slightly. "No, they are not. Nevertheless, they are a starfaring race, and so the *danui* wanted to establish relations with them by letting them settle here. That was a mistake. Not long after they came to *tanaash-haq*, the *morath* learned that one of the adjacent hexagons was inhabited by the *kua'tah*, a race whom they disliked and distrusted. This was not an acceptable situation, so they decided to launch an invasion of the *kua'tah* habitat."

"Why?" D'Anguilo's eyes widened. "I mean, it's not as if there's not enough room here for everyone."

Jahd's right eye turned toward him. "You are correct, Dr. D'Anguilo. There was no reason for the *morath* to want to take control of the *kua'tah* habitat except that they did not like the notion of a rival living so close to them. They fashioned weapons from the native materials of their habitat and made plans to use the transportation system as a means of laying siege upon the *kua'tah*. Before they could accomplish this, the *danui* learned of their intentions and settled the issue themselves."

Jahd extended a hand toward the tram platform beside them. "This node once led to the *morath* habitat." Heshe then turned toward the window. "As you can plainly see, there is nothing here. All six of their modules were jettisoned by the *danui*, without warning or chance for appeal."

Andromeda stared at the emissary, not knowing what to say. D'Anguilo was at a loss for words as well; his mouth hung open in shock. Only Zeus was able to speak. "How many people . . . I mean, *morath* . . . lived here?"

"Nearly a million."

"How many survived?"

"Only those few aboard a ship that was docked within this node at the time. The *danui* ordered it to leave at once, and the *morath* vessel was allowed to remain in orbit above *tanaash-haq* so that its crew might observe the modules as they fell into the sun."

Andromeda felt horror grip at her heart. "The *danui* jettisoned the habitat toward the sun?"

"Yes." Jahd's fin rose to its full height as heshe turned to look straight at her. "It took nearly three months for the modules to complete their fall, but their inhabitants perished before then. My people dispatched one of our own vessels to witness the end of the *morath* colony, and we listened to their radio transmissions until we could hear them no more."

"And you did nothing to save them?"

"No." Jahd's head bobbed up and down on hisher neck. "The *danui* would not allow it even though many races . . . my own among them . . . offered to come to their rescue. The *danui* wanted the destruction of the *morath* habitat to serve as an example to any other race that might consider making war upon its neighbors." Heshe paused. "Theirs was a horrible death that no one here has ever forgotten."

Andromeda suddenly understood. "That's why the *danui* asked us to come here," she said quietly. "They want us to see what happens to guests who disobey their rules."

"Yes." Jahd's fin lowered back against hisher head. "Although your race has had a peaceful coexistence with the other Talus races, we are aware that humans have a long and violent past. So you should know that, if you accept the *danui's* invitation to settle here, you must respect their mandate that all of this world's inhabitants must live together in peace, and that if you don't . . ."

"I get the idea." Andromeda felt something cold travel down her back. "You can tell the *danui* that we . . ."

A sharp chirp from her transceiver. She had almost forgotten that she was still carrying it beneath her left arm. Indeed, it had been nearly fourteen hours since the last time she'd been able to communicate with the *Montero*. Apparently her present position within the former *morath* docking node allowed radio signals to reach her.

"Pardon me," she said to Jahd. "I think I need to take this." The *hjadd's* head briefly swung back and forth as she turned away to fasten her headset against her mouth and ear. "Survey Two to *Montero*," she said quietly. "We copy, over."

"*Montero to Survey Two.*" Anne's voice was fuzzed with static. "*Glad to hear you again, skipper. I've been trying to reach you for a while.*"

"Same here. The tram tunnels have been blocking reception. What's going on?"

"*Bad news. We received word from Survey One just a little while ago. Sean says that their tram took them somewhere besides Nueva Italia. They don't know where they are, but it's clear that they're not where they're supposed to be.*"

"I don't understand." Andromeda was confused. "I gave him the coordinates. He must have entered them wrong."

"*With all due respect, skipper, he seems to think otherwise.*"

While she'd been talking to Anne, D'Anguilo had quietly walked over to stand beside her. "Your son didn't show up at our habitat?" he asked quietly, and Andromeda shook her head. "Are you sure you gave him the proper coordinates?"

Andromeda glared at him. "Of course I . . ." She stopped

as a thought occurred to her. *Oh, my God . . . what if I didn't?* "Stand by, *Montero*. I need to check something."

She muted the headset, then reached into her pocket and pulled out her datapad. Retrieving the coordinates she'd copied down at the Nueva Italia tram station, she held the pad so that D'Anguilo could read the screen. "Didn't you tell me that this should be read from right to left?"

"That's what I said, yes." He pointed to the crosshatched diamond at the right end of the sequence. "You started to enter the ones for this station the other way, from left to right, but I stopped you because . . ."

"I remember now. It was because the digits at the bottom of the screen went the other way. And we got to where we were supposed to go." Andromeda felt her face become warm. "Damn it. Damn it to hell . . ."

"Uh-oh." He stared at her. "Did you reverse the sequence when you read it to Sean?"

"I was half-asleep when he called, and we hadn't yet figured out . . ." She shook her head again, then reactivated her headset. "Anne? You still there?"

"Right here, skipper."

Andromeda let out her breath, closed her eyes. "Sean's right . . . It's my fault. I read the coordinates to him in reverse order, left to right instead of right to left. That's why he got lost." She mentally kicked herself for her carelessness, then went on. "That should be easily solved. All he has to do is enter those coordinates again, this time in the proper sequence, and the tram should take him straight to our biopod."

"I understand, Captain, but we haven't heard from him since then. He said that he and his team were going into the habitat where they arrived in hopes of finding someone who could help them." A reluctant pause. *"That was the last transmission I received from him, and there's been no response to my signals. Skipper, I think they're in trouble."*

Again, Andromeda felt a chill run down her spine. As much as she might have liked to think otherwise, she knew her communications officer was probably right. And if her son was in danger, it was because his own mother had put him there.

Before she could respond, though, she felt D'Anguilo's hand on her shoulder. "Captain, there's a way to find them," he said quietly. "If you reverse the coordinates, too . . ."

"That'll take us to them. Right." She nodded to D'Anguilo. "Did you copy that, Anne?"

"Affirmative, skipper. Is that your intent?"

She gazed at D'Anguilo. He couldn't hear what Anne was saying, but apparently he'd guessed her response, because he slowly nodded.

"Roger that, *Montero*," Andromeda said. "I'm going to go find my son."

SANCTUARY

TWENTY-ONE

"**Y**OU CANNOT SAVE YOUR PEOPLE," SASHATASMA JAHD Sa-Fhadda said.

Andromeda stared at himher through the transparent wall of hisher booth. She was still holding her datapad up so that the *hjadd* emissary could read the *danui* numbers on its screen. One look at them, and Jahd's fin had risen to its full height. Heshe was clearly perturbed, but she didn't know why.

Before she could respond, Tom D'Anguilo spoke up. "Why can't we? It's not their fault they're lost. There's no reason why we shouldn't . . ."

"You do not understand." Jahd raised a six-fingered hand to point to Andromeda's pad. "These coordinates, when read in reverse order, correspond to those of a restricted habitat. It is unfortunate that they have found themselves in this place, but the *danui* have placed it off-limits. No Talus race is allowed to go there."

"I don't understand." D'Anguilo shook his head. "What is that place? Why . . . ?"

"Allow me to explain." Jahd reached beneath his robe to produce a hand-sized object faintly resembling an ink stamp. Grasping it by its handle, heshe pressed buttons on its flat end. A blue ray painted a translucent image across the wall between himher and the humans on the other side: a holographic image of Hex. Heshe tapped at the object again, and the image expanded until only part of its northern hemisphere was displayed.

"Here is where your habitat is located." Jahd pointed a taloned finger toward a tiny hexagon halfway up the hemisphere; it became red at his touch. "Here is where we are," he continued, and another habitat, located five hexagons northwest of Nueva Italia, became scarlet when heshe touched it. "And here is where your people are," heshe finished, as a third habitat was illuminated, this one to the northeast of the second hexagon.

"That doesn't look very far away," Zeus said, stepping closer to peer at the map.

"It is not," Jahd said. "You could reach it in only a few of your hours. However, distance is not the issue. This habitat belongs to a race that should be familiar to you . . . the *taaraq.*"

The name sounded familiar, but Andromeda couldn't quite recall its significance. D'Anguilo obviously did, though, because he stared at the holo in stunned surprise. "You have *taaraq* here?" he said, his voice little more than a whisper. "Living *taaraq?*"

Jahd's head slowly swung back and forth in an affirmative. "I'm not following this," Zeus said. "Who are the *taaraq?* Why are they so important?"

"Who are the . . . ?" D'Anguilo turned to regard the chief petty officer with disbelief. "Don't they teach history in school anymore, or did you just sleep through class?" Zeus's face went red as the astroethnicist went on. "The *Galileo* expedition. Spindrift. The race that was discovered hibernating inside . . ."

"I remember now," Andromeda said. "That was Ted Harker's mission. Spindrift was the rogue asteroid that wandered past Earth's solar system back in 2288. When the *Galileo* went out to investigate it, they discovered that it was hollow. It was a sort of interstellar ark, and inside was an entire race that had put itself in biostasis and left their home system when it was destroyed by . . ."

"Kasimasta." Jahd completed the thought for her. "Yes, you remember correctly. When their homeworld was about to be destroyed by the rogue black hole called the Annihilator, the *taaraq* transformed a nearby asteroid into an enormous starship. A million and a half members of their race sealed themselves within *Shaq-Taaraq* and, in a state of long-term hibernation, set out for a planet in a distant star system that could support them. Your people discovered them by accident, and this led to first contact between your race and mine."

Andromeda peered at the holo again. "Then these are . . . ?"

"The same *taaraq* that your expedition found in the ark? No. *Shaq-Taaraq* . . . or Spindrift, as you call it . . . is still in transit, and will be for many years to come." Jahd paused. "Yet those *taaraq* are not the only survivors of their race. The *danui* saw to that."

"My God." D'Anguilo stared at himher. "You mean, they . . . ?"

"Yes." Again, Jahd's gaze fell upon the holo image. "After *Shaq-Taaraq* made its departure, but before Kasimasta arrived in the *taaraq* system, the *danui* visited the *taaraq* homeworld and took away a number of its remaining inhabitants, along with specimens of its flora and fauna. They were brought here to *tanaash-haq*, where a sanctuary was made for them. They have been here for many generations now, longer than even my own race, with their habitat a microcosm of a world that they remember only as a legend."

"Why did they do this?" Zeus asked. "The *danui*, I mean."

Jahd didn't immediately respond. Hisher fin flattened as heshe looked away from them as if in silent contemplation. "You will have to ask the *danui* this when you meet them," Jahd said after a few moments. "However, I must warn you that the chances for such a meeting will be jeopardized if you go to the *taaraq* habitat. The *danui* have told all Talus races that they must not visit them, for the safety of both the *taaraq* and themselves."

"I don't understand." D'Anguilo shook his head. "If I remember correctly, the *taaraq* are a peaceful race, with no history of warfare. At least that's what your people told mine."

"This is true, but only for the *taaraq* inside Spindrift. They represent the advanced civilization that was able to build the ark in the first place. The *taaraq* colony of *tanaash-haq* are different. They have been here several centuries, and during that time the descendents of the original survivors have socially degenerated. They are less civilized, more hostile, than their ancestors. Any contact with them may be dangerous."

"Which is exactly why we need to go there." Andromeda suddenly remembered what they'd been discussing in the first place. "My son and his friends are in that place. If what you say is true, then their lives are in danger. We've got to get them out, and I don't care if your people or the *danui* or the whole goddamn Talus objects."

Jahd's fin rose sharply as sacs at the base of hisher throat bulged. It wasn't hard to see that heshe was angry. From the corner of her eye, though, Andromeda saw D'Anguilo solemnly nod. He alone understood why she was so adamant.

"If you insist upon doing this," Jahd said, "you will risk incurring the *danui's* wrath." Heshe gestured toward the vast, empty space beyond the nearby window where the *morath* habitat once lay. "This should be a reminder of what happens to races who dare to defy them."

"What did I just say?" Andromeda stared back at himher. "I don't care what the *danui* think. I'm going to get my son back, and . . ." She took a deep breath. "And that's it."

Even Jahd seemed to recognize the finality of her tone. Heshe didn't say anything for a moment, but only regarded her with heavy-lidded eyes. "If you must," the emissary said at last. "I cannot condone your actions but only warn you of the consequences."

"You can do more than that." Andromeda sought to rein in her temper. "If you're acting as intermediaries between us and the *danui*, you can explain to them what we're doing and why."

"I can attempt to do so, but I cannot promise that they will understand." Jahd's head rose slightly upon hisher neck. "Not all races are as protective of their offspring as humans are."

"Yeah, well . . ." Zeus shrugged, not bothering to hide his sarcasm. "Poor, stupid us, huh?"

Andromeda gave him a sharp look, then turned to Jahd again. "You could also tell us what to expect from the *taaraq* habitat."

"I can, if only to give you another reason why a rescue attempt is inadvisable. Their environment is similar to our own although its surface gravity is less than that of your homeworld. Its atmosphere is only marginally breathable by humans. Without the proper apparatus, you will not be able to survive long there. Its terrain is principally aquatic, comprised mainly of water and floating moss, with very little solid ground. It is also inhabited by quite a number of animals hostile to humans. It is a very dangerous place. Even my own people have hesitated before going there."

D'Anguilo raised an eyebrow. "So the *hjadd* have visited the *taaraq* habitat."

Jahd hesitated. "Yes, we have."

"If that's so," D'Anguilo said, "then the edict against any other race entering the habitat must not be as absolute as you've made it out to be."

Again, Jahd's fin and neck sacs showed signs of *hjadd* irritation. Andromeda wanted to keep the emissary on her side, and D'Anguilo's pointing out hisher contradictions might not have helped. But Tom was right; by slip of the tongue, the emissary had revealed something about the *danui* that heshe preferred to keep secret.

If that were so, then Andromeda wasn't surprised. Not greatly. Although the *hjadd* were the Coyote Federation's closest allies in the Talus, the fact remained that they'd never been completely truthful in their dealings with humans, particularly when it came matters that might have an impact upon trade or diplomatic relations with other races. However benevolent they seemed to be, the *hjadd* always wanted to have the upper hand, and that usually took the form of withholding important information.

"In the past," Jahd said reluctantly, "the *danui* have allowed members of other races to visit another habitat without permission of its inhabitants. Such permission is rarely given, but if the intent isn't hostile, and there's a good reason for the intrusion . . ."

"This is a rescue mission," Andromeda said. "We're going in there to save my people from being killed. What better reason is there?"

Jahd said nothing for a moment; hisher eyes swiveled back and forth as if in consternation. "I can communicate this to the *danui*," heshe said at last. "I am not confident that they will accept your rationale, but I can try."

"Thank you." Andromeda let out her breath. "We would appreciate it."

"What about their language?" D'Anguilo asked. "The *taaraq*, I mean. Assuming that we can enter their habitat, will we be able to communicate with them?"

Jahd had raised hisher instrument again. "Verbal communication is impossible," the *hjadd* said as heshe tapped at it. "Our scientists were only able to decipher their written language after studying the interior of *Shaq-Taaraq*. Their verbal language remains unknown to us. As a result, translator disks like my own are useless."

"Great," Zeus murmured. "If we can't talk to 'em, then we'll have to fight 'em . . ."

"No!" Jahd's fin unfolded again as heshe looked sharply at him. "Any hostile actions against the *taaraq* will result in retaliation from the *danui*. I cannot stress that too much. Whatever else you may do, do not attack them! Even carrying weapons into their habitat would be inadvisable."

Andromeda glanced at both D'Anguilo and Zeus; their

expressions were as grim as her own. "And what if they attack us?" she asked. "What should we do then?"

"Run." Jahd touched hisher instrument one last time, and the holo map of Hex vanished. "A tram is on its way to collect me, and I have taken the liberty of summoning one for you as well. You may set its coordinates once you are aboard."

"You won't come with us?" D'Anguilo asked.

"No. My race cannot become involved in this matter. I can speak with the *danui* on your behalf, but nothing more." Heshe turned toward Andromeda. "Captain Carson, I beg you to reconsider. If you undertake this, you will put your entire mission at risk, along with the lives of yourself and your companions."

"Thank you, emissary," she said, trying not to sound cold. "I appreciate your advice."

A breeze drifted from the tunnel, signaling the approach of a tram. Again, Jahd's head shifted back and forth in an affirmative, then heshe raised hisher left hand. *"Sa'tong qo,"* heshe said. "May we meet again."

Andromeda nodded. D'Anguilo reciprocated the gesture with his own left hand. *"Sa'tong qo,"* he replied. "I hope . . . I expect . . . we will before long."

The tram rushed forth from the tunnel, slid to a halt beside the platform. Its right-side door was directly adjacent to the booth in which Jahd stood. Heshe turned to watch as the booth's walls expanded upon heretofore invisible seams until it mated with the tram, forming an airlock through which heshe could safely pass. A moment passed, then the tram doors and the rear wall of the booth simultaneously opened. Without another word, Jahd entered the tram; heshe didn't even look back as the doors closed behind himher.

The tram had barely left the station when Andromeda reached down to the transceiver slung beneath her arm. "We've got to work fast," she said quietly. "The next tram will be here any minute."

"What are you . . . ?" D'Anguilo began.

Andromeda shook her head as she raised the antenna. Stepping closer to the window, she boosted the gain to its maximum, then slipped on her headset. "Survey Two to *Montero*," she said. "*Montero*, respond immediately . . . This is a Priority One transmission. Over."

Anne's voice came through her earpiece almost at once. *"We copy, Survey Two. What's up, skipper?"*

"Patch me through to Nueva Italia and relay the signal to Survey One." Despite what Anne had told her, it was possible that Sean might receive the signal. "Patch in the logbook, too," she added. "I want this on the record."

A few seconds went by. *"All set, Captain. Logbook on vox mode. Go ahead."*

"All stations, this is a Priority One transmission," she said. "As commanding officer, I'm authorizing and taking charge of an attempt to rescue Survey Team One. The following orders are to take effect immediately."

She paused, waiting for a response. *"Roger that, Captain,"* Jason said after a moment, speaking from the base camp. *"Standing by for your orders."*

Hoping that she'd hear from Sean, Andromeda waited a few more seconds. When his voice didn't come over the comlink, her sense of urgency increased. Taking a deep breath, she went on. "All personnel are to evacuate Nueva Italia and return at once to the *Montero*. Once aboard, they will disengage from the docking node and prepare for immediate departure."

"Captain? Why are we . . ."

"Don't question my orders, Mr. Ressler. Just follow them." Andromeda didn't like adopting a formal tone with her first officer, but she had no time to waste on discussion. "Once the *Montero* has left the docking node, I want it to assume a stationary orbit above Hex, where it will continue to monitor this frequency for further messages."

She turned toward D'Anguilo and Zeus. They stood nearby, astonished by what she'd just said. "In the meantime, Survey Team Two will proceed by tram to Survey

Team One's last known location, which we've been informed is a habitat belonging to the *taaraq* race. Once we arrive at that habitat, we will transmit a signal on this frequency. When the *Montero* receives that transmission, it will lock onto its source and use it as a beacon to guide it to the nearest adjacent docking node."

D'Anguilo seemed baffled by this, but a smile slowly spread across Zeus's face. "Oh, I get it," he said quietly.

Andromeda nodded. Removing her ship and crew from Nueva Italia accomplished two things. It gave her additional men and resources for the rescue mission. More importantly, though, they would also be safe if the *danui* objected to what she planned to do and decided to retaliate by jettisoning Nueva Italia.

"Once the *Montero* is docked with the *taaraq* habitat," she continued, "the chief engineer will leave the ship and locate the nearest tram station. He will note its coordinates and relay them to Survey Two, which in turn will use them to return to the ship. Note that tram coordinates are always read from right to left. At that point, the chief engineer and the helmsman will join Survey Two for a sortie into the *taaraq* habitat." Andromeda was reluctant about having Melpomene leave the ship during a crisis, but she'd need all the help she could get once she reached the hex.

"Affirmative, Captain." Now that he understood what his CO intended to do, Jason's tone was less puzzled. *"Do you want any special equipment from the ship's stores?"*

"Yes. We'll need airpacks for everyone in the party, along with . . ." She paused to make a quick mental inventory of the ship's expedition supplies. "Rope, machetes, a first-aid kit . . ."

"Don't we have an inflatable boat, too?" D'Anguilo asked.

Andromeda nodded. "Tom suggests that we may need the inflatable," she added. "Bring that, too, along with its motor." Another thought occurred to her. "And see if we're still carrying any explosives. If so, I want ten pounds, along with detonators."

D'Anguilo stared at her. "Captain, you can't . . . !"

Andromeda angrily waved off his objection. A plan was beginning to come together in her mind. During a recent mission, the *Montero* had transported a supply of plastic explosives to an asteroid mining operation in the *soranta* home system. If she recalled correctly, the shipment had been larger than necessary, so not all of the material had been off-loaded at its destination. If that were so, some explosives might still remain in *Montero*'s cargo hold. With any luck, the airlock scanners in the *taaraq* docking node would not classify them as potential weapons. And they might be useful . . .

"Roger that, Captain," Jason said. "Anything else?"

Andromeda felt a breeze coming from the tunnel. A tram was on its way. "Negative. Get everyone out of there and back aboard ship, then launch and await further orders. Anne?"

"Skipper?"

"I know you haven't heard anything from Survey One. But are you getting any sort of signal, or is his transmitter completely dead?"

"I'm getting a carrier-wave signal . . . just no verbal modulation."

"Good." Andromeda sighed with relief. Sean's transmitter was still active; for whatever reason, he was just unable to use it. "Very good. Once the *Montero* is in orbit, I want you to try to get a fix on his location. With any luck, it won't be far from where I show up. That'll help us find Sean and his people."

"Affirmative. Is that all?"

"For now, yes. Survey Two, over and out." Andromeda switched off the headset but left it in place and didn't switch off the transceiver. Her timing was excellent, for it was at that moment that a tram hurtled into the station. As it came to a halt at the platform, she bent down to pick up her pack. "The clock's running, gentlemen. Let's get out of here."

Without question, Zeus moved to follow her. Yet D'Anguilo was hesitant. "Captain, this is . . ."

"Tom . . ." Stopping at the tram's open door, Andromeda

glanced over her shoulder at him. "I know you're reluctant about this, and I respect the reasons why. But, I swear to God, if you don't get on this thing right now, I'm going to leave you here."

That put an end to any further argument. One look at her face, and D'Anguilo knew that Andromeda wasn't kidding. Once he'd followed her and Zeus onto the tram, Andromeda pulled out the *danui* scroll.

She walked down the center aisle to the control panel, where she carefully entered the coordinates just as she'd erroneously given them to Sean. The tram doors silently closed, and with only the mildest vibration, it began to move. Saying nothing to the others, Andromeda took a seat on the nearest bench.

Hang tight, son, she thought. *I'm coming for you.*

TWENTY-TWO

THE NIGHTMARE BEGAN AS SOON AS THEY WENT ASHORE. Sean had no choice. The boats that emerged from the brush moved to either side of the one he, Kyra, and Sandy were in, and the sharp-tipped javelins of the creatures in them left little doubt as to what they wanted the intruders to do. By the time he and Sandy had paddled their boat to the narrow beach, it seemed as if the domes had emptied themselves of their denizens. They swarmed the beach as a solid mass of six-limbed bodies, their twitching antennae resembling a vast field of tall grass.

Kyra had identified them as *taaraq*, but she didn't get a chance to say anything about them before Sean beached the boat. The moment its keel ground against the rough sand, the creatures rushed toward them. Sandy squawked and raised her paddle above her head; she swung it back and forth, trying to ward off the inhabitants.

"Get outta here!" she yelled. "Go away! Scram!"

"Sandy, no!" Kyra started to rise from her seat. "They don't . . . !"

The nearest *taaraq* was knocked off its hind legs by Sandy's paddle. It sprawled across the beach, multiple-jointed limbs thrashing at the air. Chittering angrily, it hopped back up with astonishing agility and hurled itself at Sandy, this time joined by two of its companions. Sandy screamed and lashed out at them again, but the creatures were ready for her. Dodging the paddle, all three of them grabbed Sandy before she could strike again. The paddle was yanked from her hands, then they dragged her from the boat. Sandy was screaming incoherently as she tried to fight them off, but more *taaraq* were on her in seconds.

"Stop it!" Sean jumped out of the stern, boots splashing down in calf-deep water. Paddle gripped tight in both hands, he charged the beach. "She didn't mean to . . . !"

Something jabbed the left side of his ribs, causing him to yell and look around to see what it was: the javelin wielded by one of the *taaraq* who'd met them on the river. Their boat had come ashore, and its three passengers stood beside him in the shallows. The *taaraq* were his own height, perhaps an inch or two taller; in the four black compound eyes of the one who'd jabbed him, he saw his own reflection, multiplied dozens of times. Their javelins—tipped, he now saw, with serrated barbs that appeared to be carved bones—were only inches from his chest, and the pain he felt at his side told him that one had already drawn blood.

Sean dropped his paddle, raised his hands. Hearing a scream, he looked around to see three more *taaraq* hauling Kyra from the boat. He started to move toward her, but an outthrust javelin barred his way. Another sharp jab, this time in the butt, and Sean got the message. Hands still raised, he sloshed through the lukewarm water, doing his best to keep away from the spears.

Taaraq surrounded them as soon as they were together on the beach. Indeed, it seemed as if each and every one of the creatures wanted nothing more than to lay its claws upon them. Reddish brown exoskeletons pressed in upon Sean, Kyra, and Sandy from all sides; elongated heads, mandibles in constant motion, craned forward on thin necks as multifaceted eyes peered at them without any visible emotion. Their claws—two long pinchers, with a smaller third one acting as an opposable thumb—continually darted toward them, stroking, pinching, grabbing, retreating for a moment when they were batted away only to come at them again. Their voices were a cacophony of chitters, clicks, squeaks, and snaps, so loud that it was almost deafening.

One of the *taaraq* grabbed at Sean's airmask, started to pull it from his face. He snarled and shoved the creature away, only to have the one beside it tug at his oxygen line. Hearing Sandy yell again, he saw her fighting off two more *taaraq*, who'd also tried to remove her mask.

Then something slid from his right shoulder, and he looked around just in time to see his transceiver vanish into the crowd.

"Back to back!" he shouted, trying to make himself heard above the crowd noise. "Put your backs to each other's and watch your sides! They're stealing everything they can get their hands on!"

"No kidding!" Sandy yelped. "They've already snagged my light! And my knife!"

Sean glanced down at his utility belt. His own knife had disappeared, and so had his flashlight. He'd just fought off a pair of claws that had yanked at the straps of his airpack when someone bumped into him from behind. It was Kyra, putting her back against his own.

"Think you can get through to them?" he yelled. Although he couldn't make out her expression, the look in her eyes told him what she was thinking: *are you crazy?* "C'mon! You're supposed to be the expert! How do we talk to them?"

"Do you see any translator disks?" Kyra demanded. "I don't either . . . and without them, I'd have just as much luck trying to talk to a skeeter back home!"

Sean suddenly realized that he had seen few indications of civilization, and no signs of advanced technology. Some of the *taaraq* wore sashlike belts across the smooth carapaces of their chests, and a few had polished pebbles hanging from their necks by woven strands of grass, but otherwise they were naked. The only tools in sight were the javelins and an occasional scimitar-like knife. The boats were obviously handmade, and even the massive domes of their city appeared to be crudely built. This was a primitive culture, or so it seemed; the *taaraq* might have stolen his transceiver and flashlight, but he somehow doubted that they'd know what to do with them.

"Ow! Cut it out!" Sandy slapped away a claw that was exploring the sleeve of her unitard, then hastily backed herself up against Kyra. "Look, I don't care if you use smoke signals, but tell these stupid things to back off!"

Kyra glared at her. "Don't you think I would if I . . . !"

The voices suddenly increased in volume, then abruptly subsided. All at once, the crowd withdrew from around them, if only by a few feet. They were still surrounded by a ring of javelins, but at least no one was trying to rip off their airmasks.

"What's going on?" Sean asked aloud.

As if to answer his question, the mob parted to allow an individual to pass through. The *taaraq* who approached them was a little smaller than the others; its carapace was faded and cracked as if with age, and it seemed to limp as it hobbled forward on its back-jointed hind limbs. A large round quartz hung from a pendant around its neck, and a braided grass tiara lay on its head.

A chieftain, perhaps, or maybe a warlord, a priest, or a witch doctor. Whatever it was, it was obviously revered as a leader. The *taaraq* stopped in front of the humans, head moving forward on its neck as it silently inspected them.

"Try it now," Sean whispered to Kyra. "This may be your best chance."

Kyra hesitated, then stepped forward, raising her hands to show that they were empty. "Hello," she said slowly. "We are visitors." She pointed to Sean, Kyra, and herself, then gestured in the direction from which they'd come. "We come from there," she went on, then pointed toward the river. "In your boat," she added, cupping her left hand and placing three fingers of her right hand in it. "Down the river. In the boat. We—"

The chieftain interrupted her with a strident chitter, its antennae twitching like a cat's whiskers. The other *taaraq* responded with staccato clicks and chirps of their own. Kyra glanced at Sean. "I don't know if I'm getting through to him," she murmured.

"I think you are. Keep at it."

Kyra returned to her earlier pantomime. "We came down the river, in the boat," she reiterated, moving her hands to imitate the boat's motion. "To this place," she added, stopping her left hand while pointing to the nearby waterfront with her right. "We are lost, and trying to . . ."

The chieftain's mandibles made three sharp clicks, then it half turned to make a gesture with its two left claws. The *taaraq* behind them responded by poking the humans with their javelins. "Damn it!" Sandy yelled, turning to swat aside the nearest spear. "Will you knock it . . . ?"

The *taaraq* who had prodded her buried the tip of its spear in her thigh. Sandy screamed and fell to the ground, clutching her wounded leg.

"Oh, hell!" Sean hastily knelt beside her. "How bad are you . . . ?"

"Bad enough," she hissed. Between her fingers, Sean saw a red splotch spreading across the blue fabric of her unitard. "Got me right in the muscle."

"Guys, you better get up." Kyra's voice was barely distinguishable through the crowd noise. "Hate to say it, but I think I've made 'em mad."

Sean nodded. It seemed that Kyra's admission that they'd stolen a boat was the only thing that the *taaraq* chieftain had clearly understood; apparently this was a taboo that they shouldn't have broken. Looking up, he saw that their guards were jabbing at them again, their barbs stopping only inches from their bodies, while the chieftain continued to gesture angrily at something Sean couldn't see.

"We gotta move," Sean whispered as he draped his arm

around Sandy's shoulder and under her arm. She nodded and curled her arm around his waist. "On the count of three. One . . . two . . ."

"Three," she finished, and bit off a soft cry as Sean hoisted her to her feet. Holding her so that he'd support most of her weight, the two of them lurched forward, with Kyra bringing up the rear. The *taaraq* chieftain led the way, the mob once again parting to make room for their leader, the guards, and their captives.

As they slowly moved through the mob, Sean saw that they were heading away from the river. At first he thought that they were being led toward the closer of the two immense domes, but after a couple of minutes it became clear that they were moving away from the dwellings as well. The river was behind them, and although they were close to the edge of the jungle, there were far too many *taaraq* for them to escape. Not that they could have made a break for it; Sandy could barely walk, let alone run, and the couple of miles that lay between the settlement and the tram-station escalator might just as well have been light-years.

You idiot, he thought as he struggled to keep the woman beside him on her feet. *They were counting on you to get them home, and you blew it.*

And then, another thought, even more unwelcome than the first: *You've carried a grudge against your mother for a decision she once made, but you're not doing much better, are you?*

The crowd continued to follow them as the chieftain led the way past the dwellings, but Sean had just noticed that they'd dispersed immediately ahead of the procession when the *taaraq* leader abruptly came to a halt. Its mandibles clicked and squeaked as it turned again toward its captives, then its right hands made a sudden gesture. The guards prodded Sean, Sandy, and Kyra forward, and as the chieftain stepped aside, Sean saw what lay before them.

A large, open pit, about thirty feet wide and about half as deep. Or so it seemed; when Sean came closer, he saw that its walls went straight down about six feet, then began to slope downward even farther, forming a funnel that ended at a floor about fifteen feet below the pit's edge. The floor was covered with waste and debris, most of which seemed to be rotting; along the sides of the upper walls were the narrow openings of pipes through which a brown, sludgelike fluid constantly trickled.

Even though his mouth and nose were covered by the airmask, Sean could nonetheless smell the stench of excrement and decay. Either that, or he thought he could. Either way, he had little doubt as to what the place was, or why they'd been brought there.

"Oh, my God." Sandy's voice was a horrified whisper. "You don't think they want to put us down there, do you?"

Kyra yelped as a javelin barb tore the upper sleeve of her unitard, scratching the tender skin beneath it. "'Fraid so," she said, moving closer to Sandy and Sean. "Maybe they don't have any other way of keeping prisoners, or . . ."

Her voice trailed off, but Sean knew what she was about to say: *maybe this is a form of execution.* If so, though, it was hardly an efficient means of death. Gross and humiliating, perhaps, but nothing down there appeared to be particularly lethal.

The chieftain gestured toward the pit, erasing any lingering doubts as to what it wanted them to do. Sean and Kyra knelt beside the pit, then he grasped her wrists and carefully lowered her over the edge. Kyra was still a long way from the bottom, though, so he had no choice but to let her go. She slid the rest of the way down the funnel, landing in the stinking waste on the floor.

"Are you okay?" Sean called down.

"Yeah, I think so." Kyra clumsily pulled herself to her feet, planted her back against the wall. "It's not a solid surface. You'll make a soft landing."

Sandy was the next to go; she balked at the last moment, but when the guards once more began to move forward, she saw that it was either this or be on the receiving end of their javelins again. Standing unsteadily on top of the garbage,

Kyra reached to catch Sandy as she slid down the funnel, then grasped her by the waist and helped her stand up.

"She's right," Sandy said, calling up to Sean. "There's just a lot of crap down here. Nothing solid to stand on."

Sean turned to look one last time at the *taaraq* chieftain. It regarded him with its implacable gaze, and he wondered what was going through its mind. One of the guards made an urgent motion with its javelin, so Sean bit off whatever useless remark he was tempted to make and carefully lowered himself into the pit. Its walls were smooth and made slick by slime; he knew at once that it was impossible for them to climb back out. Yet he could do nothing but let go and slide down the funnel.

His boots sank up to his ankles as soon as he landed, and when he moved to get up, he found himself sinking even farther into the muck. All he could do was lie against the pit's sloping wall and brace his feet against the surface material; it seemed to be floating on layer upon layer of debris, and there was nothing beneath the filth except more filth. Much of it appeared to be vegetable matter—rotting weeds, shredded bark, something that looked like an enormous banana peel—but he noticed what appeared to be a *taaraq* carapace and pieces of chitin lying nearby. A chill went through him; apparently this was also how the inhabitants disposed of their dead.

"Great. Just wonderful." With Kyra's help, Sandy had managed to struggle to her feet. Both women stood with their backs against the funnel wall. Her eyes were accusing when they turned toward Sean. "I told you we shouldn't have . . ."

"Shut up. He knows." Kyra was still holding her up, her legs continually moving as she struggled to keep them from sliding farther into the reeking waste. She looked at Sean. "What now? Any ideas?"

Sean said nothing as he made his way over to them, careful to keep his back against the wall. Once he was beside Kyra, he looked up at the top of the pit. Dozens of *taaraq* peered down at them, but the chieftain had vanished and it seemed to him that the chittering and clicking of their voices had diminished in volume.

"I don't know," he said, "but if they lose interest and enough of them leave, we might try . . ."

All of a sudden, something was tossed over the side. Sean caught a brief glimpse of the transceiver before it fell into the pit's center about four yards away.

"The radio!" Sandy yelled. "Sean, can you . . . ?"

Before he could even think about retrieving it, though, it sank into the morass at the center of the pit. For an instant, he heard a tinny voice—". . . to Survey One, please respond . . ."—coming from its speaker, then it disappeared from sight.

"The radio!" Ignoring her injured leg, Sandy lunged forward, desperately reaching out with both hands. "Somebody get the radio!"

Kyra grabbed her by the shoulders, hauled her back. "It's no use. It's gone."

"But . . . !"

"Don't even try. It's like quicksand over there." Frustrated, Sean slammed the back of his fist into the wall. If only the transceiver had come down a little closer . . . "Maybe someone will be able to home in on its signal. If it's still functioning, that is."

"I don't understand." Sandy shook her head. "Why take away our radio, then throw it back to us again?"

Sean didn't reply. Instead, he looked to Kyra for an explanation. "I don't understand either," she said quietly. "It's almost as if they didn't know what it was, so they got rid of it. But that doesn't make sense, either. They're supposed to be a starfaring race . . . at least they were, before they went extinct."

Despite himself, Sean laughed out loud. "They don't seem very extinct to me."

Kyra sighed. "That's what Dr. D'Anguilo told us at the university. The *taaraq* were the very first extraterrestrials we encountered, back when we found Spindrift. There were millions of them in long-term biostasis, with little chance that they'd be revived anytime soon. The rest of their race was dead, their homeworld destroyed by the Annihilator. Technically, that makes them extinct." She paused. "Tom's going to be surprised when he finds out otherwise."

If he ever does, Sean thought, although he refrained from saying so. "Maybe others of their kind survived and managed to find their way here. Is that what you're saying?"

"Uh-huh." Kyra continued to backpedal in an effort to keep from sliding farther into the pit. Sean realized that he was having to do the same as well; it was as if the pit's contents were constantly subsiding beneath his feet. "But the *taaraq* we found in Spindrift were able to build a star-ship out of an asteroid. The ones here didn't even recognize a radio. They're more . . ."

She stopped, as if searching for the right word. "Sav-age?" Sean asked.

"Yeah. Savage." Kyra glanced up at the handful of *taaraq* still watching them. "I wonder if they even know where they are."

"Sure they do," Sandy murmured. "They're home, and we're the . . ."

"Uh . . . guys?" Kyra's voice had become quiet as she continued to stare upward. "I don't like to mention this, but . . . I think we're sinking."

Sean followed her gaze and saw that in the few minutes they'd been in the pit, its walls had become slightly higher, if only by a few inches. Looking down near his ankles, he examined the point on the funnel wall at which the floor began. A faint stain, brown and wet, showed the level where it had once been.

Kyra was right. The waste material upon which they were standing was sinking farther into the pit. That couldn't be possible, though, unless . . .

He peered more closely at the center of the pit. It was hard to tell, but it appeared as if there was a faint depression in the middle of the garbage, showing the presence of . . .

A hole.

Now he knew what was going on. The pit fed into a giant funnel, and at the bottom of that funnel was a hole that in turn dropped underground. Gravity, along with the sheer mass of the material thrown or piped into the pit, would eventually drag everything in the pit to the hole. But where did the hole go?

He then remembered how Mark Dupree's and Amerigo Cayce's bodies had been dissolved by microassemblers when laid upon bare ground in the *arsashi* biopod, and how Lusah Sahsan had told him that they'd been claimed by *tanaash-haq*. So if Hex broke down waste matter, then it only made sense that there would be pits much like this one, where its inhabitants could safely dispose of their garbage. Or their dead.

Or even unwanted visitors.

"Stick to the wall," he said, scrambling backward to keep himself out of the trash as much as possible. "Try to stay on top of the trash and don't let yourself get dragged down."

"Why?" Sandy asked. "What did you . . . ?" Then she looked at the center of the pit, and suddenly she understood. "Oh, God," she breathed, her eyes going wide. "Oh God, oh God, oh God . . ."

The three of them planted their backs against the sloping funnel wall and backpedaled with their feet, struggling to keep on top of the morass even as it continued to sink beneath them. But the funnel wall was slimy with sewage, with more coming in from the openings above their heads; there was almost no traction to be found, and every time Sean looked up, it seemed that the pit's edge was getting farther away.

Inch by inexorable inch, they descended into the pit. Sean's legs were getting tired; to make matters worse, he and Kyra had to hold up Sandy, who couldn't support herself because of her wounded leg. He knew that it was only a matter of time before they succumbed to exhaustion, but he also knew that if they stopped to rest for even a moment, they'd fall into the garbage and wouldn't be able to pull themselves free before they were dragged down into the hole at the bottom of the pit.

Sean gradually became aware that the light was fading. Although he couldn't see the biopod ceiling, he realized that it was beginning to polarize. In only an hour or so, night would come to the *taaraq* habitat. Even if he'd managed to keep his flashlight, it wouldn't have done them much good; indeed, Sean wondered if it wouldn't be better that they didn't see the end when it came.

By then, only a couple of *taaraq* were still present. The rest had disappeared, as if indifferent to the fate of their captives. The two that remained behind as guards stood at the pit's edge, javelins in hand as they quietly observed the three humans struggling below. Again, Kyra tried to make them understand, as best as she could with hand signals, that she and her companions meant no harm and that they'd come in peace. There was no sign that the guards understood . . . or if they did, that they even cared. As twilight set in, all they could see of the guards was two strange silhouettes against the dark grey sky.

Sean's thighs and calves felt as if they were made of lead; it took all his strength just to keep them moving. He'd pull himself an inch or two up the funnel wall, only to slide back down again. Next to him, Sandy's breath was coming in ragged gasps; she'd gone uncharacteristically quiet, but the occasional snuffle from behind her airmask told him that she was weeping. And although Kyra bravely continued the fight to stay on top of the refuse, he knew that she was just as exhausted as he was. And just as scared.

This is it, he thought. *We're going to die. No one will ever know how, or even where. Maybe the Corps will remember us as three more explorers lost in the line of duty, but . . .*

From somewhere not far away, an abrupt rumble of thunder, close enough that Sean heard it reverberate off the pit's far wall. A storm must be coming. Which only made sense; it was humid enough . . .

An instant later, another thunderclap. This time, though,

it didn't sound natural. More like a bomb going off. Kyra heard it, too, because she looked up. "Did you hear that?" she gasped, her voice ragged. "Some sort of explosion?"

"I heard it, yeah." Sean peered up at the edge of the pit. As the echoes of the second explosion died away, he heard the guards chittering to each other. Then they disappeared from sight, as if running off to see what had happened.

Oh, please, he thought. *Let this be what I think it is . . .*

A handful of seconds went by, then he heard motion just beyond the pit's edge. At first he thought it might be the guards returning. Then a flashlight beam suddenly lanced down into the pit, traveling across the funnel walls until it found the three humans trapped below.

"Sean? Are you all right?"

The voice that softly called to him was his mother's.

TWENTY-THREE

NTIL SHE ACTUALLY SAW HIM, ANDROMEDA WASN'T sure Sean was in the pit. The radio direction finder that Rolf had found among the Corps supplies in the *Montero* had made it possible for Zeus, D'Anguilo, and her to track the location of Survey One's transceiver, but she'd known that it was always possible that Sean might have lost it. So it wasn't until her flashlight beam revealed him and his companions at the bottom of a pit half-filled with muck that Andromeda allowed herself a moment of relief.

She quickly tamped down her emotions. So long as they were still in *taaraq* territory, they were all in grave danger. "Sean?" she called down to him, trying to be as quiet as she could. It wasn't hard; the airmask she wore muffled her voice. "Are you all right?"

For a second or two, he simply stared back at her, apparently astonished to see her there at all. It wasn't until Sandy made an excited whoop, and Kyra hastily shushed her, that Sean responded. "We're okay," he said, then seemed to change his mind. "No, we're not. Sandy's injured, and this pit . . ."

"We're sinking." Kyra was also careful to keep her voice low. "There's a hole in the bottom, and everything down here is falling into it. We need to get out of here."

"We're working on it." Still kneeling beside the pit, Andromeda looked to her right. "Tom . . . ?"

D'Anguilo had been at her side only a few seconds ago, but he was no longer there. Peering over her shoulder, she saw him scurrying toward one of the trees at the edge of the jungle through which the two of them had just hacked their way. He was carrying the long coil of rope they'd brought with them from the ship; as she watched, he looped it twice around the base of the tree's trunk.

"Mother?" From the pit, Sean called up to her again. "Whatever you plan to do, you'd better hurry. We're running out of time."

"Tell me about it," she muttered, too quiet for him to hear. *At least he's no longer calling me "Captain,"* she thought, although the realization gave her little satisfaction. As she waited for D'Anguilo to finish knotting the rope, she touched her headset mike. "Zeus, do you copy?" she said softly. "We've found 'em. Where are you?"

"Back where I dropped you off." The chief petty officer's voice was a whisper that she had to strain to hear. *"I've planted another charge, right where you told me to."*

"Good," she replied. "Don't blow it until I give the word. Stand by."

Andromeda had gambled that two half-pound plastic explosives would draw the inhabitants' attention. After Zeus had dropped D'Anguilo and her off on the riverbank about a quarter of a mile from the source of the transceiver signal, he'd crossed the river and, after tying up the boat, made his way through the jungle to plant the charges across from the *taaraq* settlement. He had set them off by radio detonator once Andromeda had located the pit where Survey One was being held captive. The third charge was a precautionary backup she hoped they wouldn't have to use.

She turned her head to peer at the waterfront. The place looked as if it was on fire. The bombs had ignited the dense foliage on the opposite side of the river, and silhouetted against its rising flames were the insectlike forms of the *taaraq*. They appeared to be in a state of confusion, even panic; clicking and chittering madly, they ran back and forth, trying to make sense of the calamity that had just struck their home. The river would prevent the fire from reaching their village, of course, but the *taaraq* hadn't yet realized that. So far as they were concerned, this was the wrath of whatever gods they worshipped.

They were distracted from the pit, which was what Andromeda wanted. Nonetheless, the *taaraq* were only a few hundred feet away, and there was still some daylight remaining in the biopod. If any of them happened to think about checking on their prisoners . . .

Hearing something move toward her, she looked around again to see D'Anguilo returning to the pit, crouching low as he laid out the rope behind him. Andromeda took the rest of the coil from him and yanked at the length he'd tied to the nearby tree. Two sharp tugs were enough to convince her that it was firmly anchored.

"All right," she said, quietly calling down into the pit again, "we're going to drop you a line. Who's coming up first?"

"Sandy, you better . . ." Sean began.

"No." Sandy's voice quivered with fear, yet she was adamant. "You first, then Kyra. I'm in no shape to climb, and they're going to need both of you to help drag me out of there."

"But you're hurt. You need to . . ."

"I don't care which of you comes up first," Andromeda hissed, "but hurry the hell up."

That was a lie; she wanted Sean to be first out of the pit, if only for selfish reasons. Andromeda dropped the rope over the side, and watched as her son reached out to grab it. He hesitated, then gallantly offered it to Kyra, murmuring something that Andromeda couldn't hear. The young woman shook her head, and he reluctantly turned his back to her and braced his feet against the pit's sloping walls. Bending almost double and pulling at the rope with both hands, he began to climb upward.

Although he had only about fifteen or sixteen feet to climb, it took a long time for Sean to escape from the pit. He frequently paused to catch his breath, and Andromeda could tell that he was exhausted. The last seven feet were the worst; there the funnel ended and the vertical walls began. By then, though, Sean seemed to have tapped some inner reserve of strength; he started climbing hand over hand as fast as he could.

As soon as he was near the top, Andromeda lay flat on her stomach and reached down to him, with D'Anguilo pushing down on her ankles to keep her from falling in. She first managed to grab hold of his forearms, then his shoulders, and finally his belt; her son clambered the rest of the way out, his mother hauling at him every inch of the way, until they lay beside each other, panting for breath.

"Sean . . ." Andromeda started to reach for him, wanting nothing more than to take him in her arms.

"Thanks." He allowed her the briefest of hugs, then impatiently sat up and, squatting on his knees, pulled the rope out of the pit. "Didn't anyone ever teach you how to do this?"

"Sorry." Andromeda stared at him, mildly irritated. "Some of us didn't get Corps survival training."

"You should just be happy she thought to bring a rope," D'Anguilo added.

Sean didn't reply. Instead, he twisted the end of the rope around and tied it off to form a loop. "Put this around you, Kyra," he said as he dropped it over the side again, then he looked at his mother and D'Anguilo. "Get ready to pull her up."

It took only a few minutes for the three of them to haul Kyra from the pit. Once she was with them, she helped the others bring Sandy up. She was nearly helpless; as soon as Andromeda saw her leg, she knew that it was infected.

They'd need to get her to the ship as soon as possible if they were going to save it . . . But just then, that was the least of Andromeda's concerns.

"How did you know where to find us?" Sean asked as he pulled the rope from around Sandy.

"We met a *hjadd* who—" D'Anguilo began.

"It's a long story," Andromeda interrupted. "I'll tell you later." Bending down to pick up the machete she'd dropped next to the pit, she pointed to the tree where D'Anguilo had anchored the rope. "The path we cleared is that way, and we've got a boat waiting at the other end."

Sean nodded, then reached down to help Sandy to her feet. "Let me do that," D'Anguilo said, moving to the young woman's side. "You go with your mother."

Sean hesitated, then moved to join her. Andromeda had an impulse to take him by the hand but restrained herself. "C'mon. Let's get out of here before your friends find out you're missing."

"They're not our friends," he muttered, and Andromeda almost laughed out loud at that, but she followed her anyway. Leaving the rope behind, the five of them moved as quickly and quietly as they could for the jungle, with Andromeda and Sean in the lead.

The light was getting dimmer by the minute, but Andromeda could still make out the path. Pushing aside broad-leafed fronds and massive ferns, she hurried as best as she could with an injured person in tow; she didn't want to use her flashlight unless it was absolutely necessary, for fear that the *taaraq* might spot its beam. The path took them away from the settlement, but they could still hear the angry voices of its inhabitants; they moved in silence. Every second counted; she knew it was only a matter of time before the *taaraq* discovered that their captives had escaped.

The path abruptly left solid ground and merged with the floating moss that apparently made up most of the biopod's interior. Andromeda paused to look back at the others. "We're going to have to spread out a little," she whispered, "or else we might break through the moss and get stuck. Go single file, if you can."

"What about them?" Sean motioned to Sandy and D'Anguilo, who were bringing up the rear. He was right; the floating moss might not support both of them so long as Sandy continued to rely on Tom for support.

"I can make it," Sandy murmured. "Just cut me a branch or something, and I'll . . ."

"No time for that." Andromeda took a deep breath. "We're just going to have to chance it. You two move as carefully as you can . . . but don't take too long."

Sandy and D'Anguilo both nodded, and Andromeda turned and continued forward, with Sean and Kyra not far behind. The ground turned wet and spongy; it felt as if she were walking on a waterbed. Andromeda could barely make out the path; dusk was closing in faster than she'd expected, and it wouldn't be long before she'd be forced to break out her flashlight. But it looked as if they were getting close to the river. The boat shouldn't be too far away, perhaps only a few dozen feet . . .

Her headset chirped. *"Skipper, are you there?"*

She prodded her mike. "We copy, Zeus. What's up?"

"Bad news. I think they're onto us. A few of 'em left the waterfront about a minute ago, and now there's some commotion back a ways from the beach. I can't see what's going on, but you might want to hurry."

Andromeda paused to turn her head and listen. Zeus was right; a few hundred yards behind them, from the other side of the jungle, she heard upraised *taaraq* voices. No question about it: they'd discovered that their prisoners were gone. No doubt they'd found the rope, and she cursed herself for not removing it. In a few seconds, they'd find the path, too.

"Get the engine started," she snapped, no longer bothering to keep her voice down. "Wait until you see us, then set off the last bomb." She didn't wait for a response before she clicked off the mike and turned to the others. "Run for it!"

The sloppy ground rolled and trembled beneath their

boots as they headed for the boat; subterfuge was no longer as important as speed. At one point, D'Anguilo's left foot broke through the moss; he cursed as he toppled to the ground, but Sandy managed to stay on her feet. D'Anguilo managed to pull his boot out of the muck, and he and Sandy clung to each other as they hurried to catch up with the others.

Just ahead, Andromeda saw a tiny light wink twice, pause, then wink twice again. The boat had returned to where Zeus had dropped off D'Anguilo and her; it appeared to be even closer than she'd thought. "Go, go, go!" she yelled, then reached back to grab Sean's wrist. "C'mon, you . . . hustle!"

Zeus was kneeling in the back of the inflatable Corps boat, one hand on the throttle of its idling outboard motor. "Hurry up!" he hissed loudly when he saw Andromeda and Sean break from cover. "I think they're putting their own boats into the water!"

"Blow the last one!" she yelled.

Zeus reached to the seatboard in front of him, snatched up the detonator. Andromeda was in the act of shoving Sean ahead of her when the last charge went off. Following her instructions, Zeus had planted it beside a tree near the trail about a hundred yards back the way they'd just come. It was the smallest of the charges, less than a quarter of a pound, and was meant to deter rather than kill. Or at least so she hoped; the *danui* would not look kindly upon their human visitors if they took *taaraq* lives during the rescue attempt.

As the blast briefly turned dusk into dawn, Andromeda caught a glimpse of a huge weed-tree becoming a whirlwind of flying splinters. They were well ahead of the explosion; nonetheless, the ground was rocked by its violence. It seemed to leap beneath their feet, causing all four of them to fall to their knees. Struggling to their feet again, they lurched the rest of the way to the boat, their boots making sucking noises as they plunged deep into the floating moss at the river's edge.

Andromeda could no longer hear any *taaraq* voices. If

any of the inhabitants were still behind them, they'd just been given a reason to keep their distance. Or so she hoped.

Andromeda waited until everyone else had climbed aboard, then she brought her machete down on the nylon cord Zeus had lashed to a tree. The mooring line snapped like a severed guitar string, and she threw herself into the boat, practically landing in Tom's lap.

"Go!" she shouted. "Get the hell out of here!"

Zeus revved the engine, and the boat roared away from the shore. As the chief petty officer made the 180-degree turn that would take them back toward the escalator, Andromeda looked to the left and spotted what he'd seen a few minutes earlier. A half dozen or more *taaraq* boats had left the waterfront and were heading up the narrow river, the *taaraq* in them lashing at the dark brown water with their long-handled paddles.

Obviously, they'd figured out that their captives couldn't have escaped without help and their rescuers must have come from the river. The intruders had a head start, but not much; only about a couple of hundred feet or so, Andromeda figured.

"They can't catch us." D'Anguilo calmly gazed back at the *taaraq* boats as Zeus came out of the turn to send the boat straight down the river. "We've got an engine, and they . . ."

"There's six of us aboard," Zeus said, "and our engine doesn't have much horsepower." He darted a glance over his shoulder, then looked at Andromeda. "They can still catch up with us, skipper . . . or at least get close enough to nail us with those spears they're carrying."

Andromeda nodded. Zeus was right. That last bomb might have put off the *taaraq* following their path, but there was little they could do about the ones pursuing them on the water. With the inflatable filled to capacity, its small engine might not be able to keep them ahead of a half dozen boats with enraged *taaraq* paddling as hard as they could. And she wasn't inclined to test their accuracy with

their javelins. Even a near miss would be enough to punc-
ture their craft's skin and bring the chase to an end.

"If anyone has any ideas," she said, "I'm only too willing to . . ."

"I do." Sean was sitting in front of the boat, Kyra hud-
dled beside him. He turned to look back at her. "Give me
your flashlight."

"What are you . . . ?"

"I'll show you." He held out his hand. "Your flashlight . . .
please."

Don't argue with him, she thought. *Just do it.* Andromeda unclipped the flashlight from her belt, gave it to him.
Pointing it straight ahead of them, Sean switched it on and
moved its luminescent oval across the shadowed shoreline
to their right. Apparently he was searching for something,
but Andromeda didn't know what . . .

"There," he said. "Those eggs? See 'em?"

About seventy feet away, the flashlight's beam had settled
upon several white ovoids floating in a cluster near the base
of some enormous trees. Andromeda had noticed the eggs
earlier but hadn't paid much attention to them. "Yeah? So?"

He didn't reply, but instead gazed past her at Zeus.
"Bring us near those eggs . . . but not too near. Just close
enough that our wake will hit 'em when we pass."

"Are you out of your mind?" Sandy stared at him in horror. "They're . . ."

"Do as I say." Sean ignored her as he kept the flashlight
beam on the eggs. "Keep the throttle all the way up. I'll let
you know if you're too close."

Zeus gave Andromeda an uncertain glance. She quietly
nodded, and he took a shallow starboard turn that moved
the boat closer toward the eggs. "Good, very good," Sean
said. "Keep your distance, but . . ."

Something sliced into the water a few yards from the
boat: a javelin, hurled by one of the *taaraq.* Andromeda
looked back; sure enough, the *taaraq* were rapidly closing
the distance between them. It seemed impossible that they

could paddle so fast that they could catch up with the humans, but the inflatable wasn't built for speed.

"Sean," she began, "I hope you know what you're . . ."

"Okay, that's it!" he snapped. "Cut to the left! Fast!"

Zeus twisted the rudder to the right, and the boat made a sharp turn to port. Tepid water sloshed over the gunnels as the inflatable veered away from the shore, heading again up the middle of the river. Andromeda caught a brief glimpse of the eggs as the boat swept past them; Sean used his flashlight to track their wake's leading edge as it hit the eggs, causing them to bob up and down like buoys. Why would Sean care about . . . ?

The answer came an instant later as something huge moved on the shore just past the eggs. Andromeda watched in astonishment as one of the giant trees suddenly came to life; an upper branch came down with terrifying force, plunging into the river where the boat had been just a few seconds earlier.

No, she thought. *That's not a tree. That's a creature.* And it wasn't attacking their boat, but their wake instead and the flashlight beam that illuminated it. *It thinks the wake is alive, and it's defending its eggs . . .*

The *taaraq* knew all about the walking trees, of course, and had been careful to stay away from them. But their shallow-hulled boats didn't produce waves strong enough to disturb the eggs, so they'd apparently believed that they could move past the giant predators without alerting them. Their intended prey, though, had changed all that.

Andromeda looked back just in time to see one of the walking trees attack the closest of the *taaraq* boats. Its upper branch—which she now realized was an immense beak—came down out of the darkness to crash down into the center of the small wooden craft. A horrific screech, and the beak lifted again, a *taaraq* flailing helplessly within it. The boat itself was already gone, its other passengers nowhere to be seen. The beak rose upward and opened wide, and the screaming *taaraq* vanished into its maw.

That'll teach 'em to be nice to tourists, she thought. The rest of the *taaraq* boats were falling back, trying to avoid the monster that had unexpectedly charged one of their own. *I just hope the* danui *didn't see this.*

Sandy was cheering at the top of her lungs, and Andromeda looked around to see Sean receive a long, passionate hug from his girlfriend. D'Anguilo was uncharacteristically speechless; he stared at the walking tree, apparently mortified that he hadn't recognized it for what it really was. Zeus hunched over the throttle bar, grimly determined to put as much distance between them and the denizens of this biopod as he could.

Andromeda cleared her throat and waited until Sean broke free from Kyra. "How did you know?" she asked.

Sean turned to look back at her, but didn't immediately respond. "How did you know?" he said at last, repeating her own question.

"It's a long story."

"Really? Mine is, too." A slow nod; it was impossible to tell for sure, but she thought he might be smiling behind his airmask. "Maybe we should talk about it sometime."

"I think we should, yeah . . . later." Andromeda glanced over her shoulder again. The remaining *taaraq* boats were nowhere in sight, but it was too dark to know for certain whether they'd given up pursuit. In any case, all she wanted to do was get the hell out of there.

Lifting her hand to her headset, she prodded its mike. "Survey Two to Base One. Rolf, do you copy? Over."

The chief engineer's voice immediately came over the comlink. *"Affirmative. What's going on?"*

"We've got everyone, safe and sound. Where are you now?"

"Waiting for you at the escalator. Mel's standing by at the tram station."

"I'm here, skipper," Melpomene's voice cut in. *"Good to hear you again. You say you have everyone with you?"*

"Roger that. We should be there in five or ten minutes. Soon as Rolf tells you that he has us in sight, I want you to call for a tram. I'd like to get out of here pronto."

"We copy, Captain," Rolf said. *"And congratulations."*

"Thanks. Survey Two over and out." Andromeda clicked off the mike, let out her breath. "Okay, Chief . . . take us home."

As she'd figured, it took only a few minutes for them to return to the place where she, Zeus, and D'Anguilo had inflated the Corps boat and put it in the water. Rolf was waiting for them on the shore, holding a lamp above his head to guide them in. They abandoned their craft near the same tree where Sean had stolen the *taaraq* boat, despite D'Anguilo's misgivings about leaving advanced technology in the hands of primitives.

"Let 'em have it," Andromeda said as she helped Sean carry Sandy to the nearby escalator. "They probably won't know what to do with it anyway." She glanced over her shoulder at the darkened river. "Besides, they may still be after us. I don't want to give 'em another chance to catch up."

It didn't take long for the lift to ascend to the tram station, just enough time for Rolf to break out the first-aid kit he'd brought with him and use it to tend to the deep wound in Sandy's thigh and the small cut in Sean's side. Melpomene was waiting for them at the top of the escalator. She'd moved the Corps team's belongings from the veranda to the platform just before she used the station control panel to summon a tram.

"Don't worry, skipper," she said, as Andromeda closely inspected the panel. "I made sure that I entered the coordinates the right way."

Andromeda gave her a wry smile. "The left way, you mean."

"Trust me. I'm a navigator, remember?" Melpomene pointed to the node at the upper right corner of the *taaraq* hexagon. "That's our next stop, I promise."

On the other side of the platform's transparent barrier, a tram was already waiting for them. The station scanned everyone in the group, then the barrier slid up into the ceiling, allowing them to enter the vehicle. Once its doors shut behind them, Andromeda pulled off her airmask and let it fall to the floor. Then she collapsed on a bench, exhausted as she'd ever been.

It's over, she thought. *Thank God, it's over.*

She was wrong.

TWENTY-FOUR

SEAN'S PREVIOUS EXPERIENCE WITH HEX'S TRAM SYStem had been the journey from the *arsashi* habitat to the one occupied by the *taaraq*, so he braced himself for another long ride. But it took only a few minutes for the tram to make the short trip from the biopod to its adjacent node; it felt as if he'd just pulled off his airmask when the vehicle began to decelerate.

Not that he was about to complain. All he wanted to do, really, was get out of the stinking, ripped clothes he'd been wearing the last few days, take a hot shower, have a meal that didn't come out of a wrapper, maybe even catch a nap. Once all that was done, he might feel civilized again.

And then he'd have a long talk with his mother.

Andromeda sat across from him, slouched in her seat, with her arms limp at her sides, staring at nothing in particular. Sean had never seen her that way before; she looked as if she'd just come through an ordeal even though the physical hardships she'd endured were nothing compared to his own. So it couldn't be fatigue. It had to be something else.

Oh, man, he thought, *she really was worried about me, wasn't she?*

Perhaps she'd made the mistake that had gotten his team into a mess, but she'd also risked her life, not to mention those of her crew, to get them out of it. Sean still didn't know exactly how she'd managed to find him and the others—everyone was too tired for explanations—but he had a feeling that she'd put a lot on the line to do so.

She wouldn't have done that unless she loved you. The notion wasn't something he particularly welcomed; he had spent the last few years learning how to despise her. *But that was for what she'd done to Dad, and that was a long time ago. This time, it's just about you. And this time, she didn't . . .*

Through the window beside him, the tunnel's rock walls abruptly disappeared, to be replaced by what appeared to be another platform. Andromeda seemed to wake up a little; gazing past him out the window, she sighed with relief.

"We're here," she said, her voice a little more than a hoarse croak.

"That was fast." Sean forced a smile. "You did enter the right coordinates this time, didn't you?"

He meant it to be a joke, but it didn't come off that way. Melpomene cast him an arctic glare while his mother closed her eyes with weary resignation. "I'm sorry," she said quietly. "It was a . . . a dumb mistake, and I shouldn't have . . ."

"I didn't mean it that way," he said, and she looked up at him. "I know it was a mistake, and I"—he hesitated; *oh, c'mon, say it!*—"I forgive you."

Andromeda studied him for a moment, as if not quite believing what she'd just heard. "Thank you," she said at last, little more than a whisper. "I appreciate it."

He took a deep breath. "Look, I . . ."

"Maybe we should talk about this later," Andromeda said, as the tram glided to a halt. "Right now, we need to get back to the ship and get ready to leave."

"Sure. Okay." Sean's knees cracked as he pushed himself out of his seat, his legs stiff as wood. "Where are we going? Back to the habitat you found?"

Andromeda didn't answer at once; instead, she shared a silent look with Melpomene and Rolf. "If the *danui* will let us," she said at last, slowly rising from her own seat. "They may not be very happy with us just now."

Sean started to reply, but his mother was already heading toward the tram doors. Rolf started to follow her, but not before he paused next to Sean. "I hope you're grateful," he muttered. "She sacrificed a lot to save you."

The chief engineer walked away before he could respond, and neither Melpomene nor Zeus seemed inclined to add anything more than indifferent glances in his direction. Only D'Anguilo seemed willing to explain. "It's not your fault," he said quietly as he helped Kyra pull Sandy to her feet. "The *hjadd* emissary told us that the *danui* have an edict against one race interfering with another. You ended up where you were by accident . . . but she deliberately broke the rules to rescue you."

"But don't they know that if she'd left us there, the *taaraq* would've killed us?" Sean reached over to take Sandy from D'Anguilo. Her wound had been cleaned and bandaged, but she'd need a session in *Montero*'s autodoc before she'd be able to walk on her own again. Sean himself could use a few stitches. "I don't think she had a choice."

"Believe me, she didn't." D'Anguilo reached down to pick up his pack and Sean's as well. "And I think the *hjadd* know that, too."

"So what's the . . . ?"

"The problem is that it's not the *hjadd* who make the rules . . . It's the *danui*." D'Anguilo turned to head for the door. "And no one knows what they'll make of all this."

There was a circular hatch at the end of the platform. It spiraled open at their approach, revealing a stone-walled room. An identical hatch was on the opposite side of the room; on the other side of an adjacent window was the node's docking bay, with a tubular walkway leading to the *Montero*, suspended within a cat's cradle of mooring cables. Set within another wall was what appeared to be a comp flatscreen.

"Just like the one we came through at Nueva Italia," Melpomene said. "It shouldn't scan us on the way back, though."

"Then why is the tunnel closed?" Rolf walked over to the second hatch and stopped before it. "It was open when we left it." He waited a moment, but the hatch remained shut. He looked back at the others. "Why isn't it opening now?"

"He's right . . . It should open for us." Andromeda tapped her headset. "Survey Two to *Montero*, do you copy?" She paused to listen, and a puzzled expression came upon her face. "*Montero*, this is Survey Two. Please respond, over."

"Let me try." Melpomene prodded her own headset. "Anne, this is Mel. Please come in." A second passed, then she shook her head. "Nothing. Not even static."

D'Anguilo turned to the captain. "I don't think . . ." he began, then he stopped, his eyes growing wide in astonishment. It was at that instant that a feminine voice spoke from behind her:

"Hello, Captain Carson. It's a pleasure to meet you at last."

Sean looked around to see a *danui* standing behind his mother.

He'd seen images of *danui* before. Its six-limbed body resembled that of an immense spider, but its mandibles and eyestalks looked more like those of a crustacean. Covered with wiry black hair, it wore what appeared to be a vestlike garment crossed with several belts. Standing on the other side of the room, the alien was so solid in appearance that its lack of shadow was the only clue that it was actually a holographic projection.

Startled, Andromeda involuntarily recoiled from the creature. "What the hell . . . ?" she began, then caught herself. "Hello . . . I'm sorry, but you . . . ah, surprised me, that's all."

"Why should you be surprised?" When the *danui* spoke,

its pleasant voice wasn't synchronized with the movement of its mandibles. "We were supposed to meet earlier, were we not? Our associate, Sashatasma Jahd Sa-Fhadda, indicated that you were looking forward to our encounter."

"Yes, we do."

"Very well then. Let us talk." The *danui* raised its forelegs, bent them closer to its body. "For purposes of temporary identification, you may call me Jane Doe. You would not be able to pronounce my name if I told it to you. My people have delegated to me the task of speaking with you."

"Yes, right . . . of course." Andromeda paused. "I'm sorry for the delay. We had some urgent matters that we needed to take care of. Some of my people—"

"We know this," Doe said, interrupting her without apology. "Nothing that happens in Hex . . . as you call this place . . . goes unobserved. In fact, it is your conduct that concerns us, and our discussion of your actions will determine where you go next."

Doe turned its—or was it her?—left foreleg toward the closed hatch. "On the other side of that hatch is the walkway leading to your ship. When this meeting is over, we will open the hatch and let you board your vessel. We also will permit your ship to leave this habitat, just as we allowed it to dock here in the first place. However, you should know that it's possible that we may not allow you to return to your own habitat. If you attempt to do so, you will find that its docking node will not open for you, nor for the other vessel from your world that is in our system."

Andromeda stared at Jane Doe. "Other vessel? What other . . . ?"

"Look at the screen behind you."

Along with everyone else in the room, Sean turned toward the flatscreen. It lit to display a cruciform-shaped spacecraft somewhat smaller than the *Montero*, as captured from a stern angle several miles away. It appeared to be a freighter, and since the exhaust bell of its single engine was dark, it appeared to be adrift.

"The *Pride of Cucamonga*." D'Anguilo immediately

recognized the other vessel. "That's Ted Harker's ship." He looked back at Jane Doe. "Where is this from?"

"The image is being relayed from the same starbridge you used to come here. This ship emerged from hyperspace only fifteen minutes, thirty-two seconds ago. Because our business is still unfinished, we have shut down its main drive and navigation systems until our conversation is concluded."

"Damn," Andromeda said quietly. "Harker must have gotten impatient when he didn't hear from us and decided to come through himself." She turned toward Jane Doe again. "This ship belongs to another captain from my world. I assure you, he means no harm."

"Even if he did, we sincerely doubt that he poses a significant threat." The *danui's* mandibles moved a little faster as her eyestalks made a strange bobbing motion. *Is she laughing at us?* Sean wondered. "However, his impatience and your own . . . along with several other unbecoming traits . . . are another matter entirely. They pose a danger not only to yourselves but to other inhabitants of Hex as well. This is what we need to discuss with you before we decide whether to allow you to remain or request that you leave and never return."

The *danui* touched a band on her left foreleg, and a holographic replica of Hex materialized beside her. "First, you need to know the reasons why we built this place. As Sashatasma Jahd Sa-Fhadda has told you, we did this because our original world was in peril and we had no other alternative if we wanted to preserve our race. We later developed means of interstellar travel, but by then Hex was nearly complete. Because our race has little interest in exploration for its own sake, we realized that Hex gave us a singular advantage . . ."

"You could invite other races to come here instead of your having to go to them." D'Anguilo nodded. "I'd figured that, once we saw the number of starbridges you'd built and the different kinds of vessels coming through them."

"An astute observation, Dr. D'Anguilo." Jane Doe's eyes swiveled in his direction. "In this way, we are able to reap the benefits of interstellar travel . . . namely, trade and cultural contact . . . without having to leave home. We have emissaries in the Talus, but few of my people leave our system otherwise. Yet there is another reason."

Her eyestalks moved again toward the miniature Hex. "During our continuing effort to forge alliances with the other races of the galaxy, we've developed an appreciation for the fragility of life, the thin margins upon which it often exists. In some instances, races are threatened with extinction by forces beyond their control. My own race was nearly obliterated by a natural catastrophe. The homeworlds of the *taaraq* and the *nord*, among others, were destroyed by the Annihilator. As we understand it, your homeworld has been severely damaged by environmental abuse of your own making, forcing a mass migration to your colony world. There are many ways in which a species can perish, and their options for survival are never easy."

Jane Doe tapped her wristband again, and several tiny hexagons lit up in bright blue across Hex's surface. "Here, we have provided an alternative . . . sanctuaries for endangered races." One of her eyes turned toward Sean. "Corporal Carson, you and your party found one such sanctuary . . . the *taaraq* habitat, populated by the descendents of the survivors of a world destroyed by the Annihilator. There are a few such habitats here, each designed to mimic a native environment that has long since disappeared."

"And you keep them isolated from other races?" Andromeda asked. "Why?"

"Like the *taaraq*, some were not even aware of the existence of other races until they were brought here. Keeping them apart from others prevents cultural confusion that could be just as deadly as the forces that destroyed their own worlds. And there are many races here about which even the Talus is yet unaware."

Sean glanced at Kyra, saw the look on her face. She said nothing, but D'Anguilo wasn't as reticent. "Races that the Talus doesn't know about?" he asked. "You mean . . . ?"

"Yes. Races with whom no one but we have made contact. Yet like the *hjadd*, the *arsashi*, the *nord*, and many others, they have been invited to establish colonies here for a single purpose more important than any other . . . to preserve their races should their worlds ever come to an end."

"Hex is a galactic sanctuary," Andromeda said. "Is that what you mean?"

"Yes, precisely." The *danui's* forelegs spread apart in an almost human gesture. "Once a race has established a colony here, its existence is assured. Even if its homeworld or other colonies cease to exist, its race will not perish with them."

"And in the meantime, they are able to establish trade with your race," D'Anguilo said.

"My people, yes, but also others . . . provided that those races agree to let others visit their habitats, in which case they may exchange transit-system coordinates. But for races like the *taaraq*, or even those who simply do not wish to have contact with the Talus, isolation is perhaps best for all concerned."

"So you keep them apart from the others. I understand—"

"No, Dr. D'Anguilo . . . we are afraid you do not." Sean noticed that Jane Doe used the plural pronoun; the *danui* emissary seldom referred to itself in the singular form. An individual quirk, or a social trait? "If you truly understood, then you and your companions would not have committed many of the transgressions of the past several days. The unauthorized reconnaissance of the *arsashi* colony by your landing craft, with the resultant crash landing when it attempted to evade an energy beam meant to deter it . . ."

"Our pilot did that on orders from my commanding officer," Sean said. "The pilot was killed during the crash, and the commanding officer—"

"Died as a result of a cultural misunderstanding." Jane Doe did not seem to be perturbed by the constant interruptions. "His death could have been avoided had you known in advance that you were going to be encountering *arsashi* tribesmen."

"That was an accident." Kyra stepped forward, speaking

up for the first time. "I knew the *arsashi* customs, but Cayce . . . our commanding officer . . . wasn't willing to listen to me."

"An unwillingness to listen seems to be an unfortunate tendency among your kind." Jane Doe turned to Andromeda again. "We attempted to give you advice during your approach to Hex, enlisting the *hjadd* as our intermediaries since you are unfamiliar with our language. Had you obeyed our wishes, your ship would have docked without incident at the habitat we had prepared for you. But you chose not to do so."

Andromeda said nothing, but Sean noticed that her fists were curling at her sides. He hoped that, for once, his mother would keep her temper under control. She slowly let out her breath, and he was relieved to see her hands relax again.

"I'm sorry," she said. "You're right . . . It's my fault. If I'd listened, a lot of trouble could have been avoided." She paused for a moment before going on, this time with an edge to her voice. "However, I won't apologize for rescuing my son and his companions."

Sean took a step toward her. "Mother . . ."

"Sean, be quiet . . . please." She barely glanced at him, but instead continued to look straight at the *danui*. "I know that this was trespassing. Jahd explained that to me even before we went there. But"—she nodded toward Sean—"it had to be done. I couldn't leave him behind."

"Then you admit that you knowingly broke our rules," Jane Doe replied.

"Your rules weren't explained to us until after we had broken them . . ."

"This is true, but in this instance, they were."

Andromeda hesitated. "Yes, they were explained to us," she admitted. "Jahd told us the *taaraq* habitat was off-limits, and heshe warned us of the possible consequences." Then a quizzical expression crossed her face. "But . . . wait a minute. If you were aware of what we were doing . . . even what we *intended* to do, before we actually did it . . . then why did you let us go ahead with it?"

"She's right," D'Anguilo said. "You could have stopped us at any time. You could have prevented our ship from leaving our habitat, or refused to open this habitat's docking node, or even stopped our tram from coming here. But you let us go ahead anyway even though it was against your own rules."

Sean cleared his throat. "Pardon me, but . . . isn't a rule pretty useless if the people who made it don't obey it themselves?"

"Yes, you are correct." Jane Doe's eyestalks twitched in his direction, and Sean found himself unnerved by her attention. Her resemblance to a giant spider couldn't be ignored, and he felt the chill that prey does in the presence of a predator. "Remember, though, that this particular rule was explained to you by a member of a race that does not raise its offspring."

"What do you . . . ?" Andromeda began.

"The *hjadd* don't raise their own young," D'Anguilo said. "Once they lay their eggs, they leave and never see their children after they're hatched. Their offspring are raised instead by another community. Their evolution developed this as a means of diversifying the gene pool."

"Correct," Jane Doe said. "But my race is different from the *hjadd*. In fact, our practices are similar to your own." Her eyestalks moved toward Andromeda again. "And only another mother would know how it feels to have a child in danger."

Andromeda opened her mouth, but for the first time that he could remember, Sean saw that she was unable to speak. Instead, she and the *danui* silently regarded each other for a long moment, as if they'd suddenly recognized each other for what they were.

"I see," Andromeda said at last, her voice little more than a whisper.

"I believe you do," Jane Doe replied. "As Sashatasma Jahd

Sa-Fhadda explained, some rules can be bent under certain conditions."

In that moment, Sean realized that he had something to add. "May I say something, please?" he asked, politely raising a hand.

His mother turned to glare at him; she was obviously afraid that he'd screw things up. Before she could object, though, Jane Doe looked at Sean again. "Of course . . . by all means."

He took a deep breath, then went on. "Some of the things we did . . . some of the mistakes that were made . . . are my fault. I understand that now, and I accept the blame."

"We appreciate your candor," Jane Doe said, "but that does not excuse your actions."

"I apologize. But in my defense . . ." Sean hesitated, trying to find the right words. "I'm an explorer. It's my job to learn new things." He paused. "And now that I've seen some of this place, I only want to see more."

"Sean . . ." Andromeda stared at him, plainly aghast at the idea of losing him again.

He ignored her as he went on. "If you're willing to let us remain, I'd like to have that opportunity . . ."

"So would I," Kyra said, and Sean was surprised when she stepped to his side and took his hand. "I've been through a lot . . . both of us have . . . but if it would help my people understand yours, and everyone else who is here, then the risk is worth it."

Sean stole a glance at Sandy. Looking back at him, she quietly shook her head; she'd had enough of Hex. He turned toward Jane Doe again. "I can't promise that we won't make any more mistakes, but . . . well, we can try to do our best to abide by your rules."

A wry smile appeared on his mother's face. "They're not all that hard to understand, really," she said. "Respect your neighbors. Don't take anything that isn't yours. Call first before coming over to visit . . ." She looked at Sean again. "The sort of thing mothers try to teach their children. Sometimes, they even listen."

"We believe you now understand." Jane Doe had patiently listened to all this; her right foreleg moved toward the hatch. "You may return to your ship . . . and your habitat." A short pause. "You will hear from us again."

As suddenly as it had appeared, her holo projection vanished. A moment later, the exit hatch spiraled open. Andromeda turned to Sean and was about to say something when she apparently heard something through her earpiece. She tapped her mike and said, "We copy, *Montero*. Stand by."

D'Anguilo slowly let out his breath. "I'll be damned. I never would've believed it . . . Someone won an argument with a *danui*."

Sean grinned. "That's nothing," he said, then nodded toward his mother. "Try winning an argument with her."

TWENTY-FIVE

"THIS IS . . ."

At a loss for words, Ted Harker fell silent for a moment. Instead, he stared at the landscape spread out below the tram-station veranda. "Incredible," he finished, his voice little more than an awestruck whisper. "I can't believe what I'm seeing."

Andromeda tried not to smile. She'd witnessed the reaction a couple of times before, most recently when Anne Smith was finally able to leave the *Montero* to see Hex for herself. "I know," Andromeda said. "It always gets you the first time you see it." She looked up at the sky, with its staggering view of all the other hexagons beyond Nueva Italia's barrel ceiling. "And the second time, too," she added. "I'm not sure I'll ever get used to this."

Harker continued to gaze down upon Nueva Italia. "You say there are four more . . . um, biopods? . . . just like this one?"

"So I've been told. We haven't had a chance to visit them

yet, so we don't know exactly what's there. But if we're to believe the *hjadd*, then they should look a lot like Coyote, too."

"And the sixth biopod?"

"Closed to us. The *danui* have placed it off-limits. Something to do with protecting their technological secrets." Catching the sly look on Harker's face, she shook her head. "Don't even think about it. They've made it clear to us that their rules aren't to be broken, and I've crossed that line too many times already."

"But still . . ."

" 'But still' nothing. We've had one warning already, and I don't think we're going to get any more." Andromeda turned away from the railing. "C'mon, let's go. I think your people would like to see the rest of this place."

The crew of the *Pride of Cucamonga* stood nearby, gaping at the immense vista beyond the tram station. Harker nodded to them, and they picked up their duffel bags and followed him to the escalator. The *Pride* had come prepared to establish the makings of a permanent human colony on Hex; several crates of items—prefab building material, survey equipment, miscellaneous items such as portable lights and farm tools; everything except weapons, which had been unpacked and left behind—had already been off-loaded from the freighter, and two more crewmen had just finished stacking them on the lift. They stood aside as their captain and crewmates stepped aboard. Andromeda walked over to the control panel and pushed the lowest button, and the lift began to descend.

"A thousand miles long and a hundred miles wide." Harker whistled under his breath, studying the wooded slopes as the lift slowly moved down the mountainside. "You can fit a small continent in here." He slowly shook his head. "No, I don't think we're going to run out of real estate anytime soon."

Andromeda shrugged. "If we do, we can always ask the *danui* for more." A startled look appeared on Harker's face, and she smiled. "If what Jahd told me is true, then Hex is still unfinished. Many of the hexagons around us are vacant. Even if we used up all the land in this habitat . . ."

"We could move to another one?" Harker asked, and she nodded. "So what's the catch?"

"No catch . . . except behave ourselves." Andromeda looked him straight in the eye. "Don't mess with the landlord, Ted. I'm serious. Remember what I told you about what happened to the *morath*?"

Harker's mouth tightened. He didn't say anything for a few seconds; when he did, it was to change the subject. "So . . . are you still bored?"

Andromeda looked at him askance. "Come again?"

"When I came to your house to talk about this mission, you complained that you were bored with your job." A knowing smile spread across his face. "Just curious if that's still a problem with your life."

"No . . . no, it isn't." Andromeda allowed herself a small laugh, then looked away from him. "But I've been thinking a bit about what I'd like to do now that the job is done."

"Whatever you want, you probably won't have much trouble getting it. After all, you're the captain who discovered Hex. Don't be surprised if someone throws a parade for you when you get back home." Harker moved a little closer to her, lowering his voice so that his crew wouldn't overhear them. "You can pretty much write your own ticket. Any run you want, any ship . . . you name it, and I'll see that you get it."

Andromeda smiled. "Thanks, but I have other plans."

Harker raised an eyebrow. "Such as?"

"Actually, I'm thinking about building a nice little cottage for my retirement." She pointed toward the river. "Right over there, near the edge of that apple grove . . . or maybe a little farther away, just to put a little distance between me and the rest of the colony."

"You're *retiring*?" No longer bothering to keep his voice down, Harker nearly yelled in her face. His crew turned to stare, but he was oblivious to them. "I thought you said . . ."

"I've changed my mind."

"But . . ."

"Soon as the *Montero* gets home, I'm formally tendering my resignation. Then I'm going to sell the house, pack up my stuff, and move here." She gave him a serious look. "You'll give me a break on the freight costs, won't you? I'd like to take the *Montero* back, and Jason said he'd be willing to give me a ride next time he comes out here. If you approve my recommendation that he be made captain, that is."

"Yeah, sure, but . . ." Harker floundered, not quite knowing what to say. "What the hell, Andi . . ."

"It's Andromeda, Ted. I hate that nickname." The lift had almost reached the bottom of the incline, and she looked over at the freighter crew. "Careful now. Don't get off until we've come to a full stop."

Harker held his tongue until the lift halted, then he followed Andromeda down the ramp. "But why here?" he asked. "It's going to be a while before any settlement we put here will be self-sufficient. Not exactly a comfortable retirement spot, y'know."

"That's exactly why I want to move here." Andromeda started walking toward the nearby camp. "Steady climate, no predators . . . but plenty to do to make this place a home. Won't have any time to be lazy." She shrugged. "I'm even thinking about running for colonial governor, once we get around to elections and so forth."

"Colonial governor. Right." Harker shook his head. "Andi . . . Andromeda . . . you're a starship captain. That's your calling . . ."

"What am I going to do for an encore? Discover another Dyson sphere?" She shook her head. "I'm done. Time to hang up my wings and call it a day. Besides, I . . . Oh, dear, what is this?"

Over the past few days, while they'd been waiting for the *Pride of Cucamonga* to arrive, Andromeda's crew had reestablished the base camp. And more than that. After bringing back the tents and equipment they'd taken out of

Nueva Italia, they'd made a head start on turning the camp into a permanent settlement. While several acres had been staked out to become farm fields, the area surrounding the tents was already zoned to be the town square.

This was made clear by a sign someone had fashioned from a metal rod and a couple of pieces of packing material. Standing just outside camp, it read:

WELCOME TO NUEVA ITALIA

COYOTE 214.9 L.Y. →

← EARTH 194.6 L.Y.

Her crew was gathered around the fire pit in the camp's center, waiting for Melpomene and Anne to finish cooking lunch. Spotting Andromeda, Zeus stood up from his seat and ambled over to her. "Like it?" he asked, grinning with pride as he looked up at his handiwork. "Kinda thought this place deserved a proper sign."

"Not bad." It was the last thing Andromeda had expected to see when she returned from meeting Harker's ship at the docking node, but she had to admit that it gave the place a certain rustic class. And now that she'd announced her plans to her crew, she shouldn't be surprised to have them do certain things without her consent. "Did you bring it up for a vote?"

"Approved by unanimous consent." The smile faded from Zeus's face; he hesitated a moment, then went on. "I've been doing some thinking, skipper, and so has Mel. If it's all the same to you, we'd like to stay, too. Sorry to be jumping ship, but . . ."

"No objections from me." In fact, Andromeda wasn't surprised. She'd overheard her chief petty officer and helmsman discussing this very thing just the other day, when they thought she wasn't in her tent. "I wouldn't mind having neighbors."

The grin returned to Zeus's face, and he turned to walk

back toward the others. On the other hand, Harker didn't seem to be very pleased. "That's two more members of your crew I'm going to have to replace," he muttered.

"Aw, c'mon. There are plenty of unemployed spacers back home. You won't have any problems." Harker continued to scowl, and she tried to mollify him. "Like I said, Jason wants to continue serving aboard the *Montero*. So do Rolf and Anne, and Sandy LaPointe wants to go back, too, so it's not like you'll be losing everyone . . ."

"Don't worry about it," Harker said, albeit with obvious reluctance. "I'll approve resignations for any member of your crew who wishes to remain here." He looked up at the new sign and shrugged. "Besides, if we're going to have a new colony here, we have to start with someone."

"I sort of hoped you'd say that," Andromeda said. "That's why I'm not resigning immediately. There's one more duty as captain I'd like to perform." Raising a hand, she whistled between her teeth. "You two! Over here!"

From the other side of the fire pit, Sean and Kyra stood up and sauntered over to where Andromeda and Harker stood. Their hands were clasped together, and Andromeda couldn't help but enjoy seeing the comfortable way her son and Kyra had with each other. As they came closer, she reached out to put a hand on Sean's shoulder.

"Ted, let me introduce you to my son, Sean, and his fiancée, Kyra." Andromeda was unable to keep from beaming with motherly pride. "Yesterday morning, they requested that I marry them as soon as we got enough people here to serve as a proper wedding party."

Harker stared at Sean and Kyra. "Yes," he said after a moment. "Right. Of course."

"This won't be a problem for you, will it?" Sean slipped his arm within the crook of his mother's elbow. "I couldn't ask for anyone else that I'd rather have officiate than my mother."

Andromeda swallowed what felt like a large lump that got caught in her throat. Over the course of the past few days, while they'd waited for the *Pride* to show up, the two of them had spent many hours talking about things that should have been discussed long ago.

I've got my son back, she thought. *And I'm about to have a daughter-in-law, too. With luck, maybe even a grandchild or two . . .*

"Well . . . if we're going to have a wedding, it wouldn't be decent if we didn't have enough liquor." Harker shook hands with the groom and gave the bride a quick buss on the cheek, then stepped away. "There may be a few bottles of wine somewhere on my ship. I'll ask someone to fetch them."

Andromeda watched him go. "Poor man," she said softly, once he was out of earshot. "I wonder how many more shocks he can take in one day before he has a heart attack."

"You're enjoying this, aren't you?" Sean regarded her with an upraised eyebrow.

"Yes . . . yes, I am. Thank you."

Kyra chuckled as Sean sighed and looked down at his feet. "C'mon," he said to his bride-to-be. "Let's get out of here before she pisses off someone else."

Andromeda let them go, then turned to head over to where the new arrivals from the *Pride* were gathered. She was about to direct them to where they could put up their own tents when she heard a familiar voice from behind her.

"Captain Carson? A moment, please?"

She looked around to see Tom D'Anguilo walking toward her. "It's Andromeda," she said. "I'm not going to be captain very much longer, so you might as well drop the title."

"Okay, then . . . Thanks." He stopped, looked down at his feet with uncustomary shyness. "I just wanted to tell you . . . Well, I overheard a bit of what you were saying to Captain Harker, about how you and some other people were electing to stay behind, and . . ."

"You want to do the same?"

"I'm going to request that the company transfer me here,

yes." D'Anguilo smiled as he looked up at her. "I'll do my best to stay out of your hair, but . . ."

"Don't worry about it. I couldn't have done this without you." She paused. "Besides, I have a feeling the colony is going to need a resident astroethnicist."

D'Anguilo nodded. "That's what I think, too . . . particularly if your son meant what he said about wanting to explore more of Hex. I'd like to go with him, if he and Kyra will have me along."

"You'll have to work that out with them. I think they're looking at it as a sort of honeymoon trip." She shrugged. "But even if you don't, it makes sense having you here. Eventually, we're going to be meeting the neighbors."

"Yes, you're right. We will. But"—a reluctant pause—"there's something more, too."

Andromeda folded her arms together. "What do you mean?"

"Well . . . do you remember what Jane Doe said? About there being races here that even the Talus hasn't met yet?" Andromeda nodded, and he went on. "Well, just suppose . . . What if we start exploring Hex, and come into contact with them before anyone else does?"

Andromeda opened her mouth to reply, then stopped herself. "I hadn't thought of that," she admitted. "That's a possibility, isn't it?"

"I think it is, yes . . . and even though the *danui* are aware that we intend to continue traveling through this place, they haven't told us that we can't, so long as we abide by the rules. So . . ."

His voice trailed off. "So . . . what?" Andromeda asked.

"So what did Jane Doe mean when she said, 'You will hear from us again'?"

Because she had no answer to that question, Andromeda didn't reply. Instead, she looked away, letting her gaze travel across Nueva Italia's wooded green meadows as she savored the warmth of an endless summer.

"I hope Harker gets back here soon," she said at last. "Man, I need a drink."

EPILOGUE

ONE BY ONE, THE SHIPS CAME TO HEX.

At first, only a few made the hyperspace jump from Coyote, but before long their number increased to dozens, each traveling through an alien starbridge to arrive at a world like none other. No matter how often their crew and passengers had seen images of the Dyson sphere, nothing quite prepared them for seeing it with their own eyes, the awesome sight of its immensity as it gradually grew before them, steadily increasing in size until nothing lay before them except a vast and seemingly endless wall of hexagons.

They didn't make the trip alone. In the days that it took the ships to travel from the starbridge to Nueva Italia's docking node, they heard voices coming through the comlink: greetings from passing vessels, each of them belonging to one race or another. *Hjadd, nord, kua'tah, soranta, arsashi* . . . they were all there, making their own travels to this vast creation of the *danui*.

And not only were familiar voices heard, but on occasion there were others as well, in languages that couldn't be interpreted from ships that no one had ever seen before. Inbound from other starbridges, they disappeared as quickly as they had appeared, leaving behind only fading electronic echoes and mystery.

Only one thing was certain. Humankind would never be alone again.

In fact, it never had been.

TIMELINE

EARTH EVENTS

July 5, 2070—URSS *Alabama* departs from Earth for 47 Ursae Majoris and Coyote.

April–December 2096—United Republic of America falls. Treaty of Havana cedes control of North America to the Western Hemisphere Union.

June 16, 2256—WHSS *Seeking Glorious Destiny Among the Stars for the Greater Good of Social Collectivism* leaves Earth for Coyote.

January 4, 2258—WHSS *Traveling Forth to Spread Social Collectivism to New Frontiers* leaves Earth for Coyote.

December 10, 2258—WHSS *Long Journey to the Galaxy in the Spirit of Social Collectivism* leaves Earth for Coyote.

August 23, 2259—WHSS *Magnificent Voyage to the Stars in Search of Social Collectivism* leaves Earth for Coyote.

March 4, 2260—WHSS *Spirit of Social Collectivism Carried to the Stars* leaves Earth for Coyote.

August 2270–July 2279—The Savant Genocide; 35,000 on Earth killed; mass extermination of Savants, with the survivors fleeing the inner solar system.

April 2288—First sighting of Spindrift by telescope array on the lunar farside.

June 1, 2288—EASS *Galileo* leaves Earth for rendezvous with Spindrift; contact lost with Earth soon thereafter.

January 2291—EASS *Galileo* reaches Spindrift. First contact.

September 18, 2291—EASS *Columbus* leaves for Coyote.

February 1, 2344—CFSS *Robert E. Lee* returns to Earth, transporting survivors of the *Galileo* expedition.

April–July 2352—Collapse of Western Hemisphere Union; mass exodus of refugees from Earth, halted by destruction of Starbridge Coyote.

COYOTE EVENTS

August 5, 2300—URSS *Alabama* arrives at 47 Ursae Majoris system.

September 7, 2300 / Uriel 47, C.Y. 01—Colonists arrive on Coyote; later known as "First Landing Day."

Uriel 52, C.Y. 02—First child born on Coyote: Susan Gunther Montero.

Gabriel 18, C.Y. 03—WHSS *Glorious Destiny* arrives. Original colonists flee Liberty; Western Hemisphere Union occupation of Coyote begins.

Ambriel 32, C.Y. 03—WHSS *New Frontiers* arrives.

Hamaliel 2, C.Y. 04—WHSS *Long Journey* arrives.

Barchiel 6, C.Y. 05—WHSS *Magnificent Voyage* arrives.

Barbiel 30, C.Y. 05—Thompson's Ferry Massacre; beginning of the Revolution.

Gabriel 75, C.Y. 06—WHSS *Spirit* arrives.

Asmodel 5, C.Y. 06—Liberty retaken by colonial rebels, Union forces evicted from Coyote; later known as "Liberation Day."

Hamaliel C.Y. 13—EASS *Columbus* arrives; construction of starbridge begins.

November 2340 / Hanael C.Y. 13—*Columbus* shuttle EAS *Isabella* returns to Earth via Starbridge Coyote; United Nations recognition of Coyote Federation.

Muriel 45, C.Y. 15—*Galileo* shuttle EAS *Maria Celeste* returns to Coyote via alien starbridge.

Asmodel 54, C.Y. 16—*Hjadd* Cultural Ambassador arrives on Coyote.

Hamaliel 25, C.Y. 16—CFS *Pride of Cucamonga* departs for Rho Coronae Borealis via *hjadd* starbridge.

Hamaliel 1, C.Y. 17—Exploratory Expedition departs Bridgeton for first circumnavigation of the Great Equatorial River.

Uriel 2, C.Y. 17—Destruction of the CFSS *Robert E. Lee* and Starbridge Coyote; later known as "Black Anael."

Adnachiel C.Y. 17–Barbiel C.Y. 20—Reconstruction of Starbridge Coyote; opening of trade with Talus races.

Hamaliel 48, C.Y. 22—Discovery of Hex by CFSS *Carlos Montero*.

Gabriel 10, C.Y. 23—Arrival of WHS *The Heroism of Che Guevara* from Earth.

ACKNOWLEDGMENTS

I'd like to express my appreciation to my editor, Ginjer Buchanan, and my agent, Martha Millard, for their continued support. Many thanks as well go to Rob Caswell, Winchell Chung, Horace "Ace" Marchant, and Sara and Bob Schwager for their advice and expertise, with special thanks to the staff of the Science and Engineering Library at the University of Massachusetts, Amherst campus, for their research assistance. And, as always, love and thanks to Linda Steele for putting up with me for another novel.

—WHATELY, MASSACHUSETTS
OCTOBER 2009–JUNE 2010

SOURCES

Carrigan, Richard A. Jr. "IRAS-based Whole-Sky Upper Limit on Dyson Spheres." Submitted paper, Fermi National Accelerator Laboratory, 2008.

——. "Starry Messages: Searching for Signatures of Interstellar Archaeology." Submitted paper, Fermi National Accelerator Laboratory, 2009.

Dyson, Freeman J. "Response to Letter from John Maddox." *Science*, Vol. 132, July 22, 1960.

——. "Search for Artificial Sources of Infrared Radiation." *Science*, Vol. 131, June 3, 1960.

——. "The World, the Flesh, and the Devil." *Communication with Extraterrestrial Intelligence* (Carl Sagan, editor). MIT Press, 1973.

Karashev, Nikolai S. "On the Inevitability and the Possible Structures of Supercivilisations." *The Search for Extraterrestrial Life: Recent Developments* (M.D. Papagiannis, editor). International Astronomical Union, 1985.

Kepner, Terry. *Extrasolar Planets: A Catalog of Discoveries in Other Star Systems*. McFarland & Co., 2005.

Maddox, John. Letter, *Science*, Vol. 132, July 22, 1960.

Sagan, Dorion. *Biospheres: Metamorphosis of Planet Earth*. Bantam, 1990.

Savage, Marshall T. *The Millennial Project: Colonizing the Galaxy in Eight Easy Steps*. Empyrean Publishing Ltd., 1992.

*The Coyote saga continues with two perilous journeys
undertaken at the same time—one to save a hero from
oblivion, and the other to stop a terrorist from unleash-
ing mass destruction . . .*

From three-time Hugo Award–winning author
ALLEN STEELE

COYOTE DESTINY
A NOVEL OF INTERSTELLAR CIVILIZATION

The lone passenger on a ship from Earth arrives on
Coyote bearing news: the survivor of the *Robert E. Lee*
explosion is still alive on Earth—but the person who
destroyed the ship is somewhere on Coyote.

"An engrossing tale of interstellar colonization, and a
damn good book in and of itself."   —*SFScope*

"The closest thing the science fiction world now has to
Robert A. Heinlein."   —*SFRevu*

facebook.com/AceRocBooks
penguin.com

M1029T1211

From three-time Hugo Award–winning author
ALLEN STEELE

THE COYOTE SERIES

COYOTE
COYOTE RISING
COYOTE FRONTIER
SPINDRIFT
GALAXY BLUES
COYOTE HORIZON
COYOTE DESTINY